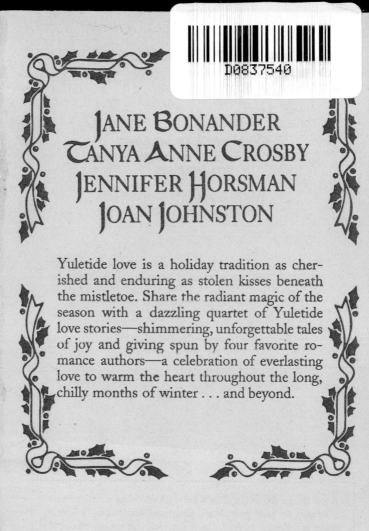

Jane Bonander
Tanya Anne Crosby
Jennifer Horsman
Joan Johnston

Yuletide love is a holiday tradition as cherished and enduring as stolen kisses beneath the mistletoe. Share the radiant magic of the season with a dazzling quartet of Yuletide love stories—shimmering, unforgettable tales of joy and giving spun by four favorite romance authors—a celebration of everlasting love to warm the heart throughout the long, chilly months of winter . . . and beyond.

For More Christmas Love
from Your Favorite Romantic Authors
Don't Miss

AVON BOOKS PRESENTS:
UNDER THE MISTLETOE

AVON BOOKS
PRESENTS

A Christmas Together

JANE BONANDER
TANYA ANNE CROSBY
JENNIFER HORSMAN
JOAN JOHNSTON

AVON BOOKS ◆ NEW YORK

AVON BOOKS PRESENTS: A CHRISTMAS TOGETHER is an original publication of Avon Books. This work, as well as each individual story, has never before appeared in print. This work is a collection of fiction. Any similarity to actual persons or events is purely coincidental.

AVON BOOKS
A division of
The Hearst Corporation
1350 Avenue of the Americas
New York, New York 10019

Contents

Angel Face

Jane Bonander

Prologue

Early September 1866—Northern Minnesota

JOEY PRESCOTT LICKED HIS PALM AND PRESSED IT against the stubborn cowlick that sprouted from his crown. He looked at his father's dark, wavy hair. "Wish my hair was like yours, Pa." They rode side by side in the wagon toward the community building, which was currently being used as the church and temporary schoolhouse.

Sam Prescott studied his ten-year-old son. He favored his mother, no doubt about that. The straight black hair, the high, proud cheekbones and the regal nose. Pure Dakota—or Sioux, as the Whites called them, a name they didn't like for it meant "enemy."

Only Joey's eyes gave him away. They were blue. "Blue as the waters of the north," his mother, Laughing Eyes, used to say with affection.

Laughing Eyes. Something hard and angry always pressed against Sam's heart when he thought about his wife. He felt responsible for her death, even though he could have done nothing to stop it.

He had been away fighting for the Union when a few restless, hungry young Dakota braves, out for revenge against the Whites, sparked a bloody revolt that left many dead on both sides, including Laughing Eyes.

Newspapers had called it the Great Sioux Uprising, slanting its views against the Indian, not allowing anyone to know the real reason behind the war. But Sam knew there had been hunger, anger and a feeling of betrayal among his wife's people. Even so, most of them had not wanted the confrontation.

When Sam had returned from the war between the states, the wife he'd reluctantly left behind, his sweet Laughing Eyes, was dead, killed by his own brother during the uprising. It may have been an accident; Sam would never know for sure. But that hadn't prevented him from nearly beating his brother to death. His family had naturally taken his brother's side; they had never approved of his marriage to a "filthy squaw" and hadn't taken to Joey as grandparents should. The rift between Sam and his family had widened, and Sam had taken Joey and moved north. There had been nothing left for him but harsh memories in the southern Minnesota lands that had absorbed the blood of so many.

The trouble was, no matter where they went, prejudice against the Indian followed.

"I'm happy with the way you are, Joey," Sam said. "Each time I look at you I'm reminded of your mother."

Joey glanced at him. "Does it hurt when you think about her, Pa?"

Sam smoothed his hand over Joey's cowlick. "Not like it used to, son." All he wanted on this earth was for Joey to be happy. That he was half Indian shouldn't matter. He was an innocent boy who didn't understand the slights and mockings of others.

"There's the building, Pa."

Sam noted his son's quiet enthusiasm, almost felt the tense excitement that coursed through Joey's body. He hadn't dared approach the school board about allowing Joey to attend. He knew he had a better chance if Joey just showed up. He'd thought this was the first day of the new school year, but as he looked around, he began to wonder. There was no sign of other children. Everything was too quiet.

"So it is. Nervous?"

Joey nodded, his eyes riveted on the white clapboard building. "Some."

Sam reined in the team. "Have a good day, Joey. See you this afternoon."

Joey gazed at his father, his light eyes showing a hint of fear. "Bye, Pa."

Giving him a reassuring smile, Sam handed him his lunch pail. "You'll do fine." He watched his son walk stiffly to the building, climb the stairs and disappear inside.

He sat a while, studying the structure, wishing he were a fly on the wall. Joey was tough; he could handle himself. But a part of him ached for his son, because he knew that all his life Joey would have to fight harder for his share of what the world had to offer.

Then the door opened and Joey stepped outside. Sam and his son locked gazes briefly before Joey looked away. Sam saw the rejection stamped all over his son's handsome face.

Slowly, Joey descended the stairs and trudged toward the wagon. When he reached it, he stared again at his father, tears filling his eyes. "They didn't want me, Pa."

Cora Nisbeth looked up from her knitting and studied the three men standing at the window, one of them her husband. They were foolishly staring after the half-breed child they'd just refused entrance to school. She quietly clucked her tongue but forced herself to say nothing.

Her husband, Clarence, turned and shook his head. "It ain't right. If God wanted man to breed with the Indians, he'd have civilized them."

Cora glanced up at Henry and Oscar Hassler, two other members of the school board, and knew that

they, like Clarence, would never change their minds
about the Indians. Every farmer for miles around
had had run-ins with them at one time or another.
Prejudice ran deep.

"The boy was quiet and mannerly," she said
softly. "His father probably isn't a bad sort."

Clarence pressed a pinch of snuff between his
cheek and gum. "How would you know, woman?
They live out there, every bit as antisocial as Torkelson and that breed squaw of his. They come into
town and don't speak to a soul. Not a living soul."

"Well, we haven't exactly made him feel welcome." She glanced around her, remembering that
just the day before, they'd all gathered in the building for the church service. It made her feel guilty at
their un-Christianlike behavior toward the man and
his half-breed son. Whether Sam Prescott had married an Indian woman or not shouldn't make a whit
of difference; he was a human being, just the same,
and God probably still loved him. The least they
could do was act civil toward him.

She thought of Eve, the new school teacher, whom
they'd taken in to board with them, and remembered the new-fangled, outspoken, often outrageous
ideas she'd hoped to implement in the classroom.
"I've a feeling if the new little schoolmistress were
here, you'd have a fight on your hands."

"Lucky for her she wasn't," Clarence said, turning
a harsh eye on his wife. "And we don't need your
two-cents worth, Cora. You're not a member of this
board. Eve Engels will do what she's told, if she
wants to keep her job."

Cora wasn't the least bit offended by her husband's blunt words. She merely sniffed at him and
went back to her knitting.

The Hassler brothers, who owned land near the
Nisbeths, exchanged glances but said nothing. Cora
knew they agreed with her husband. They all had
cause to be wary of the Indian. It was just that . . .

well, she didn't feel that a child should be punished for the sins of his father.

Oscar Hassler held the newspaper he'd been reading earlier high in the air, as if it were some kind of divine torch. "I read it before, and I'll read it again." He brought the paper down to eye level, pushed his glasses to the end of his nose and began. *"The Indians, the Sioux and the Chippewas, are having a high old time again, killing each other at every opportunity. May that opportunity be every minute of every day. May they kill each other until the last savage is dead, and we're rid of their dirty hides forever."*

Cora's fingers flew over her knitting; she could always knit like a house afire when she was angry or upset. "Have you forgotten that the little half-breed's father owns the land you want to build the new schoolhouse on?"

Clarence frowned at her; she knew that look. It said, "Wife, when will you learn to keep your mouth shut?" She pursed her lips and glanced away.

"We'll find other land, then," Clarence grumbled, turning again to the window.

She wanted to ask what harm it could possibly do to let the boy attend school. But she also understood her husband's reasons for not allowing it, and in some ways, she couldn't blame him. His only sister and her family had been killed by Indians. It would take a miracle to change his mind about any of them.

1

Early December 1866

S HE SHOULD NEVER HAVE STAYED AT THE SCHOOL
so late; she should have left with the others.
There would be plenty of time to prepare the pageant. Christmas was still more than two weeks away.

Shivering, she trudged through the deep drifts,
the cold, sharp wind hammering snow at her face,
instantly numbing her skin. Putting her hand to her
mouth, she sucked in a breath, grateful her mitten
filtered out some of the cold. She brought her scarf
across to cover everything except her eyes, then continued through the mounting snow, against the
screaming, ice-filled wind, in the direction she
thought would bring her to the Nisbeth farm.

She slogged through the drifts, her heart pumping
with exertion. Squinting into the wind, she saw
nothing. The Nisbeth barn should be directly in front
of her. A bubble of fear froze in her chest as she
realized she'd somehow lost her way. She'd known
it was possible; it was easy to get lost during a snow-
storm. The wind could easily blow a person off
course.

Her legs were numb to her knees, and she could
hardly feel her toes. Shielding her eyes, she looked
hard into the distance. A fluttering of hope spiraled
through her. Was that smoke? The outline of a
cabin?

Praying it wasn't an illusion, she forced her feet

8

to move on. Relief lifted her heart when she saw the definite outline of a log building. It wasn't the Nisbeth farmhouse, but at least it was shelter.

A dog barked, the sound muffled by the swirling flakes. As she approached the cabin, the sound became louder, until suddenly the animal was upon her, yapping and whining at her heels.

"G-g-good doggie," she stuttered, shivering against the cold and her newly found fear. She reached out, allowing the animal to sniff her mitten. He playfully bit the end, pulling it free. She gasped as the icy air hit her hand, then uttered another startled cry when the animal licked her fingers.

"Good boy," she said again as she picked up her mitten and moved toward the darkened building. "Is this your house?" Barking a response, the dog led the way to the cabin door.

She knocked, flinching as pain shot through her knuckles. No answer. With her mittened hand, she pressed the latch and opened the door, finding it dark inside except for a fire burning in the fireplace.

Shuddering with anticipation, she scurried into the room, allowing the dog inside before closing the door against the invading wind.

She stood only a moment before crossing to the fireplace. After churning up the embers, she laid more wood over the top, then stood back and watched it catch. The dog snuffled noisily at her side before dropping down in front of the flames.

She removed her wet felt boots, her coat, her mitten and scarf and draped them over a chair by the fire, then sat down next to the dog. She looked at the animal and laughed quietly. "Well, a fine watchdog you are."

He gazed at her through his long, hairy eyebrows while his furry tail thumped against the floor.

She removed her apron and wiped off the dog's wet back. "Oh, I don't care what you are or *whose* you are. You saved my life."

Exhausted from her journey through the blizzard, she pulled a blanket off the back of a chair, curled up in front of the fire and fell asleep.

"Sure is snowin, ain't it, Pa?" Joey's voice was muffled as it came from beneath the thick, warm quilt they were wrapped in.

"Worst storm of the year so far," Sam answered, feeling Joey huddle closer.

"Sure is a good thing the horses know the way home, ain't it, Pa?"

Sam could barely see the horses up ahead, pulling the small sleigh through the snow. "Smartest horses in the state, son."

Joey poked his head out from beneath the quilt. "We should be hearin' Chancy by now, shouldn't we?"

Sam listened for the dog. Hiding his concern, he answered, "He's probably found himself a warm spot next to the chimney and is sound asleep."

"I hope he ain't froze to death," Joey murmured, igniting Sam's own silent fears.

"Chancy's too smart for that," he answered, hoping to reassure the boy.

The horses stopped in front of the barn. Knowing his duty, Joey followed his father out of the cocoon of warmth and helped unhitch the team.

"I don't hear him, Pa."

Sam heard the frightened caution in his son's voice. "Let's get the horses fed and bedded down, then we'll have a look, all right?"

Minutes later, Sam and Joey waded through the snow toward the cabin.

"Here, Chancy!" Joey's voice was caught up by the wind and carried away. "Chancy! Here, boy!"

He tugged on his father's sleeve. "Where is he, Pa?"

Sam hated the thought that had eaten at him since they'd neared the farm and hadn't heard the dog.

Chancy had already had run-ins with a wolf and a skunk. Unfortunately, he never seemed to learn his lesson. Though Joey attributed his pet with the wisdom of a sage, Sam knew Chancy was just a dog.

Sam pushed the latch on the cabin door and stepped inside. His gaze was drawn to the fireplace. Startled and dumbfounded, he answered, "Chancy's here, Joey."

Man and boy inched toward the fireplace, stepping silently. A pretty, blond-haired woman lay there, wrapped in Joey's quilt. She was asleep, one arm beneath her head and the other resting on Chancy's back.

The dog raised his huge, hairy head and gave them a baleful look as his tail thumped against the floor.

Sam stopped, unable to move.

Joey inched closer, finally pausing in front of her. He sighed and slowly shook his head. "I'll be dogged. She looks like an angel." He turned, giving his father a puzzled look. "Where do you suppose she came from, Pa?"

Sam shrugged out of his sheepskin jacket, hung it on a peg by the door and ran his fingers through his wet hair. His gaze moved back toward the hearth, and the beauty who slept there. She did have the face of an angel, and her hair . . . White-gold strands had settled on her cheek, the light from the fire igniting them.

"She must have gotten lost in the storm." His gaze moved over the rest of her, and he couldn't help noticing her fine, womanly shape. Even through her clothing he could detect round, full hips and a generous bosom.

"Can we keep her, Pa?"

The longing Sam heard in his son's voice was like a knife to his gut. It pained him to know Joey needed more than he could give him.

"I'm afraid she probably belongs to someone else, Joey."

Joey kept staring at her as he sat and removed his leather boots. He rubbed his toes through his wool socks, ignoring the holes. "She sure is somethin', ain't she, Pa?"

"She sure is," he answered on a heavy sigh.

The young woman made a little sound in her throat, sending Joey scrambling backward. Chancy lifted his head again and licked the woman's face. She frowned and blinked, moaning slightly as she sat up.

Her gaze moved slowly toward them, and she pressed her hands to her mouth and gasped. "Oh! Oh, my!" She stood quickly, her frantic gaze moving toward the door. "I'm . . . I'm sorry. I . . . it was snowing so hard. I lost my way . . ." Her voice trailed off as she looked at Sam.

"It's all right, ain't it, Pa?" Joey stood before her, grinning like a fool.

"Glad we could be of help." Sam studied her, wondering who she was. Though he and Joey kept to themselves, Sam couldn't believe he'd have missed seeing her. Not that it would have made any difference; white women usually avoided him like a storm of locusts when they discovered he had a half-breed son.

She cleared her throat, breaking into Sam's thoughts. "I guess I should be going. . . ."

"You can't go out now," Joey argued. "It's still snowin' somethin' awful, ain't it, Pa?"

Sam crossed to the window and looked outside. "I'm afraid so, ma'am. I won't take my horses out again. They've been through enough for one day."

She was silent behind him, and when he turned, he caught the fear and uncertainty in her eyes. His gaze moved lower, over her ample breasts, then down over her hips. When he looked at her again, she was watching him.

"I certainly can't stay here," she murmured, sounding both frightened and perplexed.

Sam wanted a drink, but opted for coffee. "Joey, I'll bet the lady would appreciate a cup of coffee. And put Chancy back outside."

The woman gasped. "You're not going to make the poor animal sleep out in the blizzard, are you?"

Joey's eyes lit up. "Yeah, Pa. Can't Chancy sleep inside? Just for tonight?"

Judging by the look in the lady's eyes, Sam thought she wanted Chancy as a bodyguard. Ah, hell. What harm would it do? "All right. Just for tonight, then."

Joey's grin widened as he went to prepare coffee for their guest.

Rubbing her arms nervously, she went back to the fire, her back to Sam.

"Joey thinks you dropped out of the sky, just for him."

Turning, she gave him a puzzled look. "Excuse me?"

He nodded toward Joey. "My son." He grinned at her, enjoying her look of confusion. "He wants to keep you."

Her look of startlement was replaced by a shy, tentative smile. "Oh. Yes, I . . . I seem to have that effect on all boys under the age of ten."

He wanted to argue that he couldn't imagine men of any age not being affected by her. Wisely, he kept his mouth shut. He'd been rebuffed too many times by too many women even to consider saying it.

Suddenly a frown nicked her smooth, flawless brow. "Shouldn't your son be in school?"

To avoid her gaze, Sam glanced away. "He should be, but he isn't."

"But why?"

Sam barked a laugh. "You obviously didn't get a good look at him, ma'am."

"I can tell that he's of school age," she answered

tartly. "I suggest you bring him to my classroom at your earliest opportunity."

Sam's insides froze. "*Your* classroom?"

She stepped back from his dark glare. "Yes. I'm . . . I'm Eve Engels, the new schoolmistress."

2

EVE WATCHED THE CHANGE COME OVER THE man's handsome face. Anger and some private hatred suddenly hardened his features.

"So, you're the new schoolmistress. Well," he said around a snarl, "take a good look at my boy, ma'am, and then tell me you've never seen him before."

Eve swallowed a blister of fear. The boy, Joey, came toward her holding a mug of coffee. He had a wide, innocent face, and she immediately saw his Indian features. Her gaze drifted slowly to the man standing beside him. So, she thought, pressing her hands against her heart, this was Sam Prescott, the man who had married an Indian woman. She'd heard about him. Somehow she'd pictured him differently. Wilder, maybe. But she hadn't listened much to the gossip. Considering her own dubious background, having been left on the steps of a Minneapolis orphanage as a baby by a girl who couldn't face the consequences of her act, Eve had always felt she was the last person to judge another.

She gave Joey a tentative smile and accepted the coffee. She took a sip, hiding her grimace as she tasted the strong brew. When the boy retreated back into the depths of the cabin, she turned her gaze on the father. "I have never seen either of you before."

His eyes changed from expressing anger to revealing nothing. Turning away briefly, he answered. "Whatever you say, ma'am."

"You don't believe me."

"It doesn't matter what I believe. What's done is done."

"What do you mean?" For the first time she really took stock of his features. Amending her earlier assessment, she realized he wasn't truly handsome. His face was too hawklike and his eyes too piercing. His hair, wet from the snow and messed from the wind, was dark, and far too long to be fashionable. He was tall and lean-hipped, though wide through the shoulders and thickly muscled.

She didn't think he was an Indian, but it was as if he'd lived with them so long, he'd absorbed their peculiarities. It was pure conjecture; she had no idea if it were true.

"I took Joey to the school, and he was turned away."

Eve bit her bottom lip and felt a rush of sympathy. She understood rejection. "When was this?"

"The first part of September. I don't recall the exact date."

Eve realized he must have brought his son to the building during a board meeting. "School didn't start until the end of the month."

"Well, someone sure as hell turned him away."

"I'm sorry. I wasn't there that day. If I had been, I—"

His humorless laugh interrupted her. "It wouldn't have mattered."

Stung, she bristled. "How do you know that?"

He went to the hearth, nudging the dog aside with his toe before churning up the fire. "Where have you been living, anyway? In a convent?"

"These are good people, for the most part," she answered, understanding his sarcasm.

He lifted a wood chunk onto the grate. "But they still hate Indians."

"Can you blame them? I mean, some of them had families down south, around New Ulm. They lost their loved ones in the massacre."

"The Indians lost loved ones, too."

"But the Whites didn't start all the trouble," she argued.

He turned and glared at her, his stance almost vicious. "Have you any idea why it happened in the first place?"

She moved toward the dog and stroked his furry ears. When she stopped, the animal nudged her hand with his nose, so she continued. "Only what . . . what others have told me and what I've read in the papers."

He jabbed at the fire, seeming to find an outlet for his anger. "I've often wished the Indians had a similar means of communication. But I guess even if they had, no White would ever read it."

"Why do you say that?"

"Because it's true. As you read the papers, did you ever get the impression that the massacre happened because the Indians were hungry? That they were waiting for long overdue money promised them by the government? That all the land the Whites reaped had once been theirs? That they'd been confined to a small reservation, pressured to abandon their culture and religion?"

Eve swallowed. It sounded too . . . reasonable. If that had been the case, wouldn't someone have mentioned it? "Still, that's no reason to kill innocent people."

He sighed and dragged his hand over his face. "You're right, of course. What no one understands is that reason had nothing to do with it."

"Did you live with the Indians?" she ventured.

"For ten years," he answered softly.

So, she'd been right. She crossed to the window,

the dog following. It was still snowing and blowing. The wind howled mournfully. Suddenly she remembered that she couldn't leave. Turning swiftly, she caught him studying her.

"I really can't stay here," she whispered.

A hooded expression crossed his face. "You'll be perfectly safe. You can have my bed; I'll sleep in the loft with Joey."

Her stomach was in knots, and her mouth was dry. Turning to the window again she knew she had no choice but to accept what he offered.

She glanced at the bed in the corner where a patched quilt was spread carefully over the bedding. Her stomach continued to roil. It wasn't that she was afraid of this intense, angry man. Something inside her had been drawn to him immediately. She'd always found widowed men who were forced to raise their children alone very appealing. It was partly because it made them vulnerable—which she sensed most men wanted to hide. It also reminded her that her own parents, whomever they were, had refused to take on their responsibility.

"I don't see what there is to think about," he said, breaking into her reverie.

Taking a deep breath, she faced him, finding his whole bearing darkly intriguing. He'd unbuttoned his shirt and pulled it from his jeans, exposing the top of his long underwear. Hair, dark and curly, peeped out over the stitching, and his firm chest muscles were outlined beneath the fabric.

Oh, there is much to think about. She took another dizzying breath and looked away, willing herself to focus on chaste thoughts, like puppies and babies and innocence. But puppies and babies dredged up reminders of how they were conceived, and all thoughts of innocence fled.

Bringing a hand to her throat, she swallowed, scolding herself for her wayward thoughts. "You're right, of course." She glanced up at the loft; the boy was on his stomach, staring down at them, his blue eyes wide.

Suddenly her stomach growled, and she knew that Sam Prescott heard it. Her cheeks flamed.

He gave her a quick glance, then cleared his throat. "I'm . . . er . . . Joey and I ate supper with some friends. I'm sorry. Can . . . can I fix you something?"

With a nervous shake of her head, she answered. "No. Really, I'm not hungry. I'm . . . I'm fine."

"Well, if you're sure." He gave her a gruff sigh, then nodded toward a dry sink near the bed in the far corner of the room. "You can clean up there, if you want. There's a clean towel on the rod."

Still clutching the fabric at her throat, she gave him a nervous nod. "Th-thank you. I'll be fine." She waited until he'd taken the ladder to the loft, then scurried to the bed and crawled under the covers— fully dressed except for her shoes.

She could hear father and son stirring above her, trying to get comfortable. The boy's whispers were met with short answers in Sam's deep voice, and she knew the conversation was about her. She rolled to her side and took a deep breath, pulling the smell from the flannel bedding into her lungs. The private, masculine scent triggered a response from deep inside her, and she drew the bedding closer. This was his smell. Not unpleasant at all, it was strangely comforting and . . . provocative.

It had been two years since she'd left the orphanage. Two years since she'd had to share a bed with anyone. Lying in this man's bed, surrounded by his scent, was far more pleasant than sharing her bed with two other squirming girls or sleeping alone.

Eve had slept hard. When she awakened, it was still dark, but the fire had been fed, and she knew it was morning. She was also hungry. She crept from the bed and looked toward the loft. They were gone, probably out in the barn doing chores.

After quickly washing her face and hands, she hurried to the kitchen corner of the cabin and rummaged through drawers and bins, finding the fixings for breakfast. By the time Sam Prescott and his son returned from their chores, she'd sliced and fried salt pork and had batter cakes bubbling on the griddle.

"See, Pa? I told you she'd have breakfast ready."

They both stamped the snow from their boots, then left them by the door. Joey strode to the table, his eyes closed and his nose in the air, noisily pulling in the warm, delicious smells.

"Um, boy. It sure smells good, ma'am," Joey said.

Eve smiled, but it vanished when she looked at the boy's father. From beneath his dark brows, his eyes glittered dangerously.

"Joey, wash your hands and face," he ordered, his gaze still on Eve. "You didn't have to make breakfast."

She quickly flipped the batter cakes. "It was the least I could do," she answered, aware that her pulse was racing. When she turned back, he was at the dry sink and Joey was at the table, face scrubbed and hair brushed to the side, although a stubborn cowlick rose from the top of his head.

He eyed the crispy salt pork and licked his lips. "Hurry up, Pa. I'm hungry."

Eve heaped the batter cakes onto a platter she'd found in the makeshift cupboard and set it down in front of Joey just as the boy's father came to the table. His sleeves were rolled up, exposing hard forearms covered with thick, dark hair. She stared, marveling at the corded muscle that strained at the taut skin.

Blinking furiously, she looked up and caught him watching her.

He immediately began rolling down his sleeves. "I'm sorry, ma'am."

Flustered, she cleared her throat. "Oh. No. Don't be. I mean, I don't care. I mean, you don't have to roll them down..." She stopped, aware that she was babbling. "Please," she finally said, "sit down and eat."

He sat, and to her surprise, he and Joey bowed their heads and recited a prayer in a language Eve didn't understand.

Moments later, Joey was praising the breakfast to the heavens. "Umm-mmm. I ain't never tasted such good griddle cakes. Have you, Pa?"

The man swallowed a mouthful of food. "Since we're having a genuine schoolmistress to breakfast, son, I think you should think about proper speech."

Joey gave his father a puzzled look. "Huh?"

"Maybe it's time to stop saying 'ain't.' "

Eve lowered her gaze to her plate and hid a smile.

Joey nodded. "Oh, yeah. 'Ain't' ain't, I mean, isn't a very good word, is it, ma'am?"

She smiled. "No, it isn't."

They finished breakfast in silence. As father and son cleared the table, Eve said, "I fried up the ends of the salt pork, and there are a couple of batter cakes left. Is it...I mean, can they be fed to the dog?"

"Yeah," Joey answered. "Chancy'd love it, wouldn't he, Pa?"

"He'll think he's died and gone to dog heaven."

"Aw, Pa," Joey said around a laugh. "He always gets table scraps. They just ain't—I mean aren't as good as these."

"All right, son." His father returned the smile. "Take it out to him and feed him in the barn."

When Joey left the cabin, Eve found Sam Prescott at her side, helping her clean up the kitchen. He must have noticed her surprise, for he said, "We've been doing this ourselves for years, ma'am. I'd feel funny letting you do it alone."

Eve couldn't believe her ears. This man was, well,

she had to face it, the *perfect* man. Actually, she thought as his arm brushed hers, he was too good to be true. No man she'd ever known, including Clarence Nisbeth, whom she admired, had ever lifted a hand to help in the kitchen. Why, it just wasn't done. But it was so nice . . .

He glanced past her toward the window. "It's still snowing."

She pulled in a quiet breath. Translated, that undoubtedly meant she wasn't going home today, either. To her surprise, she realized she wasn't unhappy about it.

"It's about two weeks until Christmas," she began. "Do you and Joey celebrate it?"

He gave her a strange look. "Of course. Why wouldn't we?"

"Oh," she mumbled, embarrassed, "no reason. I just thought, I mean, your breakfast prayer was so—"

"I think it's important for Joey to remember his mother's culture as well as mine, which is the one he's being pushed into."

Eve glanced away. "I've heard . . . very little about you and Joey," she began.

Snorting softly, he turned down the kerosene lamp on the table. "That surprises me. I was sure that you, like everyone else in this community, knew all about me."

The way he said it brought a tingling to the base of her neck. "Is there something else to know, other than that you married an Indian woman?"

He stood across the table from her, the low lamplight casting macabre shadows across his face. "I nearly killed my own brother because he murdered my wife."

3

EVE LEANED AGAINST THE TABLE, FORCING HER
rubbery legs to hold her. "Your . . . brother
murdered your wife?"

"Yes. And I nearly killed him for it. Now, are you
anxious to leave? Doesn't it frighten you just a little
to be in the same room with a man who could have
murdered his own brother?"

It was as if he were baiting her, wanting her to be
afraid, taunting her. "But . . . but you didn't." She
held onto the back of a chair and studied him, hiding
the internal panic he had so easily riled. "You're trying to scare me."

He gave her a sultry smile. "You mean I haven't
succeeded?"

She let out a shaky breath and gave him a tremulous smile. "Oh, I wouldn't say that."

"Then, why aren't you screaming and running for
the door?"

When she reached up to repair her hairdo, her fingers shook. She hoped he wouldn't notice. "I seldom
do what's expected of me," she said with more bra-
vado than she felt. She removed the pins from her
hair and splayed her fingers through the heavy mass
that fell over her shoulder. She wanted to know
more about him, but asking meant revealing her uncertainty, and she was stubborn enough not to want
it to show.

Her fingers met tangles, and she frowned. It was
bad enough that she'd had to sleep in her clothes in

a strange bed, but worse that she had no toiletries with her.

"Here. You can use this if you want to."

She glanced up to find him standing beside her, a brush in his hand. Nodding her thanks, she took it gratefully and pulled it through her hair.

A blast of cold air rushed into the room as Joey entered. He didn't speak for so long, Eve became concerned, fearing something was wrong. She glanced at him as he stood by the door, his wide eyes riveted on her.

Alarmed, she asked, "Is something wrong, Joey?"

He continued to stare at her as he stepped into the room and removed his jacket. Reaching out toward the peg on the wall, he attempted to hang his jacket on the hook by the door. It fell to the floor in a heap. "Holy smoke," he whispered, still staring at her. "She's really got angel hair, don't she, Pa?"

Her gaze swung to the boy's father, who was staring at her as well. The brief look of agony on his face disappeared, replaced by a cold, hard stare. He was silent.

"Your hair," Joey said, still mesmerized.

Eve looked away and began weaving her hair into a braid, finding the task difficult to do with such nervous fingers.

"Pa read me stories about Christmas angels. All the while, I imagined them with hair like yours. Can't you leave it down?"

She gave him an anxious laugh, aware that although his father hadn't said a word, he hadn't taken his eyes off her, either. As she coiled the braid at the back of her head, she answered. "Now, how practical would that be? After all, you wouldn't want it to catch fire while we're baking cookies, would you?"

His eyes brightened even more, and he grinned. "Cookies? Real cookies?"

Eve laughed, still aware of Sam standing quietly across from her. "Are there any other kind?"

Sam stayed out of their way. He couldn't stand to be close; it hurt like hell. Why she'd stumbled into their lives, he couldn't imagine. He knew Joey missed his mother's gentle touch. Maybe this was heaven's way of telling him the boy needed it.

Sam knew better. He and Joey were meant to go it alone. Sam's allegiance to the Indian community and his love for his half-breed son meant that for as long as they lived among the Whites, white women would cut a wide path around them. Hell, shortly after he and Joey had moved north, Sam had met a woman who'd showed immediate interest in him— until she saw Joey. And that hadn't been the first time.

Now, as he watched the angel-haired woman mix up cookies with his son, he knew it wouldn't be the last. Baking cookies was one thing; getting involved was another.

He sensed her pride and strength, though. What had he been thinking, blurting out that he'd nearly killed his brother? Not that it wasn't true, but he shouldn't have scared her like that. Maybe he'd just wanted to get rid of her. Maybe, in some idiotic way, he was afraid of her . . .

He swore again. He knew why he'd done it. He'd felt the attraction. But he couldn't afford to let thoughts of her linger, for never mind his own pain, there was Joey's to think about. Joey was drawn to any woman who'd bake him a batch of cookies, but this woman didn't belong with them, and tomorrow she'd be gone. And good riddance.

Sam almost wanted to drag her away from his son, to tell her to quit toying with him. But the force that prevented him from doing so was stronger. Watching Joey with her gave him pleasure, but not nearly as much pleasure as watching just her.

The delicious smell of ginger-and-molasses cookies filled the cabin. Joey stood on a stool beside the woman, rolling dough into walnut-sized balls. They were talking and laughing together, and Sam wanted to bottle the scene before him and keep it forever. He knew there would be bleak days, weeks and years ahead when he'd want to remember things just as they were today.

"Hey, Pa! The cookies are ready. Here," Joey said, blowing on the hot molasses treat as he flipped it from one hand to the other. "Try one."

Sam wanted to say no, but his mouth watered. The cookie was big, round and flat and sprinkled with sugar. He bit into it and nearly groaned out loud. He closed his eyes, memories of his childhood flashing before him. He felt an ache deep inside in a place he'd kept carefully protected.

When he opened his eyes, he found a cup of coffee and a plate of cookies sitting on the table before him.

No. Don't cave in. Don't let this happen. Don't dream of things that can never be. They'll bring you pain, Sammy-boy, nothing but pain.

But even as his mind warned him of the consequences, Sam took another cookie from the plate and devoured it, washing it down with a cup of excellent coffee.

As he nibbled a third cookie, he watched the woman work. She was at home in the kitchen and seemed to enjoy it. All right, so what? Sated now, he steeled himself against his feelings for her and all of what she could mean in his life. Cookies were one thing. At least she hadn't made bread. The one thing he couldn't fight against in the whole damned world was the taste of bread, fresh from the oven, slathered with creamy butter.

Joey rushed up to him, his eyes shining. "Pa! Guess what? Miss Engels is gonna bake us some bread!"

Sam tightened his jaw and stifled a groan.

* * *

For Eve, the day flew by. Thankfully. By busying herself in the kitchen, she didn't have to think about the man who watched her every move from somewhere behind her. As she worked, she found herself surprised that he'd even had the fixings for any baked goods. By evening, besides a batch of molasses cookies and freshly baked bread, she had a pot of stew bubbling over the fire.

And Joey . . . what a charming child he was. A thought had begun to form in her busy brain. She would approach the father before saying anything about it to Joey, just in case he didn't approve.

She turned as Sam Prescott entered the room from outside. Their gazes locked briefly before he turned away. "Supper is almost ready," she said, aware of the flutter of excitement his presence caused her. "Where's Joey?"

Sam hung his jacket on a hook and crossed to the washstand. "He'll be along."

She hovered behind him, watching him scrub his hands and splash water over his face. Now was as good a time as any. "I've been thinking—"

"Most women think too much," he interrupted as he dragged a towel across his face.

Mildly stung, she lifted her fists to her hips. "And every man alive thinks he's the biggest toad in the puddle. Now, may I continue?"

A smile lifted one corner of his mouth. "I doubt I could stop you."

Pulling in a satisfied breath, she said, "If the school board won't allow Joey to attend school, at least for now," she said, certain she could do something about that, "then I think you should consider letting me come here to tutor him."

Sam continued wiping his hands on the towel, long after Eve was certain they were dry. "Why would you want to do that?"

"Because he's a delightful child and very bright.

It would be tragic if he weren't allowed to learn to read and write."

"And how do you know he can't?" The question was defensive.

"Because he told me so," she answered tartly. "I just hope your stubborn pride won't stop you from consenting to my suggestion."

He studied her for a long, quiet minute before turning to hang the towel on the peg by the mirror. "And how often will you come to teach him?"

Eve straightened the silverware beside the plates, removed the kerosene lamp from the table and replaced it with a candle. "I'd like to come three afternoons a week. We can see how it goes from there." She held her breath as she waited for his answer.

"And I suppose you'll come in and make a mess of my kitchen each time."

Eve gasped. "A mess of your—" She clamped her mouth shut before she said something she might regret. It didn't help. "Please believe me, Mr. Prescott," she said with a sweet-tart smile, "I hope you live forever on hard tack and pig swill."

He nodded briskly. "As long as we understand each other."

"Fine. I'll begin tonight."

"Tonight?" He turned as Joey came in through the door, a rush of frigid air preceding him.

"Is there any reason why I shouldn't?"

He motioned Joey to the washstand. The boy's expression was proof that he was puzzled by the tension in the air.

"No, I guess not," Sam answered.

Moments later, they were all sitting at the table, eating their supper of stew and bread. Eve bit the insides of her cheeks as Joey once again enthused about her cooking. As she glanced at the intriguing, sullen man across from her, she couldn't help wondering why he was afraid of her. She would occasionally notice the warmth in his eyes as he watched Joey, but the minute he saw her watching him, his whole face changed. He would show no emotion at all.

He just didn't want her around. That was obvious, but why? She didn't know a man in the world who would turn down home cooking, yet Sam Prescott had. Why, he'd almost made it sound revolting.

After the evening meal was cleared away, the dishes done and Chancy fed, she sat with Joey, writing letters on a slate with chalk that she carried in her purse. His father sat nearby, pretending disinterest as he read a newspaper that was probably a month old.

After an hour, he looked up. "Joey, it's time for bed."

Joey didn't argue, but he looked at her, his eyes still filled with excitement. "How'm I doin', ma'am?"

Smiling down at him, she touched his cowlick. "Very well, Joey. Very well."

He grinned and nodded. "Well, g'night, Miss Engels."

"Good night, Joey." She watched him pad to the ladder, her heart breaking when she noticed the holes in the toes of his wool stockings.

At the bottom of the ladder, he turned. "You comin', Pa?"

"In a few minutes, son."

Appeased, he nodded and climbed to the loft.

Visions of bedtime brought Eve discomfort. She'd kept busy all day, able to keep her thoughts of Sam Prescott at bay, even though he was always close by. Despite his reticence, he fascinated her.

"I should be able to take you home tomorrow."

She realized that no one knew where she was, and although she wasn't accustomed to having anyone worry about her, no doubt Cora Nisbeth would. "The Nisbeths are probably worried."

"That's where you live?"

She nodded. "You'll probably be glad to be rid of me and go back to your normal routine." When he didn't deny it, she felt a foolish stab of disappointment.

"How can I pay you for what you're doing for Joey?"

Frowning, she crossed to where he sat and dropped into the chair opposite him. "Pay me? Why, nothing. It's part of my job."

He looked away, appearing to study the fire. "No one does something for people like us for nothing."

She stiffened. " 'People like you'? What's that supposed to mean?"

He folded the newspaper roughly, tossing it aside as he stood. "You know exactly what I mean."

Oh, yes, she knew. He was feeling sorry for himself. "You can't tell me you didn't know how people would react when they learned that you'd married an Indian. Certainly you've come to terms with all of that, Mr. Prescott."

"I married an Indian because I fell in love with her. It wasn't until Joey was born that I realized what bigots my own people were."

She noted the sadness that cut into his features. Why was it so easy for some people to hurt others? It seemed that if a person were different, others coped with their lack of understanding by making fun of them and talking about them behind their backs. It was cruel, especially if a child was involved.

"It's been hard for you, hasn't it?"

He strode to the ladder. "Yes, it's been hard. But we don't need your pity, ma'am."

She frowned as he retreated up the ladder. No, he didn't think he needed anything. But she wondered if he ever stopped to think of what Joey needed. She sensed that there was still a sad little boy inside

Sam's big, hard body that felt rejected by his own people.

She watched him disappear into the loft, then made her way to the bed. She'd been in her clothes for two days, and she couldn't stand to sleep in them another night. Her corset dug into her ribs, and she felt sticky all over, despite the cool night air.

Eyeing the loft again to make sure Sam was up there to stay, she peeled off her clothes, leaving on only her chemise and drawers, then crawled into bed. As she shivered under the covers, she looked at the fireplace. The fire was almost out. He'd forgotten to bank it.

She flung the covers back and left the bed, padding quietly to the wood box. She lifted out a heavy wood chunk and dumped it onto the grate, where it appeared to smother the remaining embers. Spying the poker that rested against the wall, she grabbed it and began jabbing at the log.

"Here, I'll do that."

His voice made her jump, and she turned toward him, the poker still in her fist. Unable to look him in the eyes, she allowed her gaze to drop down to the neck of his long underwear, which was open to the middle of his chest. Dark hair curled there, clear up to the pulse that pounded at his throat and down across his hard, flat chest.

Automatically dropping her gaze lower, she saw that he'd either been in the process of removing his jeans, or pulling them back on, for they weren't buttoned up all the way. They hung low on his hips, and even though he was fully covered by his underwear, it seemed indecent.

"Seen enough?"

She felt heat rush to her face as she quickly looked up at him. That maddening half-smile and those sultry eyes made her look away. "You forgot to bank the fire."

He took the poker from her. His touch, though

surely innocent, sent a spiral of heat into her belly.

"Having a woman around seems to have caused my good senses to take a holiday."

She stepped away, yet stayed close to the fire. It was warm, yet she suddenly shivered. She really ought to scurry back to bed—

He went past her to retrieve another wood chunk, giving her a quick glance as he did so. "Nice underwear."

Her flush deepened, and she crossed her arms over her chest. "I'm sorry, I'll go back to bed—"

"No," he rasped harshly. "Stay a minute."

Her heart thudded madly, and though all her good sense told her to bolt and run, she stayed.

Once the fire was banked, he rested the poker against the wall and turned to her. His gaze raked over her, briefly stopping at places that automatically reacted. Like her breasts, which suddenly tingled, and her stomach, which quivered, and the place below. . . .

"There's more danger for you here at this very minute than you'll ever know." His voice was a husky whisper.

She was quivering inside and couldn't speak. If she had, she would have told him she knew that. Still, she didn't move away.

Stepping close, he reached over and brought her thick rope of hair over her shoulder, cradling it in the palm of his hand. The backs of his fingers rested against her breast, and she felt her nipples tighten beneath her chemise. She stood still, but inside she was shaking with the newness of her feelings.

He unbraided her hair, the rough edges of his fingers occasionally snagging it as he worked the hair loose. She forced herself to stand quietly before him. This was wrong; she knew it, but she didn't care. She'd been wildly curious about him from the beginning, and though he'd made every effort to show her he felt nothing, she sensed it wasn't true.

She glanced briefly at his face. His eyes were dark, but light from the fire made them smolder. She tried to control her breathing but noticed that he couldn't control his, either. She had a reckless urge to touch his jaw, to rub the backs of her fingers against his stubble.

Suddenly his fingers, which had been resting almost innocently against her breast, pressed against it. Her gaze shot to his again, and there was an unasked question in his eyes. Oh, sweet heaven, she should run. Scurry back to bed. . . . But she didn't. She merely closed her eyes and waited.

Slowly, as though he had all the time in the world, his fingers left her hair and moved gently over the swell of her breast. Her nipples tensed further, pulling her breasts so tight she swore she could feel them harden. There was an ache down deep, between her legs. It was as if she'd just discovered an unchartered path from her breasts to that secret place below.

He circled her breast with his fingers, then touched her pebbled nipple. She gasped for breath and stepped away, for had she not, she might have thrown herself at him, the feelings he'd stirred within her were so strong.

"Like I said," he murmured sarcastically, "you're in more danger now than you'll ever know."

Her eyes snapped open, and she saw the change that had come over him. He was no longer hungry, he merely wanted to hurt her. But he hadn't. She hadn't known him very long, but she already felt she knew him well. Whenever he was afraid, he lashed out. It was his defense. And again, she realized that for some reason, he was afraid of her.

Without bothering to answer, she stumbled back to his bed, crawled under the covers and turned to face the wall. Not until she heard him climb the ladder to the loft did she let out the breath she was holding.

She lay there, studying the darkness, beginning to feel a kernel of shame uncoil inside her. How brazen she'd been! Had he tried to kiss her, she wouldn't have pushed him away.

Suddenly, she was elated to be leaving in the morning. Her heart told her one thing while her head fairly shouted another. Wisely, she listened to the scoldings in her head. But it was still impossible to fall asleep.

4

EVE STOOD AT THE NISBETHS' PARLOR WINDOW and watched Sam Prescott drive away, the bells on the teams' bridle ringing in the cold morning air. As he'd predicted, the day had dawned sunny and still, and he'd been able to bring her home in the sleigh. He'd insisted he would pick her up from school those afternoons she was to tutor Joey, and she hadn't been able to refuse, although she wasn't sure how it was going to look.

Now that she was home, her decision to tutor Joey didn't seem quite as sound as it had when she'd made it. She didn't want to lose her job, but how could she live with herself if she didn't try to help the boy? He was very bright; that kind of child didn't come along every day.

Cora Nisbeth appeared beside her, put her arm around her and drew her close. When Eve had arrived home, Cora had hugged her so tightly, she'd been nearly suffocated. "If I weren't so happy to see you, young lady, I'd spank you like a child," she scolded. "Do you realize how many people were looking for you? Lan' sakes, the most *awful* things went through my head. I . . . I thought maybe you had frozen to death in a snowbank. Or worse yet, you could have been eaten by wolves." Cora pressed her fingers to her lips, but a quiet sob escaped anyway.

Eve felt awful. She didn't want people to worry about her; she wasn't used to it. Until the Nisbeths had come into her life, no one had really cared much about her. It was touching, and she felt like crying herself. Instead, she gave Cora a sisterly hug.

"I'm sorry you all worried about me, but I was lucky to find a place to wait out the storm." She sighed. "I'd heard about people losing their bearings in a blizzard. I just didn't think it would ever happen to me."

Cora clucked her tongue. "But of all places to be. . . ."

"Oh, it wasn't so bad. Joey's a charming child. It just makes me want to spit when I think of the school board turning him away."

"You know how Clarence feels about Indians, Eve." Cora led her from the window to the sofa in front of the fire. "One doesn't lose one's only sister to the Indians without feeling bitter and angry."

Eve shivered and rubbed her arms. "Oh, that dreadful New Ulm massacre. I understand his grief, Cora, but why does he have to take it out on a child?"

Cora poured Eve a cup of coffee and pressed it into her hands. "The subject of Clarence's family is the least of your worries, dear. Even if I don't say anything about where you've been for the past two days, word will get around, and—"

"Cora," she interrupted, "I couldn't have left had I wanted to. And Mr. Prescott was a perfect gentleman." More or less, she realized, but what had happened between them had been as much her fault as his. A pleasurable rush of gooseflesh scampered over her arms.

"Still," Cora continued, unaware of Eve's thoughts, "people will talk."

"Then I'd best let it be known right now that I'm planning to tutor Joey Prescott three afternoons a week." She held her breath, waiting for Cora to protest.

"What?!"

"Cora, I have to. It's part of my job, and no where in my contract does it say I can't tutor children in special circumstances on my own time."

She knew that Cora had been involved in writing up the terms of the contract. Now, she could sense her going over what she'd helped compose.

"But we didn't imagine anything like this would happen," Cora argued weakly.

"Well, everyone respects you, Cora. If you don't make a big issue of it, no one else will, either."

Cora heaved a sigh. "It would almost be worth it to get the boy into school rather than having you traipse over there. Why, you'll be at his mercy, Eve, you'll—"

"Oh, Cora," Eve answered on a laugh. "Believe me, he isn't too thrilled about my coming over there. He made that perfectly clear. But he's a good father, no matter what any of you think, and he only wants what's best for his son."

Cora gently patted the area over her heart, as if warding off a swoon. It was a tactic Eve had discovered the woman used mostly when she wanted something from her husband.

Eve put her coffee cup down and stood. "Don't give me that faint-hearted expression, Cora. Just be there with me if and when I have to face the school board."

Cora sighed and shook her head. "I'm afraid that under the circumstances, that will be sooner than you think. Clarence has called a meeting for to-night."

Eve's shoulders drooped. She wasn't looking forward to it. She hated confrontations, she always had. The only thing that gave her strength was to think ahead to the next afternoon, when she would see Sam Prescott again. In spite of the cold draft that whistled in under the door, she felt as though she'd captured a smoldering ember near her heart.

That evening, Eve faced the members of the school board in the Nisbeths' parlor. Cora had started decorating for Christmas. Bittersweet berries, nested in the evergreen sprigs of the fragrant red cedar, bedecked the mantel.

Unfortunately, the festive warmth of the decorations didn't reach out and penetrate the people in the room. Henry Hassler sat stoically gazing at the fire, while his brother stared at Eve from behind steepled fingers.

Cora's fingers flew over her knitting, the needles clicking rhythmically. Now and then she glanced up at her husband, who examined Eve's contract. Suddenly he stood and dropped the contract on the desk.

"Well, it appears you're right, Eve."

She held her breath.

Clarence Nisbeth crossed to where she sat and studied her for a moment. The look on his face told Eve that he wasn't happy about admitting he was wrong. "We didn't provide for such an occurrence. Seems you can tutor the boy on your own time. Just see that it doesn't interfere with the work we've hired you for."

Eve nearly sagged with relief. "Of course it won't interfere. But it would be so much easier if he could just—"

"Eve," Cora interrupted quietly but firmly, "let it go."

Eve took a deep breath and leaned back in her chair. Yes, better to let it go—for now. But somehow, someway she would get Joey Prescott into her class-room.

Although Eve was nervous about her first session with Joey since they'd been snowbound, when she saw the Prescott sleigh coming toward the building, she bundled up in her warm clothes and carried the supplies she would need for Joey outside. Also stuffed deep in her valise were darning thread and a needle. The condition of Joey's socks was shame-ful. She wouldn't bother to ask Sam Prescott if she could darn them; she'd just do it.

She saw that Sam was alone, and he didn't look happy. He really didn't want her help; she wished she knew why. Before she could even greet him, he started in on her.

"Joey and I don't need you interfering in our lives, Miss Engels. I heard about you begging to get Joey into school. We don't need pity or charity." As he assisted her into the sleigh and lifted the quilt over her knees, Eve noticed a muscle tighten in his jaw.

She ignored his reprimand. "Where's Joey?"

"He'll be there by the time we get home."

"Good. And I didn't beg," she said, answering his rebuke. "But one way or another, I'll get him into school. Until then, I'll tutor him." She turned and glared at him. "I can't see why my decision should bother you. It's for Joey's own good."

He walked around the horses and pulled himself onto the seat beside her. As he slid beneath the quilt, Eve felt a flutter of pleasure. It seemed so . . . inti-mate. She fought the memory of their night together in front of the fire.

Sam flicked the reins over the team, and the horses started down the snowy path, bells jingling. "We can fight our own battles."

"And it certainly appears that you've done a fine

job," she answered with a measure of sarcasm.

Ignoring her tone, he said, "They want my land for their new schoolhouse. That's my ace in the hole to finally get Joey into school. I don't need you."

She turned and studied him, feeling a quivering in her stomach as she realized that he was, in truth, as compelling as she'd remembered. The cold winter air had nipped his cheeks, rendering them apple-red beneath his dark stubble. His nose, so straight, seemed chiseled from granite. His cheekbones were high and sharply defined.

"Unless someone else gives them a better offer," she said, then looked away, wishing she could find him uninteresting. "Isn't there some land across the lake from the community building?"

He was silent for a moment, then answered. "Yes. But it belongs to old man Torkelson. He refuses to sell. Seems he wants to lay in a corn crop there."

Eve nodded. Jeremiah Torkelson and his wife, Mavis, were loners, too. Eve didn't think she'd ever seen Mavis in town, or anywhere else, for that matter. As far as she knew, they'd never had children, and Jeremiah wasn't too keen on having the schoolhouse built on his land, even if it meant getting paid for it.

Eve was suddenly aware that her hand had landed inadvertently on Sam's thigh beneath the quilt. Their gazes met, and she removed her hand and quickly looked away. "I . . . I hope you're right. If there's anything I can do to convince them—"

"Like I said, Miss Engels," he interrupted, "don't go meddling into my affairs. The last thing I need is some fool woman trying to fight my battles."

Eve held her tongue, but she was seething inside. *Men.* They were so . . . so stubborn. Finally, after stewing for a good minute, she said, "If you would present yourself to the community in a friendlier manner, maybe they'd be more obliging to you."

He snorted. "Yeah, like that would do any good."

"Well, it couldn't hurt. Don't you see what you're doing? You're acting exactly the way they expect you to."

He shot her a quick, angry glance that held underlying interest. "What do you mean?"

She pulled in a breath of frigid air, then watched it cloud before her as she exhaled. "I mean, because you lived with the Indians for so many years, people just figure you're one of them. You're on their side, no matter what. In essence," she added, "you're a traitor."

"Dammit! I'm *not* a traitor. Why can't they understand that?"

She shrugged. "How can they? You moved here with Joey and became a recluse. You don't mingle with any of the people in town. You avoid conversations with everyone. You bought land that no one thought you could afford, being an Indian lover and all—"

"Ah, hell," he interrupted again. "You're no better than the rest of them."

"But don't you see? That's not me saying those things. It's everyone who's ever seen you ride sullenly into town, go wordlessly about your business, then slink back to your farm. Just by your actions you've proven that you're exactly what they thought you would be."

He sat quietly beside her as if digesting what she'd said. "I don't see what I can do to change their minds."

"You could start smiling . . . just a little." She gave him a sidelong glance and felt a rush of delight when he smiled—against his will, no doubt. "See? Now, the next time you go into town, smile at the merchants. Tip your hat at the ladies. Let them know you're human and pleasant and not some crazy hermit."

He snorted again. "I can't do that."

Surprised, she looked at him. "And why not?"

He squirmed on the seat, unconsciously touching Eve's hip. She briefly closed her eyes as the pleasure threaded through her.

"Because it's just not something I could do."

"Then I suggest you work at it." She touched his knee again, this time on purpose, and didn't pull her hand away. They sat quietly, the air filled with an unusual tension. Eve's heart pounded hard, for she knew she was being forward, but she felt a recklessness that was new to her, and she just didn't care.

5

THEIR AFTERNOON SESSION WENT WELL. BECAUSE she was so pleased with Joey's progress, she told him that the next time she came, she'd tell him the story of *The Christmas Cuckoo*. Eve had made the story into a play, and the school children were practicing it and would present it to their parents at the school pageant a few days before Christmas.

Now, as she darned the socks Joey had brought her, she felt him staring at her from across the table.

"Miss Engels?"

"Yes, Joey?" she answered with a smile.

"You stayin' for supper?"

Her heart nearly broke. Supplication was written all over his face, but she forced herself to stay unaffected. "I'm sure your father has something planned."

Joey's glance shot toward the door, as if he expected his father to come in at any minute, although Sam had just left to start some afternoon chores.

"Aw, we'll prob'ly just have tater hash."

Eve couldn't suppress a smile. " 'Tater' hash? Doesn't sound too exciting, I will admit."

Joey sighed and stared at the fire. "Nothin's been as good as what you made, Miss Engels. All the cookies are gone, and I think Pa ate the last of the bread yesterday. And we ain't ... I mean, we haven't had nothin' as good as that stew you made."

Eve's determination not to interfere in their daily routine had already been broken since she was darning socks. What harm would it do to make them a bite of dinner? "All right. What are you hungry for, Joey?"

Joey sighed and gave her a blissful smile. "Pa and I caught some fish through the ice on the lake yesterday. How 'bout if we have them?"

"Hmmm. Did you clean them?"

"Yep. All cleaned and ready to fry."

Eve put her darning down on the floor beside the chair. "All right. You get the fish, and I'll do the rest."

Sam frowned as he entered the cabin. The lingering smell of batter-fried fish and onions filled the room, and he let out a quiet curse.

After hanging up his jacket, he removed his boots and stepped into the room. The little busybody stood over the stove, stirring something in a skillet. Freshly baked biscuits were heaped on a plate. The table was set for three.

"Pa! Guess what we're havin' for supper!"

Sam gave Joey a dark look, but the boy was too engrossed in food to notice. "Hard tack and pig swill?"

Eve turned from the stove and gave him a little smile. "That would serve you right, wouldn't it?"

He lifted an eyebrow at her but said nothing.

Joey, oblivious to their repartee, answered. "Heck,

no, Pa. We're havin' fried fish, creamed taters with onions and peas and fresh biscuits!''

Eve lifted the skillet and dumped the potato mixture into a bowl. "I'm surprised at the treasures you have in your cellar, Mr. Prescott. Why, I couldn't believe you actually had some peas. Don't tell me you do your own canning?"

"I got them from Mavis Torkelson last fall," he muttered.

She gave him a look of dry surprise. "Oh, you *do* get along with someone, then?"

He wanted to give her a sarcastic answer, but suddenly he couldn't think of one.

"Hurry and wash up, Pa. I'm hungrier than a bear."

With a mixture of reluctance and pleasure, Sam cleaned up for supper, his stomach growling in anticipation.

The meal was filled with Joey's chatter about his recent encounter with some of the boys from Eve's class at school. Apparently they all met down by the lake.

"I hope none of you boys are foolish enough to walk out onto the lake. It might be frozen, but it could still be dangerous," Sam said.

"I know that, Pa. But that Ernie Nisbeth. He pretends he's not afraid of nothin'. He's out on the lake, darin' everyone else to join him. He's a real skunk."

"A skunk?" Eve bit into a biscuit, relieved they were light and fluffy.

"He's kinda mean, but I don't think he wants to be all the time. He just is, like he can't do nothin' about it."

Eve thought about it. Yes, Ernest was probably the most troublesome child she had in the classroom, and she couldn't understand it because his parents were genuinely fine people who treated all their children fairly. It was almost as if Ernest had come from a bad seed.

"What did you and the boys talk about?"

Joey chewed on a piece of fish, then looked at his father. "Well, I told them I could write Indian sign language."

Eve put down her fork. "You can? Why, I think that's wonderful, Joey."

Joey looked at his father again, then shrugged. "Yeah, but Ernie didn't believe me. Said I was just makin' it all up and that anybody could make stick pictures in the snow."

Eve wanted to throttle Ernest. "Well, don't let him bother you, Joey. The other boys are nice, aren't they?"

He shrugged again. "Sometimes. But not when they're with Ernie."

Sam cleared his throat and stood. "It's time for me to take you home, Miss Engels."

Eve glanced at the cluttered table. "Oh, but the dishes—"

"Joey will tend to those."

Eve sighed. Sam wanted her gone.

"When you comin' again, ma'am?" Joey asked.

Eve allowed Sam to help her with her coat. "I'll be here on Wednesday, and you'll learn about *The Christmas Cuckoo*."

Joey grinned and nodded, but continued to stare at her, clearly wanting to say something else.

"Yes, Joey, what is it?"

He gave his father a quick glance, ignoring the stern look, then asked, "Do you s'pose we can bake some more of them cookies?"

Eve could feel Sam's hands tense on her shoulders. She remembered how little he wanted her around, but she refused to make up some silly excuse just for him. She had no reason to disappoint Joey.

"How about if we start baking some Christmas things?"

He gave her a puzzled look. "Christmas things?"

"Yes, like sweet Christmas bread with fruit and nuts, cookies with butter and sugar frosting, apple pie—"

"Oh, yes, ma'am," he said with a wide grin. "I'd like that just fine."

"All right, Joey. I'll see you on Wednesday, then." She felt Sam pushing her toward the door. Over her shoulder, she called, "Don't forget to study those letters!"

"I won't! I won't forget, ma'am!"

Sam took her arm and pulled her roughly toward the waiting sleigh. "I don't want you doing this," he said gruffly.

She settled onto the bench and pulled the quilt over her knees. When he was seated close beside her, their bodies touching to generate warmth, she asked, "Why is it so hard for you to let me do things for him?"

He was silent for a time. The only sound in the crisp, cold air was the jingling of the sleigh bells attached to the harness. "Because in the end, he'll only be disappointed."

Frowning, Eve digested his words. "I'd never disappoint him, Sam."

He cursed under his breath. "You just don't get it, do you?"

His words were harsh. Cold. And they hurt. "I guess I'm just too stupid to understand how cooking a few meals and baking cookies for a delightful little boy could possibly disappoint him. Why don't you explain it to me?"

He cursed again. "For a woman, you talk pretty boldly."

"I'm not trying to be bold, Sam Prescott," she retorted angrily. "I'm just trying to *understand* what you have against me."

"Ah, hell. It's not against you, personally. It's just that . . ." He took a deep breath. "All right, I'll say it right out. After you have your fun playing house, cooking and baking for my boy, you'll get tired of it soon enough. Then what? It's better if Joey doesn't get used to such stuff. It's better if . . . if you just let us be."

She should have been angry at his words. Instead they made her want to cry. Not for herself but for Joey. Her eyes filled and her throat closed. "Everyone deserves a little pleasure in life, Sam. Especially little boys like Joey who have so many more hurdles to jump than a white child. No one, not even a well-meaning father, should prevent him from having whatever pleasures are available to him."

They rode the rest of the way in silence. Eve knew he was trying to push her away. As for Joey, why, she'd never just up and leave him. They were friends. She could understand why Sam would be upset if she were the kind of person who would garner Joey's friendship, then drop him when she got bored, but she wasn't like that.

She had a special feeling for Sam, too, but the feeling wasn't reciprocated. Something deep inside her wished it would be, but wishing never made anything happen.

Cora met her at the door, stern-faced. "It's about time you got home."

Eve removed her boots, leaving them just inside the door before stepping into the room. "It's not that late." She feigned nonchalance, knowing that Cora had probably held supper for her.

"I suppose you've eaten?"

"Well, I could hardly deny the boy supper, Cora."

Cora followed her up the stairs to her room. "Is this going to be an ongoing thing? Eating supper with them?"

Eve was tired. School was hard enough, since this

would be her first Christmas pageant, and she wanted to do it right. Then, spending another few hours tutoring Joey made for a very long day. Not that she'd have it any other way. It was just that she wanted the holiday to be perfect, both at school and for Joey. Her seventeen Christmases in the orphanage had been bleak. She had a lot to make up for.

The school children were so excited about Christmas. Although they gladly memorized the songs and their parts for the play, and delighted in making decorations for the walls and windows, they were still a handful. Even pesky Ernest was well behaved at this time of year, but that didn't make him any less rambunctious.

"Well? Are you always going to eat with them?" Cora asked again.

"Oh, I don't know. Probably. I can't say no to little Joey. He . . . he seems to need some softness in his life, and as long as he wants something from me that I can give, I don't see any reason not to. And whatever Sam thinks—"

"*Sam?* Now it's Sam?" Cora interrupted plaintively. "I don't believe this, Eve. You're calling that man by his first name. It's . . . well, it's just not proper."

Eve closed her eyes and rubbed her neck. "Cora, you're making too much of it. It's nothing, believe me. He still calls me 'ma'am.' Now, does that satisfy you?" She unbuttoned her dress, stepped out of it and hung it in the wardrobe.

"Oh, I just worry so about you, dear. When I first saw you that day we stopped at the orphanage to deliver that load of fresh vegetables, my heart went out to you. You were the most beautiful young thing I'd ever seen. And so polite. 'Clarence,' I said, 'can't we take her home with us?' But Clarence said it would be far better for you to stay there and attend normal school in St. Paul. The nuns were grateful we wanted to pay for your education, and we were happy to do it. Now, you're like my own daughter. I don't want to see you hurt, dear."

Eve felt a measure of guilt. Clarence and Cora Nisbeth were the first real family she'd ever had. And they'd made her dream of becoming a teacher come true. She didn't want to hurt them, but she couldn't explain exactly what she was feeling for Joey. She just knew she couldn't abandon him.

And Sam . . . She wasn't sure what she felt for him, either, but whatever it was, she didn't want it to stop. That was a frightening realization.

She went over and gave Cora a hug. "You know I'll never be able to repay you and Clarence for what you've done for me. But I don't want you to worry about me. That's a terrible responsibility for you."

Cora watched as Eve folded her underthings and carefully laid them across a chair. "I just don't want you to be hurt, dear. Not by anyone, and that includes the people in this community once they hear what you're doing."

Eve felt a nudge of exasperation. As she unbraided her hair, she couldn't keep from saying, "Is it because the man is a widower with a half-breed child? I can't help but wonder how much different their reaction might be if Joey were white."

Cora took the brush from Eve and pulled it through her long, thick hair. It had become a ritual; Cora had always told her she had pretty hair. "Angel hair," she called it. Eve smiled, remembering that Joey had called it that, too.

"I won't deny that it would make a difference," Cora said. "We all just want you to be happy dear, and—"

"And you don't think I can be happy with a man who has slept with an Indian woman."

Cora gasped and brought her hand over her heart. "Eve Engels, don't talk so boldly. It's not a bit ladylike, and you know it."

Eve didn't want to argue. No one understood

what she was feeling, and they would never understand even if she tried to explain. She'd had her share of suitors, but no man she'd ever known had made her feel like Sam Prescott did. He could be the devil himself, and it wouldn't matter. For better or worse, she was drawn to him.

"I'm sorry, Cora. I didn't mean to offend you. I'm just tired, I guess."

Cora pressed her shoulders. "Of course you are, dear. I'll leave you."

Eve watched Cora quietly close the door behind her. She heard the clock on the mantel in the parlor chime nine times. After turning out her lamp, she climbed into bed, comforted by the familiarity, yet remembering the distinctly male scents from Sam's bedding. Trying to recapture the sensation, she drifted into a restful sleep.

6

ALTHOUGH THE CHILDREN HAD DECORATED THE insides of the windows with brightly colored green wreaths and red bows, Mother Nature had decorated the outside, adorning each pane with frost. The bright, cold sun spattered the frost with brilliance, often creating colorful prisms of light.

Inside, color suffused every available wall space, too. Christmas trees and manger scenes and children skating on a frozen lake papered the walls like a seasonal mosaic. Strings of threaded popcorn were draped over the door and windows, and bittersweet berries nested in evergreen branches.

The preacher, Reverend Larsen, didn't seem to mind that he had to share the room. Eve thought he was probably used to it. After all, the community building was put to a variety of uses all year long; people gathered to hear traveling speakers and musicians and to enjoy basket socials. Why, last summer they had even held a pig auction. Naturally, the pigs had stayed outside.

Eve could tell that the reverend truly loved children, because he often stopped by to admire their drawings and listen to their Christmas recitations. He was a round, jolly man with a ready smile and plump, pink cheeks. Eve had thought he would make a perfect Santa Claus, but she realized that the minister might not be the prudent choice.

The older boys had hauled in a Christmas tree. It was a graceful red cedar, and the children couldn't wait to put on the candles and light them. Eve had to remind them that they would be lit only at the Christmas program, over a week away, then again on Christmas Eve, for the church service. They all groaned good-naturedly.

Over the past weekend, Eve had visited the homes of her students. It was important for all the parents to know that they weren't to bring gifts for their children to the Christmas program. Since only a few families could afford it, it was better if no one did. Gifts for only a few would make the others unhappy.

She knew that Clarence had purchased a barrel of apples and was going to hand out one to each child that evening. It was a wonderful gesture, but every family couldn't be expected to do the same. And Eve and Cora planned to bake fresh gingerbread cookies, decorating them with frosting as a special treat for each child.

Eve wasn't sure, but she thought that perhaps other mothers would do something for each child, too. On the surface, all things pointed to a successful Christmas program.

On the surface. But each time she thought about Sam and Joey, excluded from the community, all her Christmas spirit fled.

While she waited for Sam to pick her up after school, she trudged through the snow to the stand of cedars that stood behind the church. She was looking for boughs to decorate Sam and Joey's cabin. She already had popping corn in her valise so they could pop it and string it for decoration.

A clump of bittersweet berries caught her eye, and she pulled it off and gently put it in her pocket. Perhaps Joey knew where they could find some more.

Hearing the sound of Sam's sleigh, she hurried to the road and waved as he drove up. Joey was with him, and he gave her a wide, happy smile. Sam appeared solemn. She felt immediate concern.

She climbed in, and Joey made room for her between him and his father. After greeting him warmly, she turned to Sam.

"Aren't you feeling well?"

"I'm fine."

Obviously he was in one of his stoic moods. She turned to Joey. "We have so much to do after your lessons today, Joey. I was wondering if you knew where there are any bittersweet berries."

"Sure do," he answered with enthusiasm. "What're you gonna make with 'em? Somethin' to eat?"

She laughed gaily. "Is that all you ever think about?"

He grinned back. "It is ever since you started comin' over, Miss Engels."

She nudged his shoulder. "We have to start decorating the cabin for Christmas." She held up her valise. "Guess what I have in here?"

"Is it somethin' to eat?"

She laughed again. "Yes and no. I mean, you can eat it, but you can also use it for decorations."

"Well, what is it?"

She shook her head. "I told you to guess. I'm not going to make it easy for you." He made a playful lunge for her valise, causing her to pull it away. She fell against Sam. When she turned to look at him, she stopped laughing. He truly looked ill.

Once they reached the cabin, she became so engrossed in Joey's lessons, she temporarily forgot about Sam's pique. When the lessons were done, she and Joey popped the corn she'd brought.

Eve heaped it high in a bowl on the table. She reached into her valise and pulled out a small sewing kit. As she threaded a needle for Joey, she caught him stuffing the popcorn into his mouth.

She laughed softly. "At that rate, there won't be any left to string."

Joey tried to grin, but his cheeks were puffed out like a squirrel's. "Me'n Chancy love popcorn," he said around his mouthful.

Eve glanced at the dog, who had been allowed inside more and more often since she'd started coming over, and discovered him pushing some popcorn around on the hearth with his nose. "Oh, Joey. Chancy's not eating it. He's playing with it."

"Aw, he'll eat it pretty soon. Chancy'll eat anything," he answered, swallowing what he had in his mouth. "Once he ate a mouse; I saw him. An' there was that time he dragged home a dead skunk—"

"That's enough, Joey," Sam interrupted.

Shuddering, Eve tossed Sam a grateful, although weak smile, trying not to remember how often she'd allowed Chancy to lick her face. "Well," she said, turning back to her task, "this is what we do." She showed Joey the threaded needle and carefully pushed it through a few pieces of popcorn, then a bittersweet berry, alternating them that way until she had a gay red and white chain. She showed him how to knot the ends when he was done.

Joey worked carefully, his face pinched in concentration. "Pa? You gonna help?"

His father glanced up from his newspaper, then buried his face in it again. "You're doing fine, Joey."

Eve felt a stab of disappointment. It would be so good for all of them to do this together, but she couldn't force him to participate. She sighed. So much for her silly dreams and plans of making them act like a family.

When Joey ran out of the berries Eve had brought, he bundled up and left the cabin with Chancy to find some more. Eve turned her attention back to the fresh, hot bread she'd just taken from the oven. She wiped the top of the loaf with butter, then looked at Sam. He was sitting at the table staring at her, his expression dour.

"Sam, I know you don't feel well. You've hardly said a word since you picked me up."

He continued to stare at her. "You're doing this on purpose, aren't you?"

His tone startled her. "What do you mean?"

"You know damn well what I mean."

Bravely ignoring his words, Eve walked around to where he sat and touched his forehead. He flinched, pulling her hand away. He didn't release her wrist.

She swallowed hard. "I . . . I thought you might be running a fever. . . ."

"I am, dammit, but not where you think."

She stared at him, his words both frightening and thrilling her. "That . . . that's hardly the thing to say. . . ."

His grip tightened, and he pulled her to him, his face dangerously close to her breasts. "You're driving me crazy, Angel Face."

The sound of his voice and the endearment uttered so angrily made her knees buckle. She tried to pull her arm away. He didn't release it. Instead, he stood and dragged her close.

"I'm not . . . I mean, I haven't . . ." Lord, she didn't know what she meant. Her heart felt all fluttery inside her chest. She studied his face. There was a handsome cleft in his chin beneath his stubble. His eyebrows were sharply defined, and his thick lashes fringed his hauntingly beautiful eyes.

He still clutched her wrist but put it behind her back, bringing her even closer. Excitement at his nearness won out over her fear. She was mesmerized by his touch, his dark, brooding looks. He made her weak. She relaxed against him and felt rather than heard his sharp intake of breath. Her gaze moved slowly to where their bodies touched, and she suddenly understood his reaction. Her breasts were flat against his chest.

A tingling, stinging sensation radiated through her, making her nipples hard and tight. It was exactly the same feeling she'd had when he'd touched her that night in front of the fire. Slowly she moved her gaze back to his face. A muscle twitched in his jaw. His breathing became the slightest bit erratic, and his eyes focused on her mouth.

Before she knew what was happening, he was kissing her—hard, angry kisses that were undoubtedly intended to punish. She'd never been kissed like this before.

Something sweet and warm erupted inside her, deep down between her legs, and she threw her free arm around him, answering his violent response. He forced his way into her mouth, his tongue sparring with hers. Releasing her arm, he brought his hands to her head, holding her as he ravaged her.

Eve felt a wild, uninhibited response to his kiss and found herself clutching him tightly. She heard him groan into her mouth and his touch softened; their mouths clung. His hands left her hair and roamed over her back. He lifted her slightly, pressing her close, and she felt the hard ridge beneath his jeans. The sensation heated her blood, and it pounded through her veins, expanding in her abdomen, making her want something she hadn't known existed.

Abruptly, he lowered her feet to the floor without letting her go. "That shouldn't have happened." His voice was harsh, husky.

She could barely stand; her legs felt like quivering aspen twigs. Oh, had she known what two people could feel . . . And whether he wanted to admit it or not, he felt something powerful for her, too.

Braving his mood, she reached up and touched his chin. He gripped her fingers and held them while he pierced her with his dark gaze.

"What in the hell do you want from us, Angel Face?"

"W-want from you?" That quivering little voice was actually hers.

"It's a simple enough question," he answered, his voice as gritty as sandpaper.

"I care about you and Joey. I—" She stopped, knowing she was about to tell Sam she was falling in love with him. But she couldn't say it; she could hardly believe it herself. Instead, she said, "I want us to be friends. Can't we at least be friends?"

His groin stirred against her stomach, sending rockets of desire and surprise into her pelvis. She felt a flush on her chest beneath her dress, one that flooded upward into her cheeks.

He gave her a grim half-smile, then glanced away. "Friends don't feel what we're feeling, little miss school marm."

She swallowed hard and knew she should step away from him, but his words held her fast.

Hoping to slow her pounding heart, she took a deep breath. "What's happening, Sam? Why am I feeling this way?"

He studied her intently, his gaze moving over her face, her neck, her breasts. She felt a tingling everywhere, as if he'd actually touched her.

His grim half-smile returned. "You know why."

Amazed at her own audacity, she asked, "Please . . . tell me."

Watching her carefully beneath heavy, sloping, thickly lashed lids, he said, "It started that night by the fire, and you know it. I want you. I won't deny it. Every time I see you I want to drag you against me and kiss you. I want to touch you in places I don't think you've ever been touched. I want to bury myself deep inside you, watch your face flush with pleasure, listen to your sweet sounds of contentment. In short, Angel Face, I want to take you to my bed and . . . and . . ."

Eve could hardly breathe. She found herself gasping, hanging on his every word, marveling at her ability to stay put and not run away. She hadn't imagined that men really talked to women this way. It was . . . it was as electrifying as if he'd physically seduced her.

Gracious and glory! Her body sang with desire and wonder, and she found herself asking, "And . . . and what, Sam?" Oh, she knew. She felt him, still stiff and hard against her. She was virginal, but she wasn't innocent. She'd read Hawthorne and Bronte and knew there was a sensual side to life that had, until now, eluded her.

Pulling her wrist from his grip, she rested both arms on his shoulders and gently touched the crisp, dark hair that hung below his ears.

She studied him, carefully watching his eyes. The heat she'd initially seen was gone, replaced with something else. "You're purposely trying to frighten me, or shock me, aren't you?"

"It doesn't seem to be working, though, does it?" He released her, crossed to the fireplace and stared into the flames. "A woman like you shouldn't respond to that kind of talk."

Eve touched her chest, able to feel her heart beat

beneath her fingers. "A woman like me? What . . . what does that mean?"

He turned slightly, giving her a thorough once-over, his gaze touching her everywhere. "A gentle-born school mistress who's never had a man between her sweet, milky white thighs."

Her pulse leaped into her throat and she felt a jolt way down deep in her stomach. "You . . . you're trying to do it again. Shock me, I mean."

With a sultry half-grin, he asked, "You mean I still haven't succeeded?"

Wishing he didn't confuse her so, she went to the table and started cutting up the dried fruits and nuts for Christmas bread. "Why do you want to push me away?"

He turned back to the fire. "I've already told you why. If I don't, in the end, Joey will just get hurt."

She cut up a dried apple and dropped it into a bowl. "End? Just what 'end' are you talking about?"

Sam sighed and ran his fingers through his hair. "Do you have any idea what a woman usually does when she discovers I have a half-breed son?"

Eve thought she knew. She'd heard of a few women who'd been disappointed that Sam, the eligible widower, had an Indian child. "I'm not like that, Sam. I know what Joey is, and I think he's a wonderful boy. Bright, generous and maybe too sensitive. I think he's always going to have to fight for what he wants. Harder than other boys."

Sam was quiet. "So you want to be my friend, is that it?"

She didn't like the sound of his voice. "Of course. And . . . and Joey's, too," she added as she dumped the fruit mixture into the bread dough.

"What happens when you marry your straight-laced white farmer? Or merchant? Or preacher? Then what? Will you still be my *friend*?" He turned and glared at her once again, his eyes sparkling dangerously.

She had to look away. The thought of marrying some anonymous stranger made her a bit sick to her stomach. In fact, she hadn't thought much about marriage at all. Well, that wasn't entirely true. Brief glimpses of a life with Sam and Joey had flashed through her daydreams. . . .

Her silence seemed to be his answer. "I didn't think so," he muttered.

"No, Sam. You don't understand. I . . . I have no suitors. No farmers, no merchants, no preachers." She shrugged a little and gave him a tremulous smile. "I've never had anyone really serious about me."

He studied her a long moment again, then answered. "It's probably because none of them think they'd have a chance with you."

In spite of her nervousness, or maybe because of it, laughter burst from her throat. "And why not?"

His gaze grew heated. "Don't you have a mirror?"

"Of course," she answered, wiping her hands on a towel. She knew she was a comely woman, but at the orphanage she'd been told that looks meant little. It was what was inside a person that counted. "What's that got to do with anything?"

"You have the face of an angel and a body that would tempt a saint. Your hair is the color of the most perfect, pale wheat kissed by moonlight." He looked at her, the sultry smile slipping. Suddenly he wasn't smiling at all. "Tell me, Angel Face, is it that color everywhere?"

She swallowed, his intimation crystal clear. Trying to ignore the stirring between her thighs, she vigorously kneaded the bread. "You're trying to shock me, again. If you're not interested in me, why do you keep referring to my body parts? Do you think about them often?"

If Sam was surprised at her bold words, he didn't show it. He simply gave her another heated half-smile. "More often than you can imagine."

Moistness gathered where the stirring had begun. "Then you didn't just say those things to shock me?" She tried to be calm as she braided the sweetened bread dough on a baking sheet.

He sighed and crossed to the window. "It doesn't matter why I said them, Eve."

She put a towel over her bread, then went to the stove and stirred the beans she was cooking for their supper. He was drawn to her, she knew it. He was also fighting it. Hard.

She pulled out the spoon and tasted the beans. They tasted all right, but she was so flustered, she couldn't be sure that she hadn't forgotten something. She turned to Sam.

"Um," she said, her expression doubtful. "Will you taste these? I think they need something else."

He came from the window, cupped his hand under hers and took a long sip of the broth. The touch of his warm, roughened palm on her hand sent tingles through her. She automatically took a step closer, and her breast brushed his arm. With quiet surprise she watched the desire that flooded his features.

Suddenly she knew she had some sort of power over him. The realization frightened her. She knew she could use it to her advantage, but she wasn't sure how. More importantly, she knew it was probably like a powder keg, just waiting to be struck with a match.

That evening when Sam stopped the sleigh in front of the Nisbeths', Eve shyly put her arms around him. She wanted things to be all right. She hated the tension that had arisen between them.

He stiffened, then pressed his fingers over hers, capturing her hand against his chest. "What in the hell are you doing?"

Smiling at him in the darkness, she squeezed him hard. "I'm hugging you, Sam. I hate to see you so miserable, and if I'm to blame, I'm sorry."

He swore on a lusty breath of air, then pulled her close, kissing her hard.

Eve answered the kiss, anxious for it, needing it.

Suddenly he pushed her away. "You're to blame, all right. I can't seem to keep my hands off you."

Again, she felt the stirring inside her. "Is . . . is that so bad, Sam?" She could feel his gaze in the darkness.

"It could be the worst thing that ever happened to you."

His ominous words pressed against her heart. "I don't see how," she answered softly.

He jumped from the sleigh, went around and helped her out. "Trust me, Angel Face. Trust me."

She left him and slogged through the snow, turning to watch him leave when she got to the house. Her insides were in turmoil. Something had happened tonight. There was an ache deep inside her. For somehow she sensed that although what had occurred between them had felt right, it would ultimately cause them both pain. And still, despite the warning, it was the kind of feeling she couldn't ignore.

7

WHEN SAM ARRIVED HOME, HE WALKED INTO THE cabin and hung up his jacket. His gaze went to the table where the Christmas bread, or *julekage*, as she'd called it, lay beneath a neat, white cloth. Beside it were round ginger cookies sprinkled with sugar and a dried apple pie. The place smelled damned good. He glanced at the windows, strung with popped corn and berries, and over the mantel, where a sprig of cedar hung, a red ribbon tied to the top.

How he'd wanted to join her and Joey as they decorated the cabin. But it was foolish, this pretense of her being part of his family. Even if he might want it, it would never happen. He could dream about it from hell to breakfast, but it wouldn't happen. Soon, she was going to get tired of Joey. Tired of trudging over here to give him an education. Tired of cooking and baking and playing house. Yeah, it would be soon. Yet, remembering Joey and Eve together, making cookies, stringing popcorn, sitting side by side while she read to him, made Sam envious. Envious of his son's easy manner with her. And though he was very much afraid of it, he ached to have it last.

Grumbling, he went to the fireplace and slumped into a chair. His gaze caught her darning needle and thread, and he winced. In spite of his efforts to keep Eve at arm's length, he found her invading every corner of his space. It scared him. The empty gap inside his soul was growing smaller. He actually looked forward to picking her up at the school, though he couldn't let her know that. She had felt the same desire that he had when he'd kissed her.

He dug the heels of his palms into his eyes and swore. *Get control of yourself, you horny bastard.* Yeah, but it was damned easier said than done. If he didn't find a way to stop, he'd take her to his bed. And he had a strong feeling that she wouldn't fight him. Their coupling would be hot and sweet, intense and frantic. She looked like an angel, but he'd felt her fire.

He couldn't let it happen. Not ever. Because it wouldn't last, and when her proper Indian-hating friends found out about it, as they surely would, they'd reject her. And he couldn't purposely hurt her that way.

A part of him realized how easy it was to promise never to touch her when she wasn't around. Even so, there was an anxious urge deep inside him that couldn't wait to see her again.

He'd purposely tried to discourage her, certain that his crude innuendoes would send her scurrying away like a squirrel in the wake of bird shot. He smiled ruefully. She wasn't supposed to egg him on, no matter how innocently. Just the look in her deep blue eyes, that quiet expression of puzzlement and desire, had urged him to continue baiting her. She was the most delectable woman he'd met in a long, long time, and even though she was outspoken and sometimes bold, he was certain she was still untouched.

He rose from the chair and went to the bed, vowing he'd never again do something to make her think there was anything between them but gratitude and friendship.

But after he undressed and slid into bed, he could still hear the devilish little voice in his head laughing menacingly at his foolish promises.

The next afternoon, after her lesson with Joey, Eve wiped her hands on a towel and gazed with satisfaction at another fresh loaf of Christmas bread. "Okay, Joey. Now you can sprinkle the *julekage* with cinnamon and sugar."

She watched as he carefully dusted the warm bread, using the precision of an artist to make sure every inch of the surface was covered.

When he'd finished, he stood back and studied his work. "How's that, ma'am?"

Eve watched the mixture darken slightly as it melted on top of the bread. "Perfect." She glanced at the clock set on the table by the window. "It's nearly time for Mr. Torkelson to pick you up. You'd better wash your hands."

Since Eve had arrived in the community, she'd heard nothing but negative things about Jeremiah and Mavis Torkelson. Clarence was always grumbling about "old man Torkelson's" refusal to sell his land so they could build a school. The commissioner of education had even come out from St. Paul with a generous offer, but it had been useless. Torkelson wouldn't budge.

Eve found it puzzling that the Torkelsons were so friendly and generous with Sam and Joey but shut out the rest of the community. Today, for instance, Joey was going over to their farm to help haul wood from the woodshed to the house. He would even be paid.

Sam still hadn't returned from his trip to town when she and Joey heard Mr. Torkelson's "hellooo." Joey quickly slipped into his jacket and pulled on his boots. As he stuffed his mittens into his pocket, he glanced at her.

"You want Mr. Torkelson to drive you home, ma'am?"

Eve gazed at the pile of dishes they'd used for baking. "No, that's all right, Joey. I'll stay and clean up. Your father can take me home later."

"Well," Joey said, gazing at the door, "I prob'ly won't see you for a couple of days, then. I'm stayin' the night. Mr. Torkelson says there's too much wood to haul for me to finish before dark." His face split into a wide grin. "Mrs. Torkelson is gonna make me a batch of fry bread. I ain't—I mean, I haven't—had fry bread and honey since before my ma died."

"Fry bread?"

"Yes, ma'am. We Dakotas love fry bread. Ever had any?"

Eve shook her head. "I can't say that I have."

"Maybe me and Pa can make you some. It's real easy, and it's good, too."

"I'd like that, Joey. Tell me," she added, "how did Mavis Torkelson learn to cook an Indian food?"

Joey shrugged. "I guess 'cause she's half Dakota, like me." He grinned again, then was gone.

Eve crossed to the window and watched Joey and Mr. Torkelson ride away. So, she thought. Mavis Torkelson was part Indian. Frowning, she wondered if that was the reason they kept to themselves.

She shook off thoughts of the Torkelsons, rolled up her sleeves and started cleaning up the dishes. She was just putting the last of the things away when Sam came in. She felt an immediate fluttering in the pit of her stomach.

He gave her a quick look, then hung up his jacket. "You still here?"

She'd hoped for a warmer welcome. Quickly looking away, she answered. "There were dishes to do. I couldn't just leave them."

He grunted a reply, went over to the basin and washed up. "You should have let Torkelson drive you home. Now I've got to hitch up my team again."

She felt a rush of anger. "Oh, don't bother. It isn't quite dark, and it's only a mile. I can walk."

He cursed quietly. "You'd probably just get lost."

Turning on him, knowing she'd wanted a different response altogether, she spat, "And that would suit you just fine, wouldn't it? Then I'd be out of your hair for good."

He crossed to the table and sat down heavily. "Yeah, then you'd be out of my hair, and I'd be relieved as hell never to see you again."

Eve turned away before he could see how his words affected her. She felt the foolish sting of tears and quickly overcame the need to cry. She didn't have to be struck in the face with a board to know it would hurt. And she didn't have to see Sam's face to know he'd somehow fought his desire for her and won. She might be stubborn, but she wasn't stupid.

She fixed him a plate of supper, put it in front of

him, then sat down across from him. "If it will make you happy," she started stiffly, "I'll continue to tutor Joey at school."

He gave her a questioning look.

Shrugging, she sighed and traced the faint pattern in the oilcloth with her finger, still feeling stupid tears pressing against the back of her eyes. "I'd hate to stop tutoring him just because . . . just because we can't seem to get along." She took a deep, shakey breath. It had all been so sweet, so wonderful. She'd had someone to cook for, bake for . . . care for. And love. All her life, it was what she'd wanted most.

But she knew now that nothing she did would make Sam love her. That had to come from him. If he didn't return her love, no amount of loving on her part could make up for the lack on his.

Suddenly she felt cold. Deep down cold, way into her bones. She shivered, stood and went to the fire. Even its warmth couldn't penetrate the depth of her chill. She'd grown to care for Joey so much, never mind how deeply she'd fallen in love with Sam. Had she really thought she could get to Sam through her cooking? She smiled sadly. Most men living alone would have fallen to their knees and kissed the hem of her skirt, had she cooked and done for them as she had for Sam.

A sharp gust of wind rattled the windows. She stepped closer to the fire and rubbed her arms.

"Wind's come up," he said from somewhere behind her.

She listened again and heard the continuous moaning outside. "Not another blizzard, I hope." She didn't think she could stand to be cooped up with him again, especially knowing how much he wanted to get rid of her. She heard the scrape of the chair as he left the table and went to the window.

"It's clear. There's a cold moon up there."

"Well," she said, more for conversation than anything else, "that's a relief."

"Not really."

She pulled herself away from the fire and went to where he stood. She was tempted to lean into him, into his warmth. She forced herself to keep her distance. She peered outside, noting how moonlight bathed the landscape, accentuating the whiteness of the snow. "Why's that?"

"It's going to get cold. Real cold. It always does when the wind kicks up and there are no clouds."

She shivered again, sensing the change in the weather. "I . . . I think I should leave now."

He rubbed his neck. "No."

Fear lifted her heart. "What do you mean?"

"I won't take my horses out again."

She felt a brief bite of shrewish anger. "Your precious horses have more of your concern than any human."

"I need my horses. I don't need another human." He turned away and left her standing alone.

She spun around. "I don't believe you."

His slow smile surprised her. "I didn't imagine you would."

Irritated, she turned to the window again. "So I'm forced to stay again, is that it?"

"I wouldn't suggest you try to leave. As long as you're here, I'm responsible for you. I don't want Clarence Nisbeth lashing me to a post if you go out there and freeze to death."

She didn't want to stay. She *wouldn't* stay. She'd pretend to acquiesce, then, when he was asleep, she'd bundle up and leave. At least it wasn't snowing, and she'd be able to find her way home with the moon to guide her. "All right. I'll stay, but I'm really quite tired. Do you mind if I go to bed right now?"

He shrugged and nodded toward his bed. "Be my guest."

She watched him go to the door and let Chancy in, then bank the fire. After he'd climbed to the loft, she went to the bed, took off her shoes and slid under the covers, fully dressed. She dozed, then awakened with a start. Everything was quiet.

Slipping from the bed, she crossed to the ladder and listened. She could hear his heavy, even breathing. Relieved, she put on her boots and crept silently toward the door.

Chancy whined and nudged her thigh, causing Eve's heart to leap into her throat. She knelt down in front of him, quietly ordering him to stay, then she slipped out the door, into the frigid, windy night.

Something awakened Sam. He opened his eyes, listening for the noise. *Chancy.* Rising up on his elbow, he heard the dog whine. He frowned. What was wrong with him?

He rose from the bed and pulled on his jeans, then climbed quickly down the ladder. One look at his empty bed, and he knew what the dog was fussing about.

Cursing, he put on his jacket and boots, grabbed his rifle and a blanket and, with Chancy leading the way, strode outside.

He felt the harsh pinch of guilt as he trudged through the drifting snow. It was his fault she had left. He hadn't thought she'd be so damned foolish. He should have known that her pride would make her do it. She'd tried so desperately to cook her way into his heart, and when she thought she'd failed, she'd let her emotions take over. She had no way of knowing that she'd found a way to his heart the very first day he'd seen her, asleep in front of his fireplace.

He let Chancy go ahead, for the wind was so strong, there weren't even any footprints left for him to follow. The road was already indistinguishable from the ditches on either side. Great drifts were swept into frigid mounds, hiding the fences. If Eve

had her senses about her, she'd be following the
road, even though it was the long way around. Trying to wade through the snow in the fields would
be impossible.

At Chancy's howl, Sam squinted into the distance,
straining to listen. His heart drummed hard when
he heard the distinctive snarling rumble of wolves.
With a tight grip on his rifle, he forced himself forward against the wind.

8

SAM APPROACHED CAREFULLY, QUIETLY. HIS HEART
pounded. The wolves snapped and snarled as
they circled Chancy. One of them lunged. With a
fierce growl, Chancy threw himself at the wolf, seizing him by the neck with his strong jaws. They
flailed and rolled in the snow, the other wolves in
the pack snapping and yelping wildly.

The wolf suddenly slithered from Chancy's grip
and plunged his teeth into his neck. Sam raised his
rifle to fire at the wolf, but didn't dare shoot for fear
of hitting his dog.

Instead, he fired one shot into the air, then another, until the wolf who had taken Chancy down
finally broke his hold, snarled menacingly and slunk
away. The others followed, growling and yipping
over their shoulders, their tails between their legs.

When he reached Chancy, the dog was still lying
in the snow, panting. Sam removed his glove,
reached down and pushed his fingers through the
heavy fur at Chancy's neck. He drew his hand away;

it was warm and sticky. Chancy was bleeding.

In response to Chancy's growling whimpers, Sam stroked his head, then moved his hand over the rest of the dog's body. He found no other injuries. "You're going to be all right, fella." When Chancy struggled to sit up, Sam dug into his pocket, pulled out a large bandanna, and wrapped it around the dog's neck. "That'll have to do until we get home, boy."

Chancy pushed himself to his feet and stood, still whimpering, and padded deeper into the thicket.

Sam followed. They were far off the road now. He didn't want to think that Eve might have been tracked by the wolves and tried to take a shortcut through the field. But as he looked ahead of him, he knew that's what must have happened.

Chancy had stopped about twenty feet ahead of him and was bent over, nuzzling something deep in the snow.

Sam took the space between them in long heart-pounding strides. When he reached Chancy, the dog was bent over Eve, licking her face. Sam saw a log all but hidden in the drifts of snow. He was certain she'd tripped and fallen in her frantic attempt to escape the wolves. Now she wasn't moving.

Holding his breath, he knelt beside her and felt for a pulse at her neck. Relief rolled over him in waves when he found it strong and steady. He laid the blanket over the snow, gently lifted Eve onto it, then covered her.

She made a strangled sound and came awake abruptly, fighting him off with her fists.

"It's all right, Eve. Shh, it's all right," he murmured, drawing her close. She sagged against him and began to cry softly. Sam pinched his eyes closed and held her tightly, pushing down the emotion that clogged his throat.

Chancy yipped quietly beside him.

Pulling away, Sam slung his rifle over his shoulder, then took Eve into his arms. As he started back the way they'd come, he realized she'd gotten nearly a half a mile before she'd veered off course.

Once they were back in the cabin, he laid Eve on the bed, shrugged out of his jacket and then stoked up the fire. After quickly tending Chancy's wound, he returned to the bedside. Eve was coming around again, moaning slightly and moving on the bed.

He took off her wet coat, mittens and scarf and hung them by the fire. After sliding off her boots, he gently massaged her cold feet. She began to shiver. The hems of her skirt and petticoats were soaked clear up to her knees.

She stirred again and opened her eyes. "Sam?" Her voice came out in a quivering whisper.

Relief stirred inside him like a warm fire. Fearing she'd see more than he wanted her to, he pulled his gaze away. "Damn fool thing to do, Eve."

She continued to shiver. "Don't scold me, Sam. Get me warm."

"We'll have to get your wet clothes off. Roll to your side so I can unbutton your dress."

Instead, she sat up and eagerly helped him remove her wet garments. When they got to her underwear, she peeled off her camisole and with shaky fingers, unfastened her corset, tossing it onto the floor. Wearing just her chemise and drawers, she scrambled under the covers and huddled into a ball.

The load of guilt Sam felt for driving her away lay heavily upon him. She could have died out there. Either from the cold or by the wolves. Closing his eyes, he ran his hands over his face and shuddered.

"Sam?"

He took a deep breath and gave her a questioning look.

"I think my drawers are dry enough to wear. I . . . I can't be sure though, because my hands are so cold."

Sam snaked his hand under the covers and

touched her thigh. It was cold, but dry. How tempting she was, and how vulnerable.

"Well? Can I wear them?"

His hand moved slowly to her hip. Her rounded femininity stoked the fires in his groin. Ah, damn. He wanted to continue touching her, but he knew it would end in disaster if he did. Still, he allowed his palm to move slowly over her thigh to her knee, then back up again. He paused, waiting for her to stop him. She lay perfectly still. His hand traced the seam of her drawers from her navel to just above her soft mound, and he felt her sharp intake of breath. She began to shiver again but did nothing to stop him.

He was hard and ready, but reveled in the twinges of pleasure and anticipation. God, how he wanted her. He swallowed, admitting to himself that he'd wanted her for weeks.

"S-Sam?"

He looked at her, his fingers resting on the soft mound of her womanhood. "Tell me to stop," he said on a hiss of breath. "Dammit, Eve, tell me to stop!"

She stared at him, still trembling. In the faint glow of light from the fire, he saw her grip her bottom lip with her teeth. Then she closed her eyes and slowly moved her legs apart.

Sam's heart drummed against his ribs as he slid his fingers toward her secret softness, to the open slit in her drawers. Down there, in the depths of her womanhood, she was wet and warm.

He stroked her, finding the hard bud of desire that pushed out through the swollen folds. She moved her head from side to side, eliciting sweet sounds that nearly drove him over the edge. He watched her face fill with the richness of passion as she moved toward completion. When he clamped his palm over her sweet mound, she dug her heels into the mattress, arched her back and cried out his name.

She lay there, her eyes closed as she caught her breath. Finally she turned and gave him a tremulous smile. "I had no idea . . ."

Sam was ready to burst. He unbuttoned his jeans and slid them down over his long underwear. There couldn't be another explanation but insanity for what he was doing, but he wanted her. He wanted her.

He slid into bed beside her. She came to him willingly, anxiously. He touched her breasts, memorizing their shape again, then rubbed his thumb over one nipple.

She helped him remove her chemise, then brought his fingers to her breasts. He groaned when he touched them. "Soft," he murmured against her hair. "So soft." His desire for her grew, becoming a throbbing that tunneled deep into his gut.

She moved one leg, curling it around his, opening herself to him. They kissed, carefully controlled kisses that turned hot and slick. Eve knew what she wanted, she instinctively knew what he needed. He was hard and stiff. Reaching down between them, she clumsily unbuttoned his underwear, shuddering with pleasure when his length leaped out against her hand. She touched him, learning about him until he stopped her and groaned against her mouth. He pressed her onto her back. She opened for him and held her breath as he entered her.

"It'll hurt, but only briefly," he whispered against her ear.

"I don't care, I don't care," she answered, tossing her legs around him, pulling him in.

He drove deep, the brief bite of pain gone as quickly as it came. Then he grabbed her hips and held her tightly to him while he rocked rhythmically against her.

She felt it again, that surge of uncontrollable pleasure that made her ache with a joy beyond description. She shuddered, knowing that her own pleasure was made greater only by the sound of his. When it was over, he rolled to his side and took her with him. She reached up, pulled his mouth down to hers and gave him a long, sweet kiss.

"Sam," she said in a long whisper.

He drew her close. She sighed with contentment and snuggled against him. And for the first time in many years, she was happy to share a bed.

It was barely dawn when she woke. Sam stood in front of the fireplace, appearing to study the flames. Quivering sensations of pleasure touched her.

"Sam?"

He turned briefly, then looked away. "I've got to get you home before it's light."

She flung the covers back, slipped into his shirt, and padded over to him, boldly putting her arms around him as she stood at his side. He tensed, but didn't pull away.

"You're worried about my reputation."

He gathered her close and held her. "And your job."

Anxiety nibbled at her, but she refused to let it take hold. "What I do in my personal life is no concern of theirs." She wanted to believe it; she wasn't sure she did. Either way, she wasn't sorry for what had happened.

His hands framed her face and he kissed her tenderly, a kiss that inevitably turned to fire. Her hands roamed his back, then his chest, where she hurriedly undid the buttons of his underwear.

His hands stilled hers.

"Please." She pressed her hands inside to his bare chest.

He sighed and pulled away. "Don't start again, Eve. I have to get you home before—"

"I know," she whispered, kissing his chest, "be-

fore it's light." She undid the buttons to his waist
and pulled his underwear down his arms. He helped
her get his hands loose, then allowed her to touch
and kiss his chest.

"Oh, I knew it would be beautiful," she said, moving her face back and forth against the dark hair that
covered him.

"Eve, Eve," he murmured huskily. "What am I
going to do with you?"

She hugged him again. "You're going to do to me
again what you did last night. But first," she added,
pulling away, "I want you to find out for yourself."

His gaze was hot. "Find out what?"

She felt her heart pounding hard and knew she
was being brazen. Slowly she slipped out of his shirt,
letting it drop to the floor. "Whether or not my hair
is the same color all over."

Sam stopped the sleigh far enough from the Nisbeths' farmhouse so that no one would hear it. He
turned and looked at Eve. "Will you be all right?"

She glanced at the house; it was still dark. A chill
scampered over her flesh, for if she were discovered
sneaking in before dawn, she knew she'd be in real
trouble. "I'll be fine." She squeezed his hand. "Don't
worry."

He nodded, studied her briefly, then pulled her to
him for a quick kiss.

Hunger for him returned. "Oh, Sam . . . I wish—"

He put a finger to her lips. "Don't, Angel Face."

She gave him a wobbly smile, then leaped from
the sleigh and hurried toward the front door. She
knew there were nights when everyone was asleep
by eight or nine o'clock. And Cora no longer waited
up for her to return from Sam's. She had discovered
that one night when she'd returned just before ten
and found everyone asleep, including Cora who
usually waited for her in the kitchen.

Eve stole softly into the house. She stood for a

moment, listening to the silence, when suddenly she heard Clarence on the stairs. He was always the first one up. Pressing herself against the wall, she held her breath and waited for him to go into the kitchen. When she was sure he'd gone, she quietly removed her coat and boots and slipped up the stairs.

Her room was cold. She removed her clothes, slipped into her flannel dressing gown and broke the thin layer of ice that covered the water in her washbasin. It really *had* gotten cold last night.

She'd just finished dabbing her face with the icy water when Cora knocked on her door.

With shaky fingers, Eve picked up the brush from her vanity table. "Come in, Cora."

Cora stepped into the room and looked around. "My, you're up early this morning."

Eve looked away and drew the brush through her hair with nervous fingers. "It was almost too cold to sleep."

Cora walked over and looked into the washbasin where little pieces of ice still floated on the water. "Don't tell me you didn't even go down to get the kettle of warm water off the stove."

Eve quickly put down her brush and took Cora's arm. "No, but now I'm freezing. Let's go down and have a cup of coffee, shall we?" Eve steered Cora toward the door just as she glanced at the perfectly made bed.

"Why don't I make breakfast this morning?" Eve offered. "I think it's my turn, isn't it? The children love griddle cakes. Why don't I whip up a batch?" She squeezed Cora's shoulders. "Anyway," she babbled on, "it'll warm me up."

Before Cora discovered that she hadn't been in the room all night, Eve pulled her from the room and tugged her toward the stairs.

She felt a little guilty about the deception but also a flutter of excitement. She loved Sam, and although neither of them had voiced their feelings aloud, Eve was certain he loved her . . . and would marry her. Then she could openly show the world the feelings that she'd kept hidden.

9

LATER THAT DAY, EVE STOOD ON A CHAIR AND struggled to attach a fresh cedar bough to the top of a window. The children had gone home, but the room was still filled with their excitement of anticipation for the Christmas program, which would be held tomorrow night.

Every now and then, when she was busy with something else, Eve felt a deep flutter of pleasure and briefly wondered why. Then she stopped what she was doing and remembered.

"Sam," she said on a soft smile. Her heartbeat sped at the sound of his name. He was a magnificent, loving, caring man, and he was hers.

Things between them were glorious now, but oh, how much more wonderful they'd be once they were married.

Stepping off the chair, she sat down, hugged her knees to her chest and smiled. She pictured Joey's reaction when Sam told him that Eve would be his stepmother. Oh, he'd be happy. But no one would be as happy as she would be. No one. Finally, she'd have a family of her own. A man to care for and love and a boy to watch grow into a strong, handsome man, just like his father.

Teaching was what she'd been trained for, but for as long as she could remember, she'd known that her ultimate goal was to have the family she'd lacked as a child.

She stood and dreamily glanced out the window. Her pulse raced when she saw Sam approaching in the sleigh, and she pressed her fingers to the base of her throat, feeling the throb of desire.

Quickly she donned her coat and boots and went outside. The brisk air felt good on her face, for through it, the sun was warm. Icicles hanging from the eaves had begun to melt, dripping in fat drops to the snow below. A fine layer of slick ice blanketed the snowdrifts.

She ran to the sleigh. "What are you doing here?" She couldn't keep from smiling, she was so happy to see him.

His face was solemn. "I came to make sure you were all right, and that . . . that no one discovered you'd been out all night."

Oh, how she loved his concern! Tears of love and gratitude filled her eyes. "No one found out. Oh, Sam, I—" She caught her lower lip between her teeth, wanting to tell him she loved him, that soon it wouldn't matter if the whole world knew they'd spent the night together. But something in the rigid way he held himself stopped her. "I'm fine," she finally said around a vanishing smile.

He nodded, his eyes warm. "Want a ride home to the Nisbeths'?"

Laughing with relief, she climbed in beside him and slid beneath the blanket. "I'd rather go home with you," she answered shyly, resting her head on his shoulder.

"Joey's still at Torkelson's." It sounded like a statement of fact, not a seductively voiced invitation.

She felt a niggle of apprehension, but ignored it. "I know," she answered, giving his arm a loving, knowing squeeze.

Sam didn't respond, but when they passed the turnoff to the Nisbeths' farm, Eve relaxed beside him and closed her eyes. This was where she belonged. It felt so right.

When they reached Sam's cabin, Chancy met them at the barn. Eve climbed from the sleigh, bent down and hugged the dog. "Hello, Chancy. You saved my life, you heroic dog." She glanced at Sam. "How is he healing?"

Sam opened the barn door. "He's going to be all right. Go inside, Eve. Get warm. I'll be in as soon as I take care of the horses."

Eve felt a giddy anticipation as she trudged to the cabin. Once inside, she removed her coat, boots and scarf and stood before the mirror over the commode, studying her reflection. Her eyes sparkled. Her cheeks were pink from anticipation as well as from the nippy air. She straightened the high, lace-trimmed collar of her cotton-batiste blouse, then ran her hands over her black cotton skirt. After pushing a wayward strand of hair back into place, she went to the hearth and stoked up the fire.

She gazed around the room, noting the ropes of popcorn and bittersweet berries she and Joey had made. They were draped perfectly over the windows and mantel. Joey's drawing of the Christmas cuckoo was tacked to the wall beside the ladder going to the loft, and Eve decided that was the perfect place for other drawings Joey would make once he was in school.

She wrinkled her nose at the burlap window coverings. The flowered chintz fabric she'd seen at the mercantile would make perfect curtains. Surely Sam wouldn't mind if she put up something brighter and less dreary; after all, it would be her cabin, too. Oh, she wouldn't be extreme; she knew how men hated frilly, lacy things.

Her thoughts turned to Christmas Eve, just a few days away. She could almost picture Sam and Joey sitting on either side of her at the Nisbeths' supper table.

"We always have a spartan Christmas Eve supper before church," Cora had told her. "Rice mush with cream and sugar, *lefse* and meatballs, if we have the meat. But Christmas Day . . ." Cora's face always became transformed when she thought about cooking and baking. "Ah, Christmas Day, we'll have *lutefisk* and turkey, and cranberry sauce and mince pie . . ."

Lutefisk, that white fish they soaked in lye that tasted surprisingly bland, but was mouthwatering when drenched in melted butter, and *lefse*, the round, flat, griddlecakelike food they made with potatoes . . . Eve's mouth watered.

Hugging herself, she smiled and twirled about. The nuns at the orphanage had drummed into her the meaning of Christmas, but Clarence and Cora had taught her about the love of sharing. That was the main reason she wanted the children to act out the story of *The Christmas Cuckoo*.

Sam came in and she ran to him, reached up and kissed him. She pulled away, gazing up at him. "I want to do that every day for the rest of our lives."

He gave her a tight smile, but said nothing. He merely hung up his jacket and crossed to the fire, warming his hands. He didn't look at her.

Suddenly Eve was nervous. The niggling unease she'd earlier tried to ignore came back, stronger than before. With mounting trepidation, she went to him and put her hand on his arm. He neither responded nor moved away.

"Sam?" She was suddenly afraid.

"I should have dropped you off at the Nisbeths'," he said softly.

She swallowed hard, fighting the sick feeling that spread through her chest. "I didn't want to go home. I wanted to be with you." Quickly, before she could change her mind, she added, "I love you, Sam."

He swore and pulled away. "You *can't* love me."

Her nausea spread deeper. "But I do," she answered, barely above a whisper. This was wrong.

This wasn't the way it was supposed to be! He was supposed to ask her to marry him.

As though he'd read her mind, he said, "I can't marry you, Eve."

She pressed her hands to her mouth, crossed to a chair and sat down, his words of rejection ringing in her ears. "You can't, or . . . or you won't?"

He swung around and glared at her. "I'd ruin your life, and you know it."

She swallowed an hysterical laugh. Her life would be ruined if he *didn't* marry her, and not because he'd slept with her. She loved him. She wanted no other man. "Ruin . . . ruin my life? How can you say that?"

He turned back to the fire. "Do you want to be an outcast like I am? Is that the way you want to live?" Without waiting for her answer, he added, "I wouldn't do that to any white woman. How do you think you'd feel if everyone in this community shunned you? Turned away from you as you walked down the street? Whispered about you behind your back? Dammit, I know what it's like, Eve, and I hate it, but I'm used to it. You," he said, giving her a brief glance, "you wouldn't last a week before you'd despise me for destroying your reputation and your life."

She was dazed, stunned. "But . . . but after what we did, the way we felt . . ."

He sighed heavily and stared into the fire. "I'm sorry for that."

"S-sorry? You're *sorry* you made love to me?" Oh, God, this wasn't happening. It *couldn't* be happening.

"I am now, but I wasn't then. Hell, no." Suddenly he looked at her, his eyes intense. "At the time, dammit, I had to have you. With every breath I took, I wanted you. Thoughts of you wormed their way under my skin until I itched to bury myself inside you. I wanted to hear you scream out your pleasure. I wanted to stroke your sweet, soft skin. Kiss you everywhere ... everywhere. ..."

She stared at him, her heart beating madly as she remembered their night together.

He briefly closed his eyes and massaged his neck. "But I should never have done it, Eve. Because I knew that having you once would never be enough. Never having you again," he added solemnly, "will be my punishment for selfishly taking that precious thing that a woman can give only once. To one man. I shouldn't have been that man, Eve, and I'm sorry. I'm so sorry."

She stared at him, at this man she'd come to love so deeply. "You didn't take anything from me that I wasn't willing to give, Sam."

His tortured expression squeezed her heart. "What you want won't happen, Eve. I won't let it."

Stung, she answered. "And I have nothing to say about it?"

He shook his head. "No," he answered, so quietly she barely heard him.

Quickly, before she could think about it, she asked, "What if I'm ... what if I—" She swallowed, feeling herself blush, but continued anyway. "What if I find out I'm going to have your baby?"

He turned, giving her a haunted look. "Then, by God, find yourself a good, hard-working man, Eve."

"*You're* a good, hard-working man," she cried out, on the verge of tears.

"I'm not good enough for you, Angel Face. If I were, I wouldn't have gotten you into this mess in the first place."

Trying to calm herself, she gasped for air. He'd never intended to marry her. Never. She pulled in a deep, shaky breath, unable to understand.

"But I *love* you, Sam. When you love someone, nothing else matters. It wouldn't *matter* if everyone avoided me. It wouldn't *matter* if they gossiped about me behind my back. I'd have you and Joey, and that's all I want. *That's all I want*, Sam."

He braced his arms against the mantel and stared gravely into the fire. "Go live your life as it was meant to be, sweetheart. I just hope I haven't already ruined it for you."

There was a heaviness in her chest. Her throat hurt. Her eyes stung. "Nothing I can say will change your mind?"

"Nothing," he answered, barely above a whisper.

She stared at him, knowing that what she felt for him was stamped in her eyes, on her heart . . . in her soul.

"I still want to tutor Joey. But . . . but maybe you should bring him and let me do it in the classroom, after the other children have left."

"If that's what you want."

Oh, my darling man, I want you. She crossed to the door and slipped into her coat. "I guess it's what's best." She couldn't bear coming here, to this place she'd hoped to call home, ever again. "Now, please, take me back to the Nisbeths'."

With a gruff sigh, he followed her. "The horses are still hitched up outside."

She valiantly kept her tears at bay. He'd known all along that he was going to reject her. She sat stoically beside him all the way home, but once she was in her own bedroom, she flung herself across the bed and sobbed.

The next morning, because the Christmas program was that evening, Eve didn't go to the school. Instead, she accompanied Clarence and Cora to the mercantile.

While Clarence enjoyed a cup of warm rum with his cronies around the potbellied stove, and Cora supervised the filling of her shopping list, Eve wandered to the counter where the bolts of fabric were stacked. With sad eyes she looked at the brightly flowered chintz she'd hoped to use to brighten Sam's windows.

Two women began to speak softly on the other side of the wall that separated the fabric from the groceries. It was impossible for Eve to ignore them.

"Well, if you ask me, she should be let go."

"She shouldn't have been hired in the first place," responded the other woman.

Eve frowned. She recognized their voices. They were mothers of two of her students.

"I agree," the first woman said. "We just can't have that sort of thing going on here. This is a *Christian* community, not one of those savage reservations where God only knows what goes on behind teepee flaps."

Eve's stomach caved in around a bubble of nausea. She wanted to leave, but she stayed and held her breath.

The other woman sighed. "I just don't understand what got into Clarence Nisbeth. When he hired her I thought to myself, I thought, 'Gladys, that one's going to be trouble.'"

"You knew it right off, did you?"

"Oh, yes," the other said soundly. "Vain. That girl is vain with all that fair hair and, well, you know . . . she's got them curves that she don't even try to hide. Trouble. Pure trouble."

It hurt. Oh, how it hurt! Eve had never known they felt this way. Had she always been so naive, assuming that everyone liked her?

The other woman clucked her tongue. "Then I guess it's no surprise that she's taken a shine to that Prescott fellow."

"Can you imagine?" The woman's voice swelled with self-righteous glee. "Going after a man who has . . . well, you know, *slept with a squaw*?" She finished in a loud whisper.

They both tittered nervously, and Eve could just see them, snorting like little pigs behind their lily-white hands. She hurt for herself, but it made her furious that they talked that way about Sam. Her anger came in the form of bold, hot tears that she had to force away with her handkerchief.

When she'd gotten control of herself, she squared her shoulders, stepped out from behind the wall and stopped in front of them.

"Well, Merry Christmas, Miss Engels," one of them said with a shamefaced smile. "Are you and the children ready for the pageant this evening? I know my Clarice is so excited to be the princess in the Christmas Cuckoo story."

Eve tried to force down her feelings of anger and hurt, but she wasn't successful. "Clarice will do a nice job. It upsets me, though, to hear the two of you talking so badly about Mr. Prescott. He's a fine man who is raising a child alone. Why must you condemn him?"

The two guilty women stumbled over each other's words as they hurried to get away from her.

Heat rushed into Eve's face as she went to the door, anxious to get outside where the air wasn't quite so foul. Her stomach was tied in knots. So, she thought, still fighting tears of anger, that was the sort of thing Sam and Joey had to put up with. People creeping about, pecking at them behind their backs in such a way that they couldn't defend themselves. Just how many people in the community felt as those two women did? Probably many. One was too many. They were eager for gossip but hid behind their pious outrage. It was awful, and it hurt. She didn't know how Sam could stand it. But she was sure it would be easier to withstand if he had someone beside him, giving him love and support. And she would have tried, if only Sam had asked her.

10

THE NIGHT SKY LOOMED DARKLY OVERHEAD. Clouds blanketed the moon. Only a few stars peeped through the vaporous cover, offering little guidance to those who drove their sleighs toward the schoolhouse. In spite of the gloomy night, sleigh bells rang out, heralding the special evening.

The building was alight with candles and lanterns and could be seen from a great distance. The Hassler brothers and their wives and children had taken on the responsibility of delivering the lanterns early, so people could find their way.

In spite of her sad mood, Eve had to admit the schoolroom looked spectacular. The graceful red cedar tree, beautifully lit with candles, was a sight to behold. And the packages! Even though she'd told the parents not to bring gifts, she was sure they all had, for the floor at the base of the tree was loaded, as was a table nearby.

On every conceivable wall space hung pictures and sentiments suited to the occasion—big-bellied Santas, nativity scenes, trees laden with candles— while green cedar branches and colorful bittersweet berries graced the windows and door. From the ceiling, paper cutout snowflakes dangled on threads. Twenty or more stockings were hung on the wall beside the tree, each heavy with secret treasures.

The children were ready to perform *The Christmas Cuckoo*. Even Ernest Nisbeth, who played the king, knew his lines. Eve was uncertain, though, whether he'd say them correctly or turn the production into his own personal sideshow.

Eve briefly touched the delicate silver brocade brooch fastened to the lace at the neck of her blouse. Cora had loaned her the pin, for it went beautifully with the ecru linen blouse and skirt she wore.

She glanced around the room, filled with parents and their children, all of whom chattered noisily. Forcing a happy smile, she stepped to the front of the room onto the temporary platform Clarence had erected for the program and looked out at her friends and neighbors. Briefly, since her confrontation at the mercantile earlier, she wondered how many were really friends. Someone near the front ordered everyone to be quiet so Eve could be heard.

When the noise died down, Eve clasped her hands in front of her and gazed up at the beautiful candlelit tree. "Isn't this the most beautiful sight?"

Murmurs of agreement rumbled through the room.

"I want to thank all of you for coming. The children have worked very hard, memorizing their lines for the production of *The Christmas Cuckoo*. Our beautiful cedar tree has an important part in the play tonight. It's not your typical Christmas story, but many of you know it well, since it's still told in the cold, icy north country of Norway."

There was a commotion behind the curtain, then Eve continued. "Briefly, this is the story of two brothers, the shoemakers Scrub and Spare, who inadvertently save the life of a cuckoo bird that they discover has magical powers. To thank them for his life, the bird offers them two trees. One is made of gold, and its leaves sound like coins when they drop off. Anyone who has that tree will be rich beyond his wildest dreams. The other is just a tree, but it is always green, and it never drops its leaves. Some call the latter tree a wise tree, others call it merry, for anyone who brings it into their home finds a happy, contented heart. Scrub wants the tree of gold. Spare, the merry tree. Let's find out which brother finds happiness."

Looking to the side, she nodded toward the boys who were ready to open the curtain. Slowly, the play unfolded. . . .

"Eve, you've done a wonderful job," Cora said, giving her a hug after the performance. "I couldn't believe my Ernest. He said his lines perfectly!"

The disturbance caused by Clarence making his way through the crowd dressed as Santa Claus prevented Eve from responding. He stepped to the front, near the tree, and raised his arms to quiet the room.

"You children all did a find job. A real fine job. Of course," he added, looking at Eve, "they couldn't have done it without a darn fine teacher."

In spite of her sadness, Eve felt proud. Everything had gone perfectly. She should be elated. She knew why she wasn't. . . .

Clarence tossed a casual glance toward the tree. "Now, I know the children are anxious for their treats and gifts. I've picked two fine young men to help me distribute them. But we have punch, coffee, Christmas bread and cookies in the back, too."

Eve scanned the room, her heart vaulting upward when she saw Sam standing toward the back, near the door. It took all the will power she had not to run to him and throw her arms around him. He looked so handsome. He'd shaved and his beautiful dark hair was combed back neatly against his head. Stubborn waves gave him a rakish look that made her want to swoon. With an ache in her heart, she wondered if she'd ever stop loving him.

He listened intently to a conversation between two other men, one of whom Eve knew was the commissioner of the school board, who had come in for the evening from St. Paul.

Sam's presence puzzled her. Not because he couldn't be there. Everyone in the community had been invited. But . . . why had he come? To finally get involved? To stop living like a hermit? She hoped for Joey's sake it was true.

He looked up, as if sensing he was being watched, and Eve nearly burst with longing. She held his gaze, perhaps drawing hope from it when there was none. A flicker of a smile touched his mouth, and a wealth of emotions made it hard for her to swallow.

Suddenly there was a disturbance near the door. A boy rushed into the room, his face pale with fear.

"It's Ernie," he cried. "He's fallen through the ice on the lake!"

Sam Prescott was the first man out the door.

Sam grabbed a coil of rope from his sleigh and ran toward the lake. When he arrived, several boys were standing on the frozen shore. He momentarily panicked when he couldn't find Joey among them.

"Pa!"

His gaze was drawn to the lake, his heart skipping a beat when he saw Joey lying flat on the ice, next to the jagged hole where the other boy had presumably fallen in.

"Joey? Are you all right?"

"Pa! I got Ernie by the hands, but I can't pull him out."

One of the boys on the shore ran up to Sam. "We'd have helped, but the ice is cracked all the way around, and we was 'fraid we'd all go through."

Sam nodded. By this time, some of the other men from the schoolhouse were there holding lanterns, Clarence Nisbeth in his Santa suit among them. Sam took control.

"We can make a chain out to Joey," he began, "but we'll have to crawl on our bellies. Otherwise, the ice won't hold." He made a hangman's knot in the rope and wrapped it around his arm, then handed the rest of the rope to Clarence. "Follow me, then hand the rope back to the next man."

The human chain slid cautiously over the frozen lake. Sam heard the ice crack beneath them but prayed it was thick enough to hold. He focused on Joey, knowing he had to make it out there not only for him, but also for the boy in the water. As he crept closer, he hoped it wasn't too late.

"Joey," he called, "how's the boy doing?"

Joey looked up, his expression pained. "I'm talkin' to him, Pa, but he's cryin'. Can't you hear him?"

Sam could hear the muffled sounds coming from the hole in the ice. "Tell him his pa is right behind me."

"I did, Pa. Ernie says he's real cold."

Sam reached Joey with the noose, then crawled to the edge of the hole. Looking down into the pinched face of Ernie Nisbeth, he gave him a reassuring smile. "We're going to get you out, son."

Suddenly there was a loud crack behind him, and Sam knew he was running out of time.

Eve tried to soothe Cora, who wanted to join the men at the lake.

"They have enough to worry about, Cora. They don't need to worry about us, too."

Cora squeezed Eve's hand. "Poor Ernest," she said, her chin quivering. "He's not really such a bad child, you know."

"Of course he isn't," Eve murmured, vividly remembering the time he'd put a nice, fat frog in her bed. And the dollop of molasses he'd poured on her chair. And the snake-shaped stick he'd wiggled at her last summer. Mischievous or not, no child deserved to freeze to death in icy water.

Some of the other mothers milled about, offering Cora words of comfort and encouragement. The children, sensing the tension in the room, threw curious glances at the tree and all the packages.

Eve was certain the festivities of the evening were over, when a few of the older boys rushed in, breathless from running.

"He's okay! Ernie's gonna be okay! They got him out of the lake, and his pa is takin' him home!"

Cora sagged with relief against Eve.

Eve glanced at the doorway, her heart lurching upward when she saw Sam standing there.

"Mrs. Nisbeth, I'll drive you home," he said, taking her by the arm. He gave Eve a private look, one that gave her hope, before he left the schoolhouse.

Joey ran into the room and went straight to Eve. The sleeves of his jacket were wet to his shoulders.

When he peeled off his jacket, Eve could see that his shirtsleeves were wet, too. "I was hangin' on to Ernie's arms," he said, trying to warm his hands in his armpits.

Alarmed, Eve brought him to the stove. She rolled up his sleeves and rubbed his arms and hands gently. They were icy cold.

Eve was so proud of him, she wanted to hug him. Instead, so she wouldn't embarrass him, she gave him a warm smile. "That was a very brave thing to do, Joey."

He shrugged. "Somebody had to, and I was the only one who dared crawl out onto the ice."

Oscar Hassler went to the front of the room and called for everyone's attention. "Ernest is at home now, and the doc says he'll be fine. The Nisbeths want you all to continue your party. The youngsters have been eyeing those gifts something fierce, and it would be a shame if they didn't get a chance to open them."

Eve felt detached as she watched the evening progress. She sat near the stove with Joey, unwilling to think about a future without him and Sam. There was a lump the size of an apple in her throat.

A while later, Sam returned with Clarence Nisbeth and went directly to Joey. They spoke quietly, Joey assuring his father he was all right. Eve couldn't help listening, wishing things could be different. Wishing she could respond to them the way her heart urged her to.

The boy who had announced Ernest's fall through the ice came up to Joey and handed him a package. Joey gave his father a questioning look before turning back.

"I want you to have this, Joey. If you hadn't crawled out and hung onto Ernie, he'd probably be dead now."

Another boy did the same, then another, until Joey had a lap full of gifts.

Eve felt tears press against her eyes and wondered why children were so often wiser than their parents.

Joey looked up at his father, his eyes shining. "Pa?"

Sam gave Joey a smile that tore at Eve's heart. "Go ahead, son. Open them. You deserve them."

Eve could barely hold her feelings inside. She moved away, hoping distance would help dull the pain of losing Sam. She crossed to where the other boys sat. "You've done a fine thing, boys. A very fine thing."

One of the boys blushed. "Joey done it, Miss Engels. Joey saved Ernie's life, even though Ernie was never nice to him."

"I know," she answered with a warm smile, "but—"

"I have something to say, and I want everyone to listen," Clarence Nisbeth called over the din. He threaded his way through the crowded room and stopped in front of Sam and Joey.

Eve held her breath. She prayed Ernest hadn't taken a turn for the worse.

Clarence reached out and touched Joey's shoulder. "We've all learned a lesson here tonight. Christmas is a time for giving, and this boy here, Joey Prescott, gave me back my son. If it weren't for him, Ernest would have drowned. And if it weren't for the quick thinking of his father, Sam Prescott, we might not have gotten to my boy in time." He studied them for a long minute.

The room was so quiet, Eve could hear the gentle sputter of the candles.

"We've all had our own run-ins with the Indians, and I'll be the first to admit I have a personal prejudice against them. But I'm willing to set that aside. What's done is done. This boy here," he continued, gripping Joey's shoulder, "is proof enough for me that it doesn't matter what a man's blood is. Good is good. Now, this boy's father has offered to sell us the land we need to build a new schoolhouse. At the time he made that offer, he knew darned well that we wouldn't take his son into this classroom. But I'm here to tell all of you," he added, "that we will. That is, if Mr. Prescott will forgive us all for being such narrow-minded fools."

Eve gasped, her gaze flying to Sam. She saw his shiny eyes. He was on the brink of tears. She pressed her fingers over her mouth and turned away before she made a fool of herself by flinging herself into his arms.

"Now," Clarence concluded, "let's go on with this party. There's plenty of eats left, and my Cora said no one is to go away hungry."

The boys who had given Joey gifts huddled around him, slapping him on the back, treating him like a hero. Eve dug out her handkerchief and wiped her eyes. Finally, Joey would be where he belonged in school with the other children.

Clarence stepped up to her. "Well, young lady, are you ready to go home? We all drew straws to see who cleans up, and the Hassler families lost."

She threw Sam a quick look, noting he was conversing quietly with Mr. Barnes, the carpenter. He didn't even look her way.

Dredging up a smile, she took Clarence's arm and

headed for the door. "I'm ready." She squeezed him affectionately. "The apples were a big hit. And so were you, Santa."

He coughed nervously. "Well, of course." He studied her for a moment. "I'm not nearly the bear you think I am, Eve. Why, I might even be the kind of person you could confide in."

"Oh, I know that, Clarence. I know that."

"Well, then," he continued gruffly, "the next time you come home in the wee hours of the morning, join me in the kitchen for a cup of coffee, and we'll talk."

She gasped, her face heating with a guilty flush. "You . . . you heard me?"

They stopped by the door, and Clarence helped her on with her coat. "Like I said, I'm not an ogre. I was wrong about Prescott from the beginning, and I had to do a lot of soul searching. But he's a fine man, Eve. You could do a whole lot worse."

Eve knew it too, but it was too late. If Sam had changed his mind about them, he'd have come to her and told her so this evening.

11

EVE GLANCED UP AS CORA CAME INTO THE ROOM Ernest shared with his younger brother.

"Go to bed," Cora whispered. "I'll sit with him now."

Eve stood and stretched, yawning as she made her way to the door. She was tired, but felt restless. As she passed Cora and Clarence's bedroom, the sounds of Clarence's rumbling snores made her smile. What a dear man he was. . . .

She crept softly down the stairs to the kitchen to make herself some hot cocoa. Clarence had banked a fire in the stove, and the room was warm and cozy. The chime clock had just rung four. Later that morning, she and Cora would bake mince and dried apple pies and plum pudding and prepare the wild rice stuffing for the Christmas Day turkey. Tonight, after the Christmas Eve service, she would help Cora put the finishing touches on the children's gifts.

And tomorrow, Christmas Day . . . She sighed and lifted the pan of milk before it boiled over. Until a few days ago, she'd privately planned to spend Christmas Day with Sam and Joey.

A noise behind her startled her. She turned and gasped. "Sam!"

He put a finger to his lips. "Come with me," he whispered. "Joey needs you."

She pressed a hand over her heart. "Joey? Oh, no. Is he coming down with something because of tonight?" Not waiting for Sam's answer, she hurried into the hallway and took her coat off the rack.

Sam ushered her outside into the waiting sleigh. He slid in beside her and spread the quilt over their knees.

"Does he have a fever? Chills?" she asked as they rode through the dark night. "Oh, Sam," she said, "maybe you should have called the doctor. I don't really know what to do. Oh, but I'm glad you came for me. I want to be there. Did he ask for me?"

"He never stops asking for you, Eve."

He sounded so calm. How could he be so calm? A wrenching, emotional pain twisted her stomach. "The poor darling. Oh, Sam, why did you leave him alone? Are you sure he'll be all right?"

They were approaching Sam's cabin; a tiny light flickered in the window. He'd barely drawn the sleigh to a stop when Eve leaped down and ran into the house, Sam following close behind her.

She threw off her coat, slipped out of her boots and hurried to the loft ladder when she felt Sam's hand on her arm. Puzzled, she turned and faced him. He had the strangest smile on his face.

"What . . . what's wrong? Sam, I have to go up there and see how he is—"

"He's fine. All you'll do is wake him up, Eve."

"But . . . but I thought you said he was calling for me."

Sam folded her into his arms. She went willingly, but she was confused.

"He's always calling for you, Angel Face. Not a waking minute goes by that he doesn't ask me why you aren't here."

She pulled away. "He's not sick?"

He gave her a shy, apologetic smile. "No."

She continued to brace her hands against his chest. She felt the beat of his heart, which surely matched the drumming of her own. "Then . . . then why am I here?"

"Because it's where you belong."

She sucked in a shaky, optimistic breath. "Your little prank scared me half to death. I'm very angry with you, Sam Prescott."

He bent and kissed her forehead. "Too angry to become *Mrs*. Sam Prescott?"

More emotion than she could hold filled her, and tears ran down her cheeks. She gave him a tremulous smile. "No, I'm not that angry."

"I was wrong, Eve, to deny our love for each other. After tonight, and the way the townspeople rallied around us, publicly supporting Joey and me, I realized how wrong I'd been." He pulled her to the center of the room and pointed to the ceiling. "It's not mistletoe or holly, but it will have to do."

Eve glanced up at the bittersweet berries that

hung from the ceiling on a string. She gave Sam a loving smile. "All that for me?"

His grin was lopsided. "Joey thought it was a good idea."

He bent and kissed her, the sweet start turning hungry. Pulling away, he framed her face with his hands and looked into her eyes. "If I keep kissing you, I'm going to want to take you to bed. But I won't. Not until we're married."

She pressed close, craving the desire that surged through her. "Oh, you're such an honorable man."

He hugged her tightly. "You don't sound too thrilled."

She rubbed her cheek against his shirt. "The biggest part of me isn't. But I still maintain a kernel of decency, in spite of myself."

They stood quietly for a long minute, then Sam said, "I suppose I'd better ask Clarence Nisbeth for your hand, or he'll string me up by my heels or by something else more precious to both of us."

Blushing, she laughed shyly, remembering her revealing conversation with Clarence. "I wouldn't worry, Sam. When he discovers that I'm gone, his first thought will be to give me away, and with good riddance."

Joey awakened shortly after five A.M. and didn't appear at all surprised to find Eve there. While he and his father went out to the barn to do chores, Eve prepared breakfast.

They'd barely finished eating when they heard the jingle of sleigh bells. Eve and Sam exchanged glances.

"Joey, go help Mr. Nisbeth with his team."

Joey flashed his father a puzzled look. "How do you know it's him, Pa?"

Sam stood and began clearing the table. "Trust me, Joey, it's him."

Joey pulled on his coat and went to the window. "I'll be dogged. You're right, Pa."

As soon as the boy went outside, Eve hurried to the window. Clarence Nisbeth stopped his team in front of the cabin and handed Joey the reins. He looked at the house, his expression stern. She checked to make sure there was enough coffee, then quickly rattled the cookie tin, grateful it wasn't empty. Clarence never took a cup of coffee without eating something sweet with it, even if it was just after breakfast.

She felt Sam's hand in hers and gripped it hard.

Clarence entered, greeting them both solemnly. He took a seat at the table, motioning Sam to sit across from him. Eve poured him a cup of coffee and put it down in front of him, next to the plate of cookies, then sat next to Sam. When Clarence cleared his throat, she felt her insides quiver.

He took a molasses cookie, bit into it and gave her a look of approval. There was a twinkle in his eye that told her he was prolonging her agony on purpose.

"Stole her away in the middle of the night, did you?"

Sam nodded. "Yes, sir, I did."

"She came willingly?"

"In a manner of speaking."

"He told me Joey was ill," Eve said, shooting Sam a scolding look.

"I didn't say that, you did."

His eyes were so warm and deep, she almost drowned in them.

Clarence poured some coffee into the saucer, blew on it then slurped it into his mouth. "You going to marry him?"

Eve glanced at Sam, unable to stop smiling. "I am."

Clarence slapped his knee then stood. "Thought so. Saw Reverend Larsen on my way over. Said you'd already talked to him. That right, Prescott?"

"Sam?" Eve couldn't believe it. "You talked to Reverend Larsen? When?"

He pulled her close. "Last night after the pageant, sweet Angel Face."

She melted against him. "You were pretty sure of yourself, weren't you?"

Clarence cleared his throat gruffly. "I hope you two can wait a spell. Cora wants all of us to attend Christmas Eve services tonight, and she fully intends to see that you, Sam, and your boy, join us for Christmas dinner tomorrow. Guess she wants to kinda look you over. See if she approves."

Eve flew to him and kissed his cheek. "They'll be there. Oh, Clarence! You *are* a wonderful man."

Clarence gave her a fatherly hug, then opened the door to let in Joey, who had hitched the reins to the post.

Clarence paused and smiled at all of them. "So, she's 'Angel Face,' is she? Then I suppose you know what 'Engels' translates to from the Norwegian?"

Joey stamped the snow from his boots. "What? What's her name mean, sir?"

Clarence cuffed Joey lightly on the chin. "Why, it means 'angels,' son."

He beamed at Sam. "See, Pa? I knew it. I knew the first time I saw her that she was an angel."

"And now she's going to be your new mother, Joey."

His face lit up, and his grin was so wide, Eve thought his mouth would crack. "No kiddin'?"

"No kiddin'," Clarence mimicked. He turned briefly to Sam and Eve. "Cora would feel slighted if you two didn't tie the knot in our parlor. You're like a daughter to us, Eve."

Eve's heart felt full to overflowing. "Oh, Clarence, thank you. If anyone's an angel, you are."

He studied her quietly. "I don't want to tell you what to do, girl, but Cora's got a heap of cooking to do today, and I think she's expecting your help."

Eve's hand flew to her chest. "Oh, yes. Oh, of course, Clarence." She tossed Sam a worried look.

"Go on. Joey and I will be along later," he said, helping her into her coat.

She turned and hugged him. "You promise?"

"We promise. Nothing could keep us away."

Two days later, Sam and Eve stood at the window and watched the Nisbeths leave. They had insisted on transporting them to and from the wedding ceremony and keeping Joey at their place for a few days.

"Well, how do you feel, Mrs. Prescott?"

Eve snaked her arm around Sam's waist and rubbed her cheek against his chest. "I feel like the happiest and luckiest woman alive." They were quiet for a moment, basking in the newness of their relationship.

"I never did get you anything for Christmas."

Eve stretched and kissed his chin. "Oh, yes you did."

He brought her full against him and held her. She felt his need; it matched her own. Earlier, as they accepted good wishes from their neighbors in Clarence and Cora's parlor, Sam had read the urgent hunger in her eyes. "I know, sweet angel," he'd whispered against her ear. "It's the same for me." She'd wanted him so badly, she thought she would burst into flames.

"I mean," he said, interrupting her thoughts, "you don't even have a wedding ring."

"Oh, Sam. It doesn't matter. All my life, Christmas had meant very little to me. In the orphanage, we didn't really celebrate it. We were expected to go to church, but other than that, we did nothing special. I remember visiting a friend from school over Christmas once, and her family had a Christmas tree, piled so high with presents you could barely see the top. How happy they all were to be together! The traditions they'd shared over the years ... I suddenly realized what I'd missed. Yet her family wasn't mine, so it just made me sad. Then Clarence and Cora took me into their home, and I've shared their traditions and been grateful for them, but they still weren't mine.

"Now," she said, hugging her husband close, "I have a family of my own, and the traditions we start will be ours. Not only that, but my wedding day is the day after Christmas. How much more special can Christmas be than that?"

Sam pulled away and tipped her chin toward him. There was a soft gleam in his eyes. "And every Christmas, will you bake those ginger-and-molasses cookies?"

"Of course, darling." She gave him a suggestive smile. "Didn't you know? Ginger is the spice of love."

Sam returned the smile, then glanced toward the loft. "I'm glad Joey's staying with the Nisbeths."

She snuggled close, removed the stiff collar of his shirt, then unbuttoned it. She pressed her hand inside against his chest, near his heart. "If he's gone for too long, I might miss him."

He unbuttoned her dress, pausing now and then to kiss the sweet flesh that he revealed. "I'll keep you too busy for that."

She shuddered as he drew his tongue over the top of her breast. "Oh, Sam. Joey's had so much excitement in the last two days ... I'm so happy for him ... for you ... for me. For us."

Sam slipped out of his shirt, then drew her dress down over her arms. "I know. I don't know how Joey and I got so lucky."

"Silly man," she scolded softly, trying to unfasten his trousers. "I'm the lucky one. Now," she said, pulling him toward the bed, "I think we should make a baby."

He gave a soft, delicious laugh and followed her. "I hear you, sweetheart. Let's make another little Angel Face."

WARM HOLIDAY WISHES
from . . .
JANE BONANDER

This story is for my fearless aunt, Ethel Moquin, schoolteacher *extraordinaire*, who began her career at Old Glory, a one-room schoolhouse in Highlanding Township, Pennington County, Minnesota.

As I was growing up, Christmas meant seeing grandparents, aunts and uncles, and a whole slew of cousins. We children would make snow angels, build forts, and ice skate on a frozen pond until our fingers and toes were numb. My first glimpse of the tree always took my breath away, for it was heaped nearly to the top with gifts. Nothing fancy, mind you, but gifts, just the same. And locked away in my memory are those satisfying aromas of Christmas: bread pudding, rice mush, Swedish meatballs, delicious spicy cookies, and the inevitable, and horrible (to us children), smell of *lutefisk*, codfish soaked in lye.

Now, with our families spread from one coast to the other, Christmas is entirely different. New traditions become intermingled with old. It's still a special, wondrous time of the year, and I thank my large, loving family for making it so.

Heaven's Gate

Tanya Anne Crosby

To Lyssa . . .
For all the little things . . .
Like laughing at all my little quips,
even when they're not really so funny,
To lingering on the phone . . .
Just to make certain I don't have just
one more thing to say . . .
Thanks for being such a great editor!

Prologue

EMMA DIDN'T QUITE KNOW WHAT TO SAY.

The frown lines etched about Lincoln Traherne's beautiful lips seemed to deepen every time she so much as attempted to cheer him. Pressing her hands to her sides, she had to quash the urge to lift her fingers to those creases, soothe the harsh lines from his face. It just wouldn't be proper, she knew. She was certain, though, that once they were wed she would know how to make him smile. Like an untouchable marble statue, her betrothed stood, hands linked behind his back, as he stared down at the narrow strip of beach below. He hadn't spoken for the longest time.

Above them, seagulls wailed, swooping gracefully toward the sea. "I-it's beautiful, is it not?" she asked him a little hesitantly, stepping toward the edge of the cliff and peering down alongside him. Nervously, she swiped her palms down across her new lemon-yellow morning dress. She'd worn the gown just for him, because he'd once told her the color reminded him of golden sunshine. He'd told her that he thought it a merry color, and after her father's warning this morn of the duke's sour mood, she thought it might somehow help to cheer him. And

105

she so wished to please him! Whatever it took, she wanted to be a good wife to him.

Nor did she want him ever to regret choosing her.

She'd been so very flattered when Lincoln Traherne, fifth Duke of Ascott, had first paid her notice. And then, of all the beautiful women he could have courted, he'd selected her instead. Even now as he stood before her in flesh and blood, Emma could scarcely credit that he'd asked for her hand in matrimony. Her hand. She glanced up at him in awe. Why, he was everything a woman could dream of in a husband—handsome, kind, and so very courteous—despite the horrors her friends had whispered of him.

"Beautiful?" Distractedly, he lifted his glance from the beach below, nodding as he met her gaze. "Yes," he agreed. "It rather is." He turned to look at her with a strange expression upon his patrician face; one Emma couldn't even begin to decipher. He seemed deeply troubled somehow.

"I just knew you would think so!" she told him excitedly, trying to sound bright, pleased that he thought so as well. "I've always loved this place so. Yet to see it now," she rushed on, "one would never credit the way it appears in winter." She swept her hand in a gesture that indicated the whole of the beach and cliffs. "In winter 'tis quite a barren place. Stark and . . ."

"Frigid?" he finished for her, and something about his tone sent a quiver down her spine.

Emma frowned. "Well, yes," she replied, rubbing her arms suddenly, for she felt strangely chilled, despite the sun shining brightly down upon them. Perhaps it was the intense look in his brilliant blue eyes? "It does get rather cold," she admitted, "though mostly because of the wind. It manages to ravage everything in its path—the wind that is."

He was looking at her rather curiously.

"I-in fact," she stammered, uncomfortably, " 'tis

for those winds that Newgale received its name."

"Yes, well . . . people have a way of doing that, as well," he disclosed dismally, his voice husky. And his eyes, too, seemed more melancholy all of a sudden.

Emma wondered if it were something she'd said. She tried to think of what it might have been but could recall nothing. "I don't quite understand, Your Grace," she said after a moment, confusion marring her youthful features. Her brows collided. "What is it that people do?" Surely she'd missed something, because she had absolutely no notion of what he was speaking.

His answering gaze seemed to penetrate her very soul. It managed even to prickle the hairs upon her nape.

"Ravage everything in their path, of course."

"Oh . . ." She couldn't imagine what would make him say such a thing. And he was beginning to unnerve her, besides. Truth to tell, he'd been behaving curiously all afternoon. She thought that perhaps the unflattering account of him in the *Times* her father had spoken of might have disheartened him. It was the only explanation, of course. She only wished she knew precisely what had been said, for her father had refused to enlighten her further, had only mentioned it at all, so that she might be warned of the duke's mood. But she couldn't ease him, she thought a little crossly, if she didn't know what was troubling him to begin with.

Perhaps it would serve her better to overlook his surly disposition entirely. Perhaps she should *stop* trying to cheer him and simply allow him his rotten mood. After all, everyone was entitled once in a while. She didn't seem to be able to alter it anyway. She sighed and to that effect continued as though he'd said nothing at all.

Attempting a brighter smile, if not for him, then for herself, she told him, "In the summer, as you can

see, of course, the cliffs are splendid . . . and the sun
so bright and warm. And the sea . . . 'tis so beautiful
that sometimes . . ." She turned to peer out over the
tumbling gray-blue ocean, and the slightest breeze
tugged at her bonnet. She secured it with a hand
and glanced up at Lincoln, her smile deepening.
"Sometimes," she continued wistfully, daring to
share her dreams with this man who would soon be
her husband, "I come here and stand and stare . . .
and only imagine what wonders must lie across the
sea."

His face twisted, as though somehow in pain.
"God, Emma . . ." He swallowed, the knob in his
throat bobbing as he stared down at her. "You just
don't understand, do you?"

She felt suddenly more ill at ease than she ever
had in his presence. "Your Grace," she began, "are
you quite well? You seem so . . ."

"Emma . . ." He shook his head, and she suddenly
felt as she had when she'd failed some silly quiz at
her studies. "You're too pure a soul."

Emma thought it might have been a compliment
but for the way that he'd said it. He'd somehow
made it seem a less than desirable trait. She wrinkled
her nose, feeling more than a little defensive yet having no notion as to why. "Not really so pure," she
demurred. Once again, he gave her that look, that
odd look that tugged at her heart. That look that
made her want to hold him in her arms and heal
him somehow. Still, she felt, too, a little slighted, for
the look on his face also made her feel as though she
were little more than a child. "At any rate, Your
Grace," she informed him saucily, "no more so than
you! Indeed . . . I think you like to believe yourself a
mite more dangerous than you are!"

His brow arched. "Really?" he asked, sounding
quite amused by the charge, though by the bleak
look in his eyes one would never have guessed he
was amused at all. In fact, he was beginning to look

every bit the dangerous rogue her friends had claimed him to be. "Surely you can't think me pure?" he asked her.

She nodded. "Why, yes, Your Grace, *I think I do,*" she told him pertly. "I can see it in your eyes."

He groaned and took her by the hand. "Emma— God, you've no idea."

"Oh, but I do!" she asserted, beginning to grow vexed with his insinuation that she was less than able to think for herself. She was nineteen now, after all!

He shook his head. "No. No, you don't. Sweet, sweet Emma . . . I've thought about it much . . . all day I've been trying to find a way to tell you . . ."

"No!" she broke in. Somehow, she sensed she didn't wish to hear what he was about to say. "I do know! I do! You're a good man, Lincoln Traherne, despite the rubbish the *Times* might print of you— despite what people might say!"

He continued to shake his head, denying her.

"I know you are! I know you are because . . . because . . . *I think . . . I think I love you, Your Grace.* And I just know I couldn't love—"

"Dash it all, Emma!" he exploded.

Emma cowered away from him. Before her eyes his expression had turned to one of utter disgust. Oh, Lord! She couldn't believe it, she just couldn't! Her eyes misted. He seemed to regain his composure at once, but Emma couldn't bear it. She took a step backward, toward the cliff edge.

"*I don't need you to love me,*" he told her cruelly. "I don't need anyone!"

At his hurtful words, Emma could feel hot tears stinging her eyes. "*But I think I already do,*" she could hear herself saying, and even as she said it, she could scarcely believe she was disgracing herself so.

"No!" he snapped. "You don't! You don't know the bloody meaning of the word!"

Wounded by his unexpected vehemence, Emma

dared not speak for fear that if she did, great sobs would burst forth instead. Shaking her head in dismay, she took another step backward. She just couldn't believe that she'd bared her heart to him and that he was trampling it without so much as a thought. She averted her face.

He seized her by the shoulders and forced her to face him. "God, Emma, neither do I . . . Listen to me. . . ." He shook her gently. "Don't you understand? *I don't want you to love me.*" His eyes pleaded with her. "Can't you understand? To love me, you might as well fling yourself down that bloody cliff!"

Turning to look below, Emma stifled a cry at how close she'd come to the edge, yet contrary to his hateful words, he drew her into an embrace, and Emma had never felt more flustered or more confused. Try as she might, she couldn't find her voice to speak, and then he broke away, kissing her firmly upon the forehead.

"I'm sorry," he whispered, moving her safely away from the cliff edge. "I shall speak with your father." And before Emma could clear the catch from her throat, he was walking away from her. Only then did her tears begin to flow. She couldn't imagine how things had gone so horribly. Couldn't begin to perceive what had happened. Couldn't imagine what she had done. What had she done? And then he was simply gone.

No explanation. Nothing.

And pride forbade her to go after him.

1

Newgale
Christmas 1839

GOOD LORD, IT WAS COLD!
And the morning rays streaming through
her bedroom window did precious little to ward
away the chill. Emma found herself trembling as she
dressed for the day. At least that was what she told
herself it was, the cold. Shaking like a sapling tree
in the midst of a winter gale, she refused to acknowledge that it was *his* presence that might have affected her so.

"You needn't do this to yourself," her maid remarked blithely.

"I am certainly *not* afraid to face him!" Emma declared resolutely. "If only I can find something to
wear, I shall be merry as a cricket!" With an ensuing
groan of distress, she sat upon the clothing-draped
bed. Having tried nearly every gown she owned, she
was now at a loss. Truth to tell, she'd never felt more
like weeping!

Jane lifted up, for Emma's scrutiny, a lovely bottle-green gown, trimmed in blond lace. "How about
this one?"

Emma sighed and shook her head. "No." Certainly it wasn't for *his* sake that she found herself so
persnickety this morn! The fact that he'd deigned to
call at long last, after two and a half years' absence
from her life, was of little significance to her! She'd

111

long since put him aside in her thoughts.

Still, the memory of her foolishness burned in her heart. How could she have been such a paper scull? *To hope he could have cared for her.* Scoundrel that he was, the Duke of Ascott was certainly not the sort who cared for any but himself! He'd merely wished for a breeding vessel, that's all! She understood that now—and should have then!

Why, he'd all but told her father and brother so! She could still feel the hot shame creeping into her cheeks as Andrew had informed her of the duke's humiliating visit with their father. Her poor father had gone into a rage, and only then had the duke agreed to rethink his decisions, which, to his credit, he'd done out of respect for her father, for she was well aware that he'd not been obligated to do so. Yet it was shortly thereafter that her father had taken ill, and no sooner had he passed away, when the duke had come calling again to inform Andrew of his final decision. He hadn't even bothered to give Emma a choice in the matter—or even an explanation. Nothing! He'd simply left her in limbo, awaiting a public announcement that was certain to ruin her life forever. Well, she was tired of waiting! She wanted it to be over. Never should she have allowed herself to hope.

Foolish she, for she'd mistakenly believed that because her father and mother had found love, and her dear brother, Andrew, had found it with his own wife, Cecile, that she, too, could—and would. Foolishness! She could see that very well now—thanks to the duke's bitter lesson—*but she would not allow herself to believe it again!*

She would guard her heart at all cost!

"Perhaps he's changed his mind," Jane suggested offhandedly, searching diligently through the wardrobe for another suitable gown.

Emma glanced up at her maid and frowned. "Unlikely!" For two and a half years she'd braced herself for the scandal their broken betrothal would inevitably create, and she refused to entertain the notion that he may wish to reconsider their situation. Nor did she wish him to change his mind. Really, she told herself, it was better to have discovered sooner, rather than later, just how inconstant her betrothed could be. That he'd spared her the scandal as long as he had, in light of her father's death, two years before, she was grateful for, but all else about the man rankled—everything, even down to the fact that he'd chosen such a special holiday to invade her life once more.

"How dare he simply appear!" she cried in dismay. "Now of all times!" Merely four days remaining till Christmas! "The man is as cold as Newgale in winter!"

"I'm tellin' y' . . . he might've changed his mind," Jane offered once more.

Emma gave the maid a censuring glance. Split between the duties of governess and abigail, Jane seemed to be neither, in fact. Still, the older woman was as much a part of the family as was Emma. "Really, Jane," Emma admonished. "I care not one whit whether he has or no! I wouldn't wed *that* man now if I were dying and he held the last breath! Why, I wouldn't even if he were Christmas incarnate and I a starving soul!"

"Tsk." Jane shrugged and sighed. "Such dramatics. Very well, Miss Emma." She shook her head in utter disgust over the gown she held in her hand and then tossed it upon the bed, not even bothering to offer it for Emma's consideration.

"Very well, indeed!" Emma scoffed. She could certainly play the game as well as he. If he wanted indifference, then let it be so. She vowed to be as unfeeling as he. And the very last she intended was to dress to please him. Seizing the gown Jane had only just tossed atop the scattered pile upon the bed, she exclaimed at last, "This one!"

"Hmmm?" Jane turned to look at her and, spying the gown she held in her hand, exclaimed in dismay, "Miss Emma?" She scrunched her nose. "That one?"

"This one," Emma affirmed, nodding mulishly.

"But Miss Emma . . . puce has never flattered you overmuch . . . what about the—"

"Precisely!" Emma exclaimed. "And I've never cared much for the gown, besides!"

Jane's face screwed. "Very well, then . . ." She peered at Emma as though she were mad. "I-if you're certain?"

"Of course, I'm certain."

"Very well," Jane relented once more, giving her a confounded shrug. "That one it is." She heaved a weary sigh, telling Emma, without so much as a word, that she thoroughly disapproved of her choice. Yet she said nothing more and at once proceeded to help Emma dress. Once her task was done, however, she didn't linger. She went, shaking her head, leaving Emma to brood alone.

It took Emma another full half hour, and at least a dozen glimpses into the looking glass, before she felt confident enough to leave her room. Yet once she did, she felt more than prepared to face him at last.

And face him she would.

Once and for all.

As expected, she found the fiend ensconced in the library with Andrew, the door only slightly ajar as they spoke in low tones behind it. She stood only an instant, bracing herself, and overheard *him* say, "I assure you, I have not changed my mind, Peters. As I told you two years ago . . . I feel it ultimately the best course for all."

Even as she told herself it didn't matter, Emma's heart twisted at his words.

"Well," Andrew began, "I had only hoped with time—"

Emma didn't wait to hear any more. The last thing she wished was for Andrew to *change* the scoundrel's mind! With as much dignity as she could muster, she threw the door wide and entered, lifting her chin as she met her brother's surprised gaze.

"Good morning, Andrew," she said much too cheerily. "You must pardon me," she said by way of apology. "I couldn't help but overhear. Certainly the duke is right. It *is* the best recourse," she affirmed as coolly as she was able. "I must only wonder why it took so very long for *His Grace* to finally take it." At last, she glanced *his* way, and at the sight of him, her heart tumbled violently.

As though he were master of this domain, the duke was seated in her brother's deep blue damask chair before the window, while Andrew paced before him like an uninvited guest. Cad! And demon, that *he* was, his dark brows arched at her bald declaration, though he did nothing more to acknowledge her. No greeting, nothing. He simply sat, observing her keenly, his dark blue eyes appearing slightly amused.

He wore blue, but a blue so dark as to appear a sinister black. And his boots, indeed, were black as well—black and coated with sand, she couldn't help but note. She narrowed her eyes and scrunched her nose, daring to lift her gaze to his face once more. This time she resisted the urge to wrench her gaze away. But Lord-a-mercy, his face! Well it was just the face she recalled, the one that had deceived her, the one she had fallen in love with at first glance; his mouth still that beautiful mouth, his face still shadowed, his eyes still jaded. Yes, indeed, it was the face that had mesmerized her, the face that had led her to think she could make a difference in his life. He arched a brow at her, in much the same way that had once made her heart go aflutter, but she refused to let it affect her any longer.

"You cannot mean to say you are in agreement

with this madness?" Andrew asked her, sounding appalled.

The cur! Well, Emma was through being mesmerized by the man. If her heart went aflutter when he looked at her then it was on account of her fragmented nerves and not a trifle more. Arching her own brow with equal coolness, she turned to face her brother. "Well, of course, I am! It has been sheer folly drawing this out so very long. For shame, Andrew, Papa has been gone from us now over two years. Really, we must thank *His Grace*"—she gave the duke a pointed glance, one with little benevolence—"for taking our Papa's passing into consideration, but now it is time to move forth—long past the time to make *this very mutual* decision public. In fact, we should even post it in the *Times*!"

"*Mutual*?" Both Andrew and Linc replied at once.

Devil have him if he'd meant to challenge her, but the exclamation came of its own accord. Linc straightened within his chair as she turned to face him once more, her smile frosty.

"Of course," she said without flinching. "Do you not agree, *Your Grace*?"

For the first time in his thirty-one years, Linc found himself at a loss for words. She stood daringly before him, proclaiming *his* decision a *mutual* one, challenging him with her dauntless posture and her deep brown eyes—eyes that were far more knowing than he recalled. She had seemed such a fragile little miss, with unwavering, trustful brown eyes that had managed to make him feel profane in comparison. He frowned, and her chin lifted another notch. He nearly choked at her response. "*Yes*," he relented, clearing his throat. "I do. I do, indeed."

"Gad, Emma! Post it in the *Times*?" her brother asked incredulously.

"Of course," she answered flippantly.

"You may rest assured it shall be posted," Andrew pointed out at once, irascibly, "but I assure you the account will be anything but lauding. The truth is that those hounds will write what they choose and not what you please."

"Not necessarily," Lincoln countered. "I have—"

"*Emma*," Andrew counseled, ignoring him.

"*Andrew*," she countered, returning his challenge.

Linc forced himself to settle back into the chair, respectfully ignoring their quarrel. He stole a sip of his port, and then she managed to astound him yet again, and it was all he could do not to choke as he swallowed.

She smiled and asked pertly of her brother, "Andrew, dearest, might you excuse us a moment, please? I have something I wish to say to His Grace. *Alone*."

Clearing his throat in startle, Linc discarded the half-full goblet upon Peters' desk.

"*Emma*," her brother entreated.

"Andrew, please . . . I shan't be but a moment."

Andrew heaved a weary sigh. "Very well, but I shall be waiting in the corridor." He came forward and grasped her shoulders gently, placing a tender kiss upon her forehead, and then he eyed Lincoln. "*Ascott*," he said as he withdrew, and Linc recognized it for the warning it was meant to be. He had to give the man his due. For all that he was a gentleman of the first order, mindful of his breeding, he seemed to care not a whit for the difference in their station when it came to his sister. Linc nodded his acknowledgment, then waited until Andrew had closed the door behind him before confronting the little shrew.

Curious how he didn't recall her as such.

"How dare you come here!" she exclaimed the very instant he met her gaze. Her eyes narrowed furiously, and her hands went to her slender hips in anger.

"What? No more *Your Grace*?" he asked blithely, referring to her barbed use of his title. "I was beginning to so like the sound of it," he remarked sardonically.

She took a step forward, and Linc thought she might fling herself at him in outrage. "How dare you!"

She wore the most God-awful morning dress that made her appear ancient and gray, yet something about her intrigued, nevertheless. *The glint in her eyes?* Perhaps because the cynicism expressed there so mirrored his own. Good God. What had he done? The mere thought of it twisted his gut, for he wasn't unlike Midas in that way—only instead of the golden touch, he seemed to turn everything bitter. He had to remind himself that while she was angry now, this was the right thing to do.

Hell, he could never have pleased her, could never have given her what she deserved. Never . . . for he was just as his father, a true Traherne—incurably rotten to the bone. He could only expect that, with him as her husband, the sweet smile of hers he remembered so well would only turn bitter and her tender heart would quickly harden. *As hard as his own.* He couldn't have borne it. And in the end she would have wilted, as did his mother with his father, because he couldn't reciprocate her feelings. He couldn't love her.

Damned if he even knew the meaning of the word.

No, she was better off without him, and for once in his life he intended to act honorably.

Still, he had no notion how to respond to her accusation, for he'd thought he'd done the right thing by coming to Newgale. Certainly it would have been easier to simply make the announcement and be done with it—to send her a message by courier and be along his merry way.

"I would have thought you'd prefer notice in person?" he asked her in genuine surprise.

She marched another step forward, giving him a look to curl his liver, and Linc stood at once and retreated behind the damask chair. Truth to tell, he'd never trusted snappish misses—and this one particularly less so for she was behaving entirely out of form. He sure as deuce didn't remember her this way.

"Ink and paper would have sufficed!" she informed him baldly. "You have no license to intrude here upon my family, sirrah—on such a reverent occasion, no less! Have you no concern at all for how this impromptu call of yours might distress them?"

"Distress *them*?" he found himself repeating, his tone incredulous.

"Distress *them*!" she reiterated, emphasizing the word. She gave him a cool little smile. "Did you think I would care one whit, *Your Grace*? Did you think you would find me the same bran-faced pea-goose you last beheld?"

Leaning forward upon the chair, Linc found himself inspecting the bridge of her nose for those childish freckles she referred to and found them gone, indeed. And pea-goose wasn't precisely the term he would use for the woman standing so impudently before him, her cheeks suffused with an angry blush.

She-dragon was more the like!

"Well, sirrah!" she exclaimed in a heated whisper. "If 'tis so, then you shall be delighted to discover me otherwise. I suggest you should pack your possessions upon your bloody phaeton—or whatever it is you rogues go about in—and be gone with a free conscience. Neither I nor my brother will trouble you further, I assure you!"

His brows drew together. "*Britschka*," he corrected.

She glared at him a moment in confusion and then said with conviction, "I don't care what you came in!" Her voice rose with her ire. "Nor am I particularly concerned with what you depart in—be it boot, carriage, or sleigh—merely that you *go*! Now . . . if you will pardon me, *Your Grace*—" She lifted her god-awful skirts and marched past him toward the tremendous wall of books at his back. "I shall procure what I came for and be along my merry way."

She could have fooled him, Linc thought ruefully. He'd have thought she'd come for his blood! "What *did* you come for?" he asked dubiously. God's truth, he had a sudden vision of her doing him bodily harm, and he flinched as she reached too close for comfort, plucking a green cloth book from one of the lower shelves at his left. He half expected her to box him with it, but she merely turned and marched across the room, leaving him staring openmouthed after her. Yet she didn't leave before offering a last word of counsel. Typical of females, he thought wryly, to always have the last word.

"I should caution you, however, to leave Newgale at your earliest convenience," she informed him haughtily. "Elsewise my dear brother might get the addle-brained notion that you *owe* me a bloody wedding after all." She smiled coolly and then said softly, "We wouldn't wish that, now would we, *Your Grace*?" She smiled, raising one brow and then told him smartly, "Good day!" She snatched the door closed, without so much as awaiting his response, and Lincoln for an instant could merely stare at it in bewilderment.

God's truth, whatever he'd expected of this meeting, certainly it had not been this.

2

HAVING BEEN SO THOROUGHLY DISMISSED, LINC found he couldn't go. He went so far as to order his carriage about, but couldn't stomach the notion of leaving after what he'd done to her. That he'd turned the bloody chit into an embittered shrew tormented him. For a moment he stared out of the open door of his carriage in sheer disgust of himself, and a vision of the sweet girl he'd first met loomed before his eyes.

Bloody hell, how old was she now? Twenty-one? Twenty-two? *Still too young and naive for the likes of him, even if she'd been one hundred-one!*

He needed heirs, but not so much that he could destroy some gentle creature's life for the sake of his name. While the notion of marrying had never wholly appealed to Linc, he'd been perfectly amenable to doing his duty. After all, as the fifth Duke of Ascott, he was responsible for ensuring the continuation of the family line.

He just hadn't been prepared for Emma.

God, he was much too jaded, cynical, and selfish—a combination as lethal to the soul as acid over a thriving bloom. He was just like his father, he feared, and the truth was that he hadn't loved the Emma of three years past, hadn't really known her, and while she'd certainly appealed to him in a very basic way, he didn't foresee that he would ever develop such a devotion to her.

Damn. He *had* hoped to find someone he could

like, and he *did* like her. But more than that, he'd
hoped to find someone who would be content to live
her own life and leave him be. He didn't want her
to be wounded if he took a mistress, he really didn't
want her to care. He bloody well should have known
not to look for someone so young and impression-
able!

She was just too vulnerable . . . and if she could
love him, if she did love him—and she'd once said
that she did—he could not, in all good conscience,
condemn her to a life with the devil himself. He was
determined to save her from a fate worse than death.

Hell, someday she would even thank him.

Muttering an oath, he punched the rear facing seat
with a clenched fist. God's teeth, since when had she
begun using the bloody word *bloody* anyhow?
Scowling, he lifted up his coat. Devil a bit! He'd
managed to botch even this, and he'd never liked
himself less than he did at the moment.

The least he could do was to stay and right his
wrong. He did *owe* her that much.

Alighting from his carriage and shrugging on his
coat, he at once sought out Peters, finding him
within the stables, handing the reins of his bay to a
young stable hand.

"She's a bit of blood," Andrew remarked when he
spied Lincoln.

"Emma?"

Andrew chuckled softly. "Her, too," he relented,
his dark eyes twinkling. He started out of the stables,
and Linc, frowning, turned to accompany him.

"Odd . . . I didn't recall her that way," he admitted.

Andrew glanced at him askew, and for an instant
his expression was imputing. "Perhaps, Ascott,
that's because you never stayed long enough to
know her." And then he added, "I presume you will
be departing Newgale at once?"

Linc sucked in a breath, grateful not to have discovered him to be the indignant brother of this morn. Hell, he'd half expected a fist up the nose. Scarcely believing what he was about to say, he relented. "In fact . . . I thought I'd remain another day. . . ."

Andrew halted abruptly and spun to face Lincoln, blinking at the not-so-subtle request.

Feeling as awkward as a scolded tot under Peters' scrutiny, Linc ran his fingers through his unruly black mane.

"You say you'd like to stay another day?" Andrew repeated dubiously.

Linc related his concern for Emma, and Andrew's brows drew together as he scrutinized his sister's soon-to-be-former betrothed. "You don't wish to leave her with ill feelings?" he repeated.

"Precisely," Linc yielded, standing his mark. "Perhaps there is something I can do to help ease this for her. Certainly, I had no intention of wounding her so."

"I see . . . so you think there is something you can do to ease her?"

Linc nodded. "I believe that *is* what I said, Peters," he affirmed, his eyes narrowing. He was beginning to take offense with the parroting.

"Yes, well . . . I should think you would simply wish to walk away just now. She's certainly given you leave."

Linc had no response to that bit of logic. It was God's truth, yet he found he couldn't simply walk away. Not as yet.

Andrew studied him a moment, and then as though satisfied with what he'd concluded, consented, "Confound it, Ascott! Very well. Stay. But I'm no damn fool." He shot Linc a cautioning glare. "Dishonor her now, and you'll sure as death be eating grass before breakfast. Take my meaning?"

Linc nodded soberly. "I understand, Peters, and you have my word."

Andrew nodded, and Linc watched him go, his brows drawing together in stupefaction. God, he couldn't help but wonder what in the bloody Hell he'd just gotten himself into.

Only one thing was certain . . . whatever it was, it would be trouble, because nothing he ever did was anything but. . . .

"Why . . . in Dewsbury, even to this day, the Devil's knell is tolled for that unfortunate boy!"

"Oh, Papa!" the children rang out in horrified chorus.

" 'Tis true, I say!" Andrew Peters leaned forward, removing the pipe from between his teeth long enough to defend himself.

"Who could have done such a thing?" Lettie asked him. "Who would attack a poor little boy like that and throw his body into a cold, horrible stream?" Her eyes slanted sadly.

"Now, now," her father reminded, trying to soothe her. "It happened hundreds of years ago. Nobody knows precisely what transpired, but his murderer was discovered and as a penance was ordered to give a tenor bell to the Dewsbury parish church. And to this very day that same bell tolls once for each year that has passed since the birth of Christ. Heard 'em myself," he declared with a nod, replacing the pipe between his teeth.

"Andrew!" Lady Cecile admonished her husband. "You really shouldn't terrorize the children with such horrific tales," she sighed. "Why can't you simply let Emma read her stories and you be done, if you please?"

"You won't find that one in any book." Andrew objected testily, sounding for all the world a crotchety old man, despite his youth.

Lady Cecile shuddered, her pale blonde curls quivering with the movement. "Well, I should hope not!" she told him. "It is positively unsuitable!"

"Poppycock. 'Tis a perfectly suitable Christmas tale," argued Andrew.

"Oh, hush!" Lady Cecile demanded. "Why, that one is worse, even, than the one you told last year. Ashen fagots burned on Christmas Eve in commemoration of battles is positively barbaric!" she announced with conviction.

"Well I think it's a rather venerable tradition," Andrew countered loftily, "honoring those who died in the battles of Wessex so long ago." He gave his wife a wink and a nod. "Just consider how long it has been celebrated now . . . since 878. I can only hope I should be remembered so long. Would you remember me, love?" he asked her playfully.

Lady Cecile couldn't quite smother her giggle of scandalized surprise at his affectionate query. "Oh, will you shush, at last!" She scolded Andrew, giving him a quelling glance.

Hearing them carry on so, Emma couldn't suppress her own giggle. "I do have another tale here," she interjected when she could. She held up the little green volume she'd seized from the library shelf earlier. Truth to tell, she had no notion why she'd done so, only at that moment standing before that infuriating man, she had felt suddenly flustered. The last thing she'd wished was for him to think she'd come to the library solely to see him.

"My favorite," she revealed as brightly as she could, resolutely thrusting aside a vision of him, looking more handsome than ever a man had a right to be. Taking a fortifying breath, she looked askance at her brother's children: Jonathon, the youngest at seven, his hair as golden as his mother's, his sweet little face just beginning to lose its baby roundness. And sober Lettie, who was nine, her hair only slightly darker; missing tooth and freckled nose aside, Emma was certain she would grow to be as beautiful as her heart seemed to be. And then Samantha, the prankish eldest at thirteen; her hair as dark as Emma's, she'd inherited her mother's stunning blue eyes along with her father's mischief. The three of them sat quite primly, though their eyes fairly glowed in anticipation of the story to come.

"Care to hear it?" Emma asked them coyly.

All three together shouted an emphatic, "Oh, yes, please!"

Thinking that her brother's children were, indeed, a great cheer to her, she tried not to consider her own loss. The possibility that she might never have children of her own tore at her heart. She waited patiently while they gathered nearer, taking comfort in their familiarity and the festive air of the drawing room all decorated for the holidays. Deep burgundy bows were bound at each end of the mantel, bearing between them a swag of garland. Within the hearth itself, flames crackled loudly, warming the room. "Have I ever told you of the Christmas *crèche*?" she asked them once they were settled.

"No," Jonathon whispered solemnly, and Emma suppressed a giggle at his wide expectant eyes and enthusiastic expression.

"Well in France—"

"Papa doesn't like them!" Lettie announced. She turned to ask him over her shoulder, "Do you, Papa?"

"Well, now . . ."

"Shush, Andrew!" Cecile demanded, though not unkindly. She placed her sewing into her lap to listen along with the children.

Emma flashed a conspiratorial look toward her brother's wife of fourteen years, and Cecile winked in return. "In France," Emma continued, laughing, "the little children build themselves a Christmas crèche to place before the hearth. . . ."

"What's a crèche?" Jonathon broke in.

Samantha's brows drew together as she turned toward her younger brother. "A crib, of course!" she told him and seemed quite pleased with herself for knowing the answer.

"Of course," Emma confirmed, pursing her lips.

"But why would they want to do that?" Jonathon asked.

"Why?" Emma echoed, laughing and patting his head. "Well for *le petit Jesu*, of course, *Sauveur adorable!*"

"Baby Jesus!" Samantha declared.

"Precisely!" Emma affirmed with a delighted nod. "Baby Jesus!" She grinned at the way Jonathon squirmed with enthusiasm. "Well," she told them, "you recall he was born in a stable?" All three children nodded, and Emma glanced up to find that her brother and his wife were nodding, as well. Her smile deepened at the amusing sight they presented. Trying not to wonder what it would have been like in her own home—if she'd had one—she bent forward, lending with her voice all the reverence she felt for the tale. "In France they believe, and quite vehemently, too, that on the eve before Christmas . . ." She spoke more softly yet, drawing them into her story. ". . . the skies open wide, so very wide," she embellished, "and *le petit noel* comes down in all his glory to bring the good little boys and girls wondrous gifts of love!"

"Does he really, Aunt Em?" Jonathon asked in wonder, his big brown eyes wide with childish delight. The brilliance of his smile filled her with joy.

She hugged herself, smiling. "Well, Jonathon, I, for one, would like to believe—" She glanced up . . . only to lose her good humor at once upon discovering *him* in the doorway. At the sight of him, her heart vaulted into her throat. She tried not to feel the burst of hysteria that pummeled through her, but he was leaning much too idly against the door frame, watching her intently, and the way that he watched . . . well, it unnerved her wholly.

How long had he been there?

He smiled arrogantly, and her heart tumbled wildly in response. *Ignore him*, she commanded herself, and regaining her composure, she cast a frowning glance at her brother, for he'd not even bothered to inform her that the duke would be remaining at Newgale yet another day. At this late hour she would have presumed the fiend long departed—eager to go, in fact! God plague the man!

Well, it didn't matter that he'd remained one last night, she told herself. He'd soon enough be gone.

"What then, Aunt Em?" Samantha asked softly, impatient to hear the rest of the tale.

Then? Emma couldn't help but brood, *then her life would return to order*. Forcing her attention to the children once more, she swallowed and continued, though a little shakily. "Then . . . oh, yes! Then each Christmas the children build themselves a crèche. . . ."

"You already said that, Aunt Em!" Lettie reminded her.

"Yes, well . . ." Emma forced herself to ignore his presence, once and for all. Yet it seemed an utterly impossible task, for he filled the room as surely as he stood there scrutinizing her so candidly. "I-in that very special crèche . . . each night—" She peered up at *him* and seeing that he remained, quickly averted her gaze. Botheration! "Each night," she continued a little distractedly, "the children place a single wisp of straw as a token for each and every good work and prayer they have done for the day. . . ."

To his wonder, Linc found himself, for the first time in his life, the recipient of the cut direct. Still . . . standing there, listening, he shuddered with pleasure, for despite her obvious dislike of him, Emma had a way of speaking that enthralled even the most jaded. Like himself.

His mother had been that way, he recalled.

And hell, he hadn't understood before, but he did now. For the first time since his confrontation with her this afternoon, he fully comprehended her anger over his untimely intrusion. The scene before him was unblemished . . . unblemished but for his presence.

The scent of beeswax filled his nostrils, drifting like invisible ribbons from candles that flickered gaily throughout the room, lending cheer and warmth to the fire burning so brightly within the hearth. Deep burgundy bows, threaded with golden tinsel, adorned the room everywhere, hung alongside bells that tinkled softly as though by an imperceptible breeze. As he watched the Christmas scene unveil before him, he felt like an intruder in their midst . . . unwelcome, and out of place.

". . . and if everyone has been very, *very* good," he heard Emma say, "then on Christmas Eve, Heaven's gate shall open wide—yes it will!" she assured a skeptical Jonathon. Linc glanced her way in time to catch a smile on her lips that made his heart turn violently. She tapped the lad lightly upon the bridge of his nose and continued. "The skies will burst with a beauteous holy light, and *le petit noel* shall come down from the heavens to sleep in a warm bed full with tender straw!"

"Ohhhh!" the children exclaimed in unison.

"Imagine how sweet it would be not to sleep upon the hardness of the manger's boards," she elaborated. "Only imagine how grateful—"

"He would be *sooo* pleased he would leave lots of gifts for the boys and girls!" Jonathon said excitedly.

Emma laughed, and the sound reverberated through Linc. "Oh, but only if you have been very, very, good, Jonathon," she reminded him at once.

Linc cleared his throat. "Tell us, Miss Peters," he found himself interjecting, before he could stop himself, "what precisely constitutes very, *very* good?" For some peculiar reason, he needed her to acknowledge him suddenly as part of their cozy little gathering. He needed her to look at him. . . .

The entire room fell silent while he waited for Emma to acknowledge his presence. Yet everyone but Emma did. Still he asked, despite that she didn't bother to recognize him, "Miss Peters?" Where she had not done so before, Emma quickly buried her nose into her little book, pretending not to hear, in a last blatant effort to ignore him. But he'd be damned if he'd let her. He cleared his throat, reminding her that he waited.

Aversely, he could tell, she lifted her gaze to his, and the look she gave him would have wilted the hardiest rose.

But then, he was no rose, he acknowledged ruefully, but a weed, instead.

And weeds were indestructible.

Untouchable.

She was loath to speak to him at all, he could tell, and her declaration confirmed his suspicions. "I suppose *someone of your ilk* might indeed need some direction, *Your Grace*," she yielded a little too sweetly, a little too coolly, for her words were meant to cut, he knew. Despite all of his carefully laid armor, she succeeded, for the subtle accusation was too close to his own self-opinion to be disregarded. She smiled icily, lifting a brow. "Thus I shall endeavor to illuminate," she told him a little more wrathfully. "By good deed, I shall presume they are referring to acts of devotion or virtue. You do know the meaning of these concepts, do you not?" Her eyes impugned him. *"Or shall I further enlighten you?"*

"But Aunt Em . . . I don't know what they mean," Jonathon said guiltily, responding to the accusation in her voice. His brows slanted unhappily.

Emma's expression transformed to one of dismay as she turned to her nephew. "Oh, Jon!" she exclaimed. *"You,"* she assured him, casting a withering glance Linc's way before returning a concerned gaze to the little boy, "are all that is virtuous!" She smiled sweetly down upon him, and in that smile, Linc glimpsed the very expression she'd once lavished upon him, the one with such sweetness, purity, and innocence that it had made him feel unworthy in comparison. Yet it was no longer for him, he conceded, but for the boy, and that admission left him strangely bereft.

Nor was she any longer the innocent girl he recalled. She was a woman grown, and could hold her own. *Even against him, it would seem.*

With a gentleness he envied, she tousled the boy's shining blonde mane, and for a moment he was sure he could feel her hands within his own hair; warm fingers at his nape, the sensation so real that he inhaled in shock and closed his eyes to savor it privately. But it was a mistake, for it opened a window he'd long ago slammed shut, revived a memory he'd long tucked away. . . . *Another Christmas, long ago and far away. He was in his mother's arms, and she kissed him sweetly upon the nose while she ruffled his hair. "You are my light,"* she had said to him then. But she'd been blind in her love, for he'd been born with his father's darkness. God, even then his armor had been tarnished an ugly black. Even then.

". . . remember the time you and Lettie rescued the little robin from Penelope's perilous jaws," Emma was saying, bringing him back to the present.

"Crotchety old feline!" Andrew Peters proclaimed at once.

Emma glanced up and added with an impish giggle, "And remember your Papa fostered it within the nursery. . . ."

"Lord-a-mercy!" Lady Cecile exclaimed aghast, once again casting aside her sewing. "Not in the nursery! Really, Andrew!" She gave him a chastening look. "Sometimes I do wonder who are the children in this house!"

Despite himself, Linc chuckled at their banter. He envied their easy alliance. And Emma . . . she re-

minded him too much of his mother . . . and Jonathon, himself.

More acutely than before, he felt a trespasser. . . .

"Well that would be a perfect example of a very
good deed," she informed them all. "And I've no
doubt you'd all come up with dozens of others."

"Does keeping your socks clean count?" Jonathon
asked soberly. The child peered up into Emma's face
with all the hope and adoration Linc had once felt
for his own mother, and he couldn't help but think
that Emma would have been a very, very good
mother, indeed.

She might have even been the perfect mother . . .
for his own children.

But he refused to reconsider.

She looked so dashed innocent sitting there
amongst the children. . . .

He saw her shudder. Against the chill of the room,
he thought—a chill he didn't feel because it was too
much a part of him. *Cold*. He'd be damned if he was
capable of feeling anything as redeeming as love,
and he didn't intend to do to Emma Peters what his
father had done to his gentle mother. No, crying off
was the right thing to do—*before he inflicted the same
misery on Emma that his father had on his mother*.

"Yes, of course, Jonathon. *Everything* counts," she
advised them very charitably, raising a finger in
counsel, "so long as 'tis done for the good."

"Is it really true?" Lettie echoed.

"I would very much like to think so," Emma answered with a wistful smile. She sighed. "Wouldn't
it be wondrous?"

"Oh, yes!" Samantha exclaimed. She turned
pleading eyes toward her father. "Can we do it,
Papa? Oh, can we please? Can we build a *crèche* for
le petit Jesu?"

"Hmmm?" Brought out from his stupor by his
eldest child's plea, Peters withdrew the pipe from
his mouth and shrugged. "Well, now . . . I cannot

conceive why we should not," he said after a moment's consideration.

"Yeahhhh!" the children screeched.

"Oh, thank you, Papa!" Lettie exclaimed, leaping up and flinging herself into her father's lap. "Thank you very much!"

Jonathon, too, bounded upward, flinging his little arms about Emma's neck. "We love you, Aunt Em!"

Emma laughed, and the sound was husky and earthy rather than youthful and musical as Linc recalled. It gave him an immediate physical response. "I—" She glanced up suddenly, meeting his gaze, and her face pinkened. She quickly averted her eyes. "I-I love you, too," she assured Jonathon, but her voice was shaky, and Linc couldn't help but wonder whether she recalled saying just the same to him.

He couldn't seem to forget.

Dressed brightly in a pale yellow morning dress and a Cambridge blue bonnet, she'd tilted her face shyly to his and said with all the sincerity of an adoring child, "I think . . . I think I love you, Your Grace!"

No words had ever touched him more.

No words had ever sobered him more.

"Aunt Em?" Lettie asked, turning slightly in her father's lap where she had settled herself. She looked at her aunt and then turned to glance shyly at Linc, with something slightly calculating in her somber blue eyes. "What if you try to heal people?" she asked. Once again, Lettie turned to peer at him and this time did not turn away. Linc fidgeted uncomfortably under her guileless scrutiny. "Does that count for a good deed?" She wanted to know. "If you try to heal *people* instead of baby robins?"

Linc noted that Emma, too, had noticed the direction of Lettie's gaze, as did her father. Pinned by their combined scrutiny, and targeted by the child's question, Linc had never felt more discomfited in his entire life. He straightened abruptly as Emma replied soberly, her voice a little trembly, "Yes, of

course, Lettie, though we can merely try." She cast
Lincoln an awkward glance. "Some people will not
be healed," she disclosed softly, sadly, her brow fur-
rowing. And then she lifted her chin. "And those
you must simply set free."

Linc had the immediate impression that she was
speaking of him. *Could that be what she was attempting
with her frosty demeanor? To set him free?* The thought
touched him in a way he could not quite perceive.

Lettie whispered something into her father's ear,
and he stared down at his daughter in what appeared to be surprise, and then enlightenment, and
then he turned to regard Linc as though he'd had
some sort of *coup de foudre*. He stood abruptly,
chuckling, lifting his daughter up with him and then
setting her down before him.

"You are brilliant!" he told her softly, removing
the pipe from his mouth and bending to plant a
quick peck upon her forehead. "Well," he declared
to one and all with a sudden burst of excitement. He
straightened to his full height, grinning waggishly.
"I believe I shall have the crèche constructed at
once!" He stared at Linc an uncomfortable instant,
shook his head, chortled, and then cast a wide grin
at Emma. Still chuckling, he then abruptly seized his
wife by the arm, declaring, "Come, Cecile, my dear,
we must speak at once."

"But, Andrew!" his wife exclaimed, abandoning
her sewing to the floor as he tugged her unexpect-
edly to her feet. "What are you doing?" she
screeched and then laughed. "Where are we going?"

"To build a crèche," he announced.

"I know something we can do, too!" Lettie declared to her siblings as their parents fled the room.
"I know a very special, special good deed we can
do!" As her father had done with her mother, she
urged her elder sister to rise, seizing her by the hand
and tugging excitedly. "Come, come!" she urged.
"Let me tell you!"

"I can come, too!" Jonathon announced, bounding to his feet and hurrying after them. "Can't I? Can't I?"

In a rush of flailing limbs, all three children stampeded past Lincoln as though he'd not been standing there at all, and within the space of seconds the drawing room was abandoned . . . save for Emma and himself.

Watching over his shoulder as the children bounded down the hall after their parents, he noted that Lettie glanced back at him and then quickly turned away and giggled impishly as she spoke to her brother and sister in low tones. He listened to the echoes of their clandestine whispers only an instant longer, and then couldn't help himself. . . .

He turned and stepped into the room.

3

EMMA DIDN'T DARE LOOK AT HIM—COULDN'T bear being in the same room with him—alone, at that! She couldn't imagine what could have possessed everyone to simply abandon her so!

Fervently, she prayed that he, too, would leave, but he ventured within the room instead, his footfalls echoing woodenly upon the floor as he made his way across to the hearth. Crossing the Aubusson carpet, he halted beside her, and she swallowed, not daring to look higher than his boots.

She didn't respond to his presence.

"That was quite a touching tale," he remarked after an uncomfortable moment of silence.

Slowly, Emma peered up to find him skimming his long, lean fingers along the ribbons and tinsel that stretched the breadth of the mantel, examining it, the crude strength in his hand a direct contrast to the fine strips of satin cloth and brittle foil. The candles burning upon the mantel cast alternating light and shadow upon his profile. He lifted up a cherub and then replaced it at once.

"Yes, well"—she swallowed convulsively—"I should think you would have been long since departed, Your Grace."

He sighed. "Then, you will be no doubt pleased," he revealed, turning to face her, his hands locked behind his back, "to hear that I shall be leaving first thing on the morrow." His lips curved in that sardonic manner of his, only this time she wasn't tempted to brush her fingers across them, to smooth away the hard lines and coax a smile in its place.

She tried but couldn't tear her gaze away, his eyes were so hypnotic . . . like once before, making her believe that he needed her. Well, she refused to acknowledge it this time! As he'd told her then, he *needed* no one. She lifted her chin slightly. "I should have been significantly *more* pleased to have learned you'd already gone," she replied honestly, standing to face him. She wanted to say more, wanted to ask what she had done that caused him to set her aside so resolutely, but couldn't bring herself to begin. "I-if you will pardon me," she said, flustered. Turning, she hurried for the door.

He had the audacity to chuckle at her back.

Emma halted and turned to face him, highly insulted by his mirth, yet when she did, she had the sudden sense that it had been at his own expense, and not hers, and she found herself once again speechless.

He shook his head, as though in self-disgust. "Do I frighten you so that you must rush to leave each time you find yourself in my presence?"

Emma lifted her chin. "Frightened? I think not, Your Grace. I simply have nothing left to say to you."

"No?" He advanced upon her suddenly, and she took a startled step backward.

"N-no!" she exclaimed and wasn't precisely certain whether it was in answer to his question or a desperate plea that he keep his distance.

"You've changed," he told her curtly, taking another step toward her.

"And you haven't?" she returned saucily, withdrawing another foot.

He shook his head as though in puzzlement and said bluntly, "I don't remember you being so impertinent."

Emma gasped at his rudeness. "What did you expect? That I should lie down and weep the rest of my life simply because you chose not to honor our betrothal? Well, sirrah! I am heartily sorry to disappoint you, but I shall not!"

He shook his head again. "To the contrary... though you might find this difficult to credit. I'm quite pleased to hear it. I truly never intended to wound you."

His voice was soft, too soft, reminding Emma of the danger of venturing too close; he radiated warmth, but like the sun, if you happened too near, he consumed. "Well, then, *Your Grace*," she told him, "you may rest assured that you did not. As you can see, I am quite well. You may leave Newgale in good conscience, indeed. You are *free*."

His face screwed up suddenly, his blue eyes shadowing. "Am I really?" he asked her.

Emma didn't fool herself into believing he actually regretted what had come to pass between them. If aught, his question was no more than a courtesy. And if his life was in disorder it was certainly no concern of hers! Nor was it any less then he deserved!

"Of course," she assured him.

He took another step closer, his smoky eyes boring into her own. "I take it, then, that you are ultimately pleased with the outcome?"

Pleased? Emma nearly choked. "Delighted!" she replied. Unable to bear the sight of him any longer, she swallowed and once again turned to leave him. "I-if you will excuse me, now, Your Grace." Lord help her—she had to go—had to leave before she disgraced herself before him.

To her shock, Linc caught and seized her gently by the arm, and Emma flinched at his touch, yet turned once more to face him, though the instant she peered into his eyes she wished she hadn't. They were so filled with concern for her that she thought she would weep. Good Lord, she couldn't bear his pity. Didn't want it!

"Then tell me why it is you seemed so wounded just now," he entreated. "Tell me why you cannot bear even to look at me."

Her hands began to shake and her eyes misted. "I beg your pardon, Your Grace! I am *not* wounded!" she denied fervently. "If aught, I am angry!"

"Tell me why?"

She narrowed her eyes. "I believe I already have!"

His smoky blue eyes challenged her. "Then tell me just once more, Emma," he demanded softly.

The sound of her name upon his lips sent a quiver down her spine. Freeing herself from his grip, Emma told him, a little hysterically, "Because you don't belong here, and you shouldn't have come!"

His brows lifted a little at her declaration. "Not to put too fine a point on it," he remarked softly, nodding. "Very well, Emma." He sighed and some emotion flickered in his eyes. For the briefest instant, Emma thought she saw again that same wounded look that had once made her so willing to love him. But she didn't fool herself into believing it this time. The man was no more wounded than he was compassionate. If aught, he was feeling a mite guilty for what he was about to do to her life—and not without cause. She swallowed convulsively, loathing that she was trying so desperately to release him from his guilt, when he well deserved to feel remorse—and more!

Still, she proposed, "You owe me nothing, Your Grace. Now if you will only pardon me at long last, I wish you Godspeed and a good life."

Linc nodded once more, releasing her finally.

"Godspeed," she offered once again, choking on the word, and then she turned from him purposefully.

"Farewell, Emma," he called after her.

Emma didn't turn again, nor did she halt until she reached her bedchamber. The finality of his voice pursued her all the way through the house. Once within her room, she slammed the door closed and leaned against it, straining to catch her breath. God help her, she'd done it. She'd well and truly done it! She'd said good-bye and had meant it. She'd freed him, and had still managed to retain some modicum of her pride.

Later, perhaps, pride alone might seem a pittance prize in comparison to all she'd lost, but just now it seemed like the world. It was something to build upon, she knew . . . and perchance all was not lost.

She was merely twenty-two, after all, and not quite unmarriageable as yet. And then, of course, there was her dowry. Quite a neat little sum it was, and if the scandal to come did not ruin her entirely, then perhaps one day she would still find that dream she so craved—the husband who loved her, the children she adored. Someday, though for now she was content to simply hold her dignity intact. Without it, she might as well lie down and weep.

And weeping was something she refused to do!

Nevertheless, she was feeling quite bereft at the moment, and her heart felt just a wee bit tattered, as well. As her vision stung with tears she would not shed, Emma undressed for bed and then lay down to count her blessings.

She fell asleep just so, recounting them.

4

On the third day before Christmas . . .

"WHAT THE BLOODY DEVIL DO YOU MEAN there's nothing to be done?"

Hearing the angry bellow, Emma froze where she stood just beyond the library door. Her first impulse was to turn and flee, but curiosity got the better of her, and she stayed. She'd come downstairs this morn to elicit from Andrew precisely what had possessed him to allow Lincoln Traherne to remain at Newgale when she'd made her own wishes very clear, indeed. Nor had she thought the duke any less eager to go, yet he had remained, and she heartily suspected Andrew to be at the root of it all. It seemed as though the duke may have suspected the same, for at the moment, they sounded as though at daggers drawn.

"You can find those bloody carriage wheels is what you can do!" the duke roared, his deep voice carrying even through the closed door. Emma flinched at the fury of it.

In contrast, Andrew's reply was quite calm, muffled actually, yet Emma could make it out well enough to discern that it was an apology of some sort. *Something about the strangest theft he'd ever en-*

countered . . . didn't know how they managed to steal them . . . every last one . . .

Fairly dying with curiosity, she placed her ear to the door and overheard, "Blast it, Peters! This reeks of a hum! Who the devil would snatch carriage wheels and leave pure blooded Arabians behind in their stead?"

"Demme, if I know," she heard Andrew mumble. And then, "Don't look at me, Ascott. Confounded heathens took mine, as well!"

"I want those wheels!" she heard the duke roar, and then someone slammed something—the desk, she imagined—with such rage that the door frame vibrated.

"Yes, well how do you propose I do that? I've no notion where to be—"

"I don't give a damn, Peters!" There was a moment of taut silence, and then, "Just do it!" The duke's bellow was so near the door suddenly that she panicked at the sound of it. Suppressing a mortified shriek at the thought of being discovered eavesdropping, Emma flung herself away from the door and dashed down the corridor, hurrying toward the drawing room. To her immense relief, she slipped inside and out of view within an ace of being discovered, only to startle three eavesdropping children. As she entered, all three scattered from the doorway, squawking in surprise. She let out a startled cry of her own and opened her mouth to speak, but in that moment the library door opened and slammed shut, and her face heated. "Well!" she said instead, eyeing all three suspiciously, but she could say nothing more. How could she reprimand them when she was as guilty as they?

"We didn't do nothing!" Jonathon exclaimed. Lettie elbowed him at once and he looked up at her guiltily. "Oh!" he said softly.

"And what sort of nothing did you not do?"

Emma asked him primly, straightening the folds of her skirts as she entered the drawing room, casting a nervous backward glance at the door.

"Oh . . . well . . . just nothing nothing," he answered in a small little voice, looking all the more guilty. He peered down at his feet suddenly.

"We were merely admiring the new crèche, Aunt Em," Samantha offered sweetly, giving her little brother a slight nudge.

Emma's brow lifted. "From the door?" she asked dubiously.

Samantha considered that only an instant and then admitted with a shrug, "Well, we heard the duke shouting," she said matter-of-factly.

Emma's face burned a little hotter. "Yes, well . . . so did I," she admitted a little sheepishly. "It seems someone has robbed him of his means of departure," she said, watching them and noting that all three fidgeted guiltily at the news.

"Er . . . did you see the crèche, Aunt Em?" Lettie asked suddenly, sweetly, conveniently changing the topic.

Samantha perked up. "Oh, yes—isn't it grand?" she added quickly, giving her sister a well-done nod.

"And it's already half full!" Jonathon blurted excitedly.

Emma came closer to examine the small wooden crib that now sat before the hearth. It was crudely constructed, but still and all a charming sight. Given the scarcity of time before Christmas, she imagined Andrew had troubled to build it himself, for it very much looked as though he had. "I see that it is," she said a little warily and couldn't help but wonder a little uneasily how they'd managed to fill it so high so quickly.

Jonathon shifted excitedly from foot to foot. "Just like you said, Aunt Em! There's one straw inside for each whee—"

With a horrified gasp, Samantha slapped a hand

over her brother's impetuous mouth. "Wheeeed!"
she squealed in his stead. "One for each weed!"

Emma's brows drew together. "One for each . . .
weed?"

Samantha nodded. "Oh, yes, Aunt Em! One blade
of straw for each and every *weed* we pulled from
mother's herb garden!"

"Really?" Emma said. She didn't have the heart
to remind them that they were in the midst of winter. There was no garden. And she was beginning to
understand with sudden clarity the strange conversation she'd overheard just outside the library door.
Taking in Jonathon's guilty expression, and the girls'
much too innocent smiles, she had a sudden insight
as to what dreadful mishap had befallen the duke's
wheels. Nevertheless, she also knew the children
could never have accomplished such a monumental
feat alone nor were they quite devious enough to
carry it through without aid. And she knew precisely who to hold accountable. Their father had always been such a trickster. "One for *each* weed, is
it?" she said, cursing her dear brother to Jericho and
back.

"Oh, yes, Aunt Em!" Samantha and Lettie replied
at once, both grinning with what could be nothing
more than relief. Jonathon, with Samantha's hand
still muzzling his mouth, merely glanced up at his
sisters, his brows drawing together in confusion.

"Well, now, don't you think that's a mite exces-
sive?" Emma asked them crossly. "I should think
that one for every . . . er . . . bundle of *weeds* would
be more than enough. Besides, pulling *weeds* in the
middle of winter may not precisely qualify as a *good
deed*, at all," she informed them all lamentably.

"Oh, but they were very special weeds," Lettie returned hopefully.

"And we pulled them *all* for a very good cause,
Aunt Em," Samantha declared.

"Is that so?" Emma relented. She couldn't quite

bring herself to believe they had vandalized the duke's carriage on her behalf. The thought of it was too humiliating by half.

Nevertheless, the image of them plucking carriage wheels—that and the duke's reaction to it this morn—struck a hysterical chord. She stifled a smile. For shame that her brother would stoop to such ends to prevent the duke from leaving Newgale. Not to mention that he should involve his precious young children in such a terrible misconduct. For certain, she was going to blister his ears at the first opportunity. In the meantime, it was all she could do to keep from bursting into hilarities.

"Besides, Aunt Em," Lettie countered plaintively, looking a little dismayed, "you did say one wisp of straw for *each* good deed, did you not? We only did what you said," she assured.

Emma pursed her lips together. "I did say that," she yielded, trying in vain to frown at them, "didn't I?" The little fiends! Backed by their father, she knew without doubt that they would never confess, and so she didn't bother trying to make them do so. Good Lord, she did love all of them dearly, but she had half a mind to go and tell the duke precisely what had befallen his blessed wheels so that he could take his bloody carriage and be gone! Yet the thought of him knowing mortified her. No, she simply couldn't bear it. Nor could she bear to stand before the children an instant longer without bursting into peals of laughter.

"Aunt Em," Jonathon ventured. "Do you . . . do you think the duke will be remaining for Christmas now that his—" Lettie stomped on his shiny black shoe none too softly. "Owwie!" He turned to give his sister a most wounded look. "I wasn't gonna say it!" he shrieked in indignation. "I wasn't going to!"

Emma tried in vain to give them her most disapproving glower. "I really don't know," she told them. "But, I, for one, wish he would not." Gracious

Lord, the very last thing she intended was to play
into their mischievous little hands. "Oh, my!" she
exclaimed suddenly, dramatically, placing a hand to
her temple. "I believe I am having a sudden attack
of the vapors!" And it wasn't completely feigned,
she acknowledged, for the very thought of the
duke's continued presence at Newgale left her flustered and ill at ease.

"You are?" Samantha asked, frowning, her little
brows clashing.

"Oh, yes!" she told them. "Goodness, it seems
so!"

"Oh, but Aunt Em, you never do!"

She gave them all a hearty scowl. "Well, I am
now," she apprised them. She had no notion what
they were up to, nor what her foolish brother could
possibly be thinking, but she planned to spend the
rest of the day within her bedchamber, reading. If
they wished the duke to remain at Newgale, then
they could certainly entertain the demon without
her. Surely, she thought, once they realized she was
not about to participate in this madness, they would
return his blessed carriage wheels to him, and he
would be gone before morn. She moaned and said,
"Oh, dear ... won't you tell your Papa, please, in
case he should like to know, that I shall be resting."
She shot them another reproachful glare and turned
with a swirl of her skirts. "In my room," she added
with burgeoning satisfaction, hurrying toward the
door.

"Oh, but Aunt Em!" Samantha protested.

All three rushed after her, halting abruptly as she
collided with the duke, who suddenly appeared in
the doorway.

"Oh!" Emma exclaimed, stumbling backward at
the unexpected impact. Really! She'd not heard his
approach at all and wondered irately how long he'd
been standing there watching, listening. She eyed
him a little anxiously.

Precisely how much had he overheard?

At once, he reached out to steady her, and the touch of his hands upon her arms was almost more than Emma could bear. His fingers were too strong, his hands too warm, and if he didn't remove them from her person at once, she thought she might scream.

Neither of them stirred for the longest instant nor did he loosen his grip upon her arms.

Without thinking, Linc drew her nearer and then found he couldn't quite bring himself to release her. It seemed the most natural place for her to be all at once. His heartbeat quickened, for if yesterday she'd looked ancient, today she was anything but. And her face, stained with a healthy blush, was anything but gray. Her eyes sparkled and only dimmed at the sight of him. That realization pricked at him somewhere deep within, but he didn't stop to analyze why.

Dressed in the same pale yellow she'd worn the day she'd told him so naively that she'd loved him, she looked fresh and lovely. Too lovely for his own good. And then he happened to look down and had to remind himself to exhale. His heart skipped a beat, for there *was* one thing about her dress today that was wholly dissimilar from the one she'd worn three years before: the neckline. It was far lower than he would have preferred, at least upon her, showing a fair expanse of creamy breasts. As he stared, he had to remember that he had no right to concern himself with her décolletage—or anything else that pertained to Emma Peters, for that matter.

Not any more.

He wanted to draw her up into his arms and kiss her—damn if he didn't. Instinct drove him closer still, until he could feel the warmth radiating from her lips. His heart hammered like a fresh-faced youth's. *Warmth to drive away the chill.* God, it would be so easy. . . .

Where now his honorable intentions?

Swallowing, he stood, arrested an interminable moment, shuddering, forcibly reminding himself. He couldn't afford to feel the warmth—couldn't afford to forget what he had to do. He was more than cold, he was rotten, and anything he touched would turn the same.

With some effort, Linc managed to clear his throat, but for the second time in his life, he couldn't find his tongue to speak.

"I . . . I'm quite fine, thank you," she told him a little unsteadily, squirming out of his embrace.

It took Linc a befuddled instant to realize he hadn't asked. Nor did he so willingly release her. "I'm . . ." Following her lead, he stepped away at last, once again clearing his throat, though still he did not avert his eyes. "I . . . I'm pleased to hear it," he said huskily, his voice sounding strained even to his own ears.

It was only now that she seemed to note the direction of his gaze, for she let out a startled gasp. As he watched, the blush from her face stole to her breasts, and all he could think, insanely, was that he longed to place his hand there to feel its rosy warmth.

"Must you—" She took another startled breath, and it was all he could do not to bend and touch his lips to her heated flesh. "Must you always lurk in corridors?" she accused him irately.

God's teeth, but it took Linc another full instant to govern himself and to tear his gaze away from the delicious morsel she was tempting him with so sorely. Yet even with his eyes averted, his body didn't forget. Clenching his fist and then releasing it, he acknowledged that it was a liberty he very likely would scandalously have taken had he been her husband. And he couldn't help but wonder if she would have embraced him as a lover as passionately as she had craved to be his wife. A shudder coursed through him at the mere thought, and he glanced down again to find his answer; even through her layers of clothing, her breasts were peaked against the cloth, perfect little pebbles he would have joyfully suckled within his mouth. His body quickened.

He cleared his throat. "It seems so, Miss Peters," he admitted without much regret, his voice husky as he met her soft brown eyes. Hell, eavesdropping was a far less sin than the one he would like to commit just now. "As you have said . . ." His own eyes slivered, burning with blue heat. ". . . it seems as though someone has robbed me of my way to leave. What better way to discover just who?"

Her chin lifted at his insinuation. "Well, then, Your Grace," she exclaimed, "please do continue! I, for one, have nothing to hide—nor have I any wish to keep you! Good day!"

"Haven't you?" he asked, halting her flight by seizing her hand. It was so soft. Softer than he remembered. He found himself hoping that she lied.

She looked at him appalled, the blush in her cheeks deepening, and her ripe, full mouth puckering in outrage. She shook her hand free of his. "Of course not!" Once again, he had the sudden urge to bend and kiss those lips.

Linc nodded, though why her response should disappoint him, he didn't know. He could have expected nothing less. Yet it did.

"Good day, *Your Grace*!" she said again. And this time she didn't wait for him to give her his leave, but pressed her way past him in the doorway, her dress whispering by, her sweet scent accosting him.

Hunger slithered through him like an iniquitous snake.

He stood a moment, watching her go, feeling more than a little confounded . . . until her lemon skirts had disappeared completely around the corridor, and then he turned to face the children who were all

three staring wide-eyed at him as though he would
devour them like the dragon of their worst night-
mares. He'd forgotten they were there. They had a
right to fear him so, he acknowledged, for he'd
heard enough of their discourse with their aunt to
confirm his suspicions. Glancing behind them, he
caught sight of the crèche, quaintly adorned with
satin ribbon and lace and partly filled with straw.
Remembering how much of an intruder he'd felt the
previous evening, he scowled, and all three retreated
a step. Despite their obvious fear, Linc fully intended
to interrogate them without mercy. He had that
about him, he knew, the ability to unnerve grown
men; the children before him stood nary a chance.

"Perhaps one of you knows where I might find
four carriage wheels?" he asked them pointedly, lifting a brow in his most coercing fashion.

For a moment, none of them spoke, only peered
at each other questioningly, and he found himself
strangely regretting their answer to come.

But he regretted for naught. To his incredulity all
three merely turned and said as guiltlessly as though
they were innocent, *"No, sir, Your Grace."*

The middle child actually lifted her chin and
smiled at him—smiled at him, for God's sake!—and
for an instant, Linc merely stood, dumfounded,
scarcely believing the little heathens had managed
to lie to him so effortlessly.

Nor did he relish the immediate and unreasonable
sense of relief that washed over him in that same
instant. Despite that he knew the children were lying, he further astonished himself by muttering a
curt, "I didn't think so." Turning and walking away
was perhaps the most impressive response of all.

As the duke departed, all three children rushed to
peek around the doorway.

"Now what do we do?" Lettie asked as they
watched him go. When he had at last vanished from

the corridor, all three children retreated from the doorway, their expressions thoroughly disheartened as they seated themselves about the crèche.

They stared at it in dismay.

Samantha sighed. "I fear it just won't work if she's going to sequester herself within her room," she lamented.

"How terribly sad," Lettie wailed, her eyes misting.

"And he's so very handsome," Samantha declared. "But so very, very gloomy! But you know ... I think he really does love her," she contended. "Did you see the way that he gazed at her?"

"Aunt Em could cheer him," Jonathon stated with thorough conviction. And then, "How does he look at her, Sammy?"

Samantha patted him consolingly upon the head. "Never mind, Jonathon." She shook her head in quite a matronly fashion. "You're much, *much* too young to know."

Jonathon shrugged away from her and lifted his chin. "Oh yeah? Well, Papa says they're both just too stubborn for their own good," he informed them both, impressing them with his garnered knowledge.

Lettie's brows collided. "Did he really?" she asked. She cocked her head at Samantha. "Sam ... do you really think Aunt Em loves him, too?"

"Oh, but, how could she not!" Samantha replied with certainty. "He's so terribly, terribly handsome!"

Jonathon scrunched his nose and groaned. "You already said that," he protested vehemently, his face turning pink.

Samantha ignored him. With a sigh, she lamented, and very dramatically, "What, oh what do we do now?"

"Well ... when I'm sick in my room," Jonathon interjected, speaking to no one in particular, "Aunt Em always comes to my bed."

Lettie nodded.

"She's so smart," Jonathon continued, his eyes bright with admiration.

Lettie nodded. "From reading all those books," she agreed. "Aunt Em always knows just what to do." She heaved a hopeless sigh, and yielded, "I only wish we did, too."

"If only . . . if only we could determine how to make her go to him," Samantha sighed.

"Well," Jonathon announced offhandedly, "perhaps we could make him sick."

Both girls turned to gawk at him, mouths agape.

"Don't be silly!" Lettie declared after a horrified moment, boxing his ears soundly. "We wouldn't want to make the duke sick! He's a duke, after all!"

"Owww!" Jonathon rubbed his ears. "We wouldn't really have to make him sick!" he recanted, pouting. "We could only pretend he is and simply tell Aunt Em 'tis so. She *would* go to his room!" he insisted. "I know she would because she's the one who always comes to mine! Mother *always* sends her!"

"Really, Jonathon!" Lettie scolded him, shaking her head soberly. "That would never, never do! Why," she proposed sensibly, throwing up her hands in an exasperated fashion, "however would we make him stay in bed?"

Samantha's eyes widened abruptly, and she giggled impishly. "Well," she interposed, her eyes sparkling anew with mischief, "we *could* steal his clothes . . ."

5

On the second day before Christmas ...

LINCOLN WOKE EARLY THE NEXT MORNING, FULLY intending to find his carriage wheels and be gone. And the first place he meant to search was the stables. It seemed the most logical place for three children to hide four carriage wheels—but then, again, he reminded himself, it wasn't merely four wheels, for they'd somehow managed to abscond with even those belonging to their father—the thieving little devils!

He shook his head, frowning as he reopened the drawer in which he'd last spied his personal items.

Empty.

Something wasn't quite right here.

At once he went to the wardrobe, throwing it wide.

Empty, as well.

His brows knit as he puzzled. Damned cold was beginning to get to him. Most sensible men slept in their night rails and nightcaps, while he, on the other hand, had to be one of those unconventional few who slept like a bare-bottomed infant—but dash it all, he couldn't sleep with anything other than sheets tangled about his infernal buttocks—only now he was beginning to pay the price. He was damned well freezing!

Cursing softly beneath his breath, he slammed the wardrobe shut and began a more thorough search of the room, this time with increased foreboding. Yet even after he'd investigated underneath the bed—a ludicrous place, he knew—still there was no sign of them. Nothing! Not of his shoes! Trousers! Coat! Nothing! And he began to form a certain presentiment—brats! Only then did he make out the whispers just beyond his door, children's whispers—the scoundrels were eavesdropping—and it occurred to him like a sudden bolt of lightning just what had happened.

"Bloody whelps stole my clothes!" he roared, yet even as he said it, he couldn't quite believe it was true. They'd actually stolen his clothes—first his wheels and now his bloody clothes! He made a run for the door, thinking of nothing but the restoration of his belongings, but even before he reached it, he heard their terrorized squeals as they fled the scene of the crime. In his haste to stop them, he slipped, and with a muffled curse, he tripped. He slammed into the door, and the force of his impact knocked him onto the ice-cold floor, injuring his tailbone.

The irreverent sound of his collision echoed throughout the old house, followed by his furious howl of pain.

Infernal heathen brats! Never in his life had he met their like! Never had he known a family so peculiar in their ways, that they would give mere children the run of their home—Christmas, or no! It'd serve every damned one of them right if he lifted his frozen arse from the wooden floor and burst into the corridor after them, bared to the buttocks and mad like a loon!

God's teeth . . . if only he could lift his bare arse from the floor. He tried . . . and howled in pain.

"Aunt Em! Aunt Em!"
Emma had only just completed breakfast when the children burst into the dining room. She barely had

time to rise from the table before they swarmed
about her.

"The duke is ill!" Lettie wailed.

"Very, very ill!" Jonathon expounded.

Emma couldn't quite quell the sudden sense of
panic that burst through her. Her expression was
one of horror. "What do you mean ill?"

"Well," Lettie explained on a rush of breath. "You
see . . . we were playing in the corridor . . ." She
peered at Emma, as though to gauge her reaction,
and then at Samantha. ". . . and well, you see . . ."

"He began to scream!" Samantha declared aghast.
"Horribly! Such terrible, terrible screams of pain."

"We think he's dying!" Jonathon conveyed with a
jerky nod. It was quite clear he was shaken by the
possibility.

"Emma, dear," Cecile broke in calmly, accustomed to the children's embellishments as she was.
Emma glanced up, worry lines etching her forehead.
"Perhaps you should go and see what is the matter?"

"Yes!" Emma agreed at once, her thoughts reeling.
She didn't stop to consider the rush of relief she felt
at Cecile's suggestion. "Perhaps I should, at that,"
she said a little distractedly.

"Yes, dear," Cecile agreed, her tone full of concern, and Emma nearly bolted from the dining room
in her haste. Lord, she couldn't bear the thought of
something happening to him. She wished him gone
but certainly not ill! "Children," she heard Cecile
reprove, "you must stay. Aunt Em will do much better without you in her way."

"Yes, mum," they agreed sweetly, and Emma was
certain they were the most thoughtful children she'd
ever known. Lifting her skirts, she fair ran up the
lavish stairwell to the second floor and then down
the corridor to the duke's room.

Hearing the advancing footsteps, Linc propelled
himself into the bed with a bellow of pain. He barely

had time to cover himself before the door burst open, and Emma bolted within. None too chivalrously, he spat an oath at the sight of her and jerked the sheets clear to his chin. "Doesn't anybody in this infernal house knock?" he asked, incensed.

Emma stiffened at his accusation, but it didn't keep her from entering and nearing his bedside. "Even sick you are debauched!" she told him irately, frowning. "Good Lord, can you never cease with the profanity?"

Debauched, was it? She didn't know the half of it, Lincoln thought wryly. The sight of her warmed his blood like mere blankets never could have. He groaned, lifting his knees to conceal tell tale evidence. "I seem to recall," he countered, "that you've developed quite an aptitude for the language yourself, Miss Peters. . . ."

"Yes, well . . ." She eyed him none too benevolently. "You do seem to bring out the worst in me," she conceded.

"Is that so?" he asked her caustically.

Despite the glare she gave him, she came closer still, standing beside the bed now. "Certainly," she affirmed, reaching out to place the back of her hand, almost timidly, to his cheek.

Bloody hell, it was all Linc could do not to seize it and press it more firmly against his heated flesh.

"My, you *are* warm," she told him with great concern.

No small wonder, Linc thought, when she stood before him, once again all but baring those creamy breasts of hers. Dressed in deep rose today, the color only enhanced the flush of her skin, and he couldn't help but think that she'd never looked so stunning. Her dark hair had been lifted artfully and fell in gentle ringlets about her face, framing it perfectly. And her lush lips appeared the very same color as that of her too provocative gown.

He wondered what they would look like after being thoroughly kissed.

She took in his disheveled appearance and shook her head with growing concern. "You look quite dreadful," she announced. "You should be thankful the children were playing outside your door and heard you," she added. "Were it not for them, I never would have known to come."

He lifted a brow. "Really?"

"Truly," she told him, lifting her chin. "You really should thank them." She nodded.

"At the first opportunity," he agreed sardonically, one brow arching wickedly.

Her brows knit at his tone, but her concern overrode her displeasure. "Tell me," she ventured, "where exactly does it hurt?"

Linc was quite certain she didn't really wish to know. Neither of his pains were quite suitable for tender ears to hear. He was on the verge of telling her that he was perfectly fine, that he could only be better if they would simply give him back his infernal clothes and his blasted carriage wheels, and then she knelt beside the bed and took his breath away. Her deep brown eyes peered at him with such distress that it made him feel strangely warmed.

"I," he stammered and shuddered, his eyes helplessly locked upon her luscious cleavage, now taunting him at eye level. It was all Linc could do not to roll and bury his lips into the delectable curves. God, he wanted to draw her into his bed and suckle them each, first through the cloth of her bodice . . . and then when she didn't protest, he would bare them fully to his hungry eyes and feast upon them. He wanted suddenly to make her moan with ecstasy, wanted to show her the pleasures of womanhood. He wanted to cherish her with his hands and his body. He glanced up, into her face, with the sudden, dangerous revelation . . .

He wanted to be the one. . . .

Never had he been so affected by a woman in his entire life—and it helped none at all that he was butt-naked beneath the blankets. If she only knew— God, if her brother knew. He couldn't believe they had actually sent the wench into his bedchamber unattended. It was very likely they thought him dressed to the teeth in night rail and cap like any other respectful chap would be. Even so, it made little sense. Certainly, he wouldn't have given her such leave, and he couldn't believe how lax her brother was—with his own children, for that matter—never mind that Emma was very obviously no longer a child herself! Nor did he like it one bit that she seemed so at ease in his presence considering that most chits would have died of fright at the mere sight of a man clad merely in his nightclothes.

"I-I fell," he yielded, his voice breaking, betraying him like that of a fledgling youth's.

"You fell?" she repeated a little dubiously. Yet he couldn't precisely tell if that was what he heard in her voice, for he'd yet to be able to rent his gaze from her bodice in order to gauge her expression.

He swallowed.

"*Your Grace,*" she whispered, sounding alarmed, "are you quite all right? You seem to be suddenly growing pale. . . ." Once again she placed her hand to his cheek, and his body convulsed at her gentle touch.

"Oh, my!" she exclaimed. "You truly are blistering!" She placed her hand to his chin and lifted his face until his eyes met hers, the gesture such a tender one that Linc could scarcely bear it. And then she slipped her fingers lower, curling them about his neck, as though to measure the heat of his body. "What can I do?" she asked him fretfully.

Caught in the moment, Linc couldn't quite help himself. If it meant she would stay, then he would pretend to be at death's door, if need be. Anything, anything, to keep her from moving those long, graceful fingers from his burning flesh. When she started to remove them, he seized her arm to halt its retreat. It felt so right to have her touch him so.

More right than anything had ever felt in his life.

"My neck," he said gruffly, lying easily as he met her gaze. "It does feel rather stiff." He lifted her other hand and placed it, too, upon his feverish face. "And my head," he told her huskily, his eyes becoming heavy-lidded with desire, "it aches terribly."

"It does?" Emma croaked, eyeing him dubiously. She was staring at his bare arm with something akin to horror.

"God . . . very much so. . . ."

"I-it must be the fever," she told him a little warily. Her gaze never left his arm. She stared, as though transfixed.

"Definitely . . . definitely the fever." He began to babble, stroking her hand erotically against his cheek, relishing the feel of her soft flesh against his whiskers. At the same moment, though he doubted she knew it, her fingers began moving within the disorderly curls at his nape, gliding over his skin and through his mane, caressing ever so softly, and the feel of them quickened his body. Suddenly, her eyes widened. "Your Grace" she ventured.

"Emma," he whispered, his heart hammering.

"T-there's n-no collar!"

She closed her eyes but didn't remove her hand from his nape, and he thought he would go mad if he couldn't make love to her here and now. "Yes, Emma," he said, and his breathing quickened with the knowledge that she was as affected by him as he was by her.

Proof was in the way she bent forward slightly, drawn to him even without her awareness. He guided her closer and lifted his face to meet hers, his lips touching hers, fully intending to seize the moment.

Bloody hell, the initial contact was like nothing

Linc had ever known. Lightning heat sizzled through him with the force of thunder. His body quickened when she didn't resist, and he sent his tongue on a gentle foray of her lips, lapping them, savoring them fully, restraining himself so as not to frighten her. Devil take him, but if her brother was stupid enough to allow her into his clutches . . . he was only a man, after all. He'd never claimed to be honorable . . . and God only knew, no one had ever accused him of it.

"Your Grace," she protested weakly.

"Emma," he whispered, and she trembled at the sound of her name, but didn't withdraw.

With a groan of pleasure and victory, Linc inserted his tongue between her lips, relishing the soft, sweet warmth of her mouth. Cinnamon, he thought vaguely. Her mouth tasted of cinnamon. He savored the sensation as she accepted his tongue into her mouth and met it tentatively with her own.

"Emma, Emma, Emma . . ." He whispered her name between her lips and groaned, thinking that he'd surely been rewarded with Heaven, after all, when she allowed him to lift her and guide her over his hungry body.

Stupid brother of hers, stupid, stupid, stupid . . .

He couldn't believe Andrew Peters could be so stupid as to cast his sister into the lion's den. God's blood, but he'd truly died and gone to Heaven! Yet, Heaven, he knew, would never be his in the end, and there would be a price to pay for even this. Nevertheless, for this incredible moment, he would gladly pay. . . .

Only later . . . much, much later . . .

6

EMMA JUST COULDN'T THINK TO STOP HERSELF. She knew it was wholly wrong, knew she should speak to protest . . . but couldn't manage to do so . . . so long she'd dreamed of this moment. So long, and it was everything she'd ever imagined . . . and nothing she could ever have anticipated. Just now it didn't seem to matter that he was going to leave Newgale soon, that he didn't want her—nor that he was ill. . . .

Nothing mattered in the hazy, dreamy heat of the moment.

Good Lord, she just couldn't think with him holding her so. When he drew her nearer, she could do nothing but let him, for he never ceased kissing her . . . filling her mouth with the most dazzling warmth she'd ever known. Her heart beat frantically within her breast as he guided her closer, but she dared say nothing to break the spell. If she was dreaming, dear God, then let her dream!

She felt herself crumple atop him . . . and he let out a sudden ghastly howl.

Giving a little shriek of her own, Emma disentwined herself from him and scrambled away from the bed, crying out as he yelped once more in what seemed to be pain.

"Bloody damned heathen brats!" he exclaimed. And then, as she stood before him, staring in fright, he shouted again, "Infernal brats!"

"I beg your pardon!" Emma declared, and then

horrified at what she'd done—at what had transpired in this room—she murmured, "Oh, my
Lord!" He flung himself upright in the bed, exposing
his very, very bare chest, and she squawked, "Oh,
G-God, y-you . . . you *are* indecent!"

He gave her a forbearing glance. "In more ways
than one, wouldn't you say?"

Emma couldn't find her voice to speak.

"Something else to thank your bloody nieces and
nephew for," he added scathingly.

Emma couldn't quite bring herself to turn away,
even knowing she should. She blushed furiously. "B-
but," she stammered, "I-I thought . . . I thought . . ."

"They've stolen my blasted clothing!" he told
her irritably, giving her a long-suffering grimace.
And then grunting in pain, he reached to stroke his
backside. "Damn near shattered my backside, as
well!"

Emma thought she would swoon at his declaration. Not to mention the sight of him so . . . so . . . au
naturel—and so at ease with it, besides!

"Oh, Lord!" she exclaimed once more (and looked
askance). "I . . . I shall have them returned at once!"
she assured him. "A-at once! I . . . I'm so sorry, Your
Grace!" She turned and bolted from the room, shutting the door securely behind her.

For an instant, Emma, trembling hysterically,
grasped the knob tightly, as though to hold him
within. Only after it was clear he wouldn't follow,
did she release it and race down the corridor.

Gracious Lord above! She could scarcely believe
what had very nearly happened within that room!
Couldn't believe how much liberty she'd allowed
him to take! Oh, God, she was so humiliated! Nor
could she believe what the children had done to him.

And that kiss!

There was simply no telling what he would think
of her now. So much for her show of dispassion! At

the mere thought of it all, Emma feared she would swoon with mortification.

She sought out Andrew at once and related to him what had transpired—or at least most of what had transpired. She conveniently omitted the worst of the details. If her brother thought for a single instant that the duke had taken advantage, there would be the devil to pay—for both herself as well as the duke, for while Andrew respected Lincoln Traherne immensely, for her honor he would have forfeited his own life. Or taken one. Emma could little bear either of those repercussions.

As furious as he was with the news, Andrew managed to hold himself together well enough to console her for the dreadful ordeal she'd suffered, yet that only made Emma feel all the more reprehensible. With his usual aplomb, he assured her that he would deal with the matter directly, and he did, upbraiding the children at once. No one spoke of *the ordeal* the rest of the day, and Emma busied herself preparing the gifts she would distribute on Christmas morn.

After all, tomorrow would be Christmas Eve.

As far as Emma knew, the duke had finally departed the manor, for he was nowhere to be seen, and one of her brother's mounts turned up missing. Emma, while she told herself she was grateful to have been spared a final confrontation with him, had never felt more abandoned in all her life. Not even her mother's and father's deaths compared, for while she missed them horribly, they'd left her with the memory of their love, at least.

Lincoln Traherne, on the other hand, had heartlessly given her the smallest sampling of what she would never have of him . . . and then he'd cruelly snatched it away, making a terrible lie of her pretense. Hah! She not only cared that he had forsaken

her, but it rent her heart to shreds to know that she
not only had allowed him to do so once, but yet
again!

Had she truly sworn to never give her heart
again?

It didn't matter that no one but she and the duke
knew what had really transpired in that room. *She
knew.*

And he knew.

And the despicable truth was that she'd never re-
claimed her heart to begin with.

Nevertheless, she intended to make the very best
of the holiday for the children's sake.

God help her, she intended to be joyous if it killed
her.

> *Lully, lullay,*
> *Thou little tiny child,*
> *Bye, by lully, lullay . . .*

The sound of the pianoforte keys chinked like hal-
lowed bells, ringing throughout the old house like a
haunting melody of old. Lincoln could almost imagine the accompaniment of an ancient harp.

Enchanting.

Magical. But the sound that drew him into the
drawing room was another entirely.

The sweetest singing he'd ever heard. . . .

> *. . . Oh sisters too*
> *How may we do,*
> *For to preserveth this day.*
> *This poor youngling*
> *For whom we sing,*
> *Bye, by, lully, lullay . . .*

He wasn't surprised to find Emma at the keys,
singing like an angel, her hair flowing gloriously
down her back like he'd never seen it before, rip-

pling like rich velvet as she moved to gracefully pluck at the keys. The sight of her sitting before the pianoforte, so at ease, filled him in that instant with a strange sense of peace . . . mingled with sorrow, for it reminded him of a happier time.

God, she was so like his mother before his father had managed to break her heart that it made his heart ache.

He'd spent the entire day in the village, submersed in drink, fortifying his decision to leave Newgale with every sensible argument he could possibly conceive. He shook his head, for in truth, he was no good for her. And he was certain to break her heart again at the first opportunity for, despite his noble title, he was as base as they came; like his father, he imbibed too much, consorted with women too much, and was self-indulgent.

Worst of all, he didn't have the slightest notion what it was to love.

He fully intended to hire a carriage and go. . . .

> *. . . Herod the king,*
> *In his raging,*
> *Charged he hath this day.*
> *His men of might,*
> *In his own sight,*
> *All young children to slay.*

Glancing at the hearth, he found the crèche filled to brimming with straw—no doubt one blade each for every misguided deed they'd committed against him for her sake. Loyal they were, but a more non-sensical practice he'd never witnessed . . . cradles, and straw, and unfulfilled dreams . . . *bah, humbug!*

> *And woe is me,*
> *Poor child for thee!*
> *And ever morn and day,*

He heaved a sigh, for he'd grown accustomed to finding them this way—so cozy and familiar ... the way it should have been ... the way it had never been ... they way it could have been ...

The acute sense of loss plucked at him like a discordant note.

Still, he watched ...

She had no notion that he stood there ...

None of them did.

So he continued to do so in silence, in the shadows of the corridor, taking private pleasure in the melodious sound of her voice ... in the way she turned to smile softly at her brother's children who were gathered about the pianoforte ... in the way she so gracefully performed the music.

He should leave now, he knew ...

He should turn and walk away ...

Walk away before anyone happened to notice that he was standing there ... intruding once more....

> *... For thy parting*
> *Neither say, nor sing*
> *Bye by, lully lullay ...*

He stood entranced.

And then it was too late.

Emma turned suddenly and saw him and ended the ballad with an unharmonious chord. Those disarming brown eyes of hers gazed at him with apprehension, and guilt overwhelmed him. Ill at ease with the silence that followed, Linc turned his gaze to the crèche.

There he stared.

And then he did the only thing he knew to do ...

What he should have done long before now....

He turned, at last, and walked away.

"Cecile, my dear, there is nothing I can do to prevent him from leaving," Andrew told his wife, as he crawled into the bed beside her. "We've conspired and encouraged in every possible manner, and that is that."

Her pale brows drew together. "You don't suppose he'll change his mind?" she asked him hopefully.

Dressed to the chin in his night rail and cap, Andrew cozied up to his wife in the most scandalous fashion, playfully nibbling upon her lobe.

"Andrew, my love!" she protested. "This is quite serious. If you won't listen I shall . . . I shall—" She giggled and gave a little shriek when he playfully lapped at her neck. "I shall send you back to your bed!" she warned, laughing. "Now, listen to me! Don't do that!"

He gave her a long-suffering look, and she tried not to giggle.

"We *must* do something," she told him very firmly, slapping his hand when he twisted one of her little curls about his finger.

"I'm listening!" he protested. Then very seriously, he looked at her and said, "Cecile, I have gone so far as to allow my only sister into a known rake's room—upon your request, I might remind you. Gad, when the children came to you with their cockamamie plan, I stood by and allowed it. And then when she came away from there so shaken, I stilled my hand—and my tongue—when I felt like murdering the imbecile. I don't know what happened in there, and I'm not certain I wish to know, but as far as I'm concerned, we've tried our very best and have managed only to fill a blasted cradle with idiotic straw!"

"But—"

He placed a finger to her lips, shushing her. "As far as I'm concerned, we've gone beyond the call of duty—far, far beyond. *It's over.*" He cupped her chin and raised her face to his, gazing at her adoringly. "I am touched you care so deeply for my dear sister . . .

but I do believe it is time for the duke to go."

Cecile sighed and shook her head. "I suppose you are right ... though I did *so* hope. It would have been such a merry Christmas, indeed, if it had worked out the way we had planned." She sighed. "Emma was so beautiful this morn, and I thought ... I thought perhaps they would talk." She sighed again. "It's all just so very, very sad!"

"It's over, Cecile," he repeated firmly.

"Did you not see the way he looked at her to-night? If only they had more time," she lamented.

It was Andrew's turn to sigh. "It was an uncomfortable moment at best. Nevertheless, Ascott has informed me that he shall be leaving in the morn, and to that end we have returned his carriage to order. This time," he told her inflexibly, "*none* of us shall interfere. We must let him go. Cecile?"

Cecile gave one last sigh. "Agreed," she relented with a pout, and then she turned to nuzzle her husband's neck. "You are so scandalous," she purred, "coming in to me dressed like this! Look at you! 'Tis no wonder Emma was so shaken after having seen the duke dressed so!"

"Gad, Cecile, don't remind me! Or I just may have to kill the blackguard, after all!"

7

'Twas the eve before Christmas . . .

THE NEXT MORNING WHEN JANE ENTERED THE room, Emma could barely open her eyes, she'd slept so sedately.

"Miss Emma!" Jane was saying, patting her arm none too gently. Her voice was much too bright for Emma's liking. "Wake up! Wake up!" she demanded. " 'Tis Christmas Eve!"

"Noooo," Emma wailed. "Please, please, go away! I'm much too tired!"

"Oh, but Miss Emma!" Jane exclaimed joyfully. "I cannot! You simply must get up!"

Emma groaned, lifting the coverlet up over her ears.

"But, Miss Emma!" Jane admonished, tugging it down once again. " 'Tis the duke! The duke is calling!"

Emma bolted upright in the bed.

Linc stood at the bottom of the stairwell, shifting uncomfortably under the watchful gazes of Andrew Peters and his inquisitive, incredulous wife. God's truth, he thought he would go mad with the wait! And his blasted arse was aching like blazes.

Hell, he ought to turn and go. Ought to walk right out the door, which stood a mere ten feet to his rear. Why he didn't just do so, he couldn't fathom. Instead, he stood like an imbecile, while three pair of eyes peeped from under the settee in the drawing room across the way. All three brats, no doubt, waiting to see their efforts come to fruition.

What by God was taking her so—

His eyes were drawn upward suddenly, to the top of the stairwell, to where Emma stood looking down upon him, and as he stood gazing at her, he knew at once why he'd remained. God help him . . . much as he loathed it, he was drawn to her in a way he could never have conceived possible. Once again she took his breath away. Dressed in a bottle-green, high-necked, challis gown, she wafted down the steps like a glorious angel, while her abigail watched behind her, hands clasped in ill-suppressed pride. He'd asked that she dress warmly, and she held in her hand a matching mantle, richly trimmed with white fur. Despite her lack of adornment, she looked stunning, with her dark hair parted to fall in gentle ringlets on either side of her face.

He swore beneath his breath, for in all his days he'd never been so profoundly affected. At the mere sight of her, he found himself in a renewed state of arousal.

With the memory of yesterday's kiss, he burned.

He cleared his throat. "Miss Peters," he said a little hoarsely, shifting uneasily under so much scrutiny. He cast an awkward glance at his unwelcome audience. "I thought . . . I thought perhaps you would join me for a bit of air?"

Emma's brows furrowed at his curious request.

"I wish to speak with you," he explained at once.

Emma nodded, and as gracefully as she was able with her unsteady limbs, made her way down the steps, grasping the guardrail for support. She descended nervously, unable to conceive of what he wished to speak to her. Whatever it was, was clearly of some import by the profound expression upon his face. She'd come fully prepared to wish him adieu with as much grace as she could summon, certain as

she was that he'd called upon her for the sole purpose of bidding her his farewells, but good Lord,
she'd never seen him appear more striking than he
did in that moment! It was all she could do to remind herself to breathe.

Dressed in buff-colored breeches that fit much too
snugly, and a navy morning coat that was elegantly
trimmed with gilt buttons, the sight of him made her
heart skip beats. She wanted to tell him this was
entirely unnecessary, that she wished him a good
life, and Godspeed, and then she wanted to flee to
her bedchamber before she could disgrace herself
and burst into tears. But before she could speak, he
started up the stairs, relieving her at once of her
mantle and placing it about her shoulders. And then,
almost impatiently, he drew her down the stairs and
out the front door. Turning to question her brother,
she managed to catch his shrug just before the door
closed.

All at once feeling a little desperate, Emma opened
her mouth to speak, to tell him he really needn't do
this, that she would be fine—despite that it would
be a lie—but once again he preempted her and
asked, "Has anyone ever told you how lovely you
are?"

In the chill air, evidence of his startling question
hung like frosty mist between them.

Her heart leaping a little, Emma blinked and then
belatedly she shook her head. She swallowed, as she
realized he'd yet to release her hand. His smoky blue
eyes followed the direction of her gaze, and her
heart tumbled violently as he threaded his fingers
through her own and then cradled her small hand
into his fist. She tried to shake her fingers loose at
once.

"May I?" he asked softly, resisting.

Once again Emma parted her lips to speak. Her
cheeks suffusing with heat, she shook her head, assuming that he meant to comfort her. She couldn't

bear it! "Your Grace," she protested, chagrined, "this really isn't necessary!"

His eyes danced with devilment. "Ahhhh, but it is," he countered and then began walking toward the cliffs, leading her away from the house.

Emma frowned at his back, thinking him the worst fiend she'd ever known that he should be enjoying her discomfort so immensely! "Really!" she assured him, trying to keep up with his long strides. "It isn't necessary—" She shrieked as he squeezed her hand possessively and drew her forward to walk beside him. "Yet, if you insist," she relented, confused.

"Your brother returned my carriage wheels to me this morn," he told her offhandedly, without anger. In fact, he actually grinned, flashing his dazzling white teeth, and once again Emma's heart tumbled. "It seems your nieces and nephew were the thieving culprits, after all." To her surprise he chuckled at that, and she couldn't help but think it rather peculiar that he was no longer furious over their little prank, particularly so when he'd angrily suspected them all along. In fact, she found herself annoyed that he'd been right, despite the nagging truth that she'd suspected them herself.

"Congratulations," she offered him a little sourly. "I presume that now, at last, you shall be leaving Newgale?"

"Do you?" he asked by way of a reply. He turned to gift her with a curious grin, and his blue eyes fair twinkled with mirth.

"Certainly it is for the best," she told him a little breathlessly. "And of course, I do wish you well," she assured him, trying to be nonchalant. And then she realized how far they'd come from the house and demanded, "*Your Grace*, where are we going? And what, pray tell, is the rush?"

Lincoln said nothing, and continued to lead her toward the cliffs, afraid that if he relented and re-

vealed that he merely wished to be alone with her—
that he had something to discover of himself and
needed to be alone with her to do it—that she would
refuse him and flee to the house. She had every reason to, after all. Besides, he wasn't precisely certain
what it was he was after this morn, except that he
needed to speak with her without half-a-dozen pair
of eyes affixed upon them.

The only thing that had become clear to him after
Peters had returned his carriage to order and he'd
been free to leave ... was that he didn't precisely
wish to go. He'd told himself that he felt badly for
what he was about to do to Emma and that if he
could but speak to her alone ... and she could somehow forgive him, then he would be set free. But as
he led her further away from the house, it became
clearer that there was something more. Certainly, he
could stop where they were and speak to her without any ears or eyes upon them, but he led her further away, craving absolute solitude. His heartbeat
quickened euphorically with every step he took.
Even his aching arse didn't slow his stride.

"Your Grace!" she protested, and still he ignored
her. At last they reached the cliff side, and he
stopped before the stairs that led down below to the
shore. There in the cold breeze, with the sun shining
down upon him, his heart hammered like a fledgling
youth's as he turned to face her.

"Emma," he began, and then he faltered. She was
frowning at him, and he felt suddenly strangely uncertain of himself. "Are you cold?" he asked instead,
his voice breaking.

"I'm quite fine, thank you, and shall be more so
when you leave!" she informed him baldly, wrap-
ping her mantle more securely about her. "Really,
Your Grace, you needn't be so concerned with my
welfare. I'm not at all the fragile little miss you'd
like to think me!"

Impulsively, Lincoln brought her hand to his lips,

placing his mouth gently upon it, considering her, considering his next words carefully.

Emma shivered at the gesture and wanted desperately to shake her hand free of his once and for all, yet she merely stood there staring, quaking with the cold, feeling his warm lips upon her flesh much too acutely. Perhaps for him it was the most natural thing in the world to do with a woman's hand, but it only made her want to weep, for it reminded her of another time when he'd so gallantly held her hand just so and she'd so stupidly disgraced herself by whispering in awe of him her childish declaration of love.

"Do you wish me to go?" he asked her suddenly.

Emma bristled at his question, even as it kindled a little spark of hope. She refused to consider what he meant by it, for he seemed to be able to break her heart without so much as trying. If he thought for one instant that he was going to humiliate her more than she'd already done to herself, then he was sorely mistaken! "As I've said before, Your Grace—"

"Lincoln," he interjected huskily, his warm breath against her hand sending gooseflesh racing up her arm.

She jerked her hand from his lips in growing confusion. "I've no wish to call you *Lincoln*, at all, thank you very much! I wish to call you *Your Grace*! And as I've already said you've no need to pity me! After all, whether you believe so, or no, I am quite certainly *not* on the shelf as of yet, sirrah! I promise you, I will endure this! And quite well, thank you!"

At the mere thought of her with someone else, Lincoln's stomach clenched. He stiffened, standing a little straighter. His brow lifted. "Are you trying to tell me something, Miss Peters?"

"I am trying to tell you nothing!" she assured him a little hysterically.

Lincoln didn't think then; he only acted. His hand

flew out, seized her by the wrist and wrenched her to him. His heart hammering violently against his ribs, he pressed her more intimately against him and lowered his mouth to hers, crushing it beneath his hungry lips. She resisted him at once, but he murmured her name, and she whimpered and went still in his embrace. He groaned with pleasure as she allowed him to caress her mouth with his own. "Emma," he whispered feverishly. And he didn't know if he was more tortured by her allure or by his lack of will. "Emma, Emma, Emma," he gasped between her parting lips. He kissed her thoroughly, while she stood stunned, and then he lifted his face suddenly, crushing her more possessively against the length of his body, his eyes heavy lidded as he gazed at her expectantly, searching her expression. His brow furrowed when he found nothing but anguish. "Can you honestly say to me that you were unmoved by my kiss, Emma?"

"Arrogant cur!" Her deep brown eyes appeared to him like that of a fox's at the end of a hunt, cornered and a little bit wild. "I don't know what you wish of me!" she pleaded.

Linc shook his head and released her abruptly, suddenly disgusted with himself. "I'm sorry . . . God, Emma, I'm sorry . . . I . . . I don't believe I know anymore, myself." He hung his head, unable to face her.

"Yes, well! I-I'm afraid this has been a grave mistake!" she told him and spun about suddenly, hastening away.

Before Lincoln could think to stop her, or even that he knew he wished to, she had lifted her skirts and begun to run, obviously eager to be as far from him as she could manage. As he watched her go, the waves below crashed against the cliff side, sounding as chaotic as he felt.

"Emma! Wait!" he shouted after a dumbfounded moment, but it was too late. She couldn't hear him for the pounding of the surf, and all he could think of as he stood there watching her leave him was that without a doubt this had not ended the way he'd envisioned.

He had no notion how long he remained at the cliffs, staring down at the tumbling surf. It rolled in violently, covering the beach below completely, and pummeled the cliff side relentlessly.

The way his conscience pummeled him.

When he made his way back to the manor, the sun was waning at last. He cut across the garden, intending to enter through the rear entrance and thereby avoid the drawing room, which was inevitably where the family had all gathered once more.

To his misfortune, he found them—every last one of them, for God's sake, including the governess, or abigail, or whatever she was—being led into the garden by an exhilarated Jonathon, and his heart skipped a beat as he watched them. Christ, it seemed as though he were forever destined to intrude upon them in this way, and he determined right then to leave Newgale at first light—Christmas be damned! The last thing he intended was to stay and watch them exchange gifts and fuss over one another like cooing doves.

He stood back, watching, hoping they would go, because in that instant he couldn't have moved even to save his life.

It occurred to him after a befuddled moment that they were staring up at the sky. Curiously, he peered up to see what had captured their attention, and the sight that he beheld stole his breath away: The heavens were painted with beautiful wispy white clouds and streaks of mauve and gray, and spearing through them in the dusky sky was the most incredible shaft of light he'd ever spied, so bright and luminous that it filled him with awe. It was spectacular.

"I told you!" Jonathon Peters was saying. "I told

you, Aunt Em! It is Heaven's gate! It is! You were right!"

"It must be!" Lettie agreed enthusiastically, and Lincoln, too, found himself agreeing wholeheartedly.

Emma's laughter drifted to him suddenly. Certainly, if she'd been angry with him earlier, it didn't show in her mood just now. She gazed up at the sky with wonder and laughed again in delight, bending to hug young Jonathon.

Lincoln found himself envious of the child, remembering when her laughter had been for him. In that instant, he craved it more than he'd ever thought possible. He turned to look at the sky once more and then at Emma where she stood, and it seemed to him that at that moment the heavenly light poured down like molten silver upon her, upon the entire garden, making it bloom in a way that mere flowers never could have.

He continued to stare, and as he did, he suddenly knew. As surely as she stood there, appearing to his eyes like an angel in haloed light, he knew. He peered up again in renewed wonder. God's teeth, it *was* Heaven's gate . . . but rather than sending down *le petit Jesu*, God had sent him Emma.

She was his redemption. She was his gift.

Suddenly, everything seemed to make sense.

His reason for coming to Newgale . . .

If he was wicked, then she was his salvation.

If he was unwhole, then she would make him otherwise.

If he would ever find Heaven, she was his gate.

Why had he not realized sooner? If he craved love and would ever know it, then she would have to be the one to teach him, for never had he felt more alive than he had in her presence, despite that he told himself otherwise. And never had he felt more empty than he had in the time he'd been apart from her—regardless that he'd managed to convince him-

self he would be better off without her . . . that she
would be better off without him.

And perhaps she would, indeed . . . but she was
what he needed, and he swore that given the opportunity he would never, ever let her regret loving
him.

The quandary now was that he'd pushed her so
far away that he knew of only one way to convince
her that she did love him still.

Then again, perhaps she no longer did?

Perhaps she never had?

Perhaps, in fact, she'd regretted her declaration of
love as much as he'd tried to make her regret it? And
very likely she did, for he'd certainly worked hard
at it.

Well . . . there was quite an elementary way to find
out, he reasoned, and grinning devilishly, he retreated from the garden, for on this very holiest of
nights . . . he intended to commit a most unholy act,
indeed.

All in the name of love.

And he was going to enjoy every second immensely.

8

When all through the house . . .

LINC WAITED UNTIL HE WAS CERTAIN THE HOUSE
was aslumber, and then he slipped into Emma's room. Stalking silently, purposefully, through
the shadows, he made his way directly toward her

bed. Beside it, he knelt, slipping a hand over Emma's lips to stifle her inevitable cry of surprise. He shook her awake.

Emma's eyes flew wide to find Lincoln poised above her, his face only partially illuminated by the silver light from the window. She cried out, but the sound was muffled into his palm.

"Emma," he whispered. "I'm going to remove my hand now, and when I do, you will have two choices: you can either scream, to which end your brother will respond by bursting into the room and putting me to rest tonight with a shovel . . . or . . . you can listen to what I have to say." He nodded, requesting her acknowledgment and permission.

Emma gave it, and he removed his hand. She sat up at once, taking the coverlet with her as she scooted backward against the headboard, moving away from him. "What are you doing here?" she demanded at once.

Linc took a fortifying breath. "I've come with a wager," he told her, steadily fixing his blue eyes upon her. "A simple wager, but quite a necessary one, for I cannot leave Newgale without knowing something for certain."

Emma peered at him expectantly and lifted the coverlet up a little higher. "Precisely what sort of wager?"

He saw the wariness in her eyes, which glittered in the light of the moon. "It begins with one last kiss," he told her.

"You are mad, indeed, sirrah!"

"Perhaps."

"You can't possibly expect—"

"You do wish me to leave?" he asked her silkily.

Emma nodded a little uncertainly. "Of course," she told him.

"Well, then, only hear me out. . . ." He grinned roguishly when she didn't respond. "You can't be afraid of a simple wager, Emma?'' he asked in outright challenge.

Emma frowned at him. ''O-of course not!''

''Very well, then . . . one kiss . . . and if you should win, I shall leave Newgale at first light. And furthermore, at the first opportunity, I shall have it posted in the *Times* that it was you who cried off and not I. I've connections,'' he told her, seizing her hand and holding it possessively within his own. ''I swear on my mother that I shall confess to one and all that 'tis you who did not wish to wed with me, and I will bear the scandal all to myself.''

She cocked her head. ''And what precisely will you tell them?'' she wanted to know.

''Suffice it to say, no one will blame you for jilting me,'' he told her.

The challenge in her eyes was obvious. ''Won't they? And why should they believe you, after all? You could have any woman you wished,'' she told him. ''How can you think it will not affect me when, in fact, I shall be scandalized either way?''

''Because I shall tell them all something quite despicable about myself, and I assure you *not a one* will disbelieve it.''

''I see,'' she relented uneasily. ''And if *you* should win this wager?''

''Then you must cede to only one request.''

''Which shall be . . .''

He chuckled wickedly. ''*That* we shall have to see,'' he told her with a roguish grin. ''Shan't we?''

Emma's brows knit. ''Well, it doesn't matter,'' she said with an affected air of confidence. ''I *won't* lose. And you'll go at first light?''

He nodded.

''Very well,'' she ceded, ''one last kiss. And what are the terms of this kiss?''

''Only one,'' he revealed and she peered at him dubiously. ''Very simply, if you are unmoved by it, you will tell me to cease and desist.''

Emma parted her lips to speak, but she couldn't bring herself to ask the obvious.

He seemed to read her mind, for he yielded at once, "And if you are not . . . then you must simply endure it."

"Endure it?" Something about the way he said the word, the way his eyes glittered, sent prickles down her spine, for somehow, Emma was certain it wasn't nearly so simple, at all.

"Either way," he assured her, "no one shall ever know of this. I swear it," he vowed.

"Fair enough," she agreed and sat up a little straighter, watching warily as he stood and sat beside her on the bed.

"I can't kiss you all the way over there," he told her, enticingly. "You'll have to come a little closer, Emma."

"Must I?" she asked him, shivering at the way he whispered her name.

He chuckled. "No . . . not precisely . . . I could come to you," he told her, and did. Before Emma could speak to protest, he moved closer and was leaning over her. She slid down defensively into the covers.

For the longest instant, Linc simply stared at her, drinking in the sight of her. She was so lovely it made his heart ache. And then he grinned, for if everything went the way he intended tonight, then tomorrow morn she would be his, indeed.

No turning back.

"Well," she exclaimed impatiently, her voice trembling slightly. "I'm ready now." She puckered her lips just a little. "Kiss me," she demanded.

Chuckling softly, Lincoln did as she bid him, determining that whatever happened this night would occur of her own will or not at all. Slowly, savoring each moment to the fullest, he bent, touching his lips to hers. He heard her shocked intake of breath, yet she didn't protest at once and he groaned in triumph.

"Emma," he whispered, and cheated just a little, placing a hand at her nape to keep her just where he wished her to stay. She didn't seem to notice, and he moved closer still, testing the kiss. Tentatively, he offered his tongue, wetting her lips gently, teasing, until she opened to his coaxing. Sucking in a victorious breath, he leaned more fully upon her, deepening the kiss, his heart hammering. He forced himself to go more slowly.

Emma thought she would die with pleasure!

At the moment, she couldn't seem to recall exactly what it was she was supposed to do, only that it felt too sweet to be kissed so. Good Lord! He kissed her as though he cherished her, and she couldn't seem to think long enough to recall that he didn't, much less to protest.

Not thinking, merely reacting, Emma locked her arms about his neck, only knowing that she didn't wish the kiss to end too soon.

His body quickening with her eager response to him, Lincoln pressed her back against the cool sheets, drawing her at once beneath him, never relenting in his kiss.

He kissed her as though his life depended upon it, for it did.

And still she didn't protest.

God help him, in that moment, he felt as though he'd been catapulted into Heaven itself. Seducing her required less effort than he expected, and the ease of it all, along with her guileless response to him, made him all the more determined to carry it through.

He wanted her.

He knew that now, and with a need more fierce than he had known before. Working quickly, never ending the kiss, he found the buttons of her gown, undid them, and slid his hand within to cup one delectable breast. As he'd anticipated, it filled his hand just perfectly, as though it were made only for him. And it was, he acknowledged, kneading her flesh softly. Groaning with the tremendous thrill, he rained kisses along the fullness of her lips, into the corner of her mouth, and then along her neck, and down, until he found precisely what he sought. She moaned as he drew one nipple between his lips, and he answered with his own groan of unfathomable pleasure.

God's teeth, but he'd waited far too long for this.

With his other hand he cherished her body, his long fingers playing lightly across the length of it to find the hem of her gown, raising the delicate cloth slowly, and once again he groaned when she didn't stop him.

Just a little more . . . just a little more, and she would be his. . . .

His fingers found and sought her woman's mound, and her only response was a little yelp of surprise.

Emma knew she should protest, but with every fiber of her being she knew she wasn't going to.

Never had she known such bliss!

His lips upon her breast were driving her to the most exquisite distraction. She couldn't think . . . couldn't think to protest . . . couldn't think to consider the consequences. Couldn't think at all.

Tonight she could pretend, because tomorrow he would leave her. To her dismay and desperation she lifted herself into his palm as he touched her *there*. Such wicked, wicked pleasure, he was giving her! She couldn't bear it!

When he lifted himself atop her, Emma could only deliriously welcome his weight. She gazed out beyond his shoulder, into the night, into the stars . . . Christmas stars . . . and prayed . . . never more fervently.

Pressing himself atop her, Lincoln groaned in exquisite anticipation. She was so ready for him, that it was all he could do to remove his breeches quickly enough, and still, with that brief separation, she did not protest, merely gazed at him with such a dazed expression that he needed to hear from her own lips that she desired this as well. At once, he lowered his body atop hers, nestling himself against her softness, and hesitated for a moment. And then once again, he began to rain kisses upon her.

He rocked against her, his movements slow and erotic. "Emma," he whispered, "tell me once more . . . tell me you love me. . . ."

He felt her stiffen beneath him.

"Please say it," he implored. "Just once more!"

"I-I can't," she sobbed. "Please don't make me!"

He stroked her body with his hands, refusing to relent, refusing to lose her just now . . . not when he was so close. "I need to hear it," he entreated. "Just once more," he coaxed.

God help her, she couldn't say it, yet she didn't want him to stop either. "You've won," she told him, her arms locking about his neck, lest he leave her. "What more can you want of me?"

"Your heart!" he whispered without hesitation. "I want your love, Emma."

Emma began to sob in earnest, yet she didn't release him. "I never took it back," she cried softly, in dismay.

"God, Emma!" he rasped with pleasure, and at once, he slipped lower, tilting toward her and settling himself between her thighs. He groaned as she parted her legs wider to receive him. She cried out softly as he entered her and reached the barrier of her maidenhood, but he bent to stifle her sobs with his mouth. "Be my wife," he whispered between her lips, rocking into her slowly, slowly, gently. "Be my wife," he persisted, "be my wife . . ."

Unable to bear it any longer when she lifted her hips to the rhythm of his, he cried out and thrust deeply, bursting her maidenhead in one powerful drive.

Emma's heart felt as though it would shatter within her breast. He couldn't mean it, he didn't mean it! Thus she refused to respond with words. Instead, she gave him her body, everything, until she cried out in pleasure and pain. The most beautiful pleasure she'd ever known, and the most heartrending pain, because with this last act, she'd truly given him everything she possessed. Everything! Whatever he chose to do afterward, she could not fault him, for he'd told her merely to stop him, and she had not. The blame was wholly her own.

"Emma?" he pleaded. "Say it! Just—say it!"

"Yes!" she sobbed.

That was what Linc had been waiting to hear. Thrusting his head backward, he cried out in sweet satisfaction and then held her close as his body convulsed with absolute pleasure.

After a long moment, he lifted himself to look down into her angelic face, gingerly brushing her curls from her eyes. "I asked you to be my wife," he whispered, "and I meant it, Emma. I meant every last word. Forgive me for the pain I've caused you," he entreated.

Emma buried her face against his chest, clutching his arms as she cried in desperation. "I won't let you hurt me again," she told him, shaking her head. "I can't . . ."

He cupped her face with his hands and forced her down to the bed once more to see her better. Moonlight spilled in from the window to highlight her face and her tears. They wrenched at his gut.

"Let me love you this way always," he pleaded. "Bring sunshine into my life, laughter into my house, joy and song into all my Christmases. I think I love you," he told her tenderly, honestly, and bent to kiss the corner of her mouth once more. "I think I did from the very first instant you looked at me so trustfully with those beautiful brown eyes and told me you loved me. I just didn't feel worthy, then— nor do I now, but I'll never, ever let you regret it. I swear it!"

Emma began to weep in earnest, and Lincoln frowned and told her without remorse, "You've really no choice, my love . . . because I've ruined you for certain now."

Emma couldn't stifle a horrified giggle. "You're an arrogant cur!" she told him, choking on her tears. "And you are absolutely despicable!"

Lincoln laughed softly and rolled, taking her with him. "So I've been told. Now tell me you love me," he demanded, holding her firmly about the waist.

Emma stifled a shriek of surprise to find herself suddenly reversed and looking down upon him. "Never again!" she swore vehemently. "Never!"

"I'll shout at the top of my lungs," he warned, "and wake your brother and the world and then you'll be forced to defend my honor."

"You wouldn't dare!"

Lincoln opened his mouth to prove otherwise, and Emma slapped her hand over his lips. "I love you!" she relented at once, laughing despite her outrage.

"Say it again," he requested softly.

"I love you," she told him, and then, God help her, again, "I love you." Tears spilled down her cheeks unchecked.

"Merry Christmas," Lincoln whispered huskily, reaching up to kiss her tears away. "*Your Grace*," he said, testing the words, and then he pledged, "In my heart tonight I thee wed—God, I feel like shouting it to the world, and if you only give me the chance, my love, I'll do it over, and over, again. . . ."

Epilogue

For to preserveth this day . . .

LINCOLN AND EMMA WERE WED THAT VERY
spring, and just after the nuptials there appeared in the *Times* the most scandalous bulletin of all. It was reported through quite a reliable source that the Duke of Ascott was very hopelessly and unfashionably in love with his wife! Outrageous as it was, it was the talk of the town.

As it was every Christmas Eve. For even stranger still, every year thereafter, on December twenty-fourth, the same account appeared in the *London Times* . . . followed by the strangest words . . . *in my heart tonight I thee wed . . . over . . . and over, again. . . .*

No one could ever quite decipher precisely what they meant.

As for the legend of Heaven's gate . . . it was carried on in the Traherne tradition, passed down faithfully from year to year, from one to another, old to young, while bright, young eyes glowed with expectation.

Yet no one ever spoke of the crèche with more love and faith than the fifth Duke of Ascott. To his last breath, he told with love of the crushed straw— and swore to each and every one of his seven grandchildren that he, himself, had witnessed the imprint of *le petit Jesu* within that very first crèche, on that first Christmas morn.

With wonder, he spoke of the glorious display of

the Heavens above and the holy light that had shone through the clouds to touch their lives that splendid day.

"Really, Grandfather?" they would ask with awe.

"Certainly!" he would swear and believe it with every faith, for on that magical, magical Christmas ... in that very special year, on that very special night, he had been given his greatest gift ... his wife.

And then with a particular twinkle in his old blue eyes, Lincoln would turn to Emma and gaze at her with the adoration that had inspired their own three children to marry for love. After a moment of reverent silence, he would say softly and with pride, for all to hear, "*I think ... I think I do love you, Your Grace.*" And both would smile in private remembrance of the young girl who had once so naively said the same to him. . . .

MERRY CHRISTMAS
from . . .

TANYA ANNE CROSBY

Christmas in the Crosby home is a double affair—
two dinners (on Christmas Eve and Christmas Day),
each with two sets of relatives, two story times, two
present-opening sessions, too much family! But there
is no complaining.

Well, maybe a little. This Christmas Eve past,
there were so many elbows at the table that we
spilled two glasses of water and three goblets of red
wine. My sister's addendum to my daughter's
Christmas prayer had my dear child, who sat with
yams in her lap from the platter before her, teary
eyed over the losses of her grandfather and her precious dog, Moses. And my poor brother, who'd
brought his new girlfriend to "meet the family,"
tried to look dignified through it all. In the end, dinner was a success and replete, we adjourned to the
family room where the fire blazed. As we sat to listen to the miraculous tale of the Christ child, an
amazing thing happened, as it does every Christmas:
While my father read, we were drawn together,
adults and children alike, by the miracle of Christmas and our love for each other. With stars in our
eyes, no one remembered the spilled wine any
longer, although my sister still wore the evidence on
her blouse. That's the true gift of Christmas, I think,
the gift of love. Well, in retrospect, we must not have
been too frightening that night, because my brother's
girlfriend remains to spend another Christmas. . . .

To everyone, Merry Christmas and Happy Holidays! May you not see the spilled wine or the sweet
potato in your neighbor's lap. . . . and as young
Timmy once exclaimed, *God bless us, everyone!*

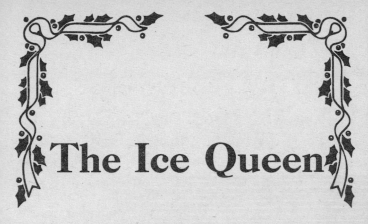

The Ice Queen

Jennifer Horsman

1

London, England, 1869

Christmas magic gathers beneath the kissing ring . . .

DR. JAMES BALFOUR'S THOUGHTS LOOMED DARKER than the misty night as he turned his prized stallion into Hyde Park. He felt the full effects of a bottle of Scotch, and yet drink had in no way diminished the despair threatening him. Desperate to escape the brutal disappointment of the day, he set his spurs sharply into the beast's side.

The great horse leaped into a gallop. James leaned forward, feeling the flex and stretch of the huge muscles beneath him and thrilling to the speed of his flight, his long cape billowing behind him like a huge dark sail. As the cold misty night flew past him in a rush of blurred images, it seemed to snatch away his dark thoughts; his bitter anger toward the antiquated doctors at London's Academy of Medicine and Science, the futile months spent petitioning them and all for naught, the absurd rigidity of the English class system and the bigotry it bred, the bigotry that reduced all his accomplishments to the invective, "Your petition has been denied. . . ."

An old woman appeared ahead, emerging from the fog like an apparition. With a startled curse, James drew back hard on the reins, tilting his weight to the left. The horse narrowly missed the old lady. Pulling the beast up, he turned him around in a hard, fast circle as he took stock of the situation.

"My heavens, Madame! I almost killed you!" James stared at the small impish figure standing before him, smiling up at him. He could scarcely believe that she stood in the deserted park in the dark middle of the night. The horse snorted angrily as James swung off so that he could make certain that the woman was indeed unhurt.

He went over to her and she looked him up and down as if taking stock. "Well, well, you are a handsome devil!"

"I beg your pardon, Madame?"

She ignored the confusion on the handsome face, nodding to herself as she took in his unconventionally tall frame and broad shoulders, a lean hardness that was the result of the rigors of his riding and his famous swordsmanship, no doubt. His olive skin and long hair created a foreign and somehow dangerous air about him, lending credibility to his reputation for arrogance, bold unconventionality and brashness. His eyes were intelligent—he was said to be a brilliant doctor and diagnostician—and they also reflected his Scottish wit and sense of mischief. She could believe all the stories about him now: that women melted like butter in the pan, that his conquests were legendary.

"You're perfect!" she continued.

James had been checking his agitated horse, speaking to the creature as if to a child, but the beast kept shuffling his feet and tossing his head with frightened neighs. His gaze returned to the old woman. "If by that you mean I emerged unscathed by this near disaster. . . " His voice trailed off as the peculiarities of the old woman accumulated and magnified in his mind. She appeared to be a lady, her tiny stature clothed in blue velvet, the very color of a summer twilight. The skirts of her cloak spread over a neat circle of expensive crinoline. Gray hair peeked from her matching cap, on which a colorful peacock feather was attached.

The old woman's extraordinary presence in a chilly winter's night in the middle of Hyde Park transformed his anger at the academy, and he shook his head as if to clear it. Damn, he must have drunk more than he realized.

"Are you quite all right, Madame?"

She nodded smartly. "Indeed I am!"

The impish quality about her struck him as if a bubble of mirth were caught in her throat. He abruptly caught sight of two footmen waiting on the side in the shadow of an enormous elm. "Ah, you are escorted, I see."

He nodded at this, as if it were just the thing. No further assistance from him would be needed. He turned back to his mount, one booted foot in the stirrup.

"I was told I might find you here," she said.

"Were you now?" he asked, the Scottish lilt to his voice replacing his slight French accent, which appeared whenever he saw humor in a situation. For he had left his two colleagues even more drunk than he back at the Firefox Inn, and no one alive knew he was here.

"Yes," she replied, nodding again as she stared. "Now Catherine does not particularly care about appearances, but I don't know many women who could resist a second look at you. Even her. The ice queen, they call her and for good reason, too." She shook her head. "That's the problem. Catherine. Her heart is covered with a chilly frost as cold as the North Sea in winter. Her husband's death, you see. She loved him madly, though no one could ever figure out why. Anyway it just keeps getting worse; she keeps getting worse. There's no more music at the manor. Her poor child is lost and becoming more lost each day. And the wonderful Christmas Eve festivities have all but disappeared. Christmas just isn't the same. Something must be done, and I need you to do it."

With a lift of his brow, James considered her nonsensical speech. Obviously, the old woman was a victim of senile dementia, sadly common among old people. What to do?

He looked to her footmen for help. The mist, the interminable London fog, billowed in clouds all around them. The two footmen waiting in the shadows had disappeared in the fog.

"Now," she said in a certain voice, a familiar voice to all who knew her. She used this voice when rearranging people's lives, which she was famous for. "Here's what I'm going to offer you for the favor. I understand you are seeking a position at the academy. Please allow me to introduce myself. I am Madame Isabel Harrington."

"Not . . . not the mother of one Sir Walter Percival Harrington?"

The old woman nodded. "The very one."

"Why this is extraordinary!" James's dark eyes searched the surrounding area as if someone might step forward to explain the ruse. And surely it was a ruse. "Why, Madame, just today your son—"

"I know all about it. My son—a good man but too stuffy by half—denied you a position at the academy, a position anyone with half a simpleton's wits could see you deserve. You were the Sorbonne's most outstanding student, were you not? Recommended by the great surgeons Laplace, Rush and von Baer! All your highly innovative research, too; why I happen to know that if given the chance you will become one of England's greatest surgeons!"

"This is all very flattering, Madame, but—"

"You know why you were denied?"

He straightened, his tone changed. "I believe it had everything to do with my heritage. My Scottish

father was damning enough, but then my dear
French mother—"

"That didn't help, I admit it, but even more than
that, those old stuffed shirts at the academy are
afraid."

"Afraid?"

"All your methods, you see. Most controversial!"
She whispered, "The dissection of cadavers, for one.
Your treatises on the church and science, for another.
Too stuck in their ways, they are. Those old men are
just not ready for you, there it is. You have to make
them and . . ." She paused, leaning forward to whisper, "I am prepared to assist you. I still exercise con-
siderable influence over my son, a few others as
well. I believe I could change his mind if you agree
to participate in the . . . ah, intrigue of my design to
save my granddaughter and her son. Besides, I suspect, I am quite certain, you will find yourself very
much in love with her as the ice begins to melt."

"Love?" James questioned, then chuckled as if it
were a completely novel prospect, and it was, at
least in his life. Once upon a time he had fallen in
love as frequently as he visited a barber shop, but
after about the twelfth time, he began to have difficulty maintaining the pretense. After the twentieth
time, he gave up the idea entirely, realizing the
world of difference between love and a base infat-
uation, or more bluntly, an appetite for lust.

As the old woman explained the most unlikely intrigue in detail, James Balfour fervently wished he
had not drunk so much. "The fencing regional finals
are to be held at Harrington Manor?" he questioned
after she was done. "Well, yes I had heard but—"

She elaborated further.

"Madame, I can scarcely believe such an outrageous proposition is coming from a woman of your
stature!"

The old woman assured him it was.

Only later did he wonder if he imagined the whole

unlikely scenario, a fantastic one borne of his desperation. As the old woman finally led him to agree to her terms, she added the last. "I neglected to mention one last thing."

"Yes?" He had mounted and turned his horse around. "What is it?"

"The deed must be done by Christmas."

"Christmas? My word, Madame, that is only two and a half fortnights away now—"

"Don't pretend to have difficulties with my time-table. I understand that you normally get your seductions underway before a single turn of the long hand!"

He heard her laughter as she backed away into the thick London fog. Perhaps he only imagined her last words, "You see, James Balfour, you're my Christmas present to Catherine. . . ."

Widow Dorset stood behind her son's chair on the edge of one of Harrington Manor's grassy fields to watch the fencing match. Her back appeared ramrod straight, her shoulders squared, her chin slightly tilted. She looked absolutely regal, utterly unapproachable, as cold as the winter's day itself. Her meticulous appearance reinforced the impression: Unruly auburn hair was pulled tightly back and neatly pinned into an unattractive knot at the nape of her neck. A net covered the whole. She wore no jewelry, lace or ribbons. Her modest blue woolen dress rose to her neck, gathering tightly at her slim waist before it dropped to the ground. A darker blue winter pelisse, open at the front, was draped over the dress.

All her passion lay hidden away. The observant eye might guess this by looking into her startling blue eyes—eyes the color of sunlight on ice. She carefully kept her emotions concealed, as if even a slight smile might expose too much. Her emotions found a vent only in front of the piano, which she rarely indulged in these days, as a wintry life closed in around her.

She pretended to watch the finalists in the sword fight. Fencing, such an archaic sport! She shook her head with disapproval as the two men paired and struck, paired and struck. Here was such ridiculous frivolity, and yet the entire audience appeared enthralled by the graceful athletic dance held on the expansive lawns of Harrington Manor.

Harrington Manor had passed into her paternal grandmother's family many generations ago from the Duchy of Lakeshire, a land grant to her great-grandfather, Baron Regional Harrington. Since she had come of age, she managed the fine house for her father. His life was in London at the Academy of Science and Medicine, and he had neither the time nor the inclination to oversee the charge of the estate.

The lawns, gardens and small lake that surrounded the three-story, Tudor-style manor were famous in the region for their beautiful seasonal variations. In days past the gardens had been opened on Sundays to the public. The surrounding communities of Lakeshire had often used the Harrington Manor gardens for all manner of exhibitions and programs. Many of these had been sporting fanfares. No more. Nowadays, she refused permission to the numerous requests to open the gardens, and much to her relief, she was no longer asked very often.

There had been some incomprehensible mistake with London's Fencing Federation. They claimed they had received permission some time ago. Of course she had granted no such request, but by the time the mistake had come to her attention, it had been too late to alter the outcome.

Her gaze dropped to Daniel in the chair before her. Three goose-down blankets covered his lap. He wore mittens, a hat and both a short and long coat, but still, it was risky letting him out in the cold. If he caught a chill . . .

Her brow creased with anxiety. The whole exhibition was extremely ill-advised. It was just that Daniel, so obstinate and headstrong, had insisted. "I'll throw a fit Mother, I swear I will and it—it could kill me!"

"Nonsense, darling," she had said but too late. The alarm in her eyes had given her away. Before anything happened, knowing she shouldn't but helpless to do otherwise, she had given in. Daniel's health was so terribly fragile, his precious grip on life itself so tenuous. . . .

This was the worst time to lose their family doctor! He was called away on a personal matter, replaced by one Dr. Michaels, recommended by her father and Admiral Guther, a neighbor. Twice already she had been forced to write her father for reassurance of Dr. Michaels' unconventional advice concerning Daniel. . . .

"Why 'e's as handsome as Satan wooing the angels, 'e is," Meredith said, excitedly, her mirthful dark eyes fixed on the taller swordsman. "If it weren't for me own Samuel, I wouldn't mind 'im warmin' me—"

Catherine cast her maid a shocked look.

"Well 'e is, ma'am. Just look at 'im."

Dr. James Balfour, Catherine knew. She watched as he expertly wielded the sword, forcing the other man back, step by step, as he attempted to gain the upper hand. She knew of the man from her father. Her father had been so distressed by certain essays the doctor had written, essays apparently everyone at the academy were talking about. She had asked to read them. She found the treatises all quite shocking, iconoclastic, barbarous really. She had dismissed them out of hand, only to discover that her thoughts kept returning to his eloquent points time and again, turning them over, finding that with some reflection a reasonable person might agree.

"He shall win, I just know it!" Daniel announced, red-faced with a seven-year-old's excitement as his small, clenched fist pounded the rim of his chair.

With alarm, Catherine leaned over, carefully tucking in the blankets covering Daniel's lap. He always became so excitable at Christmastime, and while she'd like to think his restlessness, like a normal child, owed itself to all the presents and treats, the carols and merrymaking, she knew it did not. For he was not a normal child. The tragedy had occurred at Christmas, forcing them both to relive the memory of it at this special time. The once-cherished holiday became a dreaded seasonal flux, a thing she valiantly tried to pass through as quickly and uneventfully as possible.

She put her back to the sword fight as she hovered over her son, and she thereby missed the dashing strike of the doctor's opponent. The man's sword sliced neatly through the doctor's white shirt. The audience sounded a collective gasp as he stepped safely back, his arms raised as bright red blood soaked the wide width of his chest.

The referee shouted excited exclamations about the challenger's point being bared. A number of men stepped forward. Dr. James Balfour fell against the damp grass, blood covering his shirt.

Catherine took one look, and with a lift of skirts, she started toward the injured party. "Meredith," she called over her shoulder, "cover Daniel's eyes! Take him away!"

Wide-eyed with shock, Meredith reached down to shield young Daniel's vision. She yelped as she felt two small teeth clamp down on her hand. "Why ye little ruffian—"

"I want to watch!"

"Your mum says—"

"I don't care! And don't you dare wheel me away or I'll throw a fit."

"Ye wouldn't!?"

Daniel didn't respond, for he didn't have to. They both knew he would. Besides, he was too enthralled by the sight of his mother kneeling over the injured man to pay any mind to Meredith.

Catherine was one of four figures within James's vision. She appeared before a background made of the sun piercing through a gray sky. His victim had looked beautiful from afar, but now, as she knelt at his side, leaning over his form, he saw she was a good deal more than merely beautiful. The winter sun on the rich color of her hair, the startling blue of her finely shaped eyes, too large against the pale ivory of her skin. Too pale, he saw, resisting the urge to touch her full wide lips, slightly parted to reveal a neat row of small white teeth. He caught the faintest trace of her breath mixed with her perfume: a scent of sweetened apples and lilacs.

If she was the Ice Queen, he was the fire. . . .

Hands were removing his shirt. Dr. Michaels shouted for a litter. Someone else suggested Mistress Dorset draw away from the gruesome sight of blood before she fainted. Dr. Michaels passed instructions that Dr. Balfour be removed to Harrington Manor at once. Catherine's hands had come to her face in shock, and she nodded as she drew back.

The injured man groaned, his hand shot up as if with a sudden nerve twitch. His cufflink caught a hair pin that held the net constraining Catherine's hair, and she gasped, startled, as he brought down his hand. Rich, auburn hair tumbled about her shoulders and bosom.

Catherine stared straight into the pleased smile curving on the handsome face. Of course if he were not debilitated, a hair's breadth from unconsciousness, she would have sworn the doctor had done it on purpose. Ridiculous, she realized, simply ridiculous. . . .

2

JAMES BALFOUR SAT AGAINST THE ENORMOUS CHER-rywood headboard, examining the room as if it might lend a possible clue to the owner. It did not. No doubt the house and its fixtures had been many generations in the Harrington family. It was a large, airy room overlooking the south gardens. Ancient and handsome furnishings decorated the space. Soft afternoon sunlight poured through the stately windows, falling in a stream over the polished wood floor and a corner of a dark blue-and-gold carpet. Dark blue velvet bedclothes and a matching brocade decorated the carved four poster bed. A low fire crackled in the hearth. Dutch landscapes hung on the walls. All in all a room tastefully done and wholly adequate to his convalescence.

After stitches, bandages, good natured banter and much well-wishing, old Dr. Michaels finally left to consult Widow Dorset on the care of the patient. James waited for his prey. Fortunately, he had owned the foresight to have had a trunk with him at the time of the accident. In his trunk were a number of important papers he was working on and books he was reading. As chance would have it, he had enough work to occupy him for two fortnights. Right up until Christmas.

The woman was beautiful, despite the effort she put into concealing the fact. . . .

After listening to Dr. Michaels explain the unlikely situation, and after seeing all the concerned fencing patrons out, Catherine approached the room. She appeared outwardly calm, while inside she felt her anxiety collect and mount. This was unacceptable! A wounded man, a virtual stranger, forced upon the household now. Of all times, Christmas was the worst.

She straightened as she knocked once before opening the door. Anxious blue eyes found the invalid stretched out on the enormous four-poster bed, looking so strangely hale and able she half expected him to rise for their introduction. A black silk robe draped over his shoulders, and she spied the bandage wrapped around his chest and left shoulder, noticing too, the bronze swarthiness of his skin, the well-defined muscles there. He still wore his fencing pants and tall black boots. On the bed.

Oh, no. The lawns had been quite damp. Those boots would have mud on them. Why hadn't Dr. Michaels or Meredith removed those boots? He would soil the covers—

She ignored his warm smile as she abruptly noticed his hands. Long-fingered, muscled, smooth, bronzed hands, beautiful hands like a pianist or the surgeon he was, but presently coaxing a rather loud purr from her cat, Tiger Blue. Yet his dark eyes stared up at her. She could not pinpoint exactly why, but the way he stared brought on an unnerving self-consciousness. It descended over her like a tightly woven net.

The realization brought a blush. She resisted the ridiculous urge to smooth her skirt and hair. "I do not allow the creature on the furnishings," she said primly, mentally readying the long list of rules and procedures of her house, wondering how she might delicately ask him to remove his boots—

"I don't believe we've been introduced," he replied.

She saw that he ignored her command as if she

had not uttered it. Her lips tightened, and she tilted her head. "Mistress Dorset—"

"Catherine, is it?"

The question completely disarmed her. He might have just inquired about her bathing practices, the idea of him addressing her by her Christian name was so unacceptable. She struggled for a proper retort, as if a phrase, the right word or two, would put him in his place and set things right again.

Too late. To her mounting discomfort, he added, "A beautiful name, for a beautiful lady."

The unexpected compliment sounded casual, like an afterthought. For the briefest of moments she lost herself to the deep rich lure of his voice, an irresistible voice, she realized, suffused with the hint of a French accent and as compelling as music.

"I've always loved the name Kate."

"That's not how I would have you addressing me!"

"Cat then?"

He glanced down at the cat in his hands with a smile, then back to her, as if his gaze were suggesting a similarity. The very thought made her gasp. This was not going very well at all.

"I do not appreciate your familiarity, much less your impertinence—"

His chuckle sounded warm, his stare penetrating. "Perhaps in time I can change that. . . ."

Her blue eyes widened. "How dare you! I believe you are my guest and an unwanted guest at that! To step outside propriety is an outrage—"

"Why Catherine, I'm exciting you! And to think I've only just arrived."

This was entirely too much! Her fist clenched with fury; she all but trembled with it as she stared back at him. She should have him removed at once and she would, she swore she would if not for Dr. Michaels's warning.

A tingle of alarm shot up her spine; a hand went

to her forehead in distress. She swung around, putting her back to him. She must get the upper hand here, she must. "Dr. Michaels has informed me of our predicament. For the life of me I don't understand how it is possible that your opponent's point became bared."

"A most improbable accident, I confess."

"Nonetheless, Dr. Michaels swears you cannot be removed for a fortnight, maybe longer, until your healing is well under way. Apparently the injury came very close to severing, severing—" Oh, what was that word?

"The sympathetic artery," he supplied, his hands still caressing the cat. There was no such thing of course. Doctor's daughter or not, no one outside the profession would guess it.

"Yes." She nodded as she smoothed curtains, certain his gaze was on her. She could feel the intensity of his scrutiny! "Somehow the injury has put your right hand at risk, and because you are a surgeon, Dr. Michaels concludes, this is not to be hazarded. So—"

"I'm your uninvited house guest for the holiday season," he finished for her. "All in all a most unlikely series of events culminating in a happy accidental holiday." With hardly a pause, he went on. "Would you hand me the writing block, pen, inkwell and paper there? I must inform my family of what has befallen me."

The blunt order brought her another moment's confusion, simply because she was hardly in the habit of waiting on people. She moved to ring the servants' bell.

"It's there on the desk."

She followed the direction of his finger. Of course it would be ridiculous to call a servant to perform a task that would require only the smallest effort from her. She moved stiffly to the desk. "Your family?" she asked. But she regretted the question, quite certain she should not encourage any intimacy from him.

"My parents and four sisters. My family has a château on the French Riviera. With my four older sisters and their families, the Christmas holidays have become enormous affairs. They will be heart broken to know I won't be joining them for the festivities."

The words summoned the unbidden memory of Christmas Eve past at Harrington Manor; at one time it seemed as if the whole month of December was a beautiful dream that culminated on Christmas Eve. The good people of Lakeshire, high, low and in between, all gathered at Harrington Manor on Christmas Eve to put up the Christmas tree, everyone filled with excitement and laughter, love and music. The whole house was filled with leafy garlands of spruce and holly, mistletoe, rosemary and scented candles. Fran, Meredith and she would work for weeks on the table and tree decorations and party favors: the crackers for children and their parents, the baskets of food for the elderly and poor and, oh dear Lord, the cooking. The kitchen was a sea of delicious scents and warmth as they created the Christmas feast: the turkey and goose, the plum pudding and mince pies, cheery cheeked apples, juicy oranges, the immense twelfth cake, the seething bowls of punch that made the kitchen chamber dim with its delicious steam. And most of all the Christmas music that seemed to fill the very heavens, the whole magical night ending at church for the late service. . . .

She banished the memory as she gripped the writing tray tightly, bending over to place it across his lap. She stopped, abruptly noticing his stare. Too late. They were so close. He had an attractive face from afar. Up close she could see the complexity and depth in his eyes. This was not a simple man. Her heart signaled alert, and her eyes widened to take in his handsome features.

His hand reached to her hair, his touch as gentle and compelling as his voice. "Catherine, the sorrow in your eyes just now, I wonder—"

She never let him finish. Her senses returned all at once. She nearly dropped the tray on his lap. "What my eyes are like is none of your concern, sir."

Her words were tinged with hysteria. These feelings escalated dramatically as he caught her wrist, his grip strong, utterly unyielding. She gasped, her eyes darting from his hand on her wrist to his face. "Ah, but it is my concern," he whispered. "For I'm afraid I am spellbound by the poetry in your eyes. . . ."

For one wild moment she imagined he would kiss her. Kiss her! She thought she might scream, she felt certain she would, if only she could catch her breath before she fainted—

The amusement in those eyes indicated that he was fully aware of her predicament, and what frightened her more was that he seemed utterly unconcerned about it. "Catherine." His free hand reached to her hair, and he pulled first one pin, then another. She forgot to breathe as her hair tumbled down her back. He gently spread it with his hand. "Have I mentioned? I prefer your hair worn down. . . ."

He released her hand, letting his fingers slowly slide over her clenched fist. Her confused senses returned all at once. She moved back, then stood several seconds in shock, her hands crossed over her bosom as she stared at him. The pounding of her heart was so loud she was unable to form a coherent thought.

Smiling at the sight, James returned to his letter. "I'll have tea at half past three."

"What?"

"Tea, Catherine. I'll have my tea at half past three."

She clasped her hands to stop them from trembling. "Tea is served at the fourth bell," she said tightly.

He did not look up. "You will be so kind as to inform the servants of the difference."

This was too much! She wouldn't let him do this. She wouldn't let him step out of the bounds of propriety and decency and then pretend nothing happen. "You, sir, are an outrage! I'll, I'll have you removed!"

"Will you?" He seemed maddeningly unconcerned.

Catherine realized she wanted to slap him.

"The most malicious motivations," he continued, "would not permit you to risk a doctor's career. One thought of all the children I shall no doubt be saving would naturally prohibit the measure. If you put a little thought to it, Catherine, you'd grasp the fact that you have just fallen into a quandary."

She slammed the door. Hearing his laughter, she vowed to write to her father immediately.

Meredith appeared promptly at half past three with a tea tray. "'Ere we go now," she said, smiling as she set the tea tray down on his lap. To her delight, her mistress gave her the task of caring for the handsome doctor. "Just what the doctor ordered. Some 'ot tea, buttered toast and crumpets, a bit 'o fruit and our very own raspberry jam."

James viewed the food with obvious relish and looked back at the pleasant woman. Dark curls framed an attractive face, peeking out from the ubiquitous maid's cap. Her plump figure was outfitted in a starched black gown, covered in a crisp white apron. "Are you my appointed nursemaid?"

"Meredith, at yer service," she said with a bob.

She watched James spread a liberal amount of raspberry jam on the scone as she poured the tea. "Well! Aren't you feeling well after the accident."

"It wasn't an accident, Meredith."

"What do ye mean?"

"I'm afraid it was all arranged to put me in the house for the holiday season. You see I mean to win the affection of your mistress by Christmas day."

The maid's eyes searched his face. "Ah, go on with ye now." She laughed. "Teasing a poor working woman—"

"I'm afraid it's quite true. I do mean to win your mistress's affection."

Meredith stood very still. He really meant it. All traces of merriment left her face. She swallowed as she slowly shook her head. "I do not believe ye can. I do not believe anyone can."

"Why not?" The question was asked as he sipped his tea and reached for another scone.

"Oh 'ow I wish 't'were possible." She looked around the room, her voice dropping conspiratorially. "We all do. We all remember what she was like before . . . before—"

"Before what?"

"Before the master died," she whispered with a sad shake of her head. " 'E took 'er heart when 'e went, 'e did, and she's never been the same. Nothing's been the same. Why she 'ardly ever plays 'er music anymore and the young master—" She stopped, realizing the liberty she was taking in speaking of these secrets.

"What was Catherine like before she became widowed?" he probed.

"Oh!" Meredith's hands went to her cheeks, warm affection infusing her tone as she remembered all too effortlessly what Catherine was like. "I can scarcely describe it, except to say she was like a shining light. She lit every room she walked into with only 'er smile. And 'er music! From the 'eavens, it 'tis. Oh Lord, she 'as a voice like the angels and to 'ear 'er sit at 'er piano carries a soul closer to God than any church bench, Fran, the cook, always says. Why 't'was a day when ladies and gentleman came from all over to 'ear me mistress play. She made quite a splash 'er first season, too, she did, but it never mattered to 'er for she was in love with young Charles Dorset from the start. Childhood sweethearts and all. The Dorsets live just down in South Hampton—"

"And just what virtues did this young Mister Dorset have that captured such a shining creature?"

Meredith looked perplexed. "Well . . . 'e was a kind lad, to be sure. Quiet, always the perfect gentleman. 'Tis 'ard to say really. 'E played the piano, too, though not nearly as fine. 'Twas how they met. Thrown together with the music master when they were, oh, only eleven or so. Catherine just always loved 'im, that's all. Everyone knew it. Everyone thought she'd outgrow it, especially, me thinks, Master Percival." A half-hearted grin lifted on the plump face. "Everyone knew 'e wanted her to marry a doctor like 'imself, but Catherine told everyone she would never be happy with any other match." Her face grew solemn. "That's just it. She was right. And when 'e died—"

"How did he die?"

" 'Twas a riding accident a scant week before Christmas. 'E wasn't very good with the beasts, ye see, and Master Daniel—'e was so little and 'e couldn't breath and we were so scared. 'E left to fetch the doctor and 'e got on the horse—" A hand went to her mouth; she shook her head. " 'Twas so sad. 'Asn't been the same since. . . ."

Meredith did not see the calculated appraisal James put to this brief history as she went about straightening the room, describing how it used to be at Christmastime, the feasts and the merrymaking, the caroling and the beautiful Harrington Christmas tree. Wistfully, she remembered the first time they saw a picture of the queen's tree in the London papers. How they had laughed at the foolish German custom that the queen's consort, Albert, had brought to the palace. Cutting down a tree and putting it inside, then dressing it like the queen herself!

Yet Catherine had been charmed. The next year she had ordered Mr. Walter, the head gardener, out to the garden to fetch the tallest tree that would fit in the music room, then she ordered dozens of red and silver ribbons from her dressmaker, and she instructed all of Lakeshire to start making little angels or prettily wrapped candy to decorate it with. Now, it didn't seem like Christmas without their beautiful tree, not at all, and they had not had one for five long years.

"Meredith, I believe I will need your help."

"I don't feel like it."

"Oh?" Catherine asked, her eyes fixing on Daniel with anxiety as she set the book down at his bedside. "Are you feeling ill? Is it your breathing, darling?"

"I'm tired. I should like to go to sleep."

"Oh, yes, of course." A frown creased her brow. "All our excitement. . . " She herself was still feeling the effects of the unfortunate events of the day, mainly her unwanted and most disturbing guest. She was waiting for her father's reply, certain he would direct her as to how she could have James Balfour removed. Perhaps he would arrive to remove him personally! "Good night, darling." She leaned over the bed to put out the light and thereby missed the excitement shining in her boy's eyes.

He watched his mother withdraw quietly from the room and shut the door behind her. He listened as she moved down the hall and up the stairs. The wheelchair sat near the bed. He threw back the covers and placed his feet on the floor. He struggled over to the chair, supporting his weak legs by bracing on the bed.

He fell into the chair, breathless from his exertions but excited by his small success. He wheeled the chair to the door, leaned forward to open it and, with a huge shove, pushed himself into the hall.

The swordsman was just down the hall, he knew.

He did not knock. He pushed open the door and wheeled himself inside as if he were a king in his castle. The man was sitting up in the bed. A pleasant fire crackled in the hearth. Two lanterns lit the bed space, littered with piles of books and papers. The man did not see him. He appeared deep in concentration until, with a sigh, he set down the papers and rubbed his eyes.

Daniel moved closer.

James looked up to see a youthful and quite arresting face staring back at him. The boy's face was sharp, delicate and pale, with eyes, thickly fringed with lashes, that were too large for it. Gold hair tumbled over the forehead in heavy locks, making the face seem even smaller. The boy looked peeked, perhaps even ill.

"Well, who have I here?" asked James.

"Master Daniel," the boy said smartly, his high-pitched voice never matching his tone or his big words. "You are the swordsman, am I right? You would have won, you know. I saw the whole thing," he announced, proudly. "You were splendid!"

James bowed slightly with a smile. "Young Daniel. I'm James Balfour, your guest for the time. I suppose you've heard?"

The boy nodded.

"So." James leaned back, smiling down. "Perhaps you are a budding swordsman yourself?"

"I should say not. I can't, you know. My lungs are weak."

"Weak lungs?" James looked at him curiously.

"I'm not allowed to exert myself," he explained quite matter-of-factly as he leveled his gray eyes on the swordsman. "I'm not expected to live very long."

"Who told you that?"

"Oh I hear things. . . ."

"Has your grandfather examined you?"

Daniel shrugged. "So many doctors have."

"What does your grandfather say?" James asked curiously. While he certainly did not agree with Dr. Percival Harrington on his personal admittance to the academy, he respected the man's diagnostic skills, which were unparalleled. Indeed, in his three years studying under Dr. Harrington he had learned a good deal.

"He says that my mother worries too much. She doesn't think I am normal, you see. He also says I need a stricter tutor for my studies, that I should not be allowed to run circles around old Master Wentworth."

"Yes, I see." James smiled. "About your lungs though? What does he say?"

"Oh . . . I don't know." The boy straightened before leaning forward to say pointedly: "Anyway that's not what I want to talk about."

"No?"

"No," he shook his head, his gaze narrowing with intensity. "What I want to talk about, what I really want to know is . . . is, have you killed anyone?" His voice all but trembled with excitement. "I mean killed them dead?"

"I see," James said, catching his smile. "Well." He abruptly pretended to examine the boy before him. "Can you keep a secret, Daniel?"

The boy assured him he could.

"Then the answer is I have in fact killed men. But only the most nefarious, wretched evildoers who deserved it."

"Oh my!" The large eyes widened like saucers. "Who were they? All these men you've killed?"

"Should I start at the beginning? With my secret life as the king's protector?"

"Oh yes, do tell!"

Daniel was held spellbound for the better part of an hour. No one had ever told him stories like this one. While his mother had taught him to read years ago and he spent many hours each day buried in his books, lately his mother had removed many of his favorite stories. She said he had outgrown them. Now he was finding more books such as the one she had been reading to him tonight: *Fables and Morality Tales for Young Christians*, which was only slightly better than the one before: *Manners and Protocol for the Young English Gentlemen*. And still not even his old favorites were quite as good as James's adventures as the king's protector. No matter that England had not had a king for many, many years. . . .

That night Catherine discovered just why James's sisters considered him the worst person to put the children to bed. The stories he'd tell kept his nephews and nieces awake for many hours, giggling and cringing and as wide awake as a condemned man on the morning of his hanging. Catherine opened the door just as Daniel declared, "And then did you gullet the wretched bully?!"

"Daniel!"

He turned slowly around to see his mother at the door. He looked back at James, hoping James might save him, only to see a most startled look on his new friend's face, a widening of his eyes as he stared at his mother.

She looked like a fanciful dream upon waking. Only now could James see just how much the drab modest gown and stiff hair arrangement shielded the young woman's beauty. The long auburn hair fell about her shoulders to her waist. She wore only a nightdress, made of gauze or a cotton-silk, he couldn't tell. Not with the light from the hall shining behind her, silhouetting the slender curves of a figure men dream of.

"Daniel," she said softly, though her anxiety was escalating. "Daniel. You must return to your room at once."

James forced his gaze away to meet Daniel's hopeful stare. He nodded slightly to the boy. With a sigh of disappointment, Daniel turned his chair around and headed toward the door. "Daniel," James called just as he reached the door. "I can count on you to keep my secret?"

"Oh indeed you can!" Daniel laughed.

The sound startled Catherine. She stared incredulously at her boy. Only to realize with sick dread how very long it had been since she had last heard that sound. The sound of her child's laughter . . .

Disturbed, Catherine helped her son out. She cast a meaningful look back before letting the door shut.

James could hardly wait for the encounter.

He did not wait long. Within minutes of seeing Daniel back to bed, she opened the door and stepped inside. She approached the bed. Even in the firelight he could see the hot worry in her eyes, and yes, the pleading. . . .

He ignored his pleased response to the sight of her. For the moment. "You, Catherine," he said gently, "have an extremely precocious and I must say, engaging son."

The words drew her back. Precocious, yes, everyone seemed to agree on that point, but engaging? No one had ever found Daniel engaging before. Taxing, trying, exasperating and difficult, these were the words she heard when people discussed Daniel.

She realized he had lead her from the point. She straightened. "Dr. Balfour—"

"James, please." A handsome grin lit up his face as he studied his victim cast in firelight. In her concern for Daniel, she had completely neglected the impropriety of her appearance. Dear Lord, she was more beautiful than Aphrodite in a star-filled night. And like the mendacious Vulcan, he too, would snare her in a trap. . . .

Her head tilted regally. "You might have stepped from any protocol of decency today, holding me as a most unwilling victim to your crimes, but I assure you I will not let you interfere with my son. I'm sure you noticed Daniel is not a normal child—"

"Yes, Daniel explained this himself. Not only is he not ah, 'normal' but he also told me he's not expected to live very long."

The damning words hung in a startled silence. "He didn't?!"

"I assure you those are his very words." James watched as fear changed her face and she turned away, obviously alarmed by the idea. "Daniel told me he 'hears' things," he continued, "and apparently one of those things was a prophecy of his expected longevity. Naturally, as a physician, I can only wonder why people are guessing he's not expected to live very long."

"It's his health," she said, twisting her hands nervously as her gaze danced distractedly around the room. "His lungs, you see—"

"Are weak? So Daniel said. Just what has your father diagnosed exactly?"

"Severe pulmonary asthma."

James's thoughts raced over this as he studied her. All of her anxiety seemed centered on her son's health, manifesting now in her frightened countenance and tone. As if the boy might at any moment leave the living. He grasped the problem, a problem in fact of potentially devastating, even fatal, consequences. A patient, even a young boy, who had been given the idea he was not going to live long, could very likely succumb to this suggestion. Experienced doctors had witnessed the mysterious and powerful way in which a patient's mind affects their prognosis. Furthermore, he did not believe any boy should be robbed of his boyhood unless absolutely necessary. And he suspected her father would agree.

He stated with calm authority: "That condition often improves as the child ages."

"Not so with Daniel." She shook her head. "Quite the opposite. Of course he's been seen by the most prominent doctors," she hastened to explain, adding, "including, naturally, my father. Daniel's attacks are terrible, vicious really, and some doctors believe, life threatening, a thing to be avoided at all costs. I must take great care to restrict his activities. The slightest head cold or influenza can have dreadful consequences. So that we must, I mean, I must endeavor to keep him quiet and still, to prohibit any measure that might overstimulate or excite his respiratory system. I'm sure you are familiar with the prescription for care in these deleterious cases—"

"Actually, Catherine, many doctors now believe that the asthma patient's condition can be greatly improved with a regiment of exercise and fresh air to strengthen the lungs, the physical body—"

She was shaking her head before he could finish, interrupting him with a lengthy rebuttal, but James could hardly listen. He had other things on his mind: the barest hint of her breasts beneath the nightdress, the firelight caught in her hair, the tempting curve of her lips, the faintest hint of the perfume of her skin and more than anything the sheer physicality of his attraction for her. Not since he was fourteen . . .

"So," she finished, turning to him, "I can assume you will henceforth refrain from telling Daniel these—"

A sudden muffled groan came from the patient. James grimaced as if in acute pain. Catherine's hands came to her cheeks in alarm, and, in a rustle of cotton silk, she came quickly to his side. "What is it?"

She caught his grin a split second before his hands reached up. She gasped with utter shock, too surprised to step safely back as he caught her wrists. With a playful twist, she fell against the soft cushions of the bed, and before she could even think to mount a defense, he pinned her hands above her and came partially over her.

"What is it?" he repeated, grinning, enjoying her shock. "This is the only way I could think to get you on the bed beneath me."

Her heart lurched with a sudden jolt. His huge body felt heavy, hard and warm, while his eyes seemed to laugh. As if it were a jest!

Outrage replaced her shock. "Let me up! At once!"

The feel of her soft curves beneath him became a sharp pleasure, increasing as each gasp pushed her breasts against his chest. Breasts that were tempting beyond reason. He closed his eyes briefly, only to draw her perfumed scent into his lungs. "Not yet, Catherine."

"I'll, I'll scream!"

A mischievous brow arched. "I rather doubt that would work. Who would you wake up? Daniel? He'd no doubt become very excited to see me kissing his mother. And, Catherine, I am going to kiss you." He held her hands as his free hand came to brush a silken stream of hair from her face.

She shook her head, scarcely able to believe that any man, not the lowest ruffian in all of Covent Gardens, let alone a prominent London physician, would use physical force against her for a lascivious purpose. "You can't do this! You can't—"

A warm chuckle sounded. "I believe I am."

Using all her strength, she struggled against his. A mistake. Instantly she stopped. She went very still. He watched carefully as another kind of shock replaced the first in her lovely eyes. "Ah, you feel it, too. Rather alarming, isn't it?"

Alarming was not nearly a strong enough word. Nothing prepared her for the shocking heat sweeping into her limbs, the racing gallop of her heart, the alarm tingling into shivers down her spine. She closed her eyes against the rush of sensations, only to feel a gentle finger come to her mouth where he lightly circled her lips, over and over. Hot shivers tickled her. She gasped, opening her eyes. She started to shake her head again but too late. Her eyes closed and she tensed beneath the warm press of his lips.

The kiss changed as his tongue slipped into her mouth. She managed a breath, and dear Lord, it ignited her blood like a kindling stick set to a dry summer field, and she felt herself sinking dizzily to a place she had never known as the hot warmth swept through her limbs, and he filled her with a taste of apples and spice. Way down below her stomach she felt her organs tighten into a ball, then melt in a gush of heat. Heat that spread and tingled through her in a frantic rush of chills. Like a fever. No one, not ever, not even in her imagination, had ever kissed her like this. . . .

His entire being rejoiced in the soft pliancy of her slender curves. He broke the kiss to let his lips graze over her flushed cheeks, the arch of her neck. Chills erupted from every place his lips touched, until he returned his mouth to hers with a new kiss that pressed an unknown fear into her.

She twisted her mouth from his and took a gasping breath. "Oh no . . . please!" came in a breathless rush. "You can't do this. . . ."

"Why not?"

The question was asked as if they sat at tea and she was protesting a stroll in the garden. Her mind took a full minute to catch up. Then his hands, those skilled and clever hands, smoothed the sides of her waist, testing its curves before sweeping up the side of her breast, feeding feverish shivers into her unwilling flesh. She forgot to breath again.

She was shaking her head. It was all she could do as he held her firm, as his gaze left her flushed and lovely face, the long lashes brushing against her cheek, the parted lips, to rest on the tempting lift of her breasts beneath the nightdress. "My God, you are beautiful. . . ." His fingers parted the silk strings of her nightgown above her breast.

She tensed as his hand slipped the cloth from the gentle rise of her breast. She drew a sharp breath as his hand moved lightly over the coral tip, caressing its softness. "Catherine," he said in a whisper of awe. She first felt washed in red-hot shame, but it disappeared into a hot tingle as he uncovered sensations that made her pulse race. "Oh, Catherine. . . "

She didn't realize she was saying no over and over again until the sound stopped and he was kissing her again. A kiss, slow, hot, so beguiling erotic, it gave her a new understanding of her body. He broke the kiss with a smile. "Do we like that, Catherine?"

Heat shimmered through her; she could not draw enough air into her lungs. "No . . . no!"

He pretended shock. "Catherine, you wouldn't lie to me, would you? Admit you like my kisses or I'll kiss you again."

Her eyes widened with horror. "You are a beast!"

He laughed. "And you are my beauty. Now admit it."

"Never!" She struggled against his hold with all her strength, only to be betrayed by her own body. Small little aftershocks rushed from between her legs, changing, growing, as his warm firm lips came over hers, and he was kissing her like a man dying of thirst, his tongue sliding slowly, oh so slowly, over every smooth crevice.

"James." She tore her mouth from his, now quite frightened. "Please . . . I don't know what you're doing to me. . . ."

He brushed his lips over hers and felt her tremble. "I'm using fire to melt the cold arctic place of your heart. . . ."

She shook her head again, struggling through the novel and heady sensations sweeping into her. "You're scaring me! I'm so . . . scared—"

He retreated, surprised by the anguish in her lovely eyes. "You are, aren't you?" He studied the lovely face. A gentle finger brushed her flushed cheek. "Why, I wonder?"

The question remained unanswered. She felt disastrously close to tears. In the next moment he released her hands, giving her freedom. She sat up with effort, dizzy as she came upright. Her feet came to the floor, and she felt herself rising as if in a dream.

She swiftly moved to the door.

"Catherine," he said, stopping her at the door. She did not turn around. "Until tomorrow."

"Tomorrow," she said, her voice sounding queerly, embarrassingly breathless, "I shall have you thrown into Lakeshire Creek and drowned."

The warm sound of his laughter raised the hairs on the back of her neck. "You'll be in my arms if you do."

She slammed the door.

"Merry Christmas, Catherine. . . ."

She rushed up the stairs. Once safe in her own room, she sat on the edge of her bed, trying to slow the gallop of her heart and the rush of her blood. Her body still tingled with the lingering effects of his touch, his warm body over hers, his lips pressed against her lips.

She wanted to scream, to pull her hair out, to strike him. How dare he! How dare he! To force his kisses on her. And his touch! His hand had felt her bare breasts.

Her hands rose to her hot cheeks with the shock of this memory. Charles had never kissed her like that. No. Never. Charles's kisses had been sweet, gentle expressions of husbandly affection, like their marital duties every third Saturday morning of the month. Surely Charles had never imagined touching her with such passion, yet alone desired to do it. He had been at all times extremely considerate of her natural feminine delicacy. It was not normal to make one's body weak with that fiery desire.

Of course she knew it happened. To other people. Anyone who had read any of the great romantic poets was made aware that it happened, that a physical desire can be made so consuming that it overwhelmed one's higher consciousness.

Her brows crossed in perplexity.

She and Charles had known passion, more than the next hundred people, but this had been for music. All her passion had been expressed in music. She had spent hours and hours, the whole of life really, making and perfecting those beautiful sounds that rose from her fingertips at the piano. Nothing in life came close to the beauty of hearing the music rising miraculously into the heavens. Music had become the air that sustained her very soul. This was what she had shared with Charles.

He had loved her for her music. He had not been a great musician himself, but he had the same passion for it. "Charles, you only love me for for my music," she'd tease.

"But you are the music, Catherine. . . ."

And it was true, she was and so was he. Somehow, over the years, music had become irrevocably linked to Charles, so that when he died, the music in her had died as well. . . .

Now when she sat at the piano, she was filled with a melancholy so profound, it shook her to her soul. The once effortless grace of her fingers dancing over the black and white keys was gone. Now her playing was uncertain, as tremulous as the sorrow rocking through her.

She remembered reading a biography of a famous musician who lost his passion when he fell violently in love with his married patroness. She remembered reading it and rereading it, trying to imagine losing something as essential as the air one breathes for a romantic sentiment. At the time she couldn't imagine it. At the time she felt certain that such a thing could not possibly happen to her. Until Charles had died. Just as before tonight she could not have imagined the feverish intensity of what James Balfour had forced upon her.

Her hand came to her mouth as if to stop a cry. Her distress grew inside, until she threw herself down on her bed. She whispered Charles's name over and over, as if it were a spell that had the awesome power to bring him back in time to rescue her.

Meredith approached her mistress in the parlor. Catherine sat on the sofa, staring out the window at the garden. Her pale gray taffeta skirts spread over the dark blue damask sofa; her hands kept twisting a handkerchief on her lap. She looked fraught with a secret anxiety, and with dismay, Meredith saw that now would not be a good time to ask.

But she could not resist. "Ma'am?"

Catherine gave a small start. "Oh, Meredith."

"I showed Dr. Michaels in to see Dr. Balfour."

Catherine hardly heard as she saw that Meredith also held a tray. "The posting! I have been waiting." She swept up the two cards and the letter, recognizing her father's stationery at once.

Meredith watched as Catherine tore open the letter. Now or never. "Ma'am," she began, "we were wondering about, well about Christmas. I know ye don't 'ave me put up any of the spruce, holly chains, candles or the manger or all ye beautiful angels, but well, I was just lookin' in the box, ye see and la! The angels look so forlorn. I felt as if they were all but begging me to take 'em out and set 'em up, and well, we were all thinking that we might again."

"Hummm," Catherine heard none of this.

"Wonderful!" Meredith curtsied. "I knew t'would be a Merry Christmas again." She rushed out to tell the others.

Catherine read the letter again.

My dearest Catherine,

I read your letter with keen interest. What a re-markable coincidence! Just this last week the commissioners of the board voted to deny the very same Dr. Balfour a seat at the academy. The whole unfortunate incident has incited my imagination, as I too can scarcely imagine how points became bared in a sporting match.

I must assure you, my dear, that extending the hospitality of our home to Dr. Balfour cannot be more of a burden than denying him a position at the academy. I am being inundated with letters and complaints from all corners of the world, nearly all of them questioning my reasoning in issuing the said denial. I expect to hear that the queen mother went to press with her sentiments!

Oddly, the very reasons you express for removing him from your house, even in light of the uncertainty that such a dramatic move might harm his precious health and future as a surgeon, are the very reasons his position was denied: his rash impertinence and arrogance, his liberal and iconoclastic proposals and theories.

Now we have been urged by many noble and prominent citizens to reconsider his position because of his exemplary work as a surgeon. These noble citizens are asking us to reconsider the case from the sole perspective of the wealth of Dr. Balfour's medical talent, assuring us that they will personally intervene to temper some of his more rash opinions and theories, at least as they are publicly expressed.

In any case, the man is an outstanding, even some say and I must concur, a brilliant doctor. He stood far apart from all my other young doctors. Because of this, and the pressure I am receiving, the board is reconvening the Wednesday before Christmas to reconsider our position.

For the very same reason, Catherine, you cannot

let personal prejudice in any way jeopordize the doctor's health, or his future as a surgeon. I'm afraid I must advise you, nay urge you, my dear, for the better, greater good to set aside personal prejudice in James Balfour's particular case.

Merry Christmas, dear . . .

Personal prejudice! Personal prejudice!

With the letter clutched tightly in hand, Catherine leaped from the sofa and began rapidly pacing the floor. This was too much! Personal prejudice indeed. Should she turn a shoulder to manners as low and rough as a beggar's brat, just to protect his future life as a doctor? Must she endure the humiliation and subjugation of her morals in order to protect some imaginary future patient?

Only these patients weren't really imaginary.

She stopped, remembering the taunting lilt to his voice: "One thought of all the children I will no doubt save will prohibit the measure. . . ." She closed her eyes as the image of the fine, long-fingered hands came to her mind.

She sighed; it was hopeless. Of course she would never risk such a thing. How could she?

She swooped back upon the sofa.

The memory emerged in the darkness of her thoughts: he had captured her hands, turning her so that she fell backside against his bed as he came over her. He held her hands against the bed with force. A powerful man's full strength. Where was this tender injury then?

"Why that deceitful rogue!" she thought, rising suddenly and withdrawing quickly from the room. She rushed down the main hall and to his door, just as the door opened and Dr. Michaels stepped outside. "Ah, Madame Dorset," he said, his face appearing grave and concerned. "I was just coming to speak to you. I'm afraid I have very bad news—"

A hand went to her heart. "Daniel?"

"No, no." He shook his head. "Your boy is just fine. In unusually good spirits today, it seems. The bad news concerns our patient. It appears he has had a setback."

The blue eyes narrowed suspiciously. "A setback?"

"Somehow," the doctor shook his head, "Dr. Balfour has exerted himself enough to tear the stitches. He explained he was adjusting the curtains, of all things. This is exactly what I feared. That wound must be allowed to heal properly! I cannot express the danger of it opening and bleeding again. . . ." The doctor launched into a lengthy medical explanation, but he might have been speaking German for all she understood.

The doctor did not seem to notice the guilt surfacing in the lovely eyes of his listener as she stared back at him, as if it were somehow her fault that James Balfour was led to exert himself.

Guilt indeed! she silently protested. As if she had produced an irresistible temptation for the wounded patient, one that had led him to ignore pain and discomfort and hazard the future use of his hand. Ridiculous. Of course she had been told often enough through her life that she was handsome, but for heaven's sake, hers was not a beauty that inspired poets or drew famous portrait artists to her doorstep. Nor did she in any way lead him to think she might welcome his advances, any advance, much less one of force! It was simply not her fault, she tried to tell herself. . . .

"Not that he can't enjoy a garden stroll or sit at your table in a few days."

"Sit at my table?" The idea horrified her.

"He can, but for now, the next two days at least, he must rest and stay firmly put in bed. His every need must be catered to. . . ."

"Yes, I see. . . ."

The doctor bowed. "He's resting now. Keep

checking on him throughout the day. A good day to you, Madame."

Somehow Catherine suspected that any good left in the day had just vanished. . . .

James finished the chapter and set down his book, picking up the posting Meredith had left. He spotted the letter written on the academy's stationery. With interest, he opened it. After the formal address he came right to the text of Doctor Harrington's letter:

> *My dear sir,*
> *We have been inundated with requests from high and far to reconsider our denial of your place at the academy. Your position at the academy will be discussed again on the Wednesday before Christmas. Nothing that occurs at Harrington Manor will alter this outcome. I tell you this only to save my daughter from any possible designs of malice, if indeed my judgment is wrong and she needs saving from some hidden ill will.*
>
> > *Sincerely,*
> > *Sir Walter Percival Harrington*

James set down the disquieting letter. A short time ago, just a handful of days really, he would have risen and prepared to depart after reading that his position had been all but assured. Obviously that was his initial motive in participating in this farce.

Yet a short time ago he had not known a young lady named Catherine, a young lady who once embraced life with a wealth of enthusiasm and happiness, love and . . . music. He found now, after each and every encounter, that this young lady was a maddening tease to his senses and desire.

"Your daughter, sir, is an irresistible lure. . . ."

Fancifully he imagined that she called to him from behind her icy exterior, a plea that aroused his masculine interest as nothing else could. Where had she gone to? Why did she erect this fortress of grief, a fortress no one had yet been able to penetrate?

He intended to find out. He would melt the ice and discover the woman beneath.

And Daniel needed saving just as much.

It was a simple trick to get children to eat. You simply bribe them. James had learned that from his sisters. He watched as the boy dug eagerly into the Cornish hen pie, which had been cooked with extra meat, lard and cream. He smiled. If anyone needed extra nourishment it was Daniel, so frail and thin. Dark hollows made circles under his large eyes, making them appear even larger in the pale face. He had also ordered goat's milk to replace dairy, as goat's milk was so much thicker and richer. This was the first part of his program to help the boy.

He had then invited the boy to supper when his mother had found herself suddenly indisposed. Meredith had described at length the numerous restrictions placed on Daniel's life. "Ye 'ave to witness a breathing bout to know what we go through. 'Is little face turns blue, 'is eyes bulge, 'is body convulses, and I think 'is mum dies a hundred times in a minute. . . ." She described his tantrums. ". . . Fierce terrible storms whenever 'e don't get 'is own way. 'Is mum is so afraid of 'is breathing bouts, she gives into 'im at once. Anyone who's ever known a child knows what that bodes! No good, is what! 'Tis a shame all right but 'is mum be helpless. . . ."

Apparently Daniel often spent the day in bed, actually enduring his lessons from the bedside, whenever he was too tired to rise, which Meredith said was often. For the boy was a restless sleeper, usually waking more tired than when he started. This was, of course, the malady of the infirm. After a day in bed, a night becomes a difficult, restless adventure. The boy obviously suffered from anemic dyspepsia. A new treatment was long overdue.

A sound coming from inside the door stopped Meredith in her tracks. Her young master's laughter, mixed with the deep rich timber of Dr. Balfour's amusement, reached her and made her smile as she opened the door. As she stepped inside to clear the supper trays, she paused, staring at the sparse remains of Daniel's food on his tray. "Ye even ate the potatoes and cream!"

A pleased smile grew on James's face. "Well, he's a growing boy, Meredith. He needs his strength." James winked at Meredith as she finished clearing the trays and left the room to tell Fran.

Daniel watched with alarm as James leaned back against his pillows and grimaced as if in pain. "So," James said, opening his eyes. "Daniel, do you play chess?"

"Chess?" Daniel shook his head. He didn't play any games. He didn't like them because he never won. "I don't know how. I never learned."

"I'll teach you. It's high time you learned. Fetch the brass box in my trunk, will you?"

The large slate gray eyes widened. "Me? But I can't."

James appeared confused. "Why not?"

"Meredith took my chair to be oiled."

"But you can walk, can you not?"

He shook his head. "My legs are too thin. They shake when I stand."

"Do they?" James seemed unimpressed and even more unconcerned. "You don't use them enough, I suspect. Muscular atrophy. Walking will do you good then."

Daniel swallowed nervously. "Ring for Meredith."

"Meredith? She's halfway to the kitchen with the trays right now. 'T'will take half an hour. Come now, Daniel. I can't very well get up myself now, can I?"

Daniel glanced at the trunk by the mantel. The

twenty paces might have been twenty miles. He looked back at James who now appeared to contemplate his bandages. He didn't like maneuvering without his chair in front of people. They might laugh. . . .

"I'm counting on you."

That was all he said. No one had ever counted on him before. He could not let James down. He stood slowly on unsteady legs. Leaning against the bedside where he had been sitting in a chair, he brought one leg in front of the other. He reached the end of the bed. Drawing a deep breath, he proceeded slowly to the trunk, unaware of how closely James was watching him.

The boy's movement was so slow and painful it brought James a momentary twinge of . . . anger when he thought of how his leg muscles had been allowed to deteriorate this far. Everyone was so convinced the boy was an invalid, with his every need and demand catered to as if it were his last, that he probably left the blasted chair only once or twice a day. The worst part was that as far as he and Dr. Michaels could tell, there was nothing wrong with the boy, past Daniel's certainty that he was ill, weak and soon to die. His lungs were weak from his convalescence, rather than from asthma. The terrible breathing bouts were no doubt imaginary as well, orchestrated to manipulate his mother's anxieties.

Breathing hard and fast, Daniel finally reached the trunk. Tiny drops of perspiration laced his brow, covered by a thick tumble of his hair. He bent down, taking a moment to draw a deep breath as his hand opened the lid of the trunk.

He forgot his struggle completely as the trunk offered up an unexpected treasure. "Your sword!"

"You may take it out if you like."

Daniel tried to lift it. Only to find how heavy it was. Ah, but just to hold the magnificent weapon! Few boys could resist; Daniel was not one of them.

He drew another deep breath. Using all his strength, he brought it out, its end point sinking toward the ground.

"Try wielding it," James said. "Holding it up."

For several seconds he made a valiant attempt. Color came to his face; his breathing grew deeper. He was grinning with pleasure until at last his small energies were depleted. He set it down. "It's beautiful, James."

"I could give you a few lessons." At first Daniel made no response and James added, "Fencing lessons."

The boy's flush grew in stages. "Me?"

"You are just the age at which fencing lessons normally begin. You would like to learn, would you not?"

A dream too fanciful to be real, Daniel knew. For some reason James did not seem to understand the limits of his poor health. "I'm not to exert myself."

"You just did," James pointed out.

Daniel shook his head, his voice faltering more. "My mother wouldn't let me, you see. She's afraid I'll have a breathing fit."

"Leave your mother to me, young man. Am I not a doctor, trained to evaluate these things? And you are capable of much more than people seem to think. Let's give it an experiment. I suppose we'll have to start slowly to build your strength before we begin lessons. In the meantime, fetch the box there. Every English gentleman needs to know how to play chess."

It took several more minutes for Daniel to return with the chess box, his thoughts racing as he did so. He wondered if he might learn to fence. Perhaps James was teasing him?

He looked to the bed with suspicion. James appeared intent on examining his bandage again. James would not be cruel like the others who always laughed at him, he just knew. And what if it were possible to gain his strength without succumbing to a breathing fit? Fencing lessons!

His heart pounded with excitement as he set the box down at last and fell into the chair. He felt the full effects of his exertion, along with the pleasant ones of the supper. He had wielded James's sword! He would wield it more!

James explained the queer manner in which the pieces moved. Daniel felt his breathing relax as he grasped the basics of the game. "Ah, my pocket watch," James said. "I see it up there on the mantel. Will you fetch it, Daniel?"

This time he knew he could. . . .

That night Daniel slept deeply. Youthful dreams danced through his mind: first of beautiful ladies and handsome swordsmen defending tall and airy castles. Then images of James filled his sleep: the young doctor's wonderful smile and loud laughter set amongst Daniel's familiar house, changed somehow with the wonder of the holly and evergreen garlands, the angels and the manger that Meredith had carefully and lovingly set atop the tabletops and mantels.

He was walking through the house with James when he heard a special sound. Drawn from long-ago memories, the magic of his mother's Christmas music mingled with his sleep.

The high arch of blue sky over Harrington's garden appeared as brilliant and soft as a sky over the moors, and Catherine walked briskly down the familiar path. Winter colored the garden a soft brown, save for the fir trees. Nature's magic waited to happen beneath the dark brown earth. Tangles of brown vines—Mr. Walter's famous roses—climbed the ivy-covered walls. Tiny sharp green points stuck up from the alcoves and border beds—Mr. Walter's glorious flowers in wait for spring. Soon they would be blooming with his crocuses, snowdrops and daffodils.

She had almost passed the fir trees, which were surrounded by a row of holly bushes, when she caught sight of a tall figure examining the inscription on a bench. She had so wanted to avoid his society! Perhaps she could slip past him. . . .

"Catherine! What a pleasant surprise!"

"Dr. Balfour." She nodded as her heart lurched, and to her dismay, the doctor quickly approached the place where she stood. She tried not to notice how handsome he looked in the winter light: His tall figure clothed in a long coat, brocade vest and tall black boots, the long dark hair brushing past his coat collar and more than anything his fine dark eyes offset by bronze skin. Oh, why did he have to be handsome?

"A lovely morning, is it not? May I join you?" he asked.

She smiled, pleased by a stroke of sudden ingenuity. "I was just thinking I might take a rest. Please go on without me."

"Were you?"

"Yes," she responded tightly.

"Then do allow me to ah, 'rest' with you."

His glib tone made her feel like a schoolgirl. She was reminded of his kisses, only because it was difficult to converse with him in a civilized manner after what he had done to her. She felt the uncomfortable pounding of her heart, and she could feel herself coloring under the amused scrutiny of his gaze.

There was no escape. She started to protest but saw it was of no use. She made her way stiffly to the bench and sat down, the folds of her warm woolen cloak spreading in a pretty half circle around her. She undid the matching ribbons of her bonnet, feeling suddenly warm, and as her bonnet came off, so did the net and a hairpin. She felt the brush of her hair along her neck. She must look a sight. . . .

He seemed fascinated. She cast an anxious glance behind her as he sat by her side. She resisted the urge to move, an urge that mounted as she felt his warmth chasing away the winter cold. "So." She tried to sound polite, conscious of the formal address put to him. "And how is your injury, Dr. Balfour?"

"James please," he answered, his eyes sparkling with merriment as he leaned over to whisper, "Or I might start calling you Cat after all."

She wondered if she would ever get accustomed to his impertinence.

"And I am quite on the mend, thank you," he added.

She felt his gaze upon her, and the knowledge brought color to her cheeks. How he affected her! She struggled for something to say when a loud, lovely trill sounded. "Cathrine, look." His strong hand came to her shoulder, gently turning her toward where two robin redbreasts perched on a fir tree. "You know, Catherine," he began, his arm around her on the bench and his mouth close to her ear as they stared at the pretty sight. "It is said that after Jesus was born Joseph went out to gather fuel for the fire. He was gone so long that Mary became anxious that the fire would go out. Suddenly some small brown birds flew in and began to fan the fire with their wings, keeping it lit until Joseph returned.

"Mary saw that the little creatures had scorched their breasts and said, 'From now on you will always have fiery red breasts in memory of what you have done for the baby Jesus. People everywhere will love you and they will call you robin redbreast. . . .'"

She listened, transfixed, to the story, a lovely light shimmering in her eyes, like firelight reflected in a window glass. He could only wonder at her beauty and his response to it, a response that was marked by pleasure and heightened by growing desire. A rather alarming physical desire . . .

Catherine's own grandmother had told her that story many years ago, and that dear woman had always believed the sight of robin redbreasts at Christmastime was an omen of Christmas wishes coming true. A sadness came into her eyes as she recalled how, like her music, Christmas was stolen from her. . . .

"Christmastime," he said gently, knowing to tread slowly here. "I always love the season; I suppose everyone does. Odd, though." He looked down at her pointedly. "I've noticed a surprising lack of Christmas preparations. My own dear mother and sisters seem to start with all the fussing at the very turn of the month. When do these seasonal tasks begin at Harrington Manor?"

"When?" she repeated. "Well, I—"

He had taken his coat off, and she caught a glimpse of his bandages beneath the silk shirt, and she all but cursed his wound that put her in this uncomfortable position. Her lashes brushed her cheek as she confessed, "Actually we don't do as much as we used to."

She recalled how her grandmother always claimed that one's Christmas spirit reflected the rest of one's life. It was so true. Once upon a time when they had had the merriest of Christmases she had received a never-ending stream of guests into her home. Not only would the good people of Lakeshire call often but she also saw many guests from London: friends and acquaintances of the Dorsets and her parents, and an ever-widening circle of musicians and patrons of music.

Harrington Manor had been so full of life and music. . . .

For a moment, vivid memories of the gay and lively creature she had once been swam through her mind. Music had been the whole of her life. Had she ever known a worry that was not related to a new concerto, to this or that movement? Did this contentment explain her happiness with Charles?

She thought it must be so. She had no memory of suffering an unpleasant thought, especially of the future. The future would be just like the present. In retrospect she saw what a foolish and simpleminded creature she had been. Nothing had prepared her for what fate had in store. The utter finality of death stole the very music from her life.

Everything changed after the tragedy. Common pleasantries and the polite banalities of conversation struck her as fatuous, nearly unendurable. As she sat stiffly, listening to a gentleman or lady relate their travel adventures or trials, or their opinion of the latest concerto played by the newest master, as she listened to the critique on Beethoven's last symphony or the queen's tireless edicts on Parliament, or even someone's thoughts on the weather, she found her mind gravitating to Charles. She would think of the huge rift torn in her soul, of Daniel's struggle against a dark future, and suddenly the words pouring out of her guest's mouth seemed hollow and vain, the effort she put to listening tiresome. These unpleasant thoughts would grow each moment she spent in society, and she'd have the most frightening sense of falling further into a dark despair. . . .

She saw how she had even closed her father from her life, without even realizing it. The extremities of her grief must have become too painful for him to witness, while her responses to his sympathy and tenderness were cold and unfeeling. His visits became ever shorter and less frequent. She was losing her father's love as well. . . .

"Ah," James finally said, his voice registering understanding, if not sympathy. "You haven't celebrated Christmas in faith since your husband's death."

She might have guessed there were no limits to his quest for intimacy, that he could take the most benign subject and change it into something altogether different. She nodded, looking up briefly into his eyes, which threatened to pull her into his unfathomable soul.

"I imagine that Meredith, Fran, Mr. Walter and all the others feel this same dark cloud over the season. It must keep them from participating in the full spirit of the celebrations."

Her startled eyes glanced at his. "Well, no," she answered. "Naturally they cannot be expected to feel the same poignancy of loss as I do! It's just that I . . . I—"

All at once she understood how it looked to him. That she forced her dependents, to say nothing of friends and family, to endure her frigid attitude toward the Christmas season. Piece by piece, year after year, she had been selfishly robbing them of . . . of Christmas joy, simply because she could not bear its reminder.

"I see how it looks to you—"

"Do you?"

"Yes. That it's selfish of me to steal their Christmas, that because I cannot feel any joy, neither shall they, and it's wrong, I know but I, I—" Her voice changed, she was suddenly pleading as she stood up. "You don't know what it's like. Every sprig of holly, every spice cake, every clump of mistletoe reminds me of him, of . . . what happened . . . I miss him. . . ." She whispered the simple truth. "I miss him at times so badly—" Her hand went to her mouth as her accusing blue eyes focused on his face. She spun around and ran from him, wishing she could run from the life he was gently, steadily calling her back to. For there would be, could be no more joyful Christmases for her. Not now. Not ever again. . . .

3

MEREDITH QUIETLY OPENED THE DOOR TO THE study where Catherine sat working at her father's old hand-carved desk. "Ma'am. Mr. Wentworth would like a word with ye."

Catherine looked up to examine Meredith's face. She often counted on Meredith's expression to give her an idea of how difficult a particular interview was likely to be. Discussions with Mr. Wentworth, Daniel's tutor, always required perseverance and patience, the exact amount depending entirely on how challenging Daniel had been that day. Oddly, Meredith smiled back, nodding slightly as if to encourage her. "Show him in, please."

She returned to her work, wanting to finish, if only to escape the persistent, unpleasant thoughts of her guest. Normally she had no difficulty completing tasks, any tasks, especially those required in the managing of her household. Dr. Balfour had not only forced her to cross each and every boundary of decency and intimacy but he had somehow stolen her concentration as well. . . .

Mr. Wentworth stepped quietly into the soft winter light of the study. A warm fire burned in the hearth. Catherine rose from behind the desk, bracing to hear the complaint. She noticed the elderly man's smile. With alarm she realized she had never seen Mr. Wentworth smile. Was he leaving them then? Had he reached the end of his patience?

Catherine directed him to the chairs by the window. He declined, preferring to stand, smiling as he did. With a sigh, she sank to the chair in a perfect circle of gray silk muslin. "Mr. Wentworth? You wanted to speak with me?"

"Yes, well, Madame Dorset! It's working!"

"Working?" she asked in confusion. "What's working?"

"Whatever you're doing with young Master Daniel. In all my time I've spent with the boy, I've never seen him in such high spirits as he was today. And he was most attentive to his studies. Not one complaint. Not even when we started Latin verbs."

She was so unaccustomed to hearing Mr. Wentworth praise Daniel that she suffered a moment's confusion. She hardly knew what to say. "What glad news," she managed, still confused. "He seems in . . . good spirits you say?"

The man's head bobbed up and down; his smile did not falter. "Like another creature altogether. I just felt it imperative to inform you of the change, so that you may continue his new treatment, whatever it is. That's all. I won't trouble you more, Madame."

Still smiling, the old man bowed and withdrew, leaving Catherine staring after him, wondering: What new treatment?

"My wheelchair is broken?"

"Aye," Meredith explained, biting her lip nervously. This was the one part of Dr. Balfour's program she questioned. "Don't know 'ow it 'appened but one 'o the 'orses stepped on it as Mr. Walter went about oiling it."

"He will fix it?"

"Aye but 'e needs a new wheel brought all the way from London. 'Twill be a . . . a fortnight."

A fortnight to a child might as well be a decade, Meredith knew, watching as the boy contemplated this disaster. He held perfectly still, and for a moment she braced for a tantrum. Color came to his pale cheeks; he appeared ready to cry. But no.

Daniel reached into his coat pocket and removed a crumpled note. Small hands smoothed the paper as he once again read the note James had sent him at breakfast.

> *Daniel,*
>
> *The quickest way to get through lessons is to pay attention to your schoolmaster and complete your work promptly to the best of your ability. You want to get through your lessons quickly because I will conduct your fencing instruction afterward in my room.*
>
> *James.*

As the boy read it again, the same sense of wonder filled him. James meant it! He truly meant it! He would have a fencing lesson!

He could not let James down just because his wheelchair was broken. He just couldn't. He would appear for his lesson, he would!

" 'Tisn't very far really," he told Meredith, quite calmly. He caught her smile of encouragement. "I believe I could manage it if I try. Don't you, Meredith?"

Meredith was nodding her head. "I'll step with ye the whole way," she promised, excited. She crossed her fingers, praying that God give the boy strength. The lad needed the success. If anyone ever needed a bit 'o success, 't'was young Daniel. . . .

It was in fact not a far distance. Maybe a hundred paces, no more. As Daniel slowly made his way toward James's door, an odd thing happened. The walking became easier. Step after step felt easier to manage. His legs stopped trembling. He began to smile a little as he came closer to the door.

"Look at ye!" Meredith kept exclaiming in an excited whisper, over and over as they progressed down the hall.

"It's really not so hard," the boy said, straightening suddenly, as amazed as Meredith. He stumbled a little, and Meredith gasped, reaching to catch him. Too late. Daniel righted himself, brushing away her concerned hand before continuing along. He reached the door.

His heart pounded wildly with excitement. He wanted to clap and sing. For he felt conscious of a miracle unfolding inside him, and it was a miracle, it was. He was getting stronger. . . .

Englishmen, even young Englishmen, never wear their emotions up front, and though Daniel forgot this trick when it was convenient, the tilt of his chin and determined set of his eyes indicated he used it now. He pretended his achievement was nothing of import. He turned to Meredith to tell her he wouldn't be needing her anymore. He paused, watching curiously as she wiped her eye. "What's wrong with your eye?"

"Nothing, Master Daniel. A bit 'o dust, 'tis all."

"Hum. Well, I don't believe I'll be needing you more, Meredith."

Meredith's smile was joyous as the young boy opened the door and announced, "Look, James! I say! I walked here all my self!"

Some time later Catherine anxiously saw the Reverend and Mrs. Camden to the door. It had been an unpleasant interview. Every year at Christmastime they arrived to implore her to resume hosting the Christmas Eve festivities at Harrington Manor and to resume directing the choir. Every year she declined.

"Promise me you will think about it, Catherine?" The reverend added gravely, "Our small choir has not been the same without you. Your direction is sorely missed all year, my dear, but especially at Christmas.''

Meredith watched her mistress lower her eyes as Mrs. Camden kissed her cheek good-bye. She shut the door after them, nervously biting her lip to wait for her mistress's reaction. La! To hear her mistress sing again at Christmas Eve—'twould make the merriest of Christmases. She did not dare hope for it, though. ''Ma'am,'' she said, ''Mr. Balfour has given me this note to pass to you. I did not want to pass it during the Reverend and Mistress Camden's visit.''

Catherine emerged from her troubled thoughts to see the folded letter Meredith held out. ''Oh,'' she said, taking it. She unfolded it and brought it by the lamp to read. It was directly, shamelessly, to the point:

Catherine mine, I want you . . .

Catherine's eyes widened at this outrage, and her cheeks turned crimson. Her delicate hand crushed the note. She cast a frightened look at Meredith, afraid she might have read the note. Meredith was inspecting a spot on her apron as she waited, obviously unaware of her mistress's distress.

Catherine dismissed Meredith and rushed into the drawing room she had just quit, moving directly to the fire. The crumbled paper was tossed into the flames. A small leap of orange, a trail of smoke, and it was gone.

But the sentiment remained, *Catherine mine, I want you . . .*

Her heart pounded as she considered the audacity. Never in her twenty-five years had she ever met such a person. She knew for a fact he would not be received into decent society if anyone even suspected that this brazen and licentious character lay beneath the proper accouterments of a gentleman. The trouble was she would be painted with the same black brush if anyone were to discover that she had taken such a man into her home. It would tarnish her own reputation, shrouding her character in suspicion and innuendo.

And he, reprobate that he was, was well aware of her predicament. He used it with malice, taunting her at every turn. Oh, this trial was unbearable! What could she do? What choice did she have?

During the last few days she had painstakingly avoided his society. She had not seen him once, which no doubt frustrated his dishonorable intentions and brought his iniquitous ambitions to a halt.

Catherine mine, I want you . . .

The bright orange flames leaped like dancing gypsies as blue eyes stared unseeingly into the fire. Her hand went to her mouth as she remembered the pounding sensation of his kisses, the hot feel of his hard body over hers, the sea of thick pleasure as he massaged her breast. Her breast! She closed her eyes with a slow gasp—

"Ma'am?"

Startled, Catherine leaped around to see Meredith standing there. A hot wave of panic washed over her in force, as if Meredith could read her very thoughts.

"What is it?"

"Master Daniel says he feels well enough to join you at the supper table tonight."

These last few days she had been taking her supper in Daniel's room since the wheelchair was broken. And there was no one to carry Daniel to the table, since Mr. Walter had to leave early every night. She had been amazed by Daniel's changed appearance, his happy chatter—most of this, regrettably about Dr. Balfour—his increased appetite and the color in his cheeks. The boy was obviously experiencing a brief respite from his lifelong illness. . . .

"Yes. Fine."

She hardly comprehended the import of Meredith's message, that Daniel felt well enough to jour-

ney to the table. The unpleasant train of her thoughts
consumed her. She stood before the fire for nearly
an hour, her mind traveling in so many different
directions she hardly knew anything past the fear.
Fear of what, she knew not, but a sense of doom
mushroomed inside her like winter clouds on a
horizon. . . .

A wish arose over and over in her mind. That Dr.
Balfour would fully recover. Soon. Dr. Michaels said
he might safely resume travel in two weeks. Just after Christmas . . .

"Dinner, ma'am," Meredith said.

She drew a deep breath and tried to still the unnatural flutter of her heart as she smoothed the blue
skirts of her gown. A hand went to her hair, tucking
in loose tendrils. She quickly made her way to the
dining room, accompanied by the dry rustle of her
taffeta skirts. Entering the brightly lit room, she
stopped in shock.

James stood by the hearth in the dining room talking to Daniel. Catherine failed to take in the fact that
Daniel stood, laughing apparently at some shared
jest with Dr. Balfour, and none the worse for his effort. She only saw the doctor. He looked unconventionally tall and darkly handsome in black formal
clothes. The handsome jacket concealed his injury
and its bandages. She had never imagined the effect
of a gentleman's formal dress on the man, and so it
came as a shock, altering subtly, without real awareness, her very idea of him.

She drew back, overcome with dismay. Somehow,
Dr. Balfour had mistakenly assumed he had been
invited to dine with them.

"Catherine." He bowed slightly as if not wanting
to tax himself much. "Thank you for inviting me to
dine with you and Daniel tonight."

"But I—" She stopped. She could hardly tell him
she had done no such thing. That would be more

than rude—a slight she could hardly guess how to manage. What could she do?

Nothing, she realized. She drew a deep breath, releasing her frustration with it. Just two more weeks . . .

James walked with her to the table, pulling out her chair.

"Daniel." he said, and she felt his warm breath on the back of her ear. "Have you ever noticed how beautiful your mother is?"

Daniel laughed gaily at this. "I have, James," he said as if he had just aged twoscore years. "You are as beautiful as a fairy princess, Mother."

Few women could resist the charm of these words uttered by a child. A spark of amusement caught in Catherine's enchanting eyes, though it disappeared as James assumed the seat across from her. Daniel was seated at her side.

Dazzled by how well Dr. Balfour managed everything, Meredith happily went about serving the wine he had provided. She caught sight of the angel she had placed on the mantel, and she smiled at it, imagining that the angel winked at her. A good omen if ever there was one.

The dumpling carrot soup was served next. Fran's favorite recipe was used only for special occasions. Napkins went to laps. Catherine resolved to be polite throughout the meal—she would not descend to his boorish level.

"How is your injury today, Dr. Balfour?" she inquired.

"My injury is on the mend, Madame; I am quite hale." He winked at Daniel. "I believe I am almost ready for my next adventure."

"Adventure?" she questioned, smiling a little at his romanticism, despite herself. "And what would that be, Dr. Balfour? Dare I inquire?"

"I intend to rescue a fair maiden—a sweet maid

more beautiful than any thy eyes have seen—from her most sorrowful predicament."

Catherine's thoughts rushed over these suggestive words, and her spoon dropped with a small clang to her dish. She stared into those dark eyes. "Just what do you imagine is this sorrowful predicament?"

"Ah." He smiled back. "A wicked spell has been cast about her; she lives in an icy stone fortress, isolated and alone. The magic light in her eyes, which is hope itself, grows dimmer every day as she endures her sad plight. And you see, I mean to rescue her and bring her out into the warmth of the sun again. I mean to see the light flash again in her lovely eyes."

James stared into those very eyes and thought that she looked more tempting than heaven, with wisps of half fallen hair about her face, her full breasts plumped against the blue taffeta gown and eyes gleaming in the candlelight.

Catherine felt her heart hammering beneath his look, color rising to her cheeks. She lowered her lashes, if only to save herself from being pulled into the unfathomable depth of his gaze. Oddly, it was Daniel who saved her.

"Yuk," he said. "James, that's not a very good story."

"Daniel." James chuckled. "What would you say if I told you someday you'll find yourself strangely compelled by such stories?"

"I'd say you were dreaming, James."

Catherine watched anxiously as the two bantered back and forth like old friends. Somehow James Balfour had stolen her mind and weakened her will. He was turning the neat order and sanctuary of her life into—into one of Meredith's penny dreadful novels.

James sent Meredith back to the kitchen with his compliments. "Mother," Daniel said, his eyes alight with excitement. "Guess what? James has invited us to France next year to spend the holiday season with his family!"

Catherine looked pointedly across at James. "Did he?"

"Yes, and he says it shall be grand. He has two nephews my age and he says I should enjoy fishing with them at the seashore. I've always wanted to see the seashore! I know I should love it and, and—" He stopped, realizing he could not say the other wonderful things he was to do there without giving away the secret. "He says his family's Christmas is the most merry in all of France."

Before she could respond, James asked, "Do you like to travel, Catherine?"

She shook her head slightly, relieved they were at least on a neutral subject. "I haven't had the chance to travel further than London." Of course Charles and she had intended on taking the newlyweds' traditional year abroad, but Daniel had come so soon after their marriage, nine months to be exact. He had been conceived on their wedding night, she knew, because after that embarrassing trial, Charles had not attempted the marital duties for another month, which seemed to have set a pattern. . . .

The contrast between Charles and James rose unbidden in her mind. She swallowed nervously as it occurred to her James would not likely wait a day, let alone a month, to perform the marital duties. Intuitively, she grasped the fact that James would have no reason to wait so long.

Which didn't mean anything, she told herself. . . .

Meredith appeared again to take away the soup dishes.

"So you have never been to France or Switzerland?"

The question distracted her from her disquieting thoughts. "No." She shook her head. "I haven't."

She had always wanted to go to France, Paris especially. To see the sights: Norte Dame, Chartres,

Versailles, the Louvre. Like most all people, she saw Paris as embodying the very best of culture, offering history, architecture, art, the whole ascetic experience painted with the warm colors of romantism. . . .

Her blue eyes found Daniel. His fragile health prohibited travel of course, and she could never leave him. Never . . .

"Can we go, Mother? Can we?"

Catherine delicately wiped her mouth, imagining the Balfour family barely etching a living from a small, seaside farm. That they managed to put their only son through the university was to be commended. In most cases, all but a few, actually only the most wealthy families, could afford the expense. "Daniel," she said gently, "I'm sure Dr. Balfour's invitation was premature. His mother must be overburdened with so many numbers in her family—"

"Not so," James interrupted, smiling as he thought of his mother's small army of servants. "She loves nothing more than entertaining. She has opened Blu de Sur doors to every court in Europe, including your very own English court, to say nothing of the world's artists and poets and," he grinned, "all the multitudes of pretenders to those lofty ambitions."

She looked confused. This made no sense. "The English court?"

"Indeed," he replied casually. "You English have more titled dukes and duchesses, lords and ladies, barons and baronesses than the ocean has fish; I believe I've met nearly all of them at some time or other."

"I'm confused," she confessed as Meredith served the Cornish hen and potatoes. Then she suddenly remembered her father's dismay upon discovering the personages who claimed an interest in James Balfour. "Does a title proceed your mother's name, Dr. Balfour?"

"No." He shook his head, enjoying her confusion. "Though once upon a time she was the Duchess de la Tourney, Margarite Evett Simon, but except for the properties, she gave it all up to marry my father."

The information surprised her; indeed she could not help it. She grew so absorbed in the colorful family history that she didn't even notice her son designing a fortress from his squashed potatoes. "And your father?"

"Common seafaring Scottish stock," James announced with obvious pleasure. "And my dear father is inordinately proud of the fact. I'm afraid both my parents are full of modern, egalitarian ideas and politics, including that their son should have a vocation, a life's work, despite the family's wealth and properties. In that way our families are quite similar, I understand."

It was true. Her mother's family had been wealthy and propertied, as had her father's. Both families were listed in the Baronetage. Even so, her grandparents had insisted that their father pursue a university career. He had always loved science and medicine; indeed, he was the type of man with a single focus in the world. It was difficult for him to entertain thoughts not related to his passion. Politics, religion, world affairs or even a benign subject such as gardening were of no interest to her father.

Like James's mother, Catherine too had given up a title to marry Charles, and while her family had objected, especially her grandmother who had raised her from infancy, their objections had had nothing to do with the fact that his family was not listed in the Baronetage and everything to do with the fact that Charles had no vocation or university career. Her father wanted her to marry a doctor like himself.

Catherine mused over this silently. She quite forgot her animosity toward the man across from her.

"And medicine?" she asked. "How did you choose it?"

Daniel's potato fortress reached an impressive height as James described the small naval hospital on the outskirts of the village near the château where he was raised, the doctor who worked there and their lifelong friendship. All the while Catherine's admiration grew. James seemed so much like her father. She found herself laughing at his anecdotes, drawn piece by piece into his history, and for the space of this evening she forgot her resistance to this man.

James was well aware that she was finally seeing him as something other than a beast. Not that the beast was gone—in fact James was aware of a desire that grew with each moment spent with her.

Her laughter died as she noticed his heated gaze, and her self-consciousness returned all at once. She suddenly realized the late hour, that Meredith had retired, the candles were low and Daniel had fallen asleep in his chair.

Anxiety transformed her face. "He fell asleep!" she said. "Oh, I do hate to wake him, and if he's too tired, I shan't know how to transport him to his bed—"

"I can put him to bed," James said, rising.

"Oh, but your injury—"

"I'll be sure to keep his weight on my good arm." He chuckled at her concern. "I did tell you, Madame, I am determined to rescue my fair maid, did I not?"

She watched as he swooped down effortlessly, and seemingly without pain, he lifted Daniel into his arms. The boy did not stir, and James disappeared through the doors.

Catherine stared into the lingering candlelight, telling herself over and over that it didn't matter that she had enjoyed his company—oh she had to admit it!—for the evening. It meant nothing past the fact that he could be charming and, well, decent when it suited him.

But he was still a danger to her, and that knowledge pressed heavily on her mind when he suddenly returned to the dining room. He was not smiling now. The stare of those dark eyes might have been the devil's own as he approached the place where she sat. She was maddeningly aware of each step. She felt certain he would try to kiss her again.

She felt the slow steady rise of her heart as he came behind her chair to help her up. She rose, turning to face him, stifling the childish urge to run for her life. "James." She whispered his name and then forgot why.

He only stared as he raised her small soft hand and brought it to his mouth for a kiss. A shiver shot up her arm. "Madame," he smiled. "This way." He bowed, then led her by the hand to the door. Stopping, he smiled down at her. Just as she was about to excuse herself, to leave as fast as her feet could carry her, he said mysteriously: "You know what I've done, do you not?"

"Why no, I don't."

His eyes glanced up.

Hers followed to see a Christmas kissing ring.

How she had managed to miss sight of it she would never know, but there it hung—two criss-crossed spheres wrapped prettily with evergreens and topped with a bright red bow. The danger, one she immediately saw and expressed with a slight gasp, hung by another ribbon from the bottom. Mistletoe.

Mistletoe. A remnant of their pagan Druid past. It was said that after attending the sacrificial rites, the people took home sprigs of mistletoe to put over their doors. This promoted fertility. Somehow the pagan custom changed to the English custom of kissing under the mistletoe, and James was obviously intent on celebrating it.

Meredith, I am going to kill you. . . .

She was shaking her head, held by the laughing dark eyes above her. Like a tiny bird caught in a snake's fatal gaze, she could not move to save herself. And then it was too late. His warm, firm mouth lowered to hers, and she closed her eyes. Gently, tenderly, he kissed her. His strong arms circled her waist, pulling her slender form into his. His sensitive fingers discovered the curves of her small waist beneath the rich linen of her gown, and he marveled at a softness so rich it seemed sculpted by heaven. And in the space of the magic and wonder that was this kiss, she knew how very much she wanted it to last forever. . . .

He broke the kiss. "Catherine," he whispered, tenderly pressing his lips to her forehead as his hands cradled her head. Her loose hair was like a mist, her lovely face transformed by passion.

She hardly heard him. She was barely aware of his smile as he kissed her hand again, his lips lingering briefly as he drank in the sweet perfume of her skin.

Then with a slight bow he was gone.

Catherine almost fainted.

"Is Daniel asleep yet?" Catherine asked Meredith.

"Just now, ma'am," she said. She did not tell of the miracles taking place in Dr. Balfour's room with her young man. Tomorrow they planned to have the fencing lesson in the garden, if Daniel again did well in his studies with Mr. Wentworth. The boy was that well now.

Catherine hurried through the entrance hall, passing into the long, portrait-lined corridor that led to his room. She felt the watchful gazes of her ancestors as she did so, ignoring the disapproval she imagined, irritated by this small flight of fancy her mind took. She had settled the matter, and she had no place in her heart for James Balfour.

She had not had a chance to see Daniel all day. Or Dr. Balfour. Not that she wanted to see him! She certainly did not. Still she did not have to see James to think of him, anxious thoughts that somehow wove into her sleep. She could not escape him even in the safety of her dreams. Over and over she dreamt of those laughing eyes, his irrepressible smile as he reached to take her into his arms and kiss her again—

A shiver raced through her. The dinner with James Balfour, his kisses, the whole outrageous time with him would soon be over. He would be leaving just after Christmas, and the neat order of her life would be returned to her. She had no tender feelings for him, she told herself over and over.

Forcing the memory out of her mind, she made her way to Daniel's room, which was lit by a single lamp. She quietly approached the bed, staring down at the sleeping face she loved. His breathing seemed deep, even, regular. He had not had a breathing fit for some time. . . .

Meredith said his appetite was greatly improved, despite his unfortunate confinement in his room. He seemed so happy, too, as if a secret thought kept bubbling to the surface. James's words rose unbidden to her mind: "Childhood asthma often diminishes as the child ages. . . ."

How she wished that were true! He was all she had left of Charles; Daniel was the rhyme and reason for her existence.

As if sensing her presence, his huge eyes fluttered open. "Mother. . . " he murmured, still half asleep.

She leaned over to kiss his cheek and brushed a lock from his forehead. "I missed you this evening. . . ."

"I was with James." He smiled at a secret thought. "I do like him so, Mother." He opened his eyes more to stare up at her. "Was my father like him?"

"No. He wasn't."

"What was my father like then?"

He had never asked about his father. She had felt the subject too painful to initiate herself; she had always imagined he felt the same.

He watched the familiar sadness appear in his mother's eyes. "I loved him very much. . . ." she finally said.

"I know. But what was he like?"

Her lovely eyes filled with the puzzle this question posed. How do you summarize a man in words, so that his son might know him, too, might love him as he deserves? "He was very gentle. . . ."

Daniel's brows crossed. "James is gentle."

Catherine's lips pressed together. That was a matter of perception, she thought. She tried to steer him back to his father. "Your father was very kind as well and—"

"James is very kind. His kindness is fun, too. Why he's more fun than anyone I've ever known."

"Your father loved music."

"I suspect James loves music as well," he told her happily. "Why he's always starting a song. He's got a fine voice, too. Have you heard him?"

"No," his mother said tightly. "I haven't."

"Mother, I have a surprise for you tomorrow. . . ."

"Do you?"

"Yes. James says you shall be very pleased."

"He does? What is the nature of this surprise?"

"I can't say or it won't be a surprise. He swore me to secrecy, you know, but it has to do with . . . fencing lessons."

The boy watched his mother's reaction carefully.

"With . . . what?"

"Fencing lessons! James is teaching me. Well, first we're building my strength, that's where the surprise is, but then he shall give me lessons. Oh 'twill be grand, Mother!"

Strange emotions danced through his mother's heart, but he was too tired to notice. Daniel had never felt such pleasant exhaustion, a result of Dr. Balfour's new regimen. He felt the brush of his mother's lips on his forehead, but sleep claimed him by the time she said good-night and withdrew from his room.

Catherine did not knock. She swung open the door and stepped into the brightly lit room. James was sitting up in bed, absorbed by his pile of books. He looked up.

"How could you?" she asked.

He watched her in silent fascination. She was obviously angry, but he hardly noticed as she began pacing in front of the fire, hands clasped behind her, stopping every few paces to glance furiously at him. Loose tendrils of hair fell from her tight bun, curling over the delicate forehead. Her eyes glittered. Absorbing the sight of her slender figure outlined against the gray silk of her nightgown, he drew a deep, shuddering breath which he released with a rush.

"How could you?" she repeated.

He answered with charming compunction, "Why, Catherine mine, I can hardly resist the temptation you pose. I believe you know this."

Her color deepened. "I mean about Daniel. He tells me you have suggested, that . . . that you have suggested fencing lessons!"

"Oh, that. He seems to fancy the idea, doesn't he?"

"How could you? 'Tis so cruel! I would have put it past even you! To suggest a sport to an invalid boy who can not ever hope to participate in it. How could you?"

He stated the fact quietly, seriously. "Catherine, Daniel is not an invalid."

"Not an invalid. Not an invalid," she repeated, agitated, hardly able to stop her frantic pacing. "You do not know. You have not seen a breathing fit. Dear

God, every time it happens I am weak with fear, fear that it will be his last, that I shall lose him. He coughs and sputters and cannot catch his breath. He turns blue before it is through." She looked at him, desperate to make him understand. "You cannot know how it is! You can't! I put enormous effort into creating a quiet and restful atmosphere in my house that has allowed him to survive thus far. I won't lose him; I can't. He will not have his hopes raised that he might be able to participate in a sport. I absolutely forbid your program. I forbid it!"

She stood there staring at him, her eyes flashing. James swung his long legs off the bed and took three steps to her side.

"Madame," his voice lowered with anger as he stared down at her. "Your unfounded fears are robbing that boy of his very life. His very life. I have examined him head to toe and I have found nothing wrong with him. Neither has Dr. Michaels nor, I suspect, has your very own father."

"My father admits that one cannot be sure!"

"Admits, reluctantly, under the pressure of a very determined mother who all but forces him to concede the point."

She turned away suddenly, clasping her hands tightly as if in prayer. "I will not take the chance on his health! I can't."

He grabbed her shoulders, turning her back to face him. "Listen up, Catherine—I will force you to hear me out. These asthma attacks are nothing more than a spoiled young man's desperate attempt to manipulate his mother's anxieties!"

Fury trembled through her, demanding a vent, and she raised her hand and landed a hard slap to his face.

With a gasp, startled by her inexcusable action, she turned and fled the room. James let her go, if only to spare her his response.

* * *

Mr. Wentworth conducted Daniel's lessons in his room, as the boy was often bedridden. There was a small desk arranged near the window for the days when he felt well enough. Like today. Mr. Wentworth smiled as he watched the young boy finish copying his Latin text, his small face set with determined concentration. Once again the boy proceeded through the day's lesson with studious attention and diligence. Not only did he offer no complaint, but his countenance was most cheerful as well.

Catherine appeared just as a pleased Mr. Wentworth concluded Daniel's last lesson. "Ah, Madame Dorset," he said, turning to see the boy's pretty mother standing in the doorway, clad in a black silk gown, much like a mourning dress. The black lace collar rose to her neck and seemed too tight by half. She looked extremely agitated. The color of her gown accented the unnatural paleness of her skin, the dark circles under her eyes. "Are you quite well, Madam?"

"Yes. Quite," she said shortly. She stared at her boy, who set about closing his books.

"Daniel has done very well today. Again."

"I want to be excused now. Please," said Daniel.

She stepped into the room. "Daniel," she began slowly, "I have something to say to you. I'm afraid there isn't going to be any . . . any, ah, lesson today with Dr. Balfour."

"But James said his wound was healing well—"

"No, it isn't him, Daniel. It's you. I'm afraid, Daniel . . . I'm just very much afraid you are not well enough for exercise."

"Oh, but James said I was well indeed, that really all I need is to regain my strength, and I am, Mother. I feel stronger than ever!"

"I'm afraid I can't allow it, Daniel. I won't allow it. Oh, darling." Her resolve collapsed as effortlessly as it had been built. "I can't take a chance with your health and—"

"No!" He cried suddenly, "No. I want to! I—"

"Daniel, I know you're disappointed. Perhaps someday when you get older and stronger you can learn, but for now it's quite impossible." Alarmed, Catherine watched as his face reddened and his breathing changed. "Daniel, calm down. Please dear—"

But it was too late. To her utter astonishment, he jumped to his feet and pulled quickly from her grasp. "Daniel!"

Daniel raced out of his room and into the hall. He was running. She could scarcely believe her eyes; he was running! Nothing could have alarmed her more. "Daniel, stop!" She rushed after him. "Stop! You can't run, you can't—"

The boy's legs had barely grown accustomed to walking and running proved too much. They collapsed, sending him facedown on the carpeted floor. With a scream, Catherine ran to his side, followed by Mr. Wentworth.

James stepped into the hall and rushed to Daniel's side, lifting the boy back up. "Are you all right, Daniel?"

He nodded, tears welling in his eyes. His breathing came in gulps. Catherine, who was kneeling beside him, covered her face as if to stop a scream. "My mother says I can't . . . She says I'm not well enough and I am . . . I am. . . "

"Of course you are," James responded with a furious glance at his mother. "And we shall show her, shan't we? She'll be amazed at how strong you've become."

Catherine gasped with horror. She would not stand for it! "Don't you dare do this to me! You tell him right now that it's not possible—"

"I will do no such thing, Madame!"

"How dare you! I'll not let you use him like this!"

"The boy, Madame! The boy!"

Mr. Wentworth's warning came too late. Well practiced in the technique, Daniel's throat constricted dramatically. He stopped breathing altogether.

Catherine barely knew what happened next, but she felt James's mercilessly strong arms come around her and a hand clamp over her mouth. She fought frantically to aid her son but she couldn't get free. Certain he would pass out or worse, she watched in terror as her son fought for air.

What happened next would live forever in her mind.

"Stop that at once, Daniel!"

No child would dare to disobey that command, issued with frightening authority. The words resounded in the boy's mind, and like a hard box to the ears, drew him up sharply.

Daniel took a gasping breath, staring uncertainly at James, who still held his mother. "There you go, boy. Take another breath. That's it. Now, draw a deep breath . . . that's it, that's it." The boy continued to gasp, calmer now, even as his eyes lowered with an unfamiliar emotion. Shame. This awful feeling grew as James said, "Now listen up, Daniel, you are never to pull that stunt on your mother again, do you hear?"

He did not look at his mother's face, now free of James's hand. But Daniel nodded solemnly, still breathing hard and fast. "Good. Then I have your word as a man that your mother shan't have to witness such a spectacle again. Now apologize to your mother for frightening her."

"I'm sorry. . . " he whispered.

"Are you quite well? Good. Then go in my room and wait for me there. I have something to say to your mother." He glanced pointedly at a stunned Mr. Wentworth.

With a slight bow, Mr. Wentworth withdrew.

James lifted Catherine, shaken to the bone, up to her feet, turning her to him. He held her by the arms and she was glad because her trembling legs would not support her. She looked up in his eyes, searchingly, and he stared down at her fearful gaze.

Still, he could barely temper his anger, so he did not try. "Now, Madame." His eyes narrowed. "From henceforth you will celebrate the fact that your boy is normal, that his asthma was a drama created by his mother's anxieties and his own stubborn willfulness. Is that understood?"

Her eyes shimmering with emotion, she nodded.

"Furthermore, you will start treating him as if he is normal. He will no longer have use for a wheelchair. He shall take his exercise in the garden each day. He might even reach the point where he will enjoy fencing lessons. One day he might decide to climb the Swiss Alps! Is that quite clear, Madame?"

Catherine bit her lip, hardly able to believe him, hardly able to believe what she had just seen Daniel do.

"Is that clear, Madame?"

She nodded.

He released her and turned away, shutting himself in his room.

Once the door shut, like a puppet without strings, she dropped to the floor, overwhelmed by him, this man, the whirlwind and chaos he made of the neat order of her life, the shambles he made of her grief.

For several days she could hardly put into words why she was crying, but then James's words would echo in her mind: "You shall celebrate the fact that your boy is normal. . . ." Gradually, as she watched James and Daniel in the garden every day—walking, laughing, running and playing ball, conducting all manner of normal boyhood activities—and as Daniel's strength grew by leaps and his color returned—she came to do just that: She came to celebrate a miracle, that Daniel was normal. . . .

4

DREAMS ARE WHERE WISHES COME TRUE. . . .
Catherine sat at the piano, playing a melody of favorite Christmas carols. The last notes of each song shifted and changed effortlessly beneath her fingertips to create the notes of the next melody. The harmony filled the air with the essence of Christmas: the spirit of giving and love that only music could convey, resonating joyously in the hearts of its listeners. She played. For him. At all times the music she made was for him.

Then suddenly the silence.

She felt fear, every artist's fear of an audience's response. She was keenly aware that his response could send her pummeling to hell or soaring to heaven.

Yet he leaned over the place where she sat on the piano bench. His tender hand came to her face, his fingers gently soothed her hot cheek. Something was wrong. She opened her eyes and screamed at the sight of a skeleton.

Catherine woke with a start, bolting up in her canopied bed. She looked dazedly across the darkened room, half expecting to find him standing there. The skeleton. The window had been left open a sliver. A chilly draft raced through the room, lifting the curtains, up and down, up and down. An orange glow came from the dying embers in the hearth but there was no one in the darkness.

Her heart beat irregularly, fast, then slow, then

fast again, as if uncertain of the exact nature of this emergency. Every night now she suffered through the same nightmare. She tried to make sense of it, but couldn't. . . .

She fell back against the bed, feeling confused and disoriented, and more than anything, frightened. Tiger Blue leaped up onto the bed. The cat brushed her side, and she reached for him, tenderly stroking the silky fur and finding comfort in the creature's purring.

She was now wide awake, and so, tossing back the coverlet, she slipped her bare feet into waiting slippers. She donned a pretty pearl-colored silk robe and secured it with a sash. Striking a kindling stick, she lit a lamp before quietly making her way down the stairs to the kitchen in the back of the house.

The kitchen felt chilly. The fire in the hearth had died some time ago; not even a remnant of heat remained. She shivered, pulling the robe tight about her neck, as she examined the cold oven.

What she wouldn't give for a soothing hot cup of tea! If only to settle her mind.

She had to stop thinking of him! Lately, it seemed her thoughts were only of James, though her state of mind was worse those few times when she found herself in the same room with him. He had dinner every night with Daniel and herself, entertaining them both with amazing and wonderful stories. She was at all times maddeningly conscious of his presence in her house. She even envisioned him as a woman might her . . . husband.

She pushed the alarming thought quickly from her mind. It could not be. She'd never love again. Especially not James Balfour.

She began preparing the old stove for a fire. As she went about the cumbersome business, she turned to the comfort of hundreds of memories of the many happy hours she spent in this cozy room. How many times would she sit here with Fran and

Meredith, and before that, her grandmother and Meredith's mother, too, laughing and chatting away the hours over their minor domestic concerns?

After a bit of work, at last she held a warm cup of tea.

In the doorway, James stood staring. Her long, auburn hair was tied back simply, so thick it formed a lovely halo around her face. The candlelight shone in her eyes, making them appear bright as gems. Her cheeks were flushed. He knew his feelings must cloud his judgment. For no woman was that beautiful.

"Catherine," he whispered.

She looked up with a start. He stood in the doorway, three steps up, staring down at her with a tender look of amusement. Instantly her heart understood the danger, renewing its frantic pace. It was late, and they were alone, and the kitchen was dimly lit. She heard herself say his name in fear . . . and anticipation, "James . . ."

Her lamp cast him in a small circle of gold. The intensity of his stare stretched across the distance. He wore only a midnight blue silk robe, like a smoking jacket, falling to his calves, and his feet were clad in soft, sheepskin moccasins. He stepped to the table, and her gaze fell.

A gentle hand brought her face back up. "Catherine," he said, his gaze searching hers. "What woke you in the middle of a night? A dream perhaps?"

The simple words somehow became suggestive when he uttered them, but the noteworthy idea that he had guessed her predicament hardly registered above the pounding of her heart. He was making love to her already. Her only hope, slim at that, was to escape. At once.

"I should leave. . . ." She rose suddenly from her chair, but it was too late. He was there in front of her, his strong arms encircling her protectively. She rested her hands on his upper arms, acutely aware of their muscled strength under the soft robe, the intensity of his stare as he held her and the escalating tempo of her heart.

"I think not," he said, his gaze becoming serious as he felt her fear. "Catherine," the rich timbre of his voice softened, "I, too, was wakened from a dream. A beautiful dream in which I found these soft curves against me, your breast in my palm, my lips on yours. Catherine." He kissed her forehead, his hand combing through the loose fall of hair down her back. She drew a shaky breath and released it tremulously. "I want you. I want to land on the very real shore of my dream." He kissed her once, on the lips, and then again. "Will you let me, Catherine? Will you?"

She couldn't think to save herself. He towered above her, the intensity of his desire plain in his eyes as he watched her. His body cloaked her in warmth, which stretched over her arctic heart, beckoning. Yet the only certainty amid her confusion was the power of the word no. Spoken as a plea, as if she needed his permission to retreat to the safe dark shadows of a long-ago love, her hiding place.

"Oh, James, I can't—"

It was as far as she got. A finger touched her mouth, silencing her. His gaze was unfathomable. "Catherine. . . " He pronounced her name in a caress as he reached gentle hands to her face, then let his fingertips brush through her hair. "I might ask why? Why are you so frightened of me?"

She couldn't meet the intensity of his stare, and she closed her eyes, only to feel a finger trace the contours of her mouth, barely touching.

She opened her eyes and started to shake her head, not understanding why she wasn't fighting against the sweet onslaught of his seduction. Not understanding why she wasn't running for her life. And then it was too late. . . .

He applied a gentle pressure to the back of her

neck, and her face tilted up to his. He lowered his head to hers, watching as she closed her eyes again. His kiss was like warmth and sunshine, stretching to her soul. The pleasure magnified as his tongue swept into her mouth, sending her into a soft swoon, melting, helpless.

There seemed no end to this kiss. . . .

Never had James wanted a woman more, the force of his desire felt alarming indeed, but he felt her vulnerability, too, and it allowed him to exercise a supreme gentleness. He broke the kiss and let his lips touch her closed lids and her forehead as he drank in the sweet scent of her. He whispered her name against her ear.

She felt a rush of shivers, a feverish trail where his lips touched her skin, and she was saying his name out loud. The ceaseless roar of her blood fueled the pace of her heart when the curve of his finger gently parted her lips for his next kiss. . . .

Then his hand tilted her chin slightly and he pressed his warm breath and lips to the skin on her neck, as soft as a goosling's. The clever lips found the nape of her neck before traveling to the tender curve of her ear.

He felt her tremble and knew her pulse raced as fast as his. He pressed the advantage. His lips came to hers with the gentlest pressure, and dear Lord, she tasted sweeter than life itself. He tilted her head back even further and widened his lips as his tongue delved into her delicious moistness. Hot pleasure spilled into his body as he felt the warmth of her skin beneath the flimsy robe, the full breasts pressed against his chest. He groaned deep in his throat. His hands slipped up and down her graceful back before he went on to explore the delicately voluptuous curve of her hip, luxuriating in her softness as he cupped her buttocks to pull her more tightly against him.

He broke the kiss, and all she could do was shake

her head to say no, no to the promise of his kisses, no to this ill-advised liaison. She gasped for breath and he caught those sweet breaths in his mouth as his lips caressed her upper lip, gently kneading, forcing her to share the very air he breathed.

"My God, you taste like strawberries and sunshine . . . Catherine." His large warm hands reached to her shoulders where he gently slipped off her robe and the sleeves of her nightgown. The flimsy cloth hung on her arms, revealing the beckoning lift of her bare breasts. The compelling beauty of her nudity sent his desire soaring. "You are temptation itself. . . ."

Modesty bloomed in her cheeks as she felt the penetrating heat of his gaze. She was protesting, shaking her head, even as she closed her eyes again and felt the blood rush from her head to pool around the warmth radiating from his hands as he held her breasts. He cupped them and drew erotic circles with his thumbs. Her throat constricted and helplessly she arched into his palms. "James . . . oh no, James. . . ."

Her eyes appeared as light filled jewels. "Yes and yes," he replied as he dragged her into another kiss. She swooned beneath the gentle pressure of his lips, the intoxicating taste of him, and as he deepened the kiss she forgot the danger. She had no thought past his lips on hers, the heady flavor of his mouth, the sweep of his tongue, the feel of his large warm body against hers. She had never felt anything like this except—

Except in her dreams. Dreams that turned to a nightmare of a skeleton. The image drew her up sharply, and she stiffened. With no warning, she broke the kiss and anxiously pulled up her gown. She backed away.

Stunned, he stared at her from several feet away. He didn't understand anything except the fear in her lovely eyes. She held herself tightly, looking back with eyes that revealed every emotion in her heart. "Catherine." He stepped over to her, startled by the sudden feverish light in her eyes, like a child wakened from a nightmare. "Catherine—"

"No, please." She shook her head. Panic washed away the lingering heat of his body, leaving her chilled, shaken, scared. "I can't . . . I can't do this, James!"

The finality of her statement lingered long after she had turned and fled the kitchen. James stopped himself from halting her retreat, from forcing her to confront her fear, which was a wise measure. Somewhere in the space and breadth of her kisses he had lost any semblance of control. The intensity of his desire was indeed awesome, an intensity he had not felt since he was fourteen and discovered what a certain young lady had intended by singing all her love poems in the loft of the stables. And clearly he needed some measure of control to fight the fear in those lovely eyes.

What was she so afraid of?

It seemed to have everything to do with the fortress of grief she had erected over her life, a fortress that was crumbling at her feet day by day. Was it falling in love again that terrified her, and if so why? Or was it the sensuality of that love? He understood the latter, for the force of their attraction was indeed daunting. . . .

He still had not heard her music—music that was as essential to her life as breathing. This he had plans to rectify. His hope was that her music would melt her fortress of ice, that music would chase away her fear and send her into his arms. . . .

His sigh turned into a chuckle. For while his mind pondered the benefit of waiting, his body seemed most unwilling to slow the race of his blood. At least he had no doubt what he wanted for Christmas.

And every blessed day after. . . .

* * *

Catherine paced in front of the hearth in her rooms. Twilight crept into the chamber, inch by inch, bit by bit, stealing the small warmth of the winter's afternoon. No fire lit the stone hearth. She hardly noticed the chill in the air as anxious thoughts crept into her mind.

She was thinking of Charles.

For the first time since his death, she found no comfort in memories. Not now. Perhaps not ever again. James had changed her life, casting a different light over her cherished memories, altering their shade, texture and color bit by bit, until she felt as if she looked upon a much changed past.

Charles had just turned twenty when he died. He seemed suddenly so young and boyish, and she so innocent and naive. He had been a young man, and she only a girl. She remembered his smile with startling clarity, yet she could not recall a single word he had ever said, perhaps because he had never said anything particularly memorable. Nor had he owned a single ambition past assuring her happiness and contentment. Once that had seemed a shining part of his devotion, but now it seemed more like a . . . deficiency.

The thought startled her, and she stopped pacing, coloring with sudden shame. With an anguished cry, Catherine flung herself onto her bed. She had loved Charles, so desperately that his death had cost her everything. Her music and friends, her happiness. But Charles's gentle love was nothing like James Balfour's. And her love for Charles was nothing like the love she felt blossoming in her heart for James.

Love and desire, what a potent mix! Powerful, consuming, terrifying. She could not have it. 'Twas more frightening than a leap off Dover's cliffs. *James, I'm sorry, I'm so sorry. . . .*

The bell rang downstairs. Catherine waited for Meredith to answer as she struggled with her unpleasant thoughts. Who would be calling? Harrington Manor had precious few callers these days.

The bell rang insistently again. Where was Meredith?

Footsteps sounded at last. Wait. Not Meredith's footsteps. These were sure, steady footsteps and—

"Good day, sir!"

"A good day to you, sir, as well. . . ."

Why, James had answered the door!

With a sweep of her charcoal silk dress, Catherine rushed into the hall, hurried down the stairs and swept into the entrance hall. She saw the outline of James's tall form in the doorway, lit by the greeting lamps on either side. There was no sign of his injury now. He wore black riding pants and a loose-fitting silk shirt, with no coat or vest. All her thoughts of the impropriety of his dress disappeared as he turned to her. She felt a curious leap of her heart, a sudden escalation of her pulse and breathing, and all she could think of was that night. . . .

For a brief moment, James took in Catherine's much changed appearance. Her lovely eyes were red and circled, making them look large and dramatic against the pale skin. The beautiful hair was half fallen from its pins. The sight of her struggle renewed his resolve to end it tonight.

Tomorrow was Christmas Eve.

Her gaze searched his. He gave no clue that anything had happened between them the other night, as if their encounter had slipped his mind. She colored with chagrin but ignored her feelings as best she could as she came up behind him.

"Ah, this must be Madame Dorset, I presume?" the visitor said, tipping his tall hat. He was a small man, middle aged, plump and outfitted in a gentleman's traveling coat of red—his special Christmas coat. White hair covered his rounded head, and his whiskers were too long for convention. His eyes sparkled as he looked at her. His smile was huge, and a large, black leather bag sat at his feet.

Catherine looked behind his stout form to see Mr. Walter leading the man's horse to the stables. James stood to her side and slightly behind, his arm on the door. She was queerly conscious of the intimacy suggested by his nearness. "Yes?" she answered.

"I'm Mr. Elffin. From London, Madame. Heavenly Tuning Inc."

A piano tuner! She looked for a moment, confused. "Mr. ah, Elffin, I did not order my piano tuned."

"Oh?" He bent over and removed his black book. He quickly flipped through the pages and showed her the name Madame Dorset, Harrington Manor of Lakeshire.

"Yes, I see," Catherine declared. "But still I'm afraid there's been some mistake as—"

"You do have a piano?"

"Yes. A Steinway as a matter of fact—"

"Fine instruments, if I may say so." He looked her up and down and sighed, "Though wasted on the, ah, lesser talents. . . ."

James, too, turned to stare at her.

They were implying that she was one of these lesser talents! The insult brought a sudden rush of indignation, which was ridiculous, as if Mr. Balfour and this curious Mr. Elffin were the *London Times* music critics.

"Ah!" James said. "I am told that Madame Dorset knows all the Christmas songs by heart!"

Catherine turned to him instantly, only to see his innocent smile. She might have offered a rebuttal, that not only did she know the Christmas songs by heart, as James had put it, but she had played them since she was six. By age fifteen she had been famous for her classical improvisations of these popular carols, improvisations that Mr. Schoenberg—a *London Times* critic and an old family friend—had described as "brilliant, played with such tender and intimate expression, such clarity and elegance as I have never heard before. . . ."

Of course to condescend to defend her talent— especially to James—was quite beneath her. How was it she could be tormented by the memory of his kisses and the promise of his love one minute, then irked to madness by his insolence and arrogance the next?

"I'm impressed," Mr. Elffin said mildly, not at all as if he meant it. "So, Madame! When was the last time you had your piano tuned?"

"It's been several years but—"

"Several years!" He appeared aghast at the idea. "Madame, surely you know those pianos should be tuned twice a year, that anything less can damage your instrument." He shook his head. " 'Tis a good thing I came, a very good thing."

Catherine crossed her arms, pressing her mouth to a hard line. Her father must have ordered this man to come! He had always loved her music, and once he had finally accepted Charles as his son-in-law, he used to tease him that not only had he stolen his daughter but his musician as well. After Charles's death he had tried to get her back to the bench, using one ploy after another. She had thought he'd given up. "Yes, but you see I don't play anymore—"

"Well the season is upon us, Madame!" Like a well pleased king, he patted his midsection with his chubby fingers. "All your, ah, sentimental carols and whatnot that you shall be playing soon. Now where's the piano?" He stepped past the couple into the entrance hall. "You can assist me, I hope?"

"Well, I—"

"Do not worry, Madame," the visitor hastened to add. "Nothing taxing. Just play a few scales and chords, 'tis all. The most elementary player can manage it."

Elementary player, indeed!

Mr. Elffin missed the angry flash in her eyes and

proceeded directly to the music room. James caught her elbow as she turned to follow the man. At his slight touch, a shiver coursed maddeningly through Catherine's body. He seemed not to notice. In a concerned whisper he asked, "Can you play, Catherine? I am not an accomplished musician, though I do know the basic scales. If you think you would have difficulty assisting Mr. Elffin, I would be glad to help him instead."

Catherine's face reddened, her fist tightening at her skirts. But she managed to keep most of the sarcasm from her reply. "I believe I can manage a few scales."

"Wonderful," he declared.

The music room was the finest room in Harrington Manor. As large as a tennis court and grand with its high ceilings, elegant chandelier, and polished wood floor, the room had hosted many splendid balls, to say nothing of frequent concerts. The piano sat against huge bay windows overlooking the garden, darkened now in the setting sun. The two spacious sofas and many chairs were artfully arranged around the enormous stone hearth where James immediately went about starting a fire. Four chairs and two sitting tables were arranged around the piano. The chairs were covered in an ornate green-and-rose-flowered damask that matched the sofas and other chairs. All except one.

Charles's chair . . .

Catherine felt a tingle of alarm as she sat at the bench. The strange Mr. Elffin removed his instruments from his bag, just as the fire came to life in the hearth. James set a brass candleholder, with its eight lighted candles, on the piano, then took a seat.

Catherine watched as he languidly stretched out his legs and folded his long arms across his chest, looking as relaxed and content as a cat on a sunlit windowsill. The large chair seemed to shrink as he sat in it. 'Twas Charles's chair. The one he always sat in to listen to her play. The same chair James sat on in her dreams before he had changed into a skeleton.

A shiver shot up her spine.

She began to play scales, and the tuning began. She soon discovered that Mr. Elffin was quite good at his profession and had a fine ear. This was not a surprise as she must assume it was how he made his living. She could hardly hide her astonishment however, when James offered an opinion to Mr. Elffin, demonstrating just as fine an ear. She said, "Do you have a fondness for music, Dr. Balfour?"

"Yes, Cat, I do."

Color shot to her cheeks, and she cast a quick glance to Mr. Elffin to see if he heard the endearment. He was busily engrossed in her instrument. She looked back to see James grinning with pleasure. Furious, she bristled. Cat indeed. She ought to scratch him to teach him a lesson—if only it could possibly help.

She kept resisting the urge to improvise on the simple scales Mr. Elffin had asked for. For so many years, she had not felt the urge to set her hands upon the piano, but as she sat there, memories of happier times kept flashing in her mind's eye: the endless hours she had spent filling this room with music, the countless performances given here, all the gaiety and life that was once a part of this house. . . .

Music coated each memory. Bits and pieces of it swam through her consciousness. Mr. Elffin had her play simple series of scales and minuets as he tuned the cords, testing each one over and over, and then waiting in turn for James to comment.

She remembered her grandmother giving her the first series of scales to practice for the week, remembered producing them perfectly after a half hour or so. She recalled the shocked look on her grandmother's face before her grandmother swept down and

hugged her tightly to her bosom. "My darling Catherine, I have been blessed. . . ."

"There now," Mr. Elffin said finally. "We're almost finished. I need you to play a bit for me. I prefer classical of course but I'll listen to anything you
might know. 'Tis the season, so . . . ah, how about
'Jingle Bells'? Do you know that?"

With heightened interest, James noticed Catherine's eyes narrow with irritation, she extended a stiff
index finger and tapped out the popular tune. Boing,
boing, boing . . .

Hearing a stifled sound of amusement, she
glanced at James, who appeared to be deeply engrossed in examining a button on his shirt. Irritated,
she looked to Mr. Elffin.

"Hmm, can't really get a grasp of the instrument
from that. Where do you keep your music, Madame?" He opened the lid of a nearby box. The lid
was spotless but the sheet music was dusty. "You
have quite an impressive collection here, Mrs. Dorset," he commented. Then he muttered under his
breath, "Music boxes somehow reveal the place
where ambition parts from talent. . . ."

Catherine turned ashen with fury. *Men*, she silently fumed. They always seemed to humor a woman's talents. She wondered if she had ever met
anyone half as irksome.

She remembered immediately that she had, and
he was sitting before her.

Mr. Elffin looked at Catherine skeptically as he
held up a classical booklet. "I don't suppose you
could play any of these?"

"A few," she replied primly.

"Surely not the piano version of *Eine Kleine Nacht-
musik*," he said, putting back the booklet.

Catherine drew a deep breath through tightened
lips. All men assumed women could not play that
piece! It was one of her favorite transcriptions. For,
unlike many other pianists of the time, she wor-

shiped Mozart. He had composed when the piano was still in its cradle, and many contemporary pianists, while naturally celebrating Mozart's genius, now found his music emotionless, especially since Beethoven's brilliant passion had been put to compositions. Granted, Mozart's music rarely reached the height of Beethoven's passionate *Emperor's Concerto*—

She saw Mr. Elffin flipping through her children's song booklet. This was too much. She could not stop herself. "I believe I can play that piece Mr. Elffin. If you would be so kind as to hand it to me."

"You?" A snow-white brow lifted over mischievous eyes.

"Catherine," James said, "simply to try that piece merits praise. Rest assured," he added generously, "we shall overlook your faults in the attempt."

"Thank you very much for your kindness!"

"It seems the very least we can do," he replied, deaf to her sarcasm. "Are you quite well, Catherine? You are coloring, love, as if you are upset—"

"Just hand me the music."

Mr. Elffin set the booklet on the piano.

With a much deserved look of contempt at Mr. Elffin and another at James, Catherine studied the familiar opening for a moment. Then, like a curtain falling, she panicked. Feeling the nervous tremble in her fingers, she was about to rise and excuse herself when—how strange!—her grandmother's voice echoed in her thoughts, as if she stood nearby, *Play for him, Catherine. . . .*

She bit her lip, swallowing nervously.

Play for him, Catherine. . . .

As the words sounded in her mind she felt a warmth rush from her head down, enveloping her in a sense of comfort and security from long ago. Her trembling eased. Her grandmother could always chase away her fears with the wealth of her love.

And goodness knows, she always loved that old woman. . . .

Play for him, Catherine. . . .

The music began in her mind first. Then, a miracle, all her anger, fear and confusion dissipated as the music continued to sound in her mind. Her face lost all expression. The compelling lure of the opening chords rushed straight through to her long, delicate fingers, her hands hovering over the keyboard, close, always close. And then she began.

It was then that James understood how deeply he was in love with her. It shined from his eyes as he sat in the chair spellbound, enchanted, letting the music wash over him with an intensity of pleasure quite new to him.

His musical experience was extensive. At his mother's Parisian salon he had been exposed to some of the continent's greatest pianists: Baron Rubio, Liszt, Massart, Pierret. Yet as fine and exciting as many of these concerts were, none had ever affected him like Catherine's. No concert ever would again.

He saw at once she was the type of classical pianist who exercised superior technique and skill over dramatic presentation. For all the drama and passion came forth in the music, rather than through any violent pounding of her fingertips or obvious facial expressions. Yet he had never heard such supple and responsive technique, such incredible nuance of touch and tone. . . .

Nor had Mr. Elffin. After the first three minutes he had fallen into a chair and closed his eyes. The expression of utter elation on his ruddy face might lead one to conclude he was viewing the opening of heaven's gates, but it was the music lover's response to the sound brought forth into the room. He, too, was rather famous in the Parisian music salons, a great patron to many artists and a dear friend of James's mother. He had been in England for Liszt's tour in London when he received James's note requesting his presence at this house—to lure a reluctant pianist back to her instrument. After a few discreet inquiries he had discovered that the young woman was once upon a time very much admired in music circles. James convinced him the ploy would work: "Indeed I have never met an artist whose artistic pride would not insist on demonstrating itself in such circumstances, however contrived. . . ." And so he had been right.

Now, the pleasure was his to enjoy.

Meredith and Fran stood in the doorway listening. Daniel, who had been building a block castle in his room, rushed in, slipping between Meredith and Fran, a startled look on his face. He felt Meredith's loving hands come to his shoulders, and he looked up to see the two women exchanging smiles as they wiped at tears.

The music again! The beautiful music . . .

In the midst of the final passages James silently motioned for everyone else to leave the room.

Now alone with her, he thought she had never been more beautiful. A candle bathed her face in a golden glow. At first she didn't notice that they were alone. But finally, she realized with startling clarity that only he was there and she was playing for him. For James Balfour . . .

The music was a sublime echo of her passion. . . .

The tremble started deep inside her, rising with the tempo of the music, increasing with every tap of her fingers. Then she slowed with the last notes of the final cadenza and finally stopped.

The sudden quiet of the room descended, yet it might have been a clap of thunder for all its effect on her nerves. She held perfectly still, unable to look up, aware only of the pounding of her heart.

"You did this on purpose. . . ."

"Yes."

"Mr. Elffin?"

"An old family friend, Mr. Langstaff."

Her blue eyes lifted. James sat in the chair. The grand room was dark; he was shrouded in the golden light of the candles, the more distant firelight.

"There never was an injury."

"No," he replied.

She saw at once that the whole drama had been orchestrated; starting with the first day he had fallen victim to his opponent's sword and ending now with a musical performance.

She felt as if she had suddenly wakened from a dream to find herself in an unfamiliar circumstance. For she had never witnessed such naked desire. His love had overwhelmed her over these last weeks, just as the music had so quickly and forcibly consumed her.

He stood up and quietly approached her. She was shaking her head. A look of inexpressible anguish marred her lovely face as he came to her. His eyes dared her to deny that she had been making love to him with her music. She started to shake her head but his fingers came gently to her mouth. "No. I won't let you deny it. I won't let you ruin what was so beautifully, magically constructed moments ago."

She stood up. "I don't know what happened—"

He stood up, too, taking her by the shoulders. Her blue eyes pleaded with him to let her pass. He would not. "Then let me spell it out, Catherine. The fortress has fallen. You've fallen in love. With me. And that love has made you play again. Catherine, love, the only thing left is surrender—"

"No." She shook her head. "James, please . . . You're scaring me—"

"Yes, every time I draw close to you. And, Catherine." He gently brushed an errant strand of hair from her flushed cheek. "It's becoming a problem. Because I want you. I confess I have never wanted anything more. And so, love." He slowly traced his fingers over her hairline, aware of the shivers this caused. "Now I want to know why."

She frantically searched his handsome face, her eyes wide, filled with love. " 'Tis madness! I must leave—"

His brow lifted as her small hands came to his forearms to push him away. Her desperation startled him and he reached his hands around her waist to hold her still. "Catherine—"

"No, please," she whispered, as she twisted free of his hands and dashed away. James caught her before she reached the door. She gasped as his arms encircled her from behind. With a desperate surge of emotion, a frantic cry of no, she gripped his forearms to free herself.

He had no idea how hard she struggled, but he felt her fear. "Stop fighting me, Catherine."

"No," she cried. "Please . . . James, let me go—"

"Not until I understand you."

Tears sprang in her eyes, and she collapsed into his arms. He turned her around to face him. She was shaking her head, her eyes pleading with him for something he was no longer willing to give. "Catherine, tell me."

"James," she pleaded. "James, don't you see? I can't love you! Already you're consuming me, threatening my peace, so much more than anything I've known. More than Charles. And it scares me. Look how my hands tremble," she whispered, holding them up. "I keep thinking that if I feel this way now, what shall I feel in a year? In two years? I couldn't survive if . . . I can't lose again."

He searched her eyes as she spoke. Eyes so wide and misty they seemed painted by watercolor. Eyes that validated the truth of her confession, a truth he had not been expecting, but which made perfect sense to him. She was afraid to fall in love again, to risk loss again. This magical thing which had sprung up between them was more powerful than anything she had ever felt and if she were to ever lose it she would be devastated.

He stared down at her with unmasked love in his eyes, which was as frightening to her as the prospect of his passion. She shook her head slowly, as if there were still a chance of him letting her go now, even as his arms came under her and he swept her into the air.

He carried her through the door to his room, shutting it with a kick. He brought her to the bed, where she knelt on the velvet comforter. For the longest time he stood over her, staring down at her while she looked up at him. She wasn't aware that she was still shaking her head until he leaned over and gently took her face in his hands for his kiss. "I'll be very careful, Catherine," he whispered. "Very careful . . ."

5

The morning of Christmas Eve . . .

CATHERINE SLEPT DEEPLY IN THAT SWEET HEAVEN where dreams penetrate life, a place of bliss and magic and, renaissance. Each time James had made love to her it was more deeply felt, more passionately possessive, until finally, in the quiet hours of the morning, he had carried her to the very peak of an ecstasy so high he had claimed her very soul, as no one had ever done before. She belonged to him, now and forever. She had surrendered.

Surrender. No retreat was possible now and none

was wanted. "I promise, my love," he had whispered, kissing her love-soaked form. "I promise to teach you to celebrate our love every blessed day God gives us together, so that when I do finally leave you, when you are an old woman with grown children and grandchildren, and if we are very lucky, great-grandchildren, I will leave you with a million happy memories. Catherine," he said as he kissed her, a kiss that touched her soul, "I love you. . . ."

"I love you. . . ." she replied.

A strange fragrance stirred her as she slept. It was a familiar scent drawn from Christmas past—a faint trace of Fran's famous Het Pint and hard sugared candies. She woke up a bit more, then sank down sleepily again into the goose-down pillow.

Daniel had sneaked into his mother's room and on to her bed. He tried very hard to lie still and not wake her, but it was too late. The scent of Christmas wove into her dreaming consciousness: Christmas Eve and James, love and music, family and friends, the Christmas tree and her beautiful angel collection. A smile graced her lips as she slept. . . .

Fran and Meredith, up before dawn, had let the excited boy lick the spoon after mixing the plum pudding and pour the sugar into the batter for the twelfth cake. All the while the two women had filled him with treats, excitement and laughter for the special day. Meredith had let him open one of the prettily wrapped tree decorations.

"Are we really and truly to have a Christmas Eve festival here, at Harrington Manor?"

"We are!" Meredith had exclaimed happily, swooping down to meet his gaze. "And it shall be grand, as grand as the queen's Christmas, better even because we will make up today for all the years we missed!" Then she had hugged him so tightly he thought he would burst.

A warm excitement filled Daniel as he watched his mother sleep. They had never celebrated Christmas much because it made her so sad. But James had promised him that she wouldn't be sad any more, that he would never let her be sad again. Daniel believed him. James had also made him promise not to wake his mother, and it was hard to keep this promise. Excitement made him fidget as he glanced at the huge present that sat at the foot of her bed.

Wake up, he called silently, wake up!

She opened her eyes. Daniel laughed at the miracle.

The boy's flushed face lay next to hers on the goose-feather pillows. He was smiling, his eyes filled with laughter. Seeing this charming picture of boyhood health and happiness, she was filled with a sense of Christmas magic. She smiled back as she reached a loving hand to the thick lock curling over his forehead.

"James said he'd show me exactly how the American Injuns skin people alive if I woke you, and I promised I wouldn't, but are you awake now, Mother?"

Catherine laughed. She was awake enough to know that the passion and splendor had been real. She touched her lips, lips slightly swollen and tender from the heat of his kisses. Her skin was still flushed, her every nerve satiated. The endless passion of his lovemaking formed a swift, moving stream of memories and all she could think was—

She was forever changed. . . .

"Mother, Mother, are you well? Why, you look so strange! Are you awake?" He could hardly wait for an answer. "Because 'tis Christmas Eve, Mother, and James said you will be happy to know it. He left you this pretty box, see it?"

"Oh did he?" she asked, carefully bringing the covers with her as she sat up and looking dazedly around the room. She was in her own room! She felt a flood of relief. After their endless lovemaking, when he finally relinquished his claim on her and let her fall into a deep and blissful sleep, he must have carried her up to her room.

She laughed as she beheld the enormous box tied with a pretty pink ribbon. A bright fire raged in the hearth, its warmth chasing away the winter's chill.

Daniel scrambled over and with some effort lifted the box and set it on her lap. "James says 'tis your early Christmas present, that he has lots more to give you. Open it, Mother. Let's see what's inside!"

She hurriedly untied the ribbons and lifted the lid, gasping as she beheld a beautiful rose atop a rose-colored silk gown. She took in the lingering perfume of the blossom's scent, then lifted the dress. It was quite simply the most beautiful dress she had ever beheld. Her heart quickened as she wondered if it would fit; then she spotted her very own dressmaker's card. Why, he must have discovered her dressmaker!

The card read: "Rose, the color of love. A color that shall bless the rest of our lives. . . ."

The sweet sound of his mother's laughter encouraged Daniel to ask a much anticipated question. "Mother, James asked me something important this morning. I did not know how to answer him. I thought I should ask you first."

"What, darling?"

"James said that because I am the man of the house, I must always look after you. I don't mind, Mother," he told her quite truthfully, rather fancying the idea of taking care of her. "And so he asked me for permission to marry you."

Catherine's eyes widened dramatically.

"He said if you agree to his proposal, he will be my father. I told him that was fine with me. In fact I thought I should rather like it. I don't have a father, you know, and it always makes me sad. It makes you sad, too, I can tell, and that made me even sad-der." He paused solemnly before confessing, "Sometimes it scared me, Mother, how sad you were. I always thought it was my fault. I always thought that if I hadn't had weak lungs my father wouldn't have been riding too fast on a horse."

"Oh, Daniel." She reached a hand to his face.

"I know that's wrong, James said so. He said no one can take the blame for an accident, not even God. He swore I was a blessing to you, that he suspected you loved me more than any one on Earth and that was a lot." His mother nodded, strangely silent. "Oh, Mother," he rushed on, "I do fancy James being my father! Can I say yes, Mother? Can I?" His face changed with alarm as he watched tears appear in his mother's eyes. "Why, Mother, I made you cry!"

The dress was forgotten as she drew Daniel into her arms, and for a long moment she held him, unable to speak for her happiness. "You did make me cry because, because, Daniel, he's right. I do love you so! And I'm just so happy! Do give him your permission. Go tell him now! On Christmas Eve . . . "

"Ma'am!" Meredith popped into Catherine's room. "It took three of the men to carry in the tree. Oh, do hurry. I think it is the largest and grandest tree we ever did have. The queen herself 'asn't got one as big!"

"I'll be right out!"

The good people of Lakeshire were already arriving for the Christmas Eve festivities. It had been another miracle added to all the other wonders of this day. Without her awareness, James, Meredith, Fern and the Camdens had arranged for the Christmas Eve celebration to resume at Harrington Manor, a last ploy to bring Christmas back into her life. . . .

James quietly slipped into her room, thinking that nothing, not even the rose silk dress, could do her beauty justice. The picture of her sitting in front of her looking glass as she arranged her hair seemed taken from a French romantic painting. "Catherine . . ."

She looked up in the mirror to see him standing behind her. Her breath caught and her heart leaped and time seemed to stop as he stared at her. She felt his love cascading over her with its blessing. "James . . ."

He chuckled. "Catherine," he said, leaning over to kiss the sensitive spot on the nape of her neck. "I shall cherish that blush the rest of my days. It says so much. Like your eyes, love."

She closed her eyes, savoring the lingering bliss of last night. She turned to him. For a long moment he stared down into her eyes, eyes filled with the promise of her love. Which he would bind with a betrothal ring.

Catherine watched as he presented a velvet box. "Oh James . . . I feel as if I am dreaming."

She opened it, and there it was. A betrothal ring.

He gently fitted it around her finger. A warm tingling feeling traveled up her arm, gathering in her chest as if it were magic. The room blurred with her tears, and she heard his whisper. "For you. For our love. A love I hope you will bind forever with marriage."

She was nodding and then he kissed her. Her arms circled his neck, and she clung tightly to him as the kiss deepened, renewing their desire. All James could think was that when he next saw the old lady, he would drop to his knees and kiss her small slippered feet for this gift.

The gift of true love . . .

Father Christmas carefully set down the box and then the bag of toys before stepping to the window and wiping the frost from the pane as he peered inside the music room.

'Twas a beautiful scene that greeted the old man. Friends and neighbors surrounded the Christmas tree. Gasps of wonder punctuated the silence as the people drew back to admire the magnificent tree.

James held the ladder as Catherine climbed the steps to place the silver star—made by the loving hands of Mrs. Camden's youngest daughter, Claire—on top. He knew the picture of Catherine at that moment would live in all their memories: Her face lit with joy, her cheeks flushed with Christmas merriment, the long auburn hair falling in a pretty pile over the rose-colored silk gown, which fanned over the lower rungs of the ladder. He stared up with unmasked love and admiration mixed with some worry as he watched her slender arms reaching to secure the star.

Then it was done. The majestic sight brought a sudden burst of applause and happy exclamations. Catherine started down the ladder, and James swung her down the last few feet to the ground.

Catherine closed her eyes as she felt his warm lips brush against her neck, giving her a pleasure ripe with promise. "I want you again," he whispered with frustration. Here they were on Christmas Eve with the house full of thirty good and gentle people, and he knew he should be enjoying himself—the music, laughter, gaiety and warm affection of their happy society. If only he did not have to battle the nearly irresistible impulse to sweep her into his arms and carry her off to his bedchambers.

Catherine shared his longing. His warmth penetrated her thin silk, his arms holding her to him, his breath teasing a tender spot on her neck. She could hardly think amid the vivid memories of his love-making—

"Why, Catherine." James chuckled, whispering so as not to be overheard. "Every time I look at you you seem to have applied rouge."

She laughed prettily. . . .

Father Christmas could see the love between them, and he knew gratitude. He felt it even more as he spotted Daniel circling the tree with young Boyd and Stephen. Daniel stood so tall! He looked so hale, the picture of happy youth.

The pretty scene blurred, and for a moment it confused him. Until that moment he had not realized how much he had missed his beautiful daughter, all her love and gaiety and music. But now she was returned to him.

He wiped his eyes and quietly withdrew. He spent several moments carefully retrieving his box and bag before he made his way to the door. He let himself in, marveling at the warmth of Harrington Manor. Delicious, familiar scents rose from the kitchen as he made his way through the entrance hall to the music room.

He stood in the doorway unobserved, for Meredith had called everyone to the hearth for the traditional lighting of the Yule log. The huge birch log sat in a wooden box; James made a great show of pretending he could barely lift it. Several gentlemen rushed to his aid, each struggling to fit it into the hearth, a scene that sent children and ladies into gales of laughter.

Catherine took the scissors from Meredith and leaned over, snapping off the pretty red ribbon. "Oh I do wish we had saved a piece of last year's log!" Catherine said as she stood back up. Superstition dictated that a small piece of the Yule log kept under the mistress's bed could save the house from fire all year round. Sadly she had neglected the comforting superstition along with the rest of the bustle and celebration of Christmas. "I know 'tis just silly fancy that it's protection against fire—"

"But I 'ave it, ma'am; I put it under ye bed last Boxing Day. 'Tis been there all year. Look!" Meredith held up the small piece of the log. "Wouldn't be doin' my duty if I let the house burn down, would I?"

"Oh, Meredith." Catherine laughed as she took it.

Reverend Camden lit it with a kindling stick and made the traditional announcement of the death of the devil and the coming of Christ. Everyone applauded and burst into the Yule log song as the flames wrapped around it. Catherine stood up, then looked over at the doorway and the sight of her father.

In that moment, she understood how very much she had missed her father, how she had pushed him away bit by bit until he seemed almost a stranger to her. How could she have? How could she have decided that if she could not have Charles's love, she would have no one's? Not even her dear father's. The folly of her lost years felt like a cold strike against her heart.

She noticed James watching her closely, and she turned uncertain eyes to him. He kissed her tenderly, and in that moment she understood how much he had given her: her son's health, her father's love again and the promise of a lifetime of love and music. The gratitude she felt seemed the very rhyme and reason of Christmas.

Then she rushed to Father Christmas's outstretched arms. A tender embrace, laughter and another embrace as she felt his forgiveness. Gladness washed over her with his love. They might have stayed like that until the Yule log fire died and it was Christmas morning but for the children. The children turned and saw who stood there embracing the lady of the house.

Wild exclamations of delight sounded as the children rushed upon the old man with the long white beard, red velvet cape and huge sack of toys. His enormous coat pockets were stuffed with toys, too! And he carried a big wooden box in his hands. Of course the older children, Daniel among them, understood that this Christmas fun was meant for the younger ones, many of whose little faces held a look of ebullience brought by the Christmas miracle.

James searched the room for the old woman as he came to Catherine's side, but she wasn't there. The children gathered in a semicircle around Father Christmas. Parents stood behind the children, trying in vain to quiet their exclamations. Darkness crept into the room, though the chandeliers and decorative candles spread bright light in the music room. The blazing Yule log lit the Christmas tree in all its splendor.

Feeling Catherine's small hand in his, James felt a rush of gratitude. He kissed her neck, and she smiled at him. As he stared at her lovely face he wanted to kiss that old lady responsible for this gift—a happiness and joy he had never imagined. His mother had always said true love would happen to him some day "when you are least expecting it and are completely unprepared. You will see, James, you will see. . . ." And so he had. It was odd, too, the way Catherine's grandmother had somehow known he would fall madly in love with her granddaughter even before he had met her. He assumed she would have come up from London with her son. Where was she? When would she arrive?

No one mentioned her arrival. Perhaps she would come on Christmas day. He had to know, and he motioned to Catherine, drawing her gently away from the guests for a moment's privacy. He wanted to tell her the whole absurd plot from the beginning and hear her laugh. He wanted to kiss her. He wanted to ask when her grandmother would come. She followed him to the archway leading to the dining room.

The last present waited back in the music room— the big box in Father Christmas's hands. Daniel had been given no present, but he didn't mind, for James had already given him the best present possible.

Or so he thought.

Daniel's small hand smoothed the sword lying at his side. His grandfather had probably run out of gifts. He'd surely make up for it on the morrow. . . .

Daniel abruptly became aware of the silence and that everyone seemed to be staring at him. A smile spread across his face.

In the hallway Catherine was acutely conscious of the kissing ring above her head. She was laughing waiting expectantly. "Yes?" she asked James.

"When is your grandmother coming?"

Her eyes registered her confusion. "My grandmother?"

"Yes. I want to thank her. I've been meaning to tell you since last night. You won't believe this, Catherine, but somehow that old woman knew I would fall in love with you. She knew it before I even laid eyes upon you."

She laughed. "I do find that difficult to believe."

"No more than I," he assured her. "But do you remember last night when I confessed there never was an injury, that the whole plot was intended to recommend me to your father? Until the moment I first saw you—"

She smiled at this part and finished, "And you lost your heart and wanted only to capture mine."

"Yes," he answered, smiling tenderly. "What I neglected to tell you was that the whole thing was originally your grandmother's idea. Yes! I see you are surprised." He laughed. "Yet it's true. The day I found out your father had denied me a position at the academy, I was riding through Hyde Park and almost ran smack into her. There she was in the middle of the park on a chilly night. She introduced herself and put the whole plot to win your heart before me—"

"James!" She searched his handsome face, a look

of bewilderment on her lovely features. "You're teasing me!"

"I'm afraid not, my love. I know it is hard to believe, but somehow, by some miracle of magic, she knew I would fall in love with you. She said those very words as I recall—"

"James." She laughed, guessing his story was a jest. "You must have been intoxicated that night, am I right?"

"Well I suppose I had something but—"

"It affected your wits, I'm afraid," she said. "Because my grandmother, though famous for meddling in my life, could not possibly have been in Hyde Park that night."

He stiffened ever so slightly, a chill of warning racing up his spine. "Well, why not?"

"My grandmother died several years ago." Catherine missed seeing the look on his face as she suddenly heard a small whimper coming from the large box her father had brought into the house. "Oh, Father, you didn't. . . ."

"For you, Daniel," Father Christmas said in a booming voice. "Someone to run with. . . ."

Catherine instantly forgot all about James and the amusing story of her grandmother's last sojourn into her life, forgot everything as, like countless other mothers on Christmas who find themselves confronted with their child's first puppy—and, dear Lord, such a large puppy!—all she could think about were the floors and carpets, the barking and the fleas—

These thoughts retreated as she took in the tender scene. Daniel held the large black-and-white puppy in his arms, hiding his face in its fur. The puppy sensed the import of the moment, and after a yawn, he gently nudged Daniel's face and licked him. Daniel laughed in reply.

Catherine came slowly to her son's side and knelt, gently petting the dog's silky fur. She met Daniel's tear-filled eyes as he hugged this special creature, and she heard the only word he could manage. "Please. . ." She knew she would never regret her nod of approval.

After Daniel and the other children had taken the puppy outside, they returned and gathered around the tree, trying to think of names for the animal. At last Fran called the group to the table. A loud cheer went up. Everyone paired off, and it was a joyful party that filed into the dining room. Catherine was still scolding her father, though of course with all good humor. Then her father joined ranks with another gentleman, but Catherine lingered outside the dining room doors.

James still stood under the kissing ring. "You look as if you truly have seen a ghost!" she said, laughing playfully at him. She walked over to him and stared up into his eyes, whose depth reached her very soul. "Do you really think it was my grandmother's last foray into my life?"

He searched the lovely, upturned face. "At the time, in truth, I was quite intoxicated, I confess. I don't know; I might have imagined the whole episode, I suppose—"

"It doesn't really matter," she told him, loving him so much. "Because in all these last long years I forgot something so precious. But you and your love have reminded me."

"Reminded you of what?"

"Of Christmas magic and miracles."

The love in her eyes was proof, all the proof he would ever need. "Catherine," he said, watching as her eyes filled with mischief and she looked above him. His gaze followed hers, and he laughed when she said, "I was wondering when you would notice."

He kissed her. Beneath the pretty ring of evergreen, bright red bows and mistletoe, he kissed her. And they might have gone right on kissing, missing a fine Christmas feast and all its good cheer except for one last surprise.

"Catherine," James said. His voice, heavy with passion, quickly changed to alarm. "Catherine, something is chewing on my leg. . . ."

HAPPY HOLIDAYS
from . . .
JENNIFER HORSMAN

My Aunt Mary taught me to believe in Christmas magic. She was the oldest member of our family, a spinster, and the cause of much wild speculation among relatives.

I remember sitting on her lap every Christmas day, the delicious scent of her exotic perfume, her laughter and the special warmth she radiated. She had traveled across the world and had collected one gold charm for every city she visited: a tiny Eiffel Tower, the Statue of Liberty, a London double decker bus, and my favorite, a tiny thumb-size gold box with a hundred dollar bill folded miraculously inside. It seemed the bracelet weighed her weathered arm firmly to the couch as she described each one and told of the adventures connected to each.

Because I loved her bracelet so much—I think, because I loved her so much—she bequeathed the bracelet to me when she died. Then through some mistake, no one could locate it. The bracelet had disappeared. Finally it was determined that Aunt Mary had been buried with it.

Ten years later, while my own children were carefully scouring the unwrapped packages beneath our Christmas tree, my daughter discovered a small brown package addressed to me.

With much excitement I opened it and discovered my Aunt Mary's treasured bracelet inside! No one knew how it got there. My husband had found the package on our front porch on Christmas Eve, brought it in, and put it among the other gifts.

I take it out now every Christmas . . .

May you and yours be blessed with Christmas magic too.

The Christmas Baby

Joan Johnston

1

*T*HE KILLING HAS TO STOP, EMALINE THOUGHT. *Somehow, someone has to make it stop.*

Nobody knew how the feud between the Winthrops and the Bentons had started. But for twenty years, since before the War Between the States, the town of Bitter Creek in Nolan County, Texas, had run red with the blood of both families. The most recent victims were five-year-old Sissy Benton and fourteen-year-old Rufus Winthrop. The two family patriarchs had called a week-long truce so they could bury the dead. The Bentons attended funeral services at the Bitter Creek Baptist Church in the morning. The Winthrops took over in the afternoon.

Emaline Winthrop had lost both a father and a younger brother to the feud. At twenty-two, she had spent nearly her entire life under the cloud of animosity that existed between the two families. For the past five years a particular plot of land had been the focus of hostilities. It was an idyllic spot where a stream rimmed with pecan and cypress trees crossed a pleasant grassy valley about two miles south of town. Both Winthrops and Bentons claimed possession of the land and, more importantly, the year-round source of water for their cattle.

Emaline sat in a back pew of the church mulling over a plan to end the fierce contest over those precious acres of land. She would never have a better opportunity to suggest her idea. Today she intended to confront the family patriarch, Jeremiah Winthrop, and see what he had to say.

Emaline moved to the edge of the crowd that surrounded Rufus's grave at the cemetery on the outskirts of Bitter Creek. Her eyes slid to a lone figure who stood vigil over yet another fresh grave. It was John Fleet, the town blacksmith. His daughter, Bethanne, had been a third victim of the cattle stampede through town that had killed Sissy Benton and Rufus Winthrop. Fleet's face looked ravaged, and Emaline tried to imagine the pain he must be suffering. His wife had died a year ago, and now he had lost his only child. There was no rallying clan to lend him comfort in his hour of need. He was grieving alone.

Emaline hesitated a moment before walking the twenty or so steps that took her to the huge man's side.

"Mr. Fleet?" she said quietly.

He turned to face her with red-rimmed brown eyes that seemed vacant of all feeling—until he recognized her. She recoiled at the virulent hatred that contorted his face when he spoke.

"What're you doing here?"

"I just thought you might need—"

"Get out of my sight! You Winthrops and Bentons have done enough."

"I only wanted—"

"I don't need your sympathy," he spat. "Will it bring back my Bethanne?" he said in an agonized voice. "Just go away and leave me alone."

Emaline fled, her heart wrenched by his pain, more convinced than ever that what she was about to do was right. The feud had to be stopped, not just for the sake of Winthrops and Bentons, but for the sake of everyone who lived in Bitter Creek.

After the funeral service for Rufus Winthrop, the clan gathered at the house of its patriarch for the wake. Emaline approached the elderly man, who was sitting in a rocker on his back porch with a heaped plate of food balanced on his knees.

"I need to speak with you, Jeremiah," she said.

Jeremiah spoke through a mouthful of food. "I'm listenin'."

"I have an idea. A way to end the feud."

Jeremiah stopped chewing and stared at her. He swallowed before he said, "Don't talk nonsense, girl. Been a lotta folks tried to stop the fightin'. Them Bentons just won't hear a word of it. Only way to end this feud is to kill 'em all, down to the last man, woman and child."

Emaline shivered at the venom in the old man's words. As she dropped to her knees beside him, the skirt of her eyelet lace-trimmed gingham dress billowed around her on the dusty wooden porch. "What if I could end the feud without any more bloodshed? Would you be willing to stop the killing? Would you make the men put down their guns?"

Jeremiah eyed her thoughtfully. "What fly's buzzin' in that brain of yours, missy?"

"The problem is that both Bentons and Winthrops need the water in the valley. Why can't we just offer to share it?"

"We done that, girl. Them Bentons said they own the land, and we have to pay them to use the water. Ain't meanin' to pay for what's ours!"

"I see." Emaline took a deep breath. "What if there were a way to establish that the land belonged to both Winthrops and Bentons equally? Would that solve the problem?"

"What're you gettin' at, girl? Speak up!"

Emaline grasped the arm of the rocker to steady herself. "What if a Benton and a Winthrop married and had a child? It would be half Benton and half Winthrop, right?"

"I suppose," Jeremiah conceded warily. "Only

ain't no Winthrop nor Benton neither one gonna do such a thing."

Emaline ignored him and continued. "Say the disputed land was settled on their child. The land would have to belong to both families then, wouldn't it?"

Jeremiah opened his mouth to voice another objection, then snapped it shut. His eyes narrowed as he stared at Emaline. "You got someone particular in mind to marry a Benton?"

Emaline flushed. She didn't like the way Jeremiah was eyeing her. She was a single woman long past an age when most girls married. But she saw no reason to marry when her husband was likely to die from a bullet. She had no wish to raise children when they were bound to be slaughtered in a senseless feud. She had made the conscious choice not to look for a husband, although she knew there were those who blamed her lack of a husband on her appearance. She wasn't exactly the typical young miss.

Emaline was extraordinarily tall. She had long red hair that was a riot of curls, and her face—actually her whole body—was covered with freckles. She counted her striking blue eyes and good teeth as assets. But her nose and chin were only ordinary, assuming they could be spotted past her freckles. She had a meager bosom and slender hips. Worse, she was headstrong and opinionated, two traits considered not the least attractive in a woman.

Emaline had resigned herself long ago to being an old maid. Thus, Jeremiah's speculative gaze left her feeling decidedly uneasy. "I've only made the suggestion that a Benton and a Winthrop marry," she said. "I expect it would be up to the clan to decide who should make the sacrifice. Whoever volunteered would be doing something wonderful, something for the greater good of all," she finished breathlessly. "Assuming the wedding took place right away, the feud could possibly be ended forever by a baby born at Christmas."

Jeremiah set his plate aside. "This is something needs talkin' 'bout right away, specially since we got everybody gathered in one spot."

Jeremiah raised his voice to get everyone's attention. Couples streamed out of the house and came from under the shade among the live oaks to gather around the back porch. "Emaline here has suggested a way to end the feud."

Agitated murmurs erupted from the crowd. Emaline felt her face flushing an uncomfortable red. Her blush was a mortifying thing she couldn't control. She countered the effect by lifting her chin and pretending she didn't know she looked like a boiled beet.

Jeremiah explained Emaline's plan in short, terse words.

"Who'd be stupid enough to marry a Benton?" someone shouted.

"Likely get murdered in the marriage bed!" another cried.

"Besides, how do we know them Bentons would agree to it?" still another argued.

"Why wouldn't they?" Emaline retorted. "It would end the killing. It would bring peace to Bitter Creek."

A hush descended on the crowd. Most people had lost hope that there would ever be an end to the feud. Emaline's idea had awoken in more than a few hearts a long-suppressed hunger for peace.

"Why not at least suggest the idea to the Bentons?" one woman said. "The worst that could happen is they'd say no."

"First we gotta be sure we have someone willing to marry a Benton," another woman said. "No sense getting our hopes up for nothing."

Emaline became conscious of Jeremiah's hooded eyes focused on her. Her pulse began to pound as her heart raced in panic toward her throat. She turned to the elder statesman of the Winthrop clan, her hands trembling. "No. Not me."

"Why not you?" Jeremiah said. "You're a spinster, long past the age of marriage. And it was your idea."

"I don't want to marry," Emaline protested. "And especially not a Benton."

"Why not?" Jeremiah demanded.

"I . . ." Because the Bentons had killed her father and brother. Because she hated them.

But that was the problem, wasn't it? The Bentons hated the Winthrops who hated the Bentons who hated the Winthrops. It was a neverending circle of enmity that led to death and more death. Someone had to break the cycle of violence. Someone had to be willing to forgive and forget.

Emaline looked out at the sea of faces. She saw aunts and uncles and cousins, grandmothers and grandfathers, brothers and sisters, sons and daughters. All of them were at risk so long as the feud continued. At least her idea offered hope for an end to the killing. If someone had to be the virgin sacrifice for the greater good of all, she supposed she was as likely a candidate as any other.

"If no one else is willing, I'll do it," Emaline conceded quietly.

There was a collective sigh from the crowd.

"No!" a male voice cried. "I won't let you do it, Emmy."

Emaline's older brother, Devlin, shoved his way past their relatives. He was even taller than she was, his body lean and lanky. He was blessed with hair a deep, rich auburn rather than red like hers, and his eyes were hazel instead of blue. Emaline had always envied his complete lack of freckles.

Devlin reached a spot two steps below where she stood on the porch and grabbed her hands in both of his. "You can't do it, Emmy," he said, his eyes locked earnestly with hers. "Who knows what kind of monster they'll choose to marry you?"

"I firmly believe the Bentons want peace as much as we do, Dev," she replied in a steady voice. "Whoever they choose will be making a sacrifice, too. It's bound to be someone who believes in peace as much as I do. For that reason alone, we're certain to deal well with each other."

Devlin walked up the two steps that separated them, so he could speak privately to his sister. His brow was furrowed with worry, and his face was pale. "Think what you'll be giving up," he hissed in her ear. "A chance to find a man to love, a man who loves you. Don't do it, Emmy! I don't think I could bear to lose you, too."

Emaline knew Devlin had suffered as much as she had from the loss of their father and brother. Devlin wasn't married either, and Emaline had often wondered if he had come to the same conclusion she had—that it was senseless to marry when one lived at the heart of such a violent world.

She laid a hand on her brother's arm. "I have to do it, Dev. Don't you see? It's our only hope. The killing has to stop."

She saw the struggle in Dev's features as he dealt with the enormity of what she was about to do.

"Emmy, I can't let you do it. I should be the one—" He stopped himself, biting off what he was about to say. "If I volunteered—"

"Thank you, Dev," Emaline said. "I don't think I've ever been more proud to have you for my brother—"

"But you don't understand," he said in an agonized voice, interrupting her again. "I should be doing it instead of you. But I have to talk to . . . I mean I can't just do it without asking . . ."

Emaline managed a chuckle. "If it's this hard even to talk about marriage to a Benton, how are you going to go through with the deed? No, Dev," Emaline said. "It was my idea. I'm the one who should pay the consequences."

"Well, missy?" Jeremiah prodded. "What's it to be? Do I speak to Horace Benton or not?"

"Tell Horace that I'll marry whichever Benton man they choose."

There were no cheers, no excited exclamations. Everyone present had suffered too many disappointments to believe it could be this simple to end the feud. But they were willing to try. Emaline saw that as a hopeful sign.

"I won't do it!" Conn Benton declared to the assembled Benton clan. "You can't make me do it!"

"No one's going to force you," Horace Benton said in a conciliatory voice. "But you're the most logical choice to marry a Winthrop woman. First of all, your land borders the contested property. Second, you've been a widower for long enough. It's time you got married again."

"But not to a Winthrop woman." God, how he hated all Winthrops! They had murdered his wife when she was pregnant with their first child. He could never forgive them for that. Now it seemed he had been selected to marry one of them, to take her to his bed and get a child by her. They were asking too much. How could he bear to look at another woman, especially a Winthrop, when all he could see as he closed his eyes each night was his beloved Josie lying dead in a pool of blood?

He felt a frail hand on his sleeve. "It's a chance for peace, Conn. It's a chance to stop the killing."

Conn looked into his mother's troubled eyes. She had lost a husband, two of her three sons, and a daughter-in-law to the feud. She despaired of losing Conn, who had been more reckless with his life in the two years since Josie's death. At first he hadn't wanted to live. Now he lived only to kill Winthrops.

Could he give up his need for vengeance for the

sake of his clan? Could he agree to marry a woman he hated before he even met her? Could he lie with a Winthrop woman, put his seed in her, and watch it grow, and not loathe the product of their union?

"I have to think about it," Conn said at last.

"You don't have much time," Horace Benton replied. "The truce we agreed upon for the funerals lasts a week. The Winthrops want the wedding to be held before the truce is over."

"What happens then, I mean after the wedding?" Conn asked. "Does the truce continue, or what?"

"I suppose it must," Horace said thoughtfully, stroking his beard. "A lot will depend on you and the Winthrop woman, I suppose." Horace cleared his throat uncomfortably. "On how quickly you can get her with child."

There had been some discussion about that. Both Conn and his brothers had impregnated their wives in the first months they were married. He supposed that was responsible, in part, for his being chosen as the sacrificial goat. He tried to imagine himself bedding a strange woman on his wedding night. What if she were ugly? What if she repulsed him? What if he could not . . .

Conn forced his thoughts away from failure. All women were the same in the dark, he thought grimly. He would manage to do his duty. That is, if he agreed to the insane proposition that had been made to him.

Horace cleared his throat again. "Well, Conn. I suppose there's nothing else to be said. If you won't do it—"

"I never said I wouldn't do it," Conn retorted. "I merely asked for some time—"

"There isn't any time," Horace said vehemently. "I need to give Jeremiah an answer this afternoon. Will you do it or not?"

Conn looked for some way to stall. "I want to meet the woman first," he said.

"What?"

"The Winthrop woman. I want to meet her before I agree to marry her."

"That sounds sensible," someone in the crowd said.

"In the church. At six o'clock," Conn said. "I'll give you an answer after I talk to her."

"I'll ask Jeremiah to bring the woman to meet you. I don't think he'll object. So long as you're willing to give us an answer then."

"I've said I will," Conn replied irritably.

It didn't give him much time to consider—it was already after four—but Conn welcomed the respite. He wondered what kind of woman would agree to such a harebrained scheme. It wasn't going to work. But they would still be married when all was said and done. And likely hate each other's guts.

His mother cornered him before he could leave Horace's place. "Conn," she said, "I want a moment of your time."

Conn refused to meet his mother's gaze. She had a way of making him feel guilty even when he hadn't done anything wrong. "I'm in a hurry, Ma."

Hester Benton knew her son well. She knew the pain he had suffered and perceived his righteous anger. She had left him alone for the past two years and seen him grow more and more bitter, watched him lose the laughter that had always sparkled in his eyes. The time had come for her to interfere. She couldn't allow him to ignore this opportunity to set things right. Conn had never been a cruel man. He might hate the Winthrop woman when he married her, but he would not abuse her. Their union could end the horror of the past twenty years. And perhaps when Conn held his son or daughter in his arms, he would be able to let go of the past.

"You have to do it, Conn," she said in a quiet voice. "If not for your own sake, then for the sake of your nieces and nephews. Your brothers' children deserve to live in peace."

"It's too late for that, Ma."

"No, it's not," Hester argued. "The only thing preventing peace in Bitter Creek now is your stubbornness."

"They killed Josie." Conn swallowed over the thickness in his throat as he turned to meet his mother's loving gaze. "I can't forget that."

"You may never forget," Hester said, "but you can forgive, Conn. You can give peace a chance."

"I'll think about it, Ma," Conn replied as he tore himself free of the compassion in her eyes. It was all he was willing to promise.

Conn was at the church at half past five. He needed some sort of guidance, and he wasn't finding it within himself. He was astonished to discover the Winthrop woman was there ahead of him. She whirled abruptly when she heard his bootsteps on the wooden floor.

Emaline was stunned at the sight of Conn Benton. She had never seen a man so handsome. They were totally mismatched, she realized, the ugly duckling and the beautiful swan. Except in size. Thank the Lord, he was taller than she was. His black hair was straight and a hank of it hung over his forehead. He had piercing, dark brown eyes and strong, blunt features. He was large enough to be intimidating, except she was used to holding her own with intimidating males.

Nevertheless, she felt a little breathless at the sight of him. "I didn't expect you so soon. I mean, I suppose you're the one who . . ." Her words trailed off as she stared at him, trying to imagine herself married to him.

"I am," Conn confirmed. "And you're the Winthrop woman?"

"I am." She thought of them lying next to each

other, his skin warm and golden . . . hers garishly freckled. And blushed. An incredible red. Her chin tipped up an inch in response to the incredulous look on his face.

God Almighty! Conn thought. This was the woman they proposed for him to marry? Lord, she was a long string bean! And redheaded! Conn didn't think he'd ever seen such bright red hair. She had it tied down at her nape with a green ribbon that matched her gingham dress, but it still curled every whichaway around her face. And freckles! He gave an inward groan when he thought of the child they were supposed to make together and how it would likely inherit her freckles. And no figure to speak of in that long span of female. There wasn't much he saw to her credit.

Except her eyes. They were wide and blue and utterly captivating. Then she smiled. Not a big smile, but enough to put a dimple in her cheek, and he felt the warmth of it all the way to the pit of his stomach. He steeled himself against feeling anything. She was a Winthrop.

"I don't know who thought up this blasted idea, but—"

"I did."

"What?"

"It was my idea."

"What were you thinking, woman?" Conn exploded. "Of all the cockeyed—"

"It isn't as crazy as you're making it sound," Emaline interrupted. "It will work."

"If they can find two people stupid enough to go through with a marriage," Conn muttered.

"There's nothing stupid about this idea," Emaline insisted in a voice that reverberated with feeling.

Conn could see she was set on the idea of this marriage working a miracle. Well, maybe he could change her mind. He stalked down the aisle of the church to where she was, expecting her to back away. She stood her ground, and when he stopped a foot from her, he found her eyes only an inch or two lower than his own. He took a stance with his legs spread wide and settled fisted hands on his hips.

"Look, lady—"

"My name is Emaline. Emaline Winthrop. What's yours?"

"Conn Benton. Look, Emaline—"

"My friends call me Emmy."

"I'm not your friend," Conn said in a hard voice. "And I'll never be your friend," he added. "I hate Winthrops. I'll always hate Winthrops."

"And I hate Bentons," Emaline retorted. "What does that have to do with anything?"

Conn stood with his mouth open, but no sound came out. His brow furrowed. She was about the sassiest woman he'd ever met. She kept interrupting him, and she didn't look the least bit intimidated by his presence. But then he hadn't met many Winthrop women. Maybe they were all like this. "You hate Bentons?"

"Of course," she said in a cold voice. "They killed my father. And my younger brother."

"Then why did you come up with this corkbrained idea?"

"Because I don't want to see any more killing. I have one brother left. I want to see him live to a ripe old age. And I have aunts and uncles and cousins. I'd do anything to put an end to this awful feud. Even marry you!"

Conn didn't bother acknowledging the insult. She had reason to despise him. He was a Benton. Which was why he had to talk her out of this outrageous scheme.

"Have you thought about what we'll have to do?" Conn said, his eyes gliding over her intimately. "What the terms of this agreement involve?"

Her lashes lowered, and she turned red enough to

wash out her freckles. "I know I'll have to come to your bed," she said quietly.

The slightly raspy sound of her voice glided sensuously over him and sent shivers down his spine. "They'll want us to keep trying till you're pregnant," he said flatly.

"I know." It was almost a whisper. "I never wanted to bring a child into this world before," she confessed. "But to have a baby and know it can grow up in peace . . ."

Conn felt a band tighten around his chest. If there had been peace, he would never have lost Josie. "I don't want a wife. I don't want to marry again."

Her body jerked as though she had been slapped, and her startled blue eyes sought his face. "You were married before?"

"My wife was killed by Winthrops."

"I'm so sorry."

"Save your sympathy," he snarled. "This is impossible! I won't do it!" He turned, intending to march back down the aisle toward the door to the church, but she grasped his arm and tugged at him to stop. He whirled to brush her off, and she collided with him. He had thought her rather flat-chested, but definite breasts pillowed against his chest. Because she was so tall, their bodies fit together surprisingly well. Her hair, those riotous, flyaway curls, tickled his throat.

His body roused at the feel of her, and there was nothing he could do to stop it. He could only regret it. He didn't want to feel anything. He had been faithful to Josie's memory. He hadn't wanted a woman, and when he had needed one, he had forced himself to work until fatigue made the need go away. It was just that Emaline Winthrop had caught him by surprise. She felt soft and feminine. His body had recognized the shape of her and responded.

His arms had closed around her to keep them both from falling, and he noticed she was reed slim, where Josie had been rounder, her breasts and hips more womanly. And Josie's head had barely come to his shoulder. He could feel Emaline's breath on his cheek, warm and erratic. She was frightened, he realized. For a moment he considered lowering his lips to hers, punishing her with his mouth. But he didn't make war on women and children, and kissing her would be tantamount to an assault. He bore nothing but enmity for her and her people.

"Conn."

His body tensed at the raspy sound of his name on her lips. He looked down and felt a spiral of desire as she moistened her lips with her tongue. He had missed her mouth when he was cataloging her very few virtues. It was bowed on top, and the lower lip was full and enticing. It was a mouth made to be kissed.

But not by him.

He shoved her an arm's distance away. "This won't work," he said in a guttural voice. "What's to keep everyone from killing each other in spite of this arranged marriage?"

She looked up at him, and he found himself ensnared by her innocent blue eyes.

"Everyone will start sharing the water on the disputed land at once," Emaline explained. "Supposedly that's what we've been feuding over."

"You know that's not all there is to the feud," Conn insisted.

"Why else are we fighting?"

"For vengeance," Conn said. "To pay back—"

"Don't you see that has to end?" Emaline said. "The killing has to stop somewhere, sometime. Why not now? Why not with our marriage?"

"Confound it, woman, don't you see—"

"All I see is a stubborn man, intent on killing!"

"I lost my wife!"

"I lost my father and my brother! We've all lost family. What makes you different?"

Conn wanted to rant and rave, to cry out that he had loved with a passion beyond anything he had ever thought imaginable. That his life had ended when Josie died, and he had wished to go to the grave with her. That he didn't want to live without the only love he would ever know. That he didn't want to feel again, because pain was what he felt first and foremost.

"Say yes, Conn."

Her words were a plea, but there was nothing subservient in her posture. In fact, he would probably have to wrestle her to the ground to have any chance of bedding her. Except if she wanted the peace to last she would have to bear a child. His child. She would have to submit to him. Not someday, but on their wedding day, and every day after that until his seed began to grow inside her. The thought of touching her, of discovering whether her freckles truly covered every part of her body, heated his blood.

Guilt that he felt desire when he should be feeling hate made his voice harsh. "I want nothing to do with you outside of bed. I'll do what's necessary to make a child with you, but that's all. Is that understood?"

He thought she winced, but if she did, the expression was gone as quickly as it had come, leaving only disdain for him.

"If that's the way you want it," she said. "Are we agreed then?"

"I'll marry you," he agreed. "And God help us both."

2

THE NEXT TIME CONN AND EMALINE MET WAS Saturday, the last day of the truce. They stood at the front of the Bitter Creek Baptist Church waiting for the preacher to speak the words that would bind them together for life. Anxious Winthrops sat to the left of the center aisle, nervous Bentons to the right. Conn's and Emaline's mothers exchanged concerned glances as they watched their respective children take their vows.

Emaline had made her own wedding dress. She had bought the pale peach silk with money she had earned selling eggs and butter. It had been lying folded in her cedar chest for three years. She couldn't have explained why she had spent the money for such a luxury, but when the traveling peddler had shown her the silk, she had known she had to have it. There had been no reason to make it into a dress until now.

Emaline hadn't realized until she had slipped into the pale peach princess sheath this morning just how many dreams she had sewn into the garment. She knew Conn hated all Winthrops, but he was going to be her husband. She wanted him to be proud of her. She wanted him to admire her. She wanted to feel like a bride.

She had seen Conn's eyes widen in acknowledgement when he first spied her at the church, but he hadn't given her the compliments she yearned to hear. He had simply taken her hand in his and said,

"Are you sure you want to go through with this?"

"I'm sure," she had replied.

"Then let's get it over with."

He had turned her to face the preacher, and the wedding ceremony had begun. Now Emaline felt a burning sensation in her nose that warned of tears. She swallowed hard and closed her eyes. She didn't want to be this man's wife. She was frightened of the night to come, when he would thrust himself inside her to plant his seed. Her mother had warned her it would hurt the first time, but only that one time. All Emaline could think of was the virulent hatred she had seen in Conn's eyes whenever he spoke of the Winthrops. She had always considered herself a courageous woman, but at the moment she was terrified.

Because he was holding Emaline Winthrop's hand, Conn felt her tremble as she spoke her vows. He wondered what was going on inside that pretty head of hers. And she was pretty, Conn admitted, damn near beautiful. The peach silk softened the effect of her freckles, and made her eyes look even bluer. Somehow she had managed to subdue her hair with a scant piece of netting and some paper flowers, though there were a few unruly curls around her temples and at her nape that made him want to touch her.

He should have told her she was beautiful. Every bride deserved to hear those words from her future husband on their wedding day. But the words had caught in his throat as a vision rose before him of Josie dressed all in white, her perfectly straight, dark brown hair confined securely at her nape, her bosom rising from the square neck of her linen and lace wedding gown, her hazel eyes alight with love for him. His wedding to Emaline Winthrop was merely a means to an end. Together they would stop the feud that had killed the woman he loved and so many, many others. She wasn't a real bride.

"If there is anyone present who knows any reason why these two should not be joined, let him speak now, or forever hold his peace."

The preacher's words dragged Conn from his ruminations. He waited with bated breath to hear an objection. Surely there would be one. Surely someone would put a stop to this insanity. But no one did.

The preacher had just begun to speak again when Devlin Winthrop leaped up from his seat in the front pew. "I have an objection," he said.

Every eye in the room focused on him. Emaline grabbed the skirt of her dress and swung it around to face her brother. "Please, Dev, don't."

"I have to, Emmy." Devlin turned his steady gaze on Conn. "I want a promise from you that you won't hurt my sister."

Emaline felt Conn stiffen beside her. His expression remained bland, but she sensed he was furious.

"I don't know a way to broach a virgin that doesn't hurt," Conn said in a quiet voice.

Several women gasped as they realized what Conn had said.

Emaline felt the damnable blush growing in her cheeks, but she refused to hide her face. It was no bad thing to be a virgin on one's wedding day.

"You know that's not what I mean," Devlin said, his own face flushed with anger and embarrassment.

"What *do* you mean?" Conn asked in a deadly voice.

"It's no secret my sister hates you and your kind."

Conn's face bleached white, but he said nothing as Devlin continued. "And you hate her, along with the rest of the Winthrops. I want your promise that you won't punish her for what others have done to you and yours. Otherwise, this wedding ends here."

Emaline had never been more proud of her brother. Or more frightened for him. Conn almost vibrated with animosity. She could feel the waves of tension rolling off him. Fortunately, all guns had been left outside the church. She let herself glance at Conn from the corner of her eye. The only outward evidence of his tremendous anger was a small muscle ticking in his cheek where his jaws must be clamped.

"You have my promise," he said from between clenched teeth. "Anything else?"

Emaline met Devlin's worried gaze. She knew he wanted to save her from her fate, but there was no help to be had. Someone had to marry Conn Benton.

Devlin searched Conn's dark eyes one last time, seeking reassurance. He must have found it because he said, "No. That's all."

"Well, then," the preacher said. "If that's settled, let us proceed."

Conn grasped Emaline's hand again, hard enough to hurt. With one look from her he loosened his grasp, but he didn't let go. Emaline had the feeling she had been claimed, and that Conn would kill the next man who tried to take her from him. It wasn't a bad feeling to have on one's wedding day.

Conn took a long, quiet breath and let it out as the preacher continued his incantations. He couldn't explain the rage he had felt when Emaline's brother challenged his right to marry her. But he wasn't sure whether he had been enraged at Devlin's suggestion that he would use his strength against a woman or whether he truly felt possessive of Emaline Winthrop. That seemed impossible, but the nagging feeling wouldn't leave him that she had given herself to him when she had put her hand in his at the beginning of the ceremony.

It wouldn't be long now before Emaline was his wife. The preacher was getting to the vows Conn remembered from his first wedding. "Do you take this woman . . ."

Conn had trouble concentrating on the ceremony. He couldn't be pledging these things before God. *To love and to cherish?* Everyone present knew what a mockery that was. But when the preacher demanded an answer from him, he dutifully replied, "I do."

Emaline tried not to squirm when Conn said, "I do," but a trickle of sweat was stealing down between her breasts. It made a wonderful distraction as the preacher demanded her promise *to honor and obey* her husband. What a travesty! How could she honor any Benton much less obey him? But when the preacher asked for her response, she whispered an obedient "I do."

Before Emaline was ready, the preacher was saying, "I now pronounce you man and wife." There was a slight pause before he said, "You may kiss the bride, Mr. Benton."

Emaline felt breathless. Would he dare? She raised her eyes to meet Conn's dark-eyed gaze. What was expected of them? What would do the most to help ensure the peace? She saw the question in Conn's eyes.

Emaline nodded slightly. Her eyes fell closed as his mouth lowered. His lips were firm as he pressed them fleetingly against hers. She thought the kiss was over when his arms suddenly tightened around her, and his mouth claimed hers again.

There was nothing simple about the second kiss. It was full of anger and arrogance. And need. His tongue traced the seam of her lips, and when she gasped for air it slid inside. Emaline was totally unprepared for the sensations evoked by the warmth and wetness of his invasion.

Suddenly the kiss was over. When Emaline opened her eyes, Conn was staring out at the Benton side of the church with a smug grin on his face. All hail the conquering hero, it said.

Emaline had never felt more furious in her life. Or more humiliated. So Conn thought she could be dominated by a kiss, did he? Well, she would show him!

She kept her voice pitched low as she said, "Conn, darling?"

He was so shocked by the *darling* that he turned completely around to face her. She slipped her arms around his neck, pressed her body against his, and raised herself on tiptoes to reach his mouth. He was too surprised to protest as her lips pressed against his. Her mouth curved in a satisfied smile as she heard cheering from the Winthrop side of the church.

She should have known Conn wouldn't play fair.

Before she could retreat, he had his tongue in her mouth again. She gasped at the streak of excitement that ran from her belly upward as he grabbed her by the waist and brought their bodies together.

There was hooting now from both sides of the church and a few raucous hollers.

"Give up?" Conn murmured against her lips.

"Never!" Emaline replied.

Their mothers came to the rescue.

"Conn, dear, please let me welcome my new daughter," Hester said.

"And I want to meet my new son," said Emaline's mother, Clara. It was easy to see where Emaline and Devlin had gotten their height and features. Clara Winthrop was barely an inch shorter than her son, yet she possessed a certain grace that kept her from seeming as tall as she was. She had the same auburn hair as Devlin and Emaline's blue eyes.

The two combatants were forced to disengage. Emaline turned to Mrs. Benton. Conn turned to Mrs. Winthrop. Each hugged their respective mothers-in-law. Then they turned and marched down the aisle together as the organ played a triumphant tune.

A reception was held for the bride and groom at the home of Archer Tubbston, the town banker. Besides the two families, several interested townspeople—merchants and such—had also attended the wedding, sitting in the very back pews. Archer

Tubbston was among them. When he had heard about the wedding, he had insisted on hosting the reception. "After all," he had said, "it isn't every day a feud ends."

Emaline didn't see why Mr. Tubbston was so glad to see the feud ended. The bank had made a fortune foreclosing on properties when a rancher was killed and the surviving widow couldn't meet the mortgage payments. But she supposed everyone would be glad to know the streets were safe to walk again. There had been some incidents over the years in which innocent people—neither Bentons nor Winthrops—had been hurt. The cattle stampede through Bitter Creek that had killed Rufus Winthrop, Sissy Benton, and Bethanne Fleet was just one example.

Neither Bentons nor Winthrops would admit to firing the first shot that had started the stampede. It had simply been a case of one of the numerous altercations between warring factions getting out of hand. Clearly, both sides were to blame. The senseless feud had caused three senseless deaths. No wonder Bethanne's father was inconsolable, Emaline thought.

The punch at the reception was nonalcoholic, and though there were musicians, there was no dancing. At least, not at first. One of the differences between Winthrops and Bentons was how strictly they followed Baptist tenets. Winthrops drank but didn't dance. Bentons danced but didn't drink.

Emaline should have suspected that Conn would ask his bride to dance. As soon as the violins began to play a waltz, he turned to her and said, "Shall we dance?"

She was sure he expected her to refuse, thereby creating a confrontation. She was equally determined to avoid an altercation at all costs. The solution was obvious. She simply said, "I don't know how."

"It's easy. I'll teach you," Conn replied.

He didn't offer her a choice in the matter. Emaline tensed as Conn's hand slid around her waist. It appeared there was no avoiding the situation. She laid her hand in his palm and allowed him to move her in time to the music.

"Just count one-two-three, one-two-three," Conn instructed as he swung her in ever-widening circles around the Tubbston's parlor.

Emaline felt as if she were flying. She had never realized how much fun it was to dance, otherwise she would surely have sinned much sooner. She ignored her brother's glare as she whirled by him. It was past time the Winthrops learned to be a bit more tolerant of the Bentons. Dancing was perfectly harmless.

Then she realized that Conn had closed the space between them until no more than an inch separated them. She felt his breath against her cheek, felt the heat of him along the entire length of her body, which was responding in strange and wonderful ways. No wonder the preacher had called dancing "a fornication of the spirit." She had never been so aware of a man as she was of Conn. It was like making love standing up fully clothed in a roomful of people!

When the dance ended, Emaline tore herself free and walked quickly toward an empty corner of the room. Conn followed her.

"What's wrong?" he asked.

"Nothing. I've never danced before, that's all. I had no idea . . ."

"It could be so much fun?" Conn finished.

"It could feel so sinful!" Emaline snapped back.

"Could feel so sinfully good, you mean."

"Everything we do together from now on will be subject to scrutiny," Emaline said, keeping her voice low. "I would simply prefer not to give my friends and family any more reason to talk about us than they already have."

"I see."

Conn wondered, not for the first time, what it would be like to have Emaline Winthrop beneath him in bed. He had been surprised by her willingness to dance, pleased by how quickly she had caught the rhythm of the waltz, and appalled by how much he had wanted to feel her body moving in concert with his.

He had loved dancing with Josie, but the differences in their heights had made it more difficult to stay in step. Emaline had moved with him as though they had been dancing together for years. It had been an unsettling experience, but one that he realized he was more than willing to repeat. But perhaps Emaline was right. There was no sense making a spectacle of themselves.

"All right. If you don't want to dance, perhaps we should find somewhere to sit and have something to eat."

Conn took Emaline's elbow to lead her toward the immense tables of food that had been set out. It was then he noticed Devlin Winthrop dancing . . . with Conn's own widowed sister-in-law.

Conn stopped dead in his tracks, his hold on Emaline's arm necessarily bringing her to a halt as well. She looked up at him, then followed the direction of his gaze to the dance floor. She couldn't have been more shocked. Her brother, Devlin, was dancing! She hadn't even suspected he knew how. Even more shocking was the fact he was dancing with a Benton woman.

Emaline was immediately aware of the hush that had fallen in the Tubbstons' parlor. It was all well and good for Emaline and Conn to dance. They were setting an example for the future. But it seemed the future was collapsing in on them. Emaline wondered what had possessed Devlin to approach the woman. And why she had accepted his offer to dance.

Because Emaline was watching the couple closely,

she saw something that made her blood run cold. She recognized the look on the woman's face, because she had experienced the same feeling with Conn. Carnal awareness arced between her brother and the Benton woman. They never took their eyes off each other, and their bodies seemed to hum with sensual energy.

Because she was just learning to recognize the signs herself, it took Emaline a moment to realize that Conn saw the same thing she did. Before she could stop him, he stalked past her, headed for the dance floor. Emaline hurried to catch up with him.

She used those few moments to take the Benton woman's measure. She was petite, with dark brown hair and brown eyes. She was also slender, but with the full bosom and hips that Emaline lacked. Devlin's head was bent over to listen as the woman spoke to him. There was a smile on her brother's lips.

Fortunately, the dance was just ending, so as far as the rest of the guests were concerned, it appeared that Conn and Emaline were merely greeting the other couple.

Before Conn could say a word, Emaline slipped her arm through his and said, "I didn't know you two were acquainted." Emaline faced the Benton woman. "We haven't met. I'm Emaline Win—Benton," she finished.

"I'm Melody Benton."

"My brother Andrew's widow," Conn supplied in a steely voice. He fixed a glare on Devlin. "I'm warning you now to stay away from my sister-in-law."

"Melody might have something to say about that," Devlin replied.

"She doesn't know Winthrops like I do," Conn said.

"Meaning what?" Devlin challenged.

"Please, Dev," Melody said in a quiet voice, laying

her hand on Devlin's sleeve. "Remember your promise."

The fact that Melody had used Devlin's nickname gave Emaline pause. She stared entranced as her brother laid a gentle hand over Melody's. Promise? What promise? Hadn't the two of them just met? Obviously not. But when had their romance begun, and how? Emaline wanted to get Devlin alone to question him.

"All right, Melody. I won't cause any trouble," Devlin said. He turned to Conn. "I don't want to fight with you."

"Then let go of my brother's wife."

Conn had given his order in a voice that could be heard around the room. Emaline saw the subtle shifting as Winthrops and Bentons aligned themselves on opposite sides. The truce was in danger of exploding into violence right here and now. If she'd had a skillet handy she would have used it on Conn. How could he endanger the truce now!

Emaline saw the way Devlin's fist clenched, saw Melody's face turn white, and knew she had to find a way to stop this altercation before it got started. Melody beat her to it.

"Andrew is dead, Conn. He has been for five years. I'm a grown woman. I can take care of myself."

"As guardian of my brother's children, I think I have some say—"

"You have nothing to say in this," Devlin interrupted.

"The hell I don't!"

"Dev! Conn!" Emaline put herself physically between the two men. "In case you've both forgotten, this is my wedding day. I won't have my husband and my brother coming to blows. Is that understood?" She fixed each of them with a warning glare.

Emaline noticed the way Melody's hand tightened on Devlin's arm. Her own hand tightened on Conn's sleeve. At that moment the musicians began to play another waltz.

Emaline turned to face her husband. "Shall we dance, Conn?"

Conn hesitated a moment, until Devlin led Melody off the dance floor, then he swept Emaline into his arms.

Emaline felt a palpable easing of tension in the parlor. Bentons and Winthrops mingled again and began to talk in low tones. The danger had passed.

Emaline recognized Conn's anger in the tautness of his shoulder where her hand rested. It was better, she believed, to confront the problem than to ignore it so she said, "How long do you think they've known each other?"

Conn let out a gusty sigh. "Hell if I know. But it's plain as a red barn they didn't just meet today."

"I always wondered why Dev never married," Emaline murmured. "Now I understand. How awful it must have been for them, to be in love yet not free to be together."

"Oh, they've been together. I'd lay odds on that," Conn said with a snarl of disgust.

Emaline realized suddenly the cause of all Dev's spluttering when she had first suggested a Winthrop marry a Benton. He must have wanted to shout that he and Melody would be a better couple to marry under the circumstances. Obviously, it would have been difficult to suggest such a thing when he supposedly didn't even know her. Nor could he speak for Melody without having a chance to ask her whether it was what she wanted. And things had been settled on the spot.

Emaline felt a sharp pang of regret. Her wedding to Conn might not have been necessary. On the other hand, she could see a multitude of problems that would have arisen if Dev and Melody had admitted to their clandestine relationship. Accusations and admonitions such as the ones Conn had hurled might have been made on both sides. It was better this way, she concluded. Besides, it was too late to change anything now. She was already married to Conn.

"To have to meet in secret can't have been what either of them wanted," Emaline said, raising her eyes to meet Conn's. "If I were in love—"

She cut herself off. Love wasn't any part of her arrangement with Conn Benton. Nor did it seem he had any sympathy for her brother and his sister-in-law. His hate and distrust of Bentons had been growing for years. Saying words before a preacher hadn't done a thing to ease his animosity. Emaline bit her lip to hold back the cry of despair that sought voice. She had embarked on a fool's errand. She would be lucky if she survived it whole.

Someone had secretly added liquor to the punch, and the reception gradually became rowdy. There were minor fracases, which either Jeremiah or Horace managed to quell.

Emaline looked for John Fleet at the reception, but couldn't find him. She took advantage of a moment when Conn was involved in drinking toasts with his friends and family to escape the noise and commotion. She was subjected to a few stares from passersby, which she ignored as she made her way down Main Street, but she didn't return to the reception. She needed to be alone for a little while.

Emaline hadn't realized herself where she was going until she found herself at the door to the blacksmith's shop. Fleet shouldn't have been there, since it was nearly dusk. To her surprise, he was working at the forge. Sweat glistened on his hairy torso, which was bare except for a worn leather apron. A red bandanna caught the rivulets of perspiration that ran down his neck.

Without a thought to what damage the pervasive soot or an errant spark could do to her wedding dress, she entered the darkened interior of the shop.

She stared, fascinated, as the bellows heated the embers. A horseshoe lay in the fire, turning a glowing red from the heat. Fleet held the shoe with a set of tongs, and as she watched he withdrew it from the fire and shaped it with deafening blows from a heavy hammer.

She wasn't sure how long she had been standing there when he finally noticed her. He wasn't happy to see her.

"What do you want now?" he demanded.

Emaline swallowed hard. "I suppose you know I married Conn Benton today."

"Yeah. So what?"

"The feud is over now," Emaline said. "Or it will be soon," she hurried to amend. A baby had to be born first.

"Am I supposed to be happy about that?"

"Well, yes," Emaline said. "It will mean an end to the killing."

He looked at her with sad eyes and spoke in a bitter voice. "It comes too late. My daughter is dead."

He plunged the horseshoe back into the fire and ignored her as though she wasn't even there. Emaline backed out of the shop and ran down the back alleys until she reached the Tubbstons' house, breathless and trembling. She merged with the crowd that had spread out through the back door as though she had never been gone.

It wasn't for nothing, she thought. *It may be too late for Bethanne, but not for a lot of others.*

Emaline was still a little breathless, though her trembling had stopped, when it was time for the bride and groom to head for home. Conn lifted her into a spring wagon he had brought to take her to his ranch. Sometime during the reception, the wagon had been decorated with ribbons and paper bunting. Everyone followed in wagons and carriages and on horseback. They all had an interest in making sure this marriage was consummated.

Meanwhile Emaline's virginal fears grew to monstrous proportions. It was bad enough to be facing a stranger in bed. It was a hundred times worse knowing he cared little or nothing for her feelings. This was not what she had envisioned when she thought of her wedding night. Emaline suddenly wasn't sure she could go through with it.

It was nearly dark by the time they arrived at Conn's ranch house. It was a one-story dogtrot home common to this part of Texas, with a central hallway running down the middle and rooms on either side. Emaline noticed the wood-frame structure had a fresh coat of white paint.

Conn's hands were warm through her dress as he lifted her down from the wagon seat. She was horribly aware of the blush on her face as he hefted her into his arms—what a feat that would have been for most men!—and carried her over the threshold of his home.

He kicked the door closed behind them before setting her back on her feet. She was aware of the raucous catcalls and lascivious jeers just beyond the door. Tears welled in her eyes, and she wasn't sure what to do about them. One spilled before she could blink it back.

"Well," Conn said.

That was all. Not, *Welcome to my home.* Just, *Well.*

Emaline couldn't blame him. She felt overwhelmed herself. How had they let themselves get talked into this?

"What shall we do now?" Conn said at last.

Emaline couldn't look at him. "I don't know."

"We have to—"

"Please," Emaline interrupted. "I know what I've agreed to do. Can't we wait? Just a little while?"

"It'll only get harder," Conn said.

"I can't do it," Emaline said quietly. "Not like this. I don't even know you."

"Fine," Conn said, his voice no less quiet or agitated than hers. "I'll go out there and tell them we've changed our minds."

He had his hand on the doorknob when Emaline spoke.

"All right. You win."

He turned a bleak look on her. "No, Emaline," he said, using her name for the first time, "I think we've both lost."

They stood frozen in a tableau of tragedy, of love lost and love uncelebrated. Until at last Conn reached out a hand toward her. "Let's go to bed, Emaline."

She took the two steps necessary to place her palm in his and looked up at him with somber eyes. "Please be gentle, Conn."

His hand clasped hers and gently squeezed. "I'll do my best."

Conn led Emaline to his bedroom door and left her there. "I'll be back in a little while," he said.

Emaline closed the door. It was already dusk, and there was barely enough light to see what she was doing. She noted the large four-poster bed and found the dry sink with a pitcher and bowl and a wardrobe where Conn must keep his clothing. There was also a long low cedar chest—his former wife's hope chest?—at the foot of the bed. She could feel the rag rug beneath her feet and see a slight shine on the hardwood floors in the rest of the room.

Emaline was afraid to light a lamp, knowing the wild crowd outside would realize where she was and hoot and howl all the louder. So she undressed in the dark, letting her precious wedding dress drop to the floor at her feet and then stepping out of it. It didn't take long to strip down to her chemise and pantalets. She had delivered a carpetbag of clothing to Conn's house the previous day, and it was beside the chest at the foot of the bed.

She opened it and quickly pulled out a chambray wrapper that would cover her from neck to ankles. She debated whether to leave on her chemise and pantalets, but decided it was better to take them off. If Conn planned to undress her, she didn't want to prolong the agony. She stripped down and slid the nightgown over her head. It was an old garment, and the fabric had been worn soft and smooth.

Emaline turned back the covers and slid underneath them. She sat upright, her back braced against the pillow at the head of the bed, and waited for Conn to appear.

He was nothing more than a shadow when he entered the room, it was so dark, but she could see enough to know he was wearing only his long johns. He quickly slipped under the covers to lie beside her.

"You could have lit a candle," he said.

"You know why I didn't," she retorted. "Some of the ribald things they're yelling aren't fit—" Emaline cut herself off. There was no sense angering him, especially not now.

The noise from outside of a shivaree in full swing—a serenade in pots and pans to the newly married couple by both their families—was the only sound in the silent room.

At last Conn sighed. "Emaline, I don't know a way..." He paused and started again. "I have to..."

"I know," she said. He had made his feelings clear at church. There was no way he knew to prevent a virgin's pain. Emaline inched down until she was lying flat in the bed. "Just get it over with, Conn. Please."

Conn didn't feel in the least aroused. It had occurred to him once before that he might not be able to perform on cue, but he figured things weren't going to get any better if he laid here thinking about it. So he reached over and grabbed a handful of her gown and began to move it out of his way.

He could feel Emaline's rigidity as he said, "Lift your hips." She moved so he could shove the night-gown up. He felt himself becoming aroused as his hand brushed the softness of her skin. It seemed his curiosity about her freckles wasn't going to be as-suaged, at least not tonight. The room was pitch black. He was feeling his way through what had to be done.

He eased himself onto her, bracing most of his weight on his elbows. "Spread your legs, Emaline," he murmured against her cheek. Conn realized his body was ready, even if his mind still shied from what was before him. At least he would be able to finish without entirely losing his dignity.

Emaline blessed the darkness that hid her fear and embarrassment. She grasped Conn's shoulders. "Conn. Please." She wouldn't beg him not to hurt her. She had too much pride for that. But it was frightening to be so vulnerable to him. She shivered as his hand slid down her belly. "Conn?"

"Lie still, Emaline. I just want to see . . ." His voice drifted away as his hand slid between her thighs.

Emaline pressed her legs tightly together. "What are you doing?" she demanded.

"Emaline," he said patiently, "I'm doing what a husband does with his wife."

"Oh." She forced herself to relax, allowed her legs to ease open enough to allow Conn's hand free ac-cess.

She gasped as he cupped her, then slowly parted the folds and tried to slide a finger inside her.

"That hurts, Conn," she said in a ragged voice.

His finger withdrew. "You're as dry as a bone," he said in disgust.

Emaline lay still. "Is that bad?"

"Bad enough," he admitted.

"I . . ." She swallowed over the painful lump in her throat. "Is there something I should do?"

Conn had two choices. He could take her now and get it over with, or he could spend some time arousing her first. He wanted this over with, but it was going to be hard enough for her without making it any worse.

"There are things I can do, Emaline, to make this easier."

"Such as?" she ventured cautiously.

"Your body isn't ready for mine. I have to . . . to touch you."

"Oh."

"I can do what's necessary to help your body accommodate mine better. Or I can just get it over with right now," Conn said. "The choice is yours."

Emaline thought about it a moment. "If there's a way to make it easier . . . I'd rather you do that."

"Let's get rid of this nightgown, shall we?" Conn said.

He was already tugging it up over her head as he spoke, not really giving Emaline the option to refuse. A moment later she was naked. She had sat up as he tugged off the gown, and Conn pressed her shoulder to lower her back to the pillow. It took her a few moments to realize he was stripping himself, as well. Lord, she was grateful for the dark!

"Relax, Emaline," he instructed. "I'll do all the work."

Since she had never planned to marry, she had never been courted. Not that she hadn't been kissed when she was younger, thirteen or fourteen. But those kisses had been nothing like the kisses Conn placed on her body now. And she was totally unprepared for the feelings Conn aroused as his callused fingertips caressed her. She was soon writhing beneath him. "Conn," she said desperately, "what are you doing? I feel . . . I can't . . ."

Conn told himself he was only doing as much as

was necessary to prevent hurting his wife any more than he had to when he broached her. But she was so responsive! Her back arched as his hands cupped her breasts—a bare handful. And she groaned, a wrenching guttural sound, as his lips closed on a nipple. He suckled and her hips rose to search out his own.

He didn't kiss her on the mouth. That would have made more of this than it truly was. He had a job to do, that was all. He wasn't making love to her, he was merely coupling with her.

Nevertheless, he couldn't resist touching her. Her skin was so incredibly soft. He tried to imagine the sight of her freckles beneath his fingertips, but couldn't. His hand slid down her hip, across a flat stomach and into a nest of curls, which he suddenly realized must be as red as her hair.

That was better. She was wet now. He could do what had to be done.

But he wasn't willing yet to stop touching her. She couldn't know that what he did now wasn't strictly necessary. He indulged his need to feel her flesh beneath his fingertips. His hand slid up to grip her waist, then followed the outline of her slender hip back down her thigh all the way to her knee. Then he caressed his way back up the inside of her leg to the folds that he parted for a more intimate invasion. He heard Emaline catch her breath as his finger intruded. But the way was slick now, and his finger slid easily inside.

Until he reached the proof of her virginity.

It reminded him of what he was supposed to do. Broach her. Get her with child.

It was time to get on with business.

Emaline had never felt more strange. She was in a euphoric state that made time stand still. She knew it couldn't be long now. She had recognized the difference when Conn touched her. "Conn?" she questioned.

"Lie still, Emaline. I'll try not to hurt you any more than I have to."

She braced her hands on his arms. The muscles were hard, and she realized suddenly how strong he must be. She could not stop him, not if he didn't want to be stopped. She was totally at his mercy.

Conn pushed her legs farther apart with his knees. His body was slick with a sheen of sweat. He wanted her. His body ached with wanting. It had been a long time, and his heart pounded. He tried to go slow, to enter her a little at a time, but he felt her tensing and realized the longer she had to anticipate the moment the worse it was going to be.

He thrust hard and felt the membrane give way at the same instant that she gave a sharp cry of pain.

He held himself perfectly still. "It's done now, Emaline. The painful part is over."

There was a moment of silence before she said in a small voice, "But you're not finished, are you?"

He felt his smile and was glad she couldn't see it. "No. I'm not finished yet. There is the seed to plant."

"Oh."

He began to move slightly, feeling the exquisite friction of their bodies as he lifted himself away from her and then thrust again. He felt her lift her hips to meet him and almost groaned aloud. It was a matter of embarrassingly few moments before he spilled his seed.

He rolled away, releasing his hold on her. He lay on his back with an arm across his eyes. His breathing was ragged. It had felt good. Too good. He wanted her again already, and he knew that was impossible.

The last thing he heard before he fell asleep was the sound of his new wife sobbing quietly against her pillow.

3

EMALINE WAS CRYING WITH RELIEF AND REGRET, but there was no way she could have told Conn that, even if he had asked. Which he didn't. The reason for her relief was obvious. The ordeal she had so feared was over. She had managed to survive their first coupling, and though it had hurt, she sensed the pain wasn't as bad as it would have been if Conn hadn't taken the time to prepare her first. She would always be grateful to him for that kindness.

It was the regret that kept her awake long past the time when Conn's steady breathing told her he was asleep. She was glad he had fallen asleep so quickly, leaving her alone to contemplate the past few hours of her life. Only, her thoughts were so confused that perhaps it would have been better if she wasn't doing any thinking. Because all she could imagine was what might have been. If there had been no feud. If a handsome beau had courted her. If she had married a man who loved her.

She heard the shivaree winding down until at last all the revelers were gone. She must have fallen asleep, for she woke as the first rays of dawn lightened the room.

It seemed strange to have someone else in bed with her. She was alarmed at first because she and Conn were lying nose to nose, their foreheads nearly touching. She gradually inched her way back until she could observe him sleeping. His face had a stub-

334

ble of dark beard, and she noticed for the first time
how long and full his lashes were against his cheeks.
There was a tiny scar that cut through one eyebrow,
and she could see a faint tan line where his Stetson
kept the sun off his forehead.

His hair looked silky. When she reached out
slowly, carefully, to touch it, he awoke. She jerked
her hand back and lowered her lids so he couldn't
see her eyes.

"Good morning," he said in a sleep-husky voice.
"Did you sleep well?"

"Well enough," she said in a more than normally
raspy voice. She was watching Conn, so she saw the
moment when he remembered who she was, and
who he was.

Enemies in bed together. Enemies forced to pretend that everything was normal. Enemies forced to
spend their lives together.

The amiability in his voice was gone when he
asked, "What are the chances of getting some breakfast?"

Breakfast? They were lying naked in bed together,
and his mind was on breakfast? She would have
grinned if the situation wasn't so dire. Emaline had
often chided her brother for thinking often and only
of his stomach, but it appeared it was a trait common to the male sex. "I'll be glad to fix you something. That is, if you'll give me a moment to dress."

Emaline waited for him to realize she wanted him
to leave the room. He was a perceptive man. What
she didn't count on was that he would have no modesty himself. He simply shoved the covers aside and
stood, completely naked, and stretched.

She knew she shouldn't look, but once she glanced
toward Conn, she couldn't take her eyes off him. In
the daylight he was a magnificent creature of bone
and sinew, tall and lean without an ounce of extra
flesh. The languid stretch reminded her of a sleek
cat, supremely confident and at ease. He crossed to

the wardrobe and drew out another set of long johns, which he quickly donned. Minutes later he was completely dressed, right down to his boots.

"I'll go light a fire in the stove and put on the coffeepot," he said. "I usually shave after breakfast, unless that's a problem for you."

"No problem." Emaline wouldn't have said she minded even if she did. She wasn't about to ask any favors of Conn. Once he was gone, she scrambled out of bed and hurried over to the pitcher she had noted last night on the dry sink to see if there was water to wash herself. There was, and she quickly finished her ablutions and dressed in another outfit from her carpetbag. The rest of her belongings were to be delivered to Conn's ranch today.

Emaline took one look at the smear of blood on the sheets and quickly stripped them. She usually did laundry on Monday, but unless Conn had extra sheets, she was going to have to do the washing today.

Conn was amazed at how soon Emaline appeared in the bedroom doorway dressed in a calico skirt and a long-sleeved cotton shirtwaist that buttoned all the way up to the round-necked collar. There was nothing the least bit enticing about what she was wearing, yet his heart thumped once when he laid eyes on her, and his groin tightened at the pleasurable memory of what it felt like to be inside her. It wasn't going to be as easy to ignore his new wife as he had hoped.

Emaline took a deep breath. "The coffee smells good." She stood in the small kitchen and realized she didn't know where anything was. And she had promised to make breakfast. She wasn't sure whether to start rummaging through cupboards or simply join him at the table.

Thankfully, Conn seemed to realize her problem. He stood and began rummaging through the cupboards himself. "Pots and pans are stored here," he said, pulling out a skillet and dropping it on top of the stove. "Dishes and silverware are in the sideboard. Cups are hung there, too. Eggs are in the wire basket in the icebox, along with the milk. Bacon hangs in the pantry along with preserves and canned goods and such like."

Conn had been collecting items as he showed her where they were, so that soon Emaline had everything she needed to make eggs and bacon. "If you want biscuits, you're going to have to show me where to find flour, salt, lard and baking soda," she said.

"Don't have time to wait for anything to bake this morning," he said. "Have to get started right away on some fence mending. Just eggs and bacon will be fine."

Emaline became increasingly flustered as Conn watched her with an intent stare while she worked. "How do you like your eggs?" she asked as she cut strips of bacon and laid them in the skillet.

"Fried with the yellow soft," he said. "And I like my bacon crisp."

Emaline must have cooked a thousand eggs in her life, but this morning she managed to break the yolks. The three eggs were as hard as shoe leather by the time she set them in front of Conn. Worse, in her attempt to get the bacon crisp, she had burned it nearly black. She knew nothing about her husband, whether he had a temper, whether he was tolerant, whether he could become violent. It was with some trepidation that she set the plate in front of him.

"I'm sorry, Conn. I'm a good cook. I don't know what went wrong this morning."

She expected him to gripe, but to her surprise he simply ate the hardened eggs and the blackened bacon.

"I expect you'll get better," he said through a mouthful of food.

Emaline wasn't sure whether his comment was intended as encouragement or warning.

"Actually, this breakfast reminds me of the first meal Josie made for me. We were so busy kissing that she forgot all about—" Conn cut himself off.

Emaline's face paled. So that was her name . . . Josie. The last thing she wanted was for Conn to compare her to his dead wife. She especially didn't want to be reminded how much in love with her he had been. Conn must have realized his mistake, because he didn't say another word until he had finished eating.

"I've got some chores to do in the barn before I leave. I'll eat chow with the hands at noon and be back around sundown. Make yourself to home."

"You haven't shaved," she reminded him.

"Sometimes I don't," he admitted as he closed the kitchen door behind him and headed for the barn.

He didn't kiss her as he left for the day. He didn't even look at her.

Emaline sat frozen in her chair at the trestle table that dominated the kitchen. Everywhere she turned there were reminders of Conn's first wife. The lace-edged yellow curtains in the kitchen window. Flowers embroidered on a sampler that had been framed and hung on the wall. The homemade rag rug in front of the sink. The vase in the center of the table that must have once held flowers. The tiger-coated cat that sat patiently by a bowl in the corner, waiting for it to be filled with leftover milk from breakfast.

Emaline jumped up and ran into the parlor. It held a piano covered with a lacy doily and two carved wooden candlesticks with the candles half burned down. The horsehair sofa was barely worn, but doilies covered the arms. She searched the room and found what she was looking for: a brass-framed daguerreotype of the loving couple on the mantel above the brick fireplace.

Conn looked so young! As she had suspected, Josie was more than pretty: she was beautiful. There wasn't a wayward curl or a freckle on her. Emaline set the photograph back where she had found it and hurried to the bedroom she had shared with Conn the previous night. She yanked up the lid of the chest at the foot of the bed and gave a cry of despair.

It was filled with baby clothes.

Emaline sank to the floor beside the chest. Conn hadn't just loved Josie, they were apparently planning to have a child together when her life was cut short.

How awful it must be for Conn, how awful it was for both of them, to be trying to have a child now, not because they wanted one, but to end a years'-long feud.

Emaline reached into the chest and took out one of the cotton sacques Josie Benton had sewn. It was so tiny! She pulled out a small crocheted cap and booties. Another sacque. And diapers, dozens of diapers. At the bottom she found a linen and lace dress. It had to be Josie's wedding dress. She dropped it as though it had burned her.

Emaline laid her head on her arms on the edge of the chest and wept. It was all well and good to decide upon a noble sacrifice, but the reality of the situation was daunting. She tried to imagine what her future with Conn would be like, but the picture was grim.

It wasn't just that they were enemies. She assumed that with time they would become familiar with each other, and the strain she had felt this morning would eventually dissipate. She hadn't let herself consider what it would be like if they never became more than strangers. Although she couldn't imagine how they could remain strangers with the intimacy they were forced to endure.

Emaline tried not to resent the evidence of another woman in this house. But she was only human. This was *her* home now. Yet the ghost of Josie Benton, a

woman her husband had obviously loved, still re-
sided here. Not that she wanted Conn to love her.
She didn't care if he hated her until the day she died.
But she refused to live the rest of her life in another
woman's shadow.

Emaline's head rose from her hands until her chin
was angled pugnaciously. Conn had told her to
make herself at home. Well, that was just what she
would do! That meant putting her own imprint on
the house. And removing every trace of Josie Benton.

Conn spent most of the morning distracted by
memories of the night just past. He remembered
how vehemently he had fought against marriage to
a Winthrop. He remembered how shocked he had
been at Emaline's height and appearance the day he
met her. And he remembered making love to her last
night.

He tried not to compare it to his wedding night
with Josie, but that was impossible. It was painful to
admit that he had been a better husband to Emaline
than to Josie. Of course, the years he'd spent with
Josie had taught him how to treat a woman in bed.
But it was more than that. Quite simply, the two
women were different.

He had never thought much about it, but he had
expected Emaline to be just like Josie, to act and react
like her. But she wasn't Josie, and her responses had
made him respond differently to her. His sister-in-
law, Melody, had explained a similar phenomenon
to him with regard to her two sons.

When Timmy had come along, she had expected
him to be just like James. But the two boys were
completely different, she had said, one sleeping
through the night, the other up at odd hours. One
liked peas, the other didn't. One had hazel eyes, the
other brown. It didn't make one more lovable than
the other. It just made them different.

That was what he had discovered with Emaline.

She wasn't Josie. She was a separate person, with feelings and hopes and dreams that were nothing like his first wife's. Emaline was not more or less lovable. Just different.

By mid-morning Emaline had gathered up every bit of evidence that another woman had ever occupied the house and had piled it on the kitchen table. She opened the door to the stove, prepared to throw in the embroidered sampler that had adorned the kitchen wall.

But she couldn't do it.

She stared at the flames, wondering what on Earth had come over her. Even if she burned everything in the house, it wasn't going to erase the memories of Josie Benton that Conn carried in his mind and heart. And why was she so anxious to have Conn forget Josie, anyway? Theirs was strictly a marriage of convenience. Nothing more was necessary than that they tolerate each other long enough to produce a child.

Emaline wanted more than that. She wanted her husband to like her. Oh, fiddle. She wanted her husband to love her. Only, she had this slight problem. Conn was a Benton. And Bentons had always hated Winthrops.

But the feud was over. Or would be as soon as she birthed a child to inherit the disputed land. If the peace was to continue, it was necessary for everyone to forgive and forget past transgressions. She had lived her whole life hating Bentons, but that had to cease. Why not begin her forgiveness with Conn?

Conn was the man who would be the father of her children. He was the man who would take her to his bed for all the years to come. She found it impossible to face the thought of how lonely her life would be if she and Conn never learned to care for each other.

And she wasn't going to win Conn's heart by destroying everything that had to do with Josie. She would have to find another way to supplant the memories of his first wife. But she had no idea how a woman made a man fall in love with her. Especially when it was necessary for him to stop hating her first.

Emaline carefully replaced everything she had removed, including the tiny, delicate sacques and the christening gown she had found in the cedar chest at the foot of the four-poster.

By the time Devlin arrived with her things, she was in the middle of scrubbing floors and washing sheets. She was perfectly willing to stop what she was doing to ask Devlin about his relationship with Melody Benton, but Devlin refused to be interrogated.

"Let it be, Emmy," he said. "Melody and I have to work things out for ourselves. More importantly, how are you doing?"

Emaline had difficulty meeting his eyes. "I'm fine, Dev."

"He didn't hurt you?"

Emaline felt the heat begin at her throat and head toward her cheeks. "No," she said in a whisper.

Devlin put a hand on her chin and tipped it up so she was forced to meet his gaze. "Don't lie to me, Emmy."

"I'm not lying, Dev. I'm fine."

He seemed satisfied with what he saw and let her go. "Do you want help unloading the wagon?"

"I'm not ready to bring anything into the house just yet," she said. "I can handle it myself later."

"I'll be leaving then," Devlin said. "I'll be back to pick up the wagon later." He untied the horse that was hitched to the back of the wagon and mounted. "Take care of yourself, Emmy."

Emaline put a hand across her brow to shade her eyes from the sun as she looked up at her brother. "Maybe you can bring Melody to supper sometime."

"Maybe," Devlin said. "We'll see."

Emaline spent the rest of the day cleaning house and rearranging things, not removing signs of Josie, but adding tokens of her own. Conn had kept his house neat, but she wondered how long it had been since someone had taken a mop to the floors or a dustrag to the furniture. She felt a tremendous sense of satisfaction when she was done.

Conn was mending fence when he heard someone approaching on horseback. He put down his fence pliers and picked up his Winchester even as he turned to meet whoever had come calling. The truce wasn't old enough yet to set aside caution.

"Howdy," Devlin said as he halted his horse ten feet from the bore of the rifle Conn had pointed at him.

"I thought we finished our business yesterday," Conn said.

Devlin took his time dismounting, careful to keep his hands in plain sight at all times. "I just left a wagon at your place piled high with the rest of Emmy's things. I would have stayed to help her unload them, but she said she has some cleaning to do first."

"So why are you here?"

"I've got something to discuss with you."

"I'm not interested in anything you have to say, Winthrop."

"I want to marry Melody. As her closest male relative—"

"No."

"Melody and I love each other."

"No."

"We've loved each other for three years."

Conn's lips flattened and a muscle in his jaw worked. "Been sneaking around behind my back to see her?"

Devlin flushed, but there was nothing apologetic in his expression. "We couldn't be seen together without causing trouble. It seemed safer for everyone to be discreet. It hasn't been easy to love each other, but we do."

"The answer is still no."

"You can't stop us," Devlin said in a voice that was all the more threatening because of its quiet firmness.

"I can take Melody's boys from her if she marries you," Conn threatened.

Devlin's face paled. "She loves James and Timmy more than life. It would kill her to lose her sons."

"Then leave her alone."

"You're being unreasonable," Devlin said, his temper beginning to slip. "Why is it wrong for me and Melody to marry? There's an open-ended truce between Bentons and Winthrops now. The feud is over."

"*Maybe* it's over," Conn corrected.

"What's that supposed to mean?"

"It means I don't trust a Winthrop any farther than I can throw one," Conn replied. "It means this truce may last forever, or it may be over tomorrow if some Winthrop breaks the peace."

"Nobody's that stupid," Devlin said. "We're sharing the water now. There's no reason to fight anymore."

As he finished speaking, gunshots rang out.

"I knew it wouldn't last," Conn muttered.

"Those came from the creek," Devlin said.

Both men raced for their horses and galloped them in the direction of the gunshots. They arrived in time to see Winthrops and Bentons lined up on opposite sides of Bitter Creek with their guns drawn, while cattle milled about in the water.

"What's going on here?" Conn demanded.

"Someone took a shot at me from up in those trees," Eustis Benton said, pointing across the creek to a spot behind the Winthrops.

"If a Winthrop was shootin' at you, you'd be dead!" Slim Winthrop retorted. His gun was still in his holster, but there were three Winthrops behind him with rifles in their hands. "Seemed to me that shot was meant to gun *me* down," Slim said.

"Bentons ain't in the habit of shootin' people in the back," Eustis said.

"No telling what a lily-livered, low-down skunk of a Benton would do," Slim replied.

Conn could see what was coming. The name calling would escalate until blood was shed. He gave an inward sigh of disgust. He wasn't going to let that happen. Not when he was stuck married to a Winthrop.

"That's enough!" Conn said. "Looks to me like someone just wanted to make trouble. Seems anybody bent on killing couldn't have missed from that distance."

They turned to look at the shaded area on the hill above the creek. It wasn't more than fifty yards away. What Conn said made sense.

"You all know Devlin Winthrop, my brother-in-law," Conn said, not above using Devlin's presence for his own purposes. "He and I are going to stand watch to make sure there are no more mishaps while you boys finish watering your cattle. From now on, do your watering at different times of day."

"Aw, Conn," Eustis said.

"No arguments, Eustis. I've got as big a stake as anyone in seeing this truce succeed. Now get those cattle moved out of there."

Conn and Devlin sat on their horses, guns at the ready, until all the cattle had been watered and moved back out on the range to graze.

When the last of the cowboys had ridden away, Conn turned to Devlin. "I'd like to take a look up there in that stand of trees. Someone's bent on ending the truce. If he left some sign, I intend to find it. Want to join me?"

"Sure," Devlin said. "Let's go."

What the two men found baffled both of them.

"Look at this shell," Devlin said as he held it out to Conn. "It looks homemade. You ever seen anything like it?"

"Nope. Forty-five caliber, but the casings are a little odd. Nobody I know makes his own shells," Conn said, relieved to have evidence it wasn't Bentons who had fired the shots.

Devlin shook his head. "Looks damned suspicious to me. These shots were fired by someone who has some very special skills. So who hired him?"

"Not Bentons," Conn said certainly.

"It wasn't Winthrops, either."

"It must have been one or the other," Conn said. "Why?"

"Who else hates Winthrops or Bentons enough to kill them?" Conn said with a wry smile.

"Why does the killing have to be motivated by hate?" Devlin asked.

"What other reason is there to kill?"

"Greed."

Conn stared out over the valley before them, with the shining ribbon of water weaving through it. "You figure someone else wants this land? And plans to let us kill each other off so he can have it?"

"Something like that," Devlin agreed.

"You have someone particular in mind?"

Devlin pursed his lips. "There are some other ranches that could use this water. Bob Taylor's Bar T for one. Buck Simmons's Double B for another. Maybe they brought in some gunslinger to heat things up again."

Conn frowned. He had placed all the blame for the evils in his life on Winthrops, because they had been his mortal enemies. But what if someone was playing each side off against the other for his own purposes? Conn felt a deep, searing anger at the thought that he, along with a lot of other people, had been so despicably manipulated.

He voiced the thought that was uppermost in his

mind. "If it is someone outside the two families, we have to find him and put him out of business."

"Do we tell anyone else what we've found here?" Devlin asked.

Conn shook his head. "We've got enough people looking cross-eyed at each other. Maybe the two of us will just have to do some investigating on our own."

"You and me?" Devlin arched a disbelieving brow. "I thought you hated my guts."

"I do," Conn said. "But you've got a good head on your shoulders, so I might as well make use of it."

Devlin's lips curled in a rueful smile. "I'm willing. So long as you'll consider what I talked about this morning."

Conn eyed Devlin askance. "I'll think about it."

Beyond the next ridge a man lay on his belly and watched the two men on horseback dismount and search the area where he had so recently been. He had suspected they might come looking, so he had taken himself where he could watch in safety. He cursed the appearance of Conn Benton. Without him, things might have erupted into bloodshed. He wouldn't mind seeing Bentons and Winthrops die. He didn't even have to kill them himself; he had seen how willing they were to kill each other. He had failed on this occasion, but there would be others. He had plenty of time to do what had to be done. By the time that fool woman managed to get pregnant—if she ever did—he would have the feud back in full fury.

It was late when Emaline brought the clean sheets in from the line she found strung between two trees in back of the house and remade the bed. It was dark by the time she started supper, and she was busy

making up excuses to Conn why she was so late
getting food on the table.

She also took the time to clean herself up, to make
herself pretty for Conn. She knew she was being
foolish to think he would care one way or the other.
But if there was any chance Conn could be attracted
to her because of her looks, she wanted to take advantage of it. She put on a dress and combed her
hair back, taming the worst of the curls. She patted
on a dab of powder to moderate her freckles, and
returned to the kitchen to await Conn's arrival.

It was two hours past sundown, and still he hadn't
come.

She reminded herself that he had told her he
would be home after dark. But Emaline felt a deep
sense of foreboding. What if someone had decided
to end the truce by killing Conn? What if he had
made her pregnant last night and her child grew up
without a father after all?

Because of the time he'd spent at the creek, Conn
was later than he wanted to be completing the fence
repairs. It was two hours past dark when he finished
rubbing down his horse and headed for the kitchen
door. He wondered if his new wife had waited supper on him. Probably not, he conceded. Better not to
hope for it. Then he wouldn't be disappointed when
he had to fend for himself.

Conn stood stunned at kitchen door. There were
candles and silverware on the table and the vase that
had sat empty since his wife's death was filled with
wildflowers. He could smell something good cooking on the stove. But there wasn't a sound to be
heard in the house. Where was Emaline?

Emaline knew she was being silly. But the later
Conn was, the more she worried. And the more she
worried, the angrier she got with Conn for making
her worry. So when he called to her, she rose from

the rocker in the bedroom like an avenging fury and strode out the bedroom door headed toward the kitchen.

She met him in the hall and stopped so abruptly that her calico skirt whirled around her. Her fingers folded into fists that were hidden in her skirt. "Where have you been?" she demanded. "It's been dark for hours!"

"I told you I'd be late," Conn said, keeping the edge from his voice. After all, he wasn't unmindful of the effort she'd gone to preparing supper.

"Late?" Emaline hissed. "I imagined you shot dead and buried." She backed him down the hall stabbing her finger in his chest. "You knew I would worry and—"

"How the hell would I know something like that?" Conn said. "I'm not used to answering to anyone, least of all a wife!"

"Well, so you finally remembered you have one," she snarled. "And decided to come home."

"And I'm damned sorry I did," Conn fired back as he stumbled backward across the threshold of the parlor. "If I'd known there was a shrew waiting for me—"

"Shrew!" Emaline shrieked. "I spent the day scrubbing and cleaning and cooking for you."

"Nobody asked you to do anything of the sort." Conn looked around and noticed the shine on the floor, the knickknacks on the piano and end tables, the extra pictures on the mantel. "What the hell is all this stuff doing here?" He gestured with a broad sweep of his hand.

Emaline stood in the parlor doorway, enraged at Conn's dismissal of her efforts, of her things, of *her*. "That *stuff* is mine! I live here, too, in case you've forgotten. I'm entitled to have a few of my own possessions around me."

"They don't belong in here. I liked this place the way it was." He quickly gathered a handful of items off the mantel and shoved them into her arms. "Get rid of this stuff."

Emaline marched past him and slammed everything back down exactly where it had been. "No! I've as much right to put things in here as you do."

"This house is mine!"

"And mine!" Emaline snapped back. "I'm your wife!"

"Much to my regret!"

"Oh, how I hate you!" Emaline said through gritted teeth. "When I think how I tried . . . What I hoped . . ."

"This was all your idea," Conn reminded her. He was having trouble keeping his hands off her. She looked magnificent with her blue eyes flashing, her back ramrod straight, thrusting her small breasts out at him. He wanted her, and she had given him the excuse he needed to take what he wanted. "There was only one reason I married you. And I intend to do what I promised to do."

Too late Emaline recognized the look in Conn's eyes. When had rage turned to desire? When had hate turned to passion? "No, Conn. Not now. Not like this."

"Right now. Like this."

When he reached for her, she ran. He caught her arm and yanked her around to face him. His arms closed tightly around her and his mouth came down hard on hers. They were both gasping when he lifted his head to stare down into her dazed eyes.

"You can fight me if you want, Emaline, but we both know that neither of us has any choice about this."

"You can't force me, Conn."

"I can, Emaline," he said in a harsh voice. "But it's not what I want. I'd rather have you willing."

"So you can tell yourself it's not rape?"

"As you've been so quick to remind me, you're

my wife. I'm asking no more of you than what you promised when you married me."

"You know why I married you!"

"To bring peace through a child of ours," Conn said. "Are you saying you've changed your mind?"

Emaline bit her lower lip. Conn was wrong to demand she submit to him in this way, but submit to him she must, or else risk losing everything she had sacrificed to achieve. And though she had provoked him into showing his hand, she had learned something very important in their confrontation.

He desired her. It wasn't love, but it was a start.

Conn knew the moment she surrendered. Her body relaxed against his, her breasts pillowing against his chest, her hips slipping into the cradle of his. Her arms, which had been buckled between them, slid up around his neck.

"All right, Conn. You win. I'll couple with you."

He felt a stab of desire so swift and strong it nearly made him gasp. His hands cupped her buttocks and pulled her against him so she could feel his arousal. He looked down into blue eyes that were heavy lidded. She wanted him as much as he wanted her.

Conn lowered his mouth and claimed the woman in his arms.

4

EMALINE WAS PREGNANT. SHE HUGGED THE knowledge to herself, unwilling to share it because they had been married for a mere six weeks, and it had occurred to her that once Conn knew, he would no longer have any reason to bed her. Emaline didn't want those interludes to end, because for those few hours she and Conn were as close as any two people could be.

It was only in bed that things were going so well. In their daily lives, toleration had grown to acceptance, but that was all. There were no signs of love between them. Yet.

But Emaline had done her level best to get to know Conn better and to help him get to know her.

On the first two Sundays of their marriage they had gone to dinner at the homes of their widowed parents, Clara Winthrop and Hester Benton. The exchange had been Emaline's idea. She had hoped to learn about Conn by getting to know his family and to help him get to know her better by spending some time with her mother and brother. It had seemed like a good idea at the time. It hadn't turned out exactly the way she planned.

Emaline had been appalled, when she and Conn arrived at her mother's one-story wooden house on the outskirts of town, to discover that the patriarch of the Winthrop clan, Jeremiah Winthrop, and his wife, Belle, had been invited as well. The tension that would ordinarily have existed at such a family gathering was multiplied tenfold.

She had felt the tautness in Conn's arm as he led her up the steps to greet her mother and brother on the shaded front porch. She had given her mother a hard hug and been squeezed breathless by her brother before she turned to include Conn in the welcome.

"Conn, you've met my mother, Clara, and my brother, Dev."

If Conn had been a real husband coming to call the first week after their marriage, he would have hugged her mother and heartily shaken her brother's hand. It was a sign of how different their relationship truly was that he tipped his hat to her mother

and nodded curtly to her brother. That was when
Jeremiah appeared in the doorway. Emaline could
almost feel Conn's body recoil, though he didn't
move an inch.

"How'd'do," Jeremiah said. He had a way of looking down his nose at people that should have
seemed condescending, but the spectacles perched
on the end of that protuberance gave him an excuse
for his peculiar habit.

"I thought this was going to be a family dinner,"
Conn said.

"That it is," Jeremiah said with a smile. "Clara's
my niece." Jeremiah reached out a hand to Conn. It
was an offer of peace, an offer to let bygones be bygones.

Conn shot a startled look at Emaline before he
slowly reached out to shake Jeremiah's hand once,
then let it drop.

"Dinner's all ready," Clara said. "Shall we all go
inside?" She was shooing everyone back inside,
which was when Emaline saw Conn get another
shock.

Her mother had an upright piano very similar to
the one in his home, right down to the candlesticks
and doilies on top. "You play?" he asked sharply.

She nodded. "Mother taught me."

"Why haven't you played for me?"

"I . . . I didn't think you wanted me to."

Conn grimaced. "It's foolish to let the thing sit
there gathering dust. Feel free to use it whenever
you like."

By then they had followed everyone to the dining
room where Emaline found herself sitting on one
side of Jeremiah, who was seated at the head of the
table, while Conn sat across from her on Jeremiah's
other side. Belle sat beside Conn and across from
Devlin, while her mother sat at the far end of the
table.

The table was already laden with food, and Emaline watched the dishes being passed as everyone served themselves. Conn had a confused look on his face as he ladled food onto his plate.

"What's the matter?" Emaline asked.

"What is this?"

"Cornmeal mush and black-eyed peas. It's a dish my grandmother used to make in Arkansas."

"I never had it before," Conn said flatly as he helped himself to several slices of ham.

"If you don't like it, you don't have to eat it." Emaline had trouble keeping the irritation out of her voice. It was rude to complain about what was served when you were a guest in someone else's house.

Conn's lips flattened grimly. "I didn't say I wouldn't eat it, only that I hadn't ever seen it before."

"Like I said—"

Her mother interrupted. "Shall we say grace now?"

Emaline watched to see whether Conn was going to participate. She saw him hesitate when he realized they were all joining hands, but then he took Jeremiah's and Belle's hands. To her surprise, he knew the grace and said it along with them.

She watched anxiously as he took a bite of mush and peas. He chewed slowly and swallowed. Then he reached for some butter and salt and applied both liberally before taking another bite. That one seemed to go down easier.

"Well, Conn," Jeremiah said, "I hope you've had a chance to realize what a wonderful woman you've married, even if you didn't exactly choose her for yourself."

Emaline nearly choked on her food. She spoke with her mouth full, not wanting to give Conn a chance to reply to such a personal, and potentially explosive, comment. "How's the roundup going, Dev?"

"Don't talk with your mouth full, Emaline," her mother chided.

Emaline flushed as Conn gave her a ruefully sympathetic look. Apparently mothers were the same the world over.

"Things are going fine," Devlin said. "Only we're missing some cattle."

"Rustlers?" Conn asked with interest. That was something every ranch had to worry about.

"Maybe," Devlin replied. "Or maybe Bentons."

Conn's fork stopped in mid-air, and he lowered it with a clatter to his plate. "I didn't marry your sister so you could keep on making accusations like that."

"Boys, boys," Jeremiah soothed. "It's only been a week. I trust whatever happened in the past is in the past."

Emaline shot a pleading look at her brother. He relaxed in his chair. "Probably disappeared sometime during the winter," he conceded. "Got no way of knowing."

Conn started to make a retort, but Emaline caught his eye and gave him the same pleading look she had given her brother. Not that she expected it to work as well, but to her surprise, Conn picked up his fork and began eating again.

After that Clara and Jeremiah were careful to keep the conversation on neutral topics. When Clara offered dessert, Conn confessed to a full stomach and said he had chores to do anyway and that he and Emaline had to leave.

Emaline wasn't sure what she had accomplished with the dinner, aside from proving that Conn was still sensitive about his situation. On the way home he merely said, "Your mother's nice. She reminds me a lot of my own."

Dinner the following Sunday with Hester Benton was an enlightening experience for Emaline. In the first place, there were no men left in the family, just the widows of Conn's two brothers and their children. However, Horace Benton showed up. It didn't take Emaline long to figure out the Benton family patriarch was courting Hester. Horace was at least fifteen years older than Hester, but his hair showed only a few streaks of gray, and he had a toothsome smile that flashed often, giving him a youthful, almost mischievous appearance.

Emaline wondered how Conn could stand all the noise and commotion caused by the children who ran through the house whooping like Indians and slamming doors. He seemed totally oblivious as he sat talking animatedly with Melody and his other sister-in-law, Penny, who ran the milliner's shop in town. Emaline had never seen Conn smile so much, never seen him so carefree. He looked so much younger and very handsome.

Hester came up beside her in the doorway to the parlor and stood with her watching the three of them talking together.

"Conn used to laugh all the time," she said. "But in the past two years it's been very hard for him. He loved Josie a great deal, and he was devastated by her death."

Emaline started to pull away, but Hester stopped her with a hand on her arm.

"I'm glad he married you," she said. "It's time for him to stop grieving and get on with his life."

"You don't hate the Winthrops?" Emaline asked.

Hester sighed. "I hated the feud and what it stole from all of us. You're a very courageous woman, Emaline."

"I didn't do anything—"

"Shucks, girl, you couldn't know you'd end up with a man as good as my Conn. But things'll be better now for everyone." She smiled. "And I'll have another grandchild to dandle on my knee."

Emaline flushed beet red. "Mrs. Benton—"

"Call me Hester," the older woman said. "After all, we're family now."

Emaline watched with fascination at the supper table as Conn teased his mother about Horace's intentions. *So he doesn't mind that he's about to have a stepfather.*

She asked Conn about it on the way home. "I didn't realize your mother and Horace were sparking."

He managed a lazy grin. "She's been putting him off for a couple of years." The grin faded. "Maybe now that the feud's over she'll take him more seriously."

"The feud has interfered with all our lives more than we realize," Emaline murmured.

"Yeah," Conn agreed.

"I didn't know you liked children so much," Emaline said.

"What makes you think I do?"

She grinned. "You gave yourself away when you got into the pea-spitting contest with James. I thought Melody was going to take you both by the ears and lead you out to the woodshed."

Conn laughed. "I guess it shows, huh. Josie and I—"

He cut himself off, and that was the last he said on the subject. He would make a good father, she had realized. She and the child she would one day have were very lucky in that.

Emaline had no reason to feel particularly optimistic after those two dinners, but she did. Little things gave her hope. Like the fact that Conn kissed her good-bye each morning before he left. That he always came home before dark and made a point of complimenting her suppers. And that he joined her in the parlor after supper to sit by the fire and read while she worked on a sampler to hang in the kitchen.

Emaline knew he could just as easily have gone into his office in the back of the house to work and left her alone. He never said he enjoyed her company, he just spent time with her when he could. And their lovemaking had become the high point of her day.

Conn couldn't seem to get enough of touching her, caressing her, kissing her. He prolonged the moment when he would thrust inside her and spill his seed, so that by the time he did, she cried out from the pleasure he had given her. Then he would spoon her hips into his groin and slide an arm around her, bury his nose in the curls at her nape, and fall asleep.

Conn never spoke of his feelings, and she was too afraid to ask. Now those precious moments might be coming to an end, because he had accomplished what he had set out to do. She was expecting a child that should be born in time for Christmas, so the new year could truly begin with peace and goodwill toward all men.

She was going to have to tell Conn soon, unless she chose to pretend that her monthly courses had arrived on schedule.

Emaline bit her lower lip. Did she dare lie? Surely Conn wouldn't suspect anything for a month or two. And she could use the time she bought by her deceit to work on their relationship outside the bedroom.

Having made her decision, Emaline immediately put her plan into motion.

"Conn," she said that evening when they were sitting together in the parlor, "I wondered if we could go on a picnic this Saturday."

"What?"

"A picnic."

"I suppose so. If you'd like."

He had been secretly watching Emaline over the top of his newspaper, wondering whether enough time had passed for him to take her to bed. He had a hunger for her that made him ache all day. He could barely wait through the daylight hours until he could assuage it, then he wanted her again.

Conn blamed his obsession on the fact that they

were constrained to couple nightly until Emaline
was pregnant. Somehow, what should have been a
burden had become such a source of pleasure that
he couldn't imagine not loving Emaline at the end
of the day. He thought about making love to her on
Saturday under a tree somewhere, with the sunlight
on her freckled skin. Would she be willing?

"I thought we could invite Devlin and Melody,"
Emaline said.

Conn frowned. He didn't like the idea of another
couple joining them. He wasn't as opposed to the
idea of Devlin and Melody getting married as he had
been six weeks ago. Actually, he and Devlin had
spent enough time together, breaking up altercations
between Winthrops and Bentons, that he had
learned to like and respect Emaline's brother. But he
didn't completely trust him. Or any Winthrop.

Still that had nothing to do with his objection to
having Devlin and Melody come along on their Saturday picnic. Frankly, if another couple joined them,
they wouldn't have the privacy he needed to make
love to Emaline. However, he wasn't willing to admit it. How he felt about Emaline was his own business. So he said, "You know how I feel about the
two of them."

Naturally, Emaline brushed away that excuse. "I
think they make a lovely couple, and they're clearly
in love." She set her sewing aside and crossed to
kneel at Conn's feet, laying a hand on his thigh and
looking up at him with beseeching blue eyes. "Say
yes, Conn."

Conn was lost. "All right, Emaline. We'll go pic-
nicking on Saturday. And I'll invite your brother
when I see him tomorrow and ask him to bring Melody."

Conn dropped his newspaper beside the chair and
lifted Emaline into his lap, tucking her head against
his shoulder. She seemed willing enough to be there.
Her hand slid up to his shoulder and around to his

nape, where she played with his hair. A shiver of longing spiraled down his spine.

"Emaline," he said in a husky voice, "I want you."

"I want you, too, Conn," she murmured back.

He couldn't wait till bedtime. He lowered his mouth and kissed her as his hand closed over her breast.

Emaline moaned, and her hand tightened in Conn's hair, holding his mouth against her own as his tongue slid in and out, mimicking the love act.

It was the first time they had made love outside the bedroom since the second night of their marriage, when Conn had taken her in anger, and she had submitted in resentment. This was totally different. There was a willingness on both sides to please and to take pleasure. They were making love.

Conn shifted Emaline to the Turkish carpet that covered the parlor floor and lowered himself onto her. He was already aroused. He could hardly keep from ripping off buttons as he tugged Emaline's high-necked blouse from her skirt. Emaline was equally busy, eagerly unfastening Conn's shirt.

When Conn finally had Emaline naked to the waist, he stopped to admire her. Had he ever thought her freckles unattractive? He didn't now. He slid his fingertips across her ribs, across the silky flesh that always felt so good beneath his hand, then roamed upward to cup a breast and tease the nipple with his lips and tongue. Emaline arched upward, so incredibly responsive, so marvelously giving as he took more of her breast in his mouth and suckled her.

Emaline's hands caught in Conn's hair, and she held his mouth against her. "Conn," she whispered. "Conn." She realized suddenly that she cared very deeply for this man who had been her enemy. But she didn't trust her feelings. Was it only this powerful physical attraction that drew them to each other? Was the taking and giving of pleasure all that existed between them? What did it mean to love? Was what she felt now love? Emaline had no answers, only the certain knowledge that it was no longer possible to face a future that didn't include Conn Benton.

When Conn had spilled his seed inside her, he carried her to the bedroom and made love to her again there. After he fell asleep, Emaline reached over to brush a stray curl from his forehead. Her heart ached with the knowledge that she was going to bear the child of a man who didn't love her. There had to be a way to make Conn realize that what they had found together was special, worth cherishing despite the circumstances that had united them.

Emaline kissed Conn good-bye the next morning as usual, then hitched up the wagon and drove herself the few miles to town. She had a visit to make to Doc Swilling. She knew she was pregnant, but she wanted to ask the doctor a few questions about childbearing that she couldn't ask any of the ladies of her acquaintance without giving away her delicate condition.

Doc Swilling confirmed that she could expect to bear Conn's child about the middle of December. He promised to let her make the announcement, but she could see from the beaming smile on his face that he was happy for her and for the town of Bitter Creek.

"You're about to put me out of work, Mrs. Benton," he said. "And high time, if you ask me!"

Emaline left Doc Swilling's office with a smile of her own, her step light. It was really happening. She was going to have a baby. She felt like grinning from ear to ear. She swung her reticule to let out some of the energy she felt. She was just passing an alley when she felt a hard hand grab hold of her arm and yank her into the darkness.

"Who—"

At first she thought it must be a thief intent on stealing her purse. She hadn't anything of value in it and would willingly have surrendered it, but she wasn't given the chance. An arm quickly closed around her neck, completely cutting off her air.

Emaline writhed to free herself and clutched at the restraining arm with both hands, clawing at it with her fingernails. She heard a grunt of pain, but her captor didn't lessen his hold. She panicked in earnest when the man—it had to be a man, he was so big and strong—covered her mouth and nose with his other hand.

Emaline felt faint and knew that if she didn't free herself quickly, she would die. And her baby would die with her. She wrenched her whole body in one gigantic effort to escape and almost won free. Almost. But not quite. She was nearly sobbing with fear and frustration as the villain tightened his hold once more.

"Hold still, or I'll kill you here and now."

Emaline froze. The man, whoever he was, had uncovered her nose at last. She took a deep breath, but she was so frightened she still felt suffocated. Her whole body was trembling.

"Why are you doing this?" she said behind his hand. It came out muffled, but intelligible.

"Bitch! It's disgusting how you spread your legs for a Benton. Murdering sons of bitches, all of them! Saw you coming from the doc's office. You got a Benton bastard planted in your belly yet? Answer me, girl!"

Emaline's throat was so constricted she couldn't get out any sound. Did he mean to kill her? Would it make things worse if she admitted she was carrying Conn's child? She frantically shook her head no.

"I don't believe you," he spat. "Better to kill you now and not take the chance."

Emaline felt the man's grasp tightening and panicked. He was going to kill her. She was going to die without ever holding her child in her arms or having Conn look at her with love in his eyes.

Not without a fight, she wasn't.

Emaline was tall and strong. She started by lifting one well-shod foot and kicking backward at the man's kneecap. She heard him howl, and his grasp loosened around her mouth. She let out a bloodcurdling scream.

Immediately, faces appeared at the end of the alley. Her attacker must have realized he had no time to finish what he had started. A moment later, Emaline was free. She turned to see if she could identify the man, but all she saw was a fist flying toward her face. Before she could dodge, she felt a tremendous pain in her jaw, and she was rocked backward. Blackness closed in, and Emaline crumpled to the ground.

Conn hadn't realized just how much he cared for Emaline until a man from town had come riding hell-bent-for-leather to find him and told him that she was hurt and had been taken to Doc Swilling's office. He had thrown himself on his horse and galloped back to town.

She looked incredibly fragile lying on the iron cot in the doctor's office. Her face was pale and her eyes were closed. For a terrified moment he thought she was dead.

He sank down beside her on the cot. "Doc?"

"As far as I can tell, Conn, she just fainted," Doc Swilling said. "But she's had quite a scare. Apparently some man dragged her into the alley. She screamed, and some folks showed up and scared him away."

When Emaline opened her eyes, she was lying on an iron bed in Doc Swilling's office. She found herself staring into the eyes of a grim-faced man sitting beside her. It was Conn. She tried to smile but winced at the pain in her swollen jaw. "Hello, Conn," she whispered.

"What happened, Emaline?"

His voice was harsh, with no sympathy for what she had been through. Emaline began to tremble as she remembered how close she had come to being killed. As tears welled, she closed her eyes. "A man grabbed me when I was walking past the alley. He . . . he threatened to kill me."

Conn felt his heart turn over in his chest and realized he felt a great deal more for Emaline than he had ever admitted to himself. He pulled her into his arms, needing to feel the warmth of her, needing to know she was alive and that he hadn't lost her forever. He felt such a rush of rage and hate for the man who had threatened his wife that it made him tremble.

Conn was holding her so tightly that Emaline could barely breathe. "I'm fine, Conn," she said against his shoulder.

"You could have been killed. Who was it, Emaline? Who did it?"

She wasn't about to admit it was most likely a Winthrop. Who else hated Bentons so much? "I didn't get a look at him. It was too dark in the alley."

Either she truly didn't know, or she did know and wasn't saying, Conn thought. In any case, it wasn't hard to guess. It was someone who hated him or hated her for marrying him. It was the senseless feud beginning all over again. Bile rose in his throat, caused by a crawling fear of what might happen to Emaline.

"Can we go home now, Conn? Please?"

When Conn looked to Doc Swilling, he said, "I've checked, and there's been no harm done to the baby."

Conn looked stunned. "Baby?"

"Why, yes. I just confirmed Mrs. Benton's suspicions this morning. The baby should arrive in time for Christmas."

Conn felt elation. And terror. Any threat to Emaline was now also a threat to their unborn child. His voice sounded amazingly calm to his ears as he said, "Then if it's all right with you, I'll take my wife home."

He lifted Emaline into his arms and carried her outside, where a crowd of people had gathered.

"Who did it, Conn?" one of the Bentons demanded.

"Who attacked her?" one of the Winthrops called.

A Winthrop shoved a Benton, who shoved back.

"Who you shovin' around?" the Winthrop shouted.

"A dirty, rotten, Benton, that's who!"

The Benton man swung his fist. The Winthrop ducked, took two steps backward and laughed. "Missed!"

A second Benton turned on a second Winthrop and without warning slammed a fist into the man's jaw. "I didn't!" he said triumphantly.

There were a dozen Winthrops and Bentons gathered, and it looked as if a free-for-all was going to erupt right in the middle of Main Street.

Emaline could see that the truce was in serious danger. "Put me down, Conn," she said. "And see what you can do to stop that fight before it gets started. We've come too far to lose everything now."

Conn stared at her with a strange look in his eyes but did as she asked. He drew his gun and fired twice to get the attention of both Winthrops and Bentons.

"Emaline and I have an announcement to make," he said to the surly and sullen faces before him. "We're expecting our first child before Christmas."

There was a moment of profound silence before men who had been contemplating a fight with each other exchanged grins.

"Well, I'll be a pig in slop," said a Winthrop. "He did it!"

"Damn fast work, Conn," said a Benton, slapping Conn on the back.

Conn wasn't sure whether he felt more like blushing or grinning. He did both. At first, only Bentons congratulated him, but they were soon joined by the Winthrops, who shook his hand before tipping their hats to Emaline.

Winthrops and Bentons looked sheepishly at each other. Fighting no longer seemed like a very good idea.

"This calls for a drink!" a Benton said.

"More than one, if you ask me," a Winthrop replied. The crowd headed off toward the saloon. There were whoops and hollers of exultation along the street as they spread the news to anyone who would listen.

When they were gone, Conn turned back to Emaline, who was feeling light-headed again. "Conn, I think . . ."

He caught her as she started to fall and lifted her into his arms. "Let's go home, Emaline."

Once home, Conn put Emaline to bed and insisted she stay there. That evening, instead of making love to her, he merely pulled her into his arms and held her.

"You're in no shape to do anything but rest," Conn said. "Besides, there's no reason . . . now."

Emaline felt an ache in her chest. So, it was over, just as she had suspected it would be the moment Conn found out she was pregnant. At least he hadn't left her bed entirely. He was holding her lightly around the waist and her hips were spooned against his.

Conn's arms tightened around Emaline until he heard her moan slightly in her sleep. He loosened his grasp. He was terrified that he wouldn't be able to keep her safe. That some gunman would find her alone and kill her as Josie had been slain. Or that someone might sabotage the rigging on the wagon, and she would be thrown when the horses broke free. Or that she would be caught by some madman in an alley and strangled. He couldn't sleep for the visions that haunted him.

Now there would be a child by Christmas, an heir, to end the fighting forever, another life for which he was responsible.

Conn's hand slipped down to cover Emaline's abdomen. His son or daughter was growing inside her. He tried to remember how it had been with Josie. She had been four months pregnant when she was shot. Yes, there was just a tiny rounding of Emaline's belly now. His hands reached for her breasts. Were they tender yet? They seemed the same size as always, but he knew they would increase as the child grew inside her. Had she been sick? He hadn't seen any signs of it, though he believed it was common for women to be ill in the first months.

His handling of her woke Emaline. "Conn?"

"Go back to sleep." He wanted to make love to her, but it was selfish to think only of himself. He knew her jaw was painfully bruised. And there was no reason for him to be loving her. She was already pregnant.

But when she turned to face him, he lowered his head and kissed her. And she kissed him back. He told himself he was just going to caress her shoulders to ease the tension there, but his hands roamed over her until at last he felt her hands on him. Another moment, and he knew he wouldn't be able to stop.

He grasped her shoulders and pushed her away. "Stop, Emaline."

He heard her cry of anguish and thought he must have hurt her. "Emaline? Are you all right?"

"I'm fine, Conn," she said in a quiet voice. "Go to sleep."

She didn't protest when he pulled her back into

his arms. There might be no reason for making love, but there was nothing to keep him from holding her. Conn contented himself with the knowledge that when her jaw was well he could—and would— make love to her again.

By Saturday the bruise on Emaline's jaw had faded to a pale yellow, and she was insisting over Conn's protest that she felt well enough to go on the promised picnic with Melody and Devlin.

"I told Devlin yesterday when he came to visit that we're still going," Emaline said, "so they should be here any time. I've got everything packed and ready. There's no reason not to go."

Except there may be a gunman waiting in ambush to kill you, Conn thought. But he could see there was no persuading her to stay home. When Devlin arrived, he could see his brother-in-law felt as anxious as he did about the situation. But Emaline was insistent, and they gave in. The two men rode horseback, while the women took the spring wagon loaded with picnic supplies.

Devlin dropped back so he could speak with Conn without being overheard by the women. "I sure wish you could have talked Emmy out of this."

"I tried," Conn said. "She wouldn't budge. You know how stubborn she can be."

"I sure do!" Devlin said with a wry grin. "Have you found out any more about who attacked her?"

Conn shook his head. "All I can do is guess."

"I had such high hopes for this truce," Devlin said bleakly. "It seems all I've done the past six weeks is run around putting out little fires."

"Meanwhile, someone has started a blaze that we may not find until it's burning out of control," Conn said.

The women welcomed an opportunity to speak privately as much as the men had, but their discussion ran along a completely different track.

"I've been talking to Conn about your situation," Emaline said to Melody, "trying to convince him that he should consent to your marriage to Dev. I don't think he's as opposed to the idea as he was at first, but he insists on waiting a little longer to see if the truce lasts."

"What if it doesn't last?" Melody asked. "What happens to the two of you?"

"I'd never leave Conn for any reason."

"Why, you love him!"

"I think so," Emaline said with a shaky laugh. "I'm not sure what love is, but the feelings I have for Conn are different from anything I've ever felt before."

They picked a spot for the picnic along Bitter Creek not far from the house. The two men tethered their horses and helped the women down from the wagon. All four of them laid out blankets in the shade along with the picnic basket. Then they settled down to enjoy the sound of the creek rushing by and the wind in the cypress trees above them. As they ate, they talked about this and that, never broaching any subject that might cause friction among them . . . until Emaline turned to her brother and said, "You've never told me how you and Melody met."

Devlin shot a quick glance at Conn before he answered. "Not much to tell. I came upon a broken-down wagon a few miles outside of town. A woman and two little boys were trying to get the wheel back on. I stopped to help."

"And fell in love at first sight?" Emaline asked with a teasing grin.

Devlin laughed. "Hardly. The woman poked a gun in my chest and told me to leave her alone, that she'd sit there till doomsday before she took any help from me."

Melody flushed. "He was a Winthrop. I had reason to hate Winthrops."

Emaline watched as Melody and Devlin joined

hands and gazed into each other's eyes. She began to realize they had conquered quite a few obstacles in coming to the understanding that now existed between them.

"So who held out the peace pipe?" Conn asked.

"I unbuckled my gunbelt and let it drop," Devlin said. "Then I told her she could keep the gun aimed at me as long as she felt she needed it, but I was going to fix that wheel for her. Otherwise she was going to end up stuck miles from town in the dark."

"After that incident," Melody continued, "it seemed we were constantly crossing paths in town. At first we just nodded to each other. Then we started saying hello. And then, one day I asked Dev to come to dinner, to repay him for the kindness of fixing that wheel."

"After the boys went to bed, we sat on the front porch and just talked," Devlin said. "It was as though we had known each other forever. Things developed pretty quickly after that. But there was nothing we could do. Not considering the feud, and all. Neither of our families would have allowed us to live in peace. Until now."

"When are you planning to get married?" Emaline asked.

Melody and Devlin exchanged glances, then looked at Conn.

"What about sometime after Christmas?" Conn said.

Melody launched herself at Conn and gave him a hug. "Oh, thank you, Conn! Thank you!" Just as quickly she threw herself back into Devlin's open arms. "Oh, Dev, at last! At last!"

Emaline was happy for her brother, but envious as well, and uncomfortable with his vigorous demonstration of affection for his new fiancée. "Shall we go for a walk, Conn?" she suggested, extending her hand so he could help her to her feet.

Conn grinned wryly. "That sounds like a good

idea." In fact, he planned to take advantage of the opportunity to act out his fantasy of having Emaline bared to the sunlight.

Emaline threaded her arm through Conn's, and they walked along the edge of the creek with the sun at their backs.

"I'm so pleased that you've agreed to let Melody marry my brother. I can't wait to help her plan the wedding."

"Just don't plan anything until after Christmas," Conn reminded her.

"Why not?"

"Because there's still a chance all of this could blow up in our faces. I don't want Melody to become a target because she's hitched to someone on the wrong side when battle lines are drawn again."

"Do you really think things are as precarious as all that?"

"After what happened to you, I'm willing to believe anything. It's hard for everyone to change the habits of twenty years. I just don't want to take any chances."

Conn realized they had rounded a bend in the creek, and the other couple was out of sight. He turned Emaline toward him and cupped her face in his hands. "Have I told you how beautiful you look today with the sun shining on your face and the wind blowing in your hair?"

Emaline couldn't believe what she was hearing. It actually sounded like the sort of thing a beau might say to his sweetheart when he was courting her. In fact, the way Conn was looking at her, she no longer felt like an ugly duckling. He made of her a gracious swan.

"Am I beautiful, Conn?"

"You are to me, Emaline."

She lifted her mouth as he lowered his, and their lips clung. It was a moment of recognition that there was more between them than the forced vows they had taken on their wedding day. If only the rest of the world would let them live in peace.

Conn leaned his forehead against Emaline's. "I want to make love to you here by the creek with the sunlight overhead and the grass beneath us. That's why I wanted to come alone today, Emaline," he confessed.

"We're alone now, Conn," she said in a soft voice.

"Would you be willing?"

She was already unbuttoning her shirtwaist. She grinned as she met his dark eyes. "Oh, yes, Conn. I definitely would."

There, with the sun streaming through the trees overhead, and the creek burbling alongside them, Conn made love to his wife. He had never laughed so much or felt such heights of passion as he did that day with the cool grass beneath their naked bodies and the sunlight on her freckled skin. He was ready to love her. He wanted to love her.

And yet, he could not love her. Not yet. It was simply too dangerous to give his heart to her. He couldn't survive another tragedy like the last one. It would destroy him to lose another wife, another child. So he made love to her with his body, cherished her with his mouth and hands, but he kept his soul to himself.

Emaline knew what Conn had given her and what he had not. It was more than she had let herself hope for. Maybe he didn't love her as wholly, as completely, as she loved him. But they had the rest of their lives together. Anything could happen.

5

EMALINE WAS HEAVY WITH CHILD. SHE SPENT HER days sewing clothes for the baby and playing every Christmas carol she could remember on the piano. She had insisted that she and Conn have a tree, and he had gone into the mountains to cut one. They had decorated it with ornaments they had made together out of pine cones, juniper berries and the lids cut from tinned food. They had also arranged candles around the tree to provide light at night. As she stood with Conn and admired their efforts, Emaline felt the baby move inside her.

"Feel, Conn," she said as she reached for his hand and laid it on her swollen girth. She could visibly see a hand or foot moving beneath her flesh. "He wants to be here to celebrate with us."

"He's a week late already. If he doesn't hurry, he's going to miss Christmas altogether," Conn said.

"He's still got another week to go," she replied.

Conn circled Emaline from behind, weaving his hands together over her abdomen so he could feel the restless child moving inside her. "What makes you think it's a boy?" he asked.

"It might be a girl," she said. "I'd be happy with either one. I just want our child, boy or girl, to be able to live in peace."

"That's what this marriage is all about," Conn said quietly. He paused and added, "Are you sorry, Emaline?"

"Sorry? For what?"

"For having married me."

She relaxed back into his embrace. "No, I'm not sorry, Conn. I'd do it again." *I love you, Conn*, she thought. But she didn't say the words aloud. She was waiting for him to say them first.

"Are you happy about the baby?"

"You know I am. Because it will bring peace at last." *And because it's a part of you and me.* But she didn't tell him that, either. She wasn't willing to speak before Conn made his feelings known. She felt too vulnerable. She couldn't take the chance that he didn't share her feelings.

Conn said nothing more, just turned her toward the bedroom and followed her there.

He had watched Emaline pray for peace each night and marveled at her faith in mankind. There wasn't going to be any peace he thought cynically. At the last minute something would happen to spoil it all. He could feel it in his gut.

And yet it was impossible to ignore the child growing inside her day by day, week by week, month by month. He had felt it kick. He had seen it move beneath her flesh. He had listened for the sound of its heartbeat in her womb. He knew it was alive, that it was real. But until he held it in his arms, he refused to let himself believe that everything would turn out all right. He kept waiting for the other shoe to drop.

Overnight, Emaline became convinced that something was wrong with the baby. It was already a week overdue, and there were no signs that it was coming anytime soon. She didn't want to worry Conn, but she needed some reassurance that everything was all right. The instant he left the house the next morning, she headed for town in the spring wagon to see Doc Swilling.

"There's nothing wrong," the doctor assured her after his examination. "Babies simply have a habit of coming when they're good and ready."

"But I'm ready now," Emaline said with a grimace. She could no longer see her feet. Getting up and down without assistance was impossible. And she was tired of having to make so many visits to the john. She wanted this done and over with. She wanted to hold her child in her arms. She wanted Conn to believe that it was all right to love her. She wanted peace at last.

The summer and autumn had passed without any incidents of violence between Winthrops and Bentons that resulted in death. There were, however, several unexplained "accidents." The well was fouled at Tom Benton's ranch by a dead chicken. Winthrop cattle ended up in a pasture full of crazyweed and a bunch got sick and died. Wolf poison was laid too near Zeb Winthrop's barn and his prize hunting hounds ate it and died. And someone shot at a wagonload of Bentons on their way home from church. One of the horses was killed and had to be cut from the traces.

In the past, such incidents would have called for some sort of retaliation against the other side. Even if the exact perpetrator remained unknown, they knew who to blame for the crime. But no human beings had been harmed. For the sake of the truce, both Bentons and Winthrops let the incidents remain unresolved and unrevenged.

Instead, new, peaceful habits were being formed. With the impending birth of a child who would possess the blood of both sides, and thus secure the disputed water rights to Winthrops and Bentons alike, hope was growing that the killing feud might be over at last.

It was bitterly cold outside. A blue norther had recently swept through, leaving behind a dusting of snow and drifts along the fence lines. All day Conn had been trying to talk Emaline out of attending the Grange Christmas social. "It's too cold outside, Emaline," he argued. "You'll catch a chill riding all the way into town. And what if your labor starts?"

"I'll bundle up warmly, Conn. And if my labor starts, we won't have to send for the doctor, because Doc Swilling will be right there. I'm as strong as a horse. I'll be fine. Besides, I want to dance."

Conn took one look at his wife's bulk and laughed out loud. "I'll be lucky if I can get my arms around you!"

"Then I'll find someone who can!"

Conn caught her arm and whirled her into his embrace. He wasn't far off the mark. His arms barely made it around her girth to close behind her. "All right," he conceded. "We'll go to the dance. But you're going to rest between numbers. And we're coming home early."

Emaline readily agreed to Conn's conditions. She hadn't planned to dance a great deal anyway. Mostly she wanted a chance to visit with Melody and talk with the ladies present about the impending birth of her child. The immense size of her belly made the idea of giving birth a little daunting. She feared the pain and wanted some reassurance that she could manage it.

As Conn drove Emaline into town in the wagon, his eyes constantly shifted to cover the horizon. He hadn't forgotten, even if she had, that someone had tried to kill her in the spring. The culprit had never been found, and Conn knew he was out there somewhere waiting for another opportunity to finish what he had started. Conn had guarded Emaline well over the past months, never letting her travel without an escort, always making sure she had someone with her in town. She had chafed at the constraints he put on her but had conceded that there was just cause for his concern.

He wondered what he would do if he ever caught the man responsible for attacking his wife. Shoot him and risk starting the feud all over again? Turn him over for trial by a jury of his peers? Hell, if he was a Winthrop a jury of Winthrops would just let him go again.

"What are you thinking?" Emaline asked when she saw the furrows of worry on Conn's brow.

"I'm thinking it'll be a long time before Bentons and Winthrops ever learn to trust each other."

"I trust you. Melody trusts Devlin."

"That's not trust, it's love," Conn said.

"You have to trust first, before love can grow."

"Oh, is that how it is?"

"That's how it is."

It took a moment for Conn to realize that Emaline was suggesting her love for him had grown once she had learned to trust him. On some level he had known for a long time that she loved him. She had never said the words, but then, neither had he. He wasn't sure what she was waiting for. Plain old fear was stopping him.

Several weeks ago he had taken the daguerreotype of himself and Josie from the piano, where it had been since the day Josie had died, and carried it into his office. He had sat for a long time staring at it with eyes that eventually blurred with tears. He had never grieved for Josie, he realized. He had been too consumed by hate. Now, two years later, he felt an ache in his chest, and there was a painful lump in his throat. He had fought the tears that threatened, but couldn't hold back a choking sob. He pressed the heels of his hands against his eyes as anguish dammed for years gushed over a wall that had somehow come tumbling down.

Conn wasn't sure when he first realized Emaline had come into the room, but he turned to her and buried his face against her growing belly and cried for what had been lost. She had closed her arms around him and stroked his hair and murmured words of comfort that he understood even though he never heard them.

When he had fallen silent again, he had been embarrassed because she had seen him like that. But Emaline had brushed aside his apologies.

"You loved her, Conn," she had said. "You should grieve that she's gone."

He had captured her mouth, grateful for her understanding, seeking solace for the pain, and discovered something unexpected in her arms. The emptiness, the place that had become a void when Josie died, had been filled again. He didn't have to face life alone. He had Emaline.

He had put the daguerreotype in his desk drawer for safekeeping. It was no longer necessary to remind himself every day of his pain, to nurture his hatred of Winthrops. He was going to have to stop hating if there was to be any future for himself and Emaline. And their child.

His thoughts were brought to a halt when they pulled up at the barn where the dance was being held.

"Hey, you two! We've been waiting for you," Devlin called. "What took you so long?" Devlin had his arm around Melody, and he let go of her to help Emaline from the wagon. Before he could touch her, Conn was at her side, his hands at her waist.

"I've got her," he told Devlin.

They could hear the music coming from the barn. A couple of violins and a piano could make a lot of ruckus, Conn thought. He could see that Emaline's toes were already tapping.

"Come on, wife," he said, slipping an arm around her and leading her toward the noise. "Let's go kick up our heels."

Emaline eyed the green and red wreaths strung across the ceiling as Conn whirled her in the dance. She was so dizzy from looking up that she felt breathless, yet she had a smile on her face that spread from ear to ear. It was wonderful dancing with Conn. It was wonderful looking around the room and seeing faces that were smiling instead of sullen with suspicion.

Emaline's happiness fueled the hatred of the man who had attacked her in the spring until his heart pounded in his chest, and he felt dizzy. Christmas was awful for him this year, because he was alone. But they all seemed happy. Especially her. His heavy fists opened and closed, as he yearned to close them around the flesh at her throat. Nor should the child in her belly be allowed to live. Because his child had died. Emaline had become a symbol of all he despised, and he would know no peace until she was dead.

No guns had been allowed in the barn for obvious reasons, but he had hidden a pistol in his coat pocket. He didn't care what happened to him, as long as Emaline Benton died before he did.

He was aware of the music only as a raucous noise in his head, aware of the people around him only as sources of heat and movement, aware of the lanterns hung around the barn only as a sort of burning radiance, guiding his way to vengeance. His eyes were focused on her as he crossed the barn. At last he would be free of the pain. He would kill it when he killed the woman.

Conn couldn't take his eyes off Emaline's face. He had never seen her so happy. She seemed to glow with warmth. He felt a swelling of love in his breast so strong it made him want to shout. But Conn did nothing more than smile himself, a small tilting of his lips that did little to reveal the upheaval inside. Because he was watching her, he saw the growing uncertainty on Emaline's face, followed by a dawning horror.

"Emaline? What's wrong?"

He followed her gaze and felt his heart skip a beat. John Fleet, the blacksmith who had lost his daughter in the stampede, was pointing a gun at Emaline.

"It's all your fault," Fleet said in a voice loud enough to garner attention from the dancers nearby. "And now you have to pay."

When the gun in Fleet's hand became visible, the dancers edged backward out of harm's way. Until only the three of them, Conn and Emaline and John Fleet, stood in a corner of the barn.

The musicians abruptly stopped playing. In the sudden silence, the frozen Bentons and Winthrops could easily hear what was being said.

"My little girl is dead because of Bentons and Winthrops," Fleet continued. "And now you want them to stop fighting." He shook his head. "They have to keep killing each other off, until they're all gone. That's the only way my little girl will ever have any peace, if all of them, every last Benton and Winthrop, is dead. I tried to get them to fight. I shot at some. And pulled down fences. And poisoned wells. And killed their dogs. But they wouldn't fight.

"So you see, I have to kill you. And the baby. Because you want peace, and I can't have that." He turned to Conn, standing no more than a foot from Emaline. "Get out of the way, Conn. I only want her."

Conn shook his head. A muscle in his jaw jerked. "I won't let you do this, Fleet. I can't let you do it. She's my wife. I love her."

There were several gasps at Conn's declaration of love for a Winthrop woman. They all knew how he had hated Winthrops when he married her. And there wasn't a man or woman in the room who didn't wonder just how far his love would take him. Would a Benton give his life for a Winthrop?

A bleak look appeared on Fleet's face. "I don't have any choice, Conn." He cocked the gun and pointed it at Emaline's heart. "It has to be done."

"I love you, Conn," Emaline said, fearing that if she didn't speak she would never have the chance.

Their gazes locked and suddenly Emaline realized what Conn planned to do. "No, Conn!"

He had less than a second to act. At the same instant that Fleet fired, Conn launched himself toward Emaline. The bullet caught him in the back as he fell with her, doing his best to lessen the effect of his fall on her pregnant body. Once they were down, his body sagged against her.

At the same time that Conn threw himself at Emaline, Devlin drove his shoulder into Fleet's belly and shoved him off his feet. The gun went flying. Moments later, Bentons and Winthrops alike had gathered to subdue the blacksmith. The sheriff was summoned to take him to jail.

Bentons and Winthrops stared at each other with new eyes. Clearly each side had been innocent of the incidents over the summer that had raised so much furor. If that was true, maybe both sides did want peace. They had seen how a Benton had offered his own life to save a Winthrop. And how Devlin Winthrop had leapt forward to help a couple of Bentons. Maybe it was time to let go of the past and look forward to the future.

Everyone crowded around Conn until Doc Swilling had to yell, "Get back and give me some room to work."

Emaline sat on the floor, cradling Conn's head on her lap. "Please don't die, Conn," she whispered in his ear. "Please don't die."

"How is he?" Devlin asked as he crouched beside his sister.

"If someone would give me some room to see, maybe I could tell you," Doc Swilling replied irritably.

Devlin moved the crowd back until they stood in a wide circle around Conn and Emaline. With the space he needed, Doc Swilling examined Conn and announced, "Didn't hit any vital organs, but that bullet has to come out."

"Will he be all right?" Emaline asked.

"His chances are good," he said. He turned to the crowd. "A couple of you carry him over to my office."

Bentons hurried to do the doc's bidding and found themselves facing Winthrops on the other side. By mutual agreement both Winthrops and Bentons shared the labor of carrying Conn down the street to the doc's office.

Emaline followed after them, Devlin on one side supporting her and Melody on the other. Emaline felt the first pain as she set foot outside the barn. It was just a twinge really, but she had learned enough to recognize it as the beginning of her labor.

She refused to leave Conn's side while the doctor performed surgery. "If he dies, I want to be with him."

The surgery didn't take long, but Emaline was grateful that Conn remained unconscious throughout it. Once he had been bandaged, Doc Swilling took one look at her pale, sweat-bedaubed face and said, "You need some rest, young lady."

Emaline smiled. "I'm afraid I'm not going to be getting much rest for the next few hours, Doc." She laid a hand on her belly. "This baby has decided to be born."

There was a furor among those waiting for news of Conn when they heard Emaline was in labor. Doc asked for another bed to be brought to his office and several hardy souls retrieved one from the boardinghouse.

"Are you sure you wouldn't rather go somewhere else to have this baby?" Doc Swilling asked.

"I want to stay with Conn."

Doc Swilling directed the men to set the second bed a foot away from the first and as soon as they were gone, relegated Emaline to it. "I don't want to see a toe on the floor, young lady, until that baby is delivered."

Devlin and Melody were allowed in to see Emaline, but Doc Swilling's office wasn't large enough for them to stay long, especially with the two beds crowded so close together.

Emaline had wished for a mercifully short labor, but her body didn't cooperate. She had been in labor for eight hours when Conn finally awoke. She turned on her side to face him "Good morning."

"It's still dark out," he replied in a raspy voice.

"It'll be dawn soon."

There was a pause before he asked, "Where are we?"

"In Doc Swilling's office. They brought in an extra bed for me."

"You should have gone home, Emaline," Conn chided.

"I didn't want to leave you. Besides, I needed to be close to Doc Swilling, too."

He tried to rise and fell back with a groan. "You were shot, too? Are you all right? Is the baby—"

"I wasn't shot," Emaline said, reaching out a hand to grasp Conn's. "It's the baby. It finally decided to come."

A stunned look appeared on Conn's face. "You're in labor?"

Emaline nodded. Then she gasped and bit her lip. Her hand clenched around Conn's. "Just . . . having a . . . contraction . . . now," she said panting.

Conn used his stomach muscles to get himself into an upright position and managed to place his feet on the floor. But he was dizzy and his back and shoulder hurt abominably. A lantern had been left burning on a table near the beds. Conn looked around and realized they were alone.

"Where the hell is Doc Swilling?" he demanded.

"He went upstairs to get some sleep. He said it would be hours before I need him, but if I did to yell for him."

"Why didn't you yell?" Conn demanded when he saw how tired and pale she was.

"Because I don't need him."

Conn shifted from his bed to sit on the side of hers. "You're in pain," he said, brushing damp curls from her forehead.

"That's the general idea in labor," Emaline said with a hard-won smile. "It won't be much longer," she reassured him. She hoped she was right. The pains were much closer now, and longer, and she was having greater difficulty not crying out. She grasped Conn's hand again and squeezed hard as another contraction rolled over her, absorbing her, wracking her body with excruciating pain.

"Emaline!" Conn said. "Is there anything I can do to help?"

She didn't answer until the contraction was finished. Then she took a shaky breath. "Just knowing you're here helps."

He leaned over to brush her forehead with a kiss. "I was afraid I was going to lose you, Emaline. I couldn't have borne that."

"I love you, Conn. I wish I'd said it sooner. I've felt it for a long time."

"And I love you, Emaline. I was just afraid . . ."

"I know, Conn. But I think tonight was a turning point for all of us. Poor Mr. Fleet. He must have gone crazy when his daughter was killed. But his confession means that Winthrops and Bentons really have managed to get through all these months without attacking each other. Maybe everyone is willing to change for the better. Maybe there will be peace at—"

Emaline gasped as another contraction caught her in mid-sentence.

"Should this be happening again so soon?" Conn asked as Emaline grasped his hand with enough strength to crush it. How did women bear such pain? he wondered.

"Conn," Emaline said a moment later. "Call the doctor."

"Emaline? What's wrong?"

"Call the doctor," she insisted.

"Swilling!" Conn yelled at the top of his voice. "Get the hell down here where you belong!"

Conn heard the doctor's shout of acknowledgement and then the sound of footsteps on the stairs. A moment later, the rumpled physician appeared.

"There's something wrong," Conn said anxiously. "Help her, Doc!"

Conn shifted back to his own bed while the doctor examined Emaline. "Is she going to be all right?"

"Right as rain," Swilling pronounced. "But this baby is on its way."

Conn wished for a moment that he was somewhere else, anywhere else, and didn't have to go through this with Emaline. It hurt him to see her in pain. But there was nothing he could do for her. She had to bear the child alone.

A guttural sound forced its way past Emaline's lips. "I—have—to—push," she said through gritted teeth.

"Then by all means push," Doc Swilling said.

"It—hurts," Emaline said in a grating voice.

"I'm here, Emaline," Conn said, grasping her hand.

"Go—away—Conn." But even as she said the words she tightened her hold on his hand.

"Push, Emaline," Conn said. "Keep pushing."

"I see the head. It won't be long, Emaline."

Emaline panted as she waited for the next contraction. "Do you want a girl, or a boy, Conn? You've never said."

"I'd like a son," Conn confessed. "But a daughter would be nice, too, Emaline."

Conn felt her tense as another contraction began. She raised her shoulders and bore down. "Conn!" she cried.

He watched, amazed, as the child slid out of her body and into the doctor's waiting hands.

"It's a boy!" the doctor said.

The baby let out a wail at the indignity of being forced out of his warm haven into the cold world. Once the cord was cut, Doc Swilling wrapped him in a blanket he had ready and placed him in Emaline's arms. When the birthing was done, the doctor rinsed his hands and rolled down his sleeves before getting his coat from the rack near the door. "I'll just go spread the news and leave you two alone for a little while." He left his office, quietly closing the door behind him.

Emaline met Conn's misted gaze and smiled. "It's a boy, Conn. A son."

"Thank you, Emaline," he said in a husky voice. He leaned over and pressed his lips to hers. "Thank you so very much."

"What shall we call him?"

"I haven't thought about a name."

"How about . . . Winthrop Benton?" she suggested.

"It fits," Conn said with a wry grin. "He's half one and half the other. It'll help remind people that we have a stake in getting along."

Emaline moved the blanket aside so she could see her son's face. "Well, Winthrop Benton, welcome to Bitter Creek."

Emaline had barely finished speaking when the first visitors came barging through the door in a rush. It was her mother with Jeremiah and Belle, followed closely by Dev and Melody. Dev was carrying a small Christmas tree on a wooden base, which he stood in the corner of the doctor's office.

"Wasn't sure when you and Conn would get out of here, Emmy, and I didn't want you two to miss Christmas," Dev said as he bent to kiss his sister, meanwhile getting a good look at the new baby. "Hey, the kid has your red hair!"

"But no freckles, thank God," Emaline said with a grin.

"I want to see my grandchild." Clara reached to take the baby from Emaline's arms. She held it so Jeremiah and Belle could see. "Isn't he the most precious thing you've ever seen?"

"He's got the Winthrop eyes, all right," Jeremiah said. "Blue as a cornflower."

A swirl of cold air blew in as Conn's mother arrived with Horace. "Conn? Are you all right?" she asked anxiously.

"I'm fine, Ma."

"Brought a gift for the baby," Horace said, offering Conn a package.

"Why don't you give it to Emaline?"

Horace turned and handed the package over. "Just a little something for the tyke."

Emaline opened the package and found a beautiful christening gown. "Thank you, Horace."

"Hester made it," Horace said, winking and grinning broadly.

"Thank you, Hester," Emaline said. "It's lovely."

"You'll be wanting to see this child," Clara said as she handed the baby over to its other grandmother.

Hester opened the blanket and stood with tears in her eyes, looking down at the child, Horace at her shoulder. "He's so beautiful," she said in an awed voice. "His mouth and chin are the same as Conn's when he was a baby."

"He's a Benton, all right," Horace said.

"He's more Winthrop than Benton," Jeremiah retorted. "Got the Winthrop hair and eyes."

"Got a Benton nose," Horace argued.

"He's both!" Emaline said with asperity. She reached out. "May I have Win back?"

"Is that his name?" Hester asked.

"It's Winthrop Benton," Conn said. "After *both* families."

Jeremiah looked down his nose at Horace. Horace grinned back. "Winthrop Benton it is!"

By now Doc Swilling's news had made it up one side of Main Street and down the other. More knocks came at the door as Bentons and Winthrops began to arrive. They crowded inside with gifts for the child, which they placed beneath the tree Dev had brought. The room was soon filled to overflowing with signs of Christmas cheer.

Emaline reached for Conn's hand and held it as they gazed into each other's eyes. There was no need for words. A child had been born on a cold winter's night. And like that other child, who had been born so many years ago, he would bring peace, at last, to this tiny bit of earth.

Christmas had come to Bitter Creek.

SEASON'S GREETINGS
from...

JOAN JOHNSTON

Christmas is my favorite time of year. We always have a special reason to celebrate because I have "A Christmas Baby" of my own. My daughter, Heather Lynne, was born on Christmas day in 1973. I woke up at 7 A.M. in labor, went to the hospital around noon, and Heather was born at 6.00 P.M. You can imagine what a Christmas present that was! She has continued to be a joy in my life, along with my son, Blake. We always set up the tree the first weekend in December and don't take it down until after the new year in an effort to make the season last as long as we possibly can. I hope your Christmas is a happy one and that it is filled with love and all the blessings of the holiday season.

Avon Romantic Treasures

*Unforgettable, enthralling love stories,
sparkling with passion and adventure
from Romance's bestselling authors*

FORTUNE'S FLAME *by Judith E. French*
76865-8/ $4.50 US/ $5.50 Can

FASCINATION *by Stella Cameron*
77074-1/ $4.50 US/ $5.50 Can

ANGEL EYES *by Suzannah Davis*
76822-4/ $4.50 US/ $5.50 Can

LORD OF FIRE *by Emma Merritt*
77288-4/$4.50 US/$5.50 Can

CAPTIVES OF THE NIGHT *by Loretta Chase*
76648-5/$4.99 US/$5.99 Can

CHEYENNE'S SHADOW *by Deborah Camp*
76739 2/$4.99 US/$5.99 Can

FORTUNE'S BRIDE *by Judith E. French*
76866-6/$4.99 US/$5.99 Can

GABRIEL'S BRIDE *by Samantha James*
77547-6/$4.99 US/$5.99 Can

Avon Romances—
the best in exceptional authors and unforgettable novels!

MONTANA ANGEL   **Kathleen Harrington**
77059-8/ $4.50 US/ $5.50 Can

EMBRACE THE WILD DAWN   **Selina MacPherson**
77251-5/ $4.50 US/ $5.50 Can

VIKING'S PRIZE   **Tanya Anne Crosby**
77457-7/ $4.50 US/ $5.50 Can

THE LADY AND THE OUTLAW   **Katherine Compton**
77454-2/ $4.50 US/ $5.50 Can

KENTUCKY BRIDE   **Hannah Howell**
77183-7/ $4.50 US/ $5.50 Can

HIGHLAND JEWEL   **Lois Greiman**
77443-7/ $4.50 US/ $5.50 Can

TENDER IS THE TOUCH   **Ana Leigh**
77350-3/ $4.50 US/ $5.50 Can

PROMISE ME HEAVEN   **Connie Brockway**
77550-6/ $4.50 US/ $5.50 Can

A GENTLE TAMING   **Adrienne Day**
77411-9/ $4.50 US/ $5.50 Can

SCANDALOUS   **Sonia Simone**
77496-8/ $4.50 US/ $5.50 Can

America Loves Lindsey!

The Timeless Romances
of #1 Bestselling Author

KEEPER OF THE HEART	77493-3/$5.99 US/$6.99 Can
THE MAGIC OF YOU	75629-3/$5.99 US/$6.99 Can
ANGEL	75628-5/$5.99 US/$6.99 Can
PRISONER OF MY DESIRE	75627-7/$5.99 US/$6.99 Can
ONCE A PRINCESS	75625-0/$5.99 US/$6.99 Can
WARRIOR'S WOMAN	75301-4/$5.99 US/$6.99 Can
MAN OF MY DREAMS	75626-9/$5.99 US/$6.99 Can
SURRENDER MY LOVE	76256-0/$6.50 US/$7.50 Can

Coming Soon

YOU BELONG TO ME	76258-7/$6.50 US/$7.50 Can